Praise for the bestselling authors of

Bespelling JANE AUSTEN

New York Times and *USA TODAY*
Bestselling Author Mary Balogh

"Noted for romances that stretch the boundaries, Balogh
is one of the premier writers of Regency-set historicals."
—*Library Journal*

Colleen Gleason

"Witty, intriguing and addictive."
—*Publishers Weekly* on *The Gardella Vampire Chronicles*

New York Times and *USA TODAY*
Bestselling Author Susan Krinard

"Susan Krinard was born to write romance."
—*New York Times* bestselling author Amanda Quick

Janet Mullany

"Mullany…takes the reader on a funny romp
in this delightful Regency farce."
—*RT Book Reviews* on *The Rules of Gentility*

MARY BALOGH

COLLEEN GLEASON
SUSAN KRINARD
JANET MULLANY

Bespelling JANE AUSTEN

HQN™

ISBN-13: 978-0-373-77607-8

BESPELLING JANE AUSTEN

Copyright © 2010 by Harlequin Books S.A.

The publisher acknowledges the copyright holders of the individual works as follows:

ALMOST PERSUADED
Copyright © 2010 by Mary Balogh

NORTHANGER CASTLE
Copyright © 2010 by Colleen Gleason

BLOOD AND PREJUDICE
Copyright © 2010 by Susan Krinard

LITTLE TO HEX HER
Copyright © 2010 by Janet Mullany

Recycling programs for this product may not exist in your area.

This edition published by arrangement with Harlequin Books S.A.

For questions and comments about the quality of this book please contact us at Customer_eCare@Harlequin.ca.

® and TM are trademarks of the publisher. Trademarks indicated with ® are registered in the United States Patent and Trademark Office, the Canadian Trade Marks Office and in other countries.

www.HQNBooks.com

Printed in U.S.A.

CONTENTS

Introduction

Two and a half years ago, I was thinking about Jane Austen. And vampires.

I'd been writing paranormal romance for fifteen years, and had been a fan of Jane Austen for much longer than that. I'd read *Emma* many times with great pleasure, had seen every version of *Pride and Prejudice* that had ever appeared on big or small screens, and could look back on Georgette Heyer and the Regency Romance authors of the '80s and '90s as having given me my first introduction to the world of romance novels.

Today, the combination of Austen and paranormal may seem an obvious one. But in January 2008, as I sat on my couch near midnight and began scribbling my story idea in longhand on a steno pad, it was one of the most exciting notions that had ever popped into my head. The words flowed as they had seldom flowed before, and I found a story taking shape… the retelling of *Pride and Prejudice* as a contemporary vampire romance.

Who was better qualified to be an urbane, handsome, slightly arrogant vampire but Fitzwilliam Darcy? And Lizzy would be a modern woman, with all the concerns of a modern woman but the same family problems and romantic qualms. Lydia would still be a troublemaker. Jane would still be the sister everyone would love to have. I could see the retelling as a first-person narrative, presented in the modern Lizzy's affectionate, wry and sometimes acerbic voice.

And so "Blood and Prejudice" was born.

The rest happened quickly. I knew there was a great anthology here, and so I approached my agent, Lucienne Diver, about a prospective collection of Austen/paranormal novellas. Each author would choose an Austen novel to re-imagine in the paranormal milieu, and we'd call it *Bespelling Jane Austen*.

My agent was enthusiastic. Now it was a matter of finding the right authors! I was joined by Janet Mullany, who calls herself a writer of "funny romantic historicals," including *Improper Relations*, a "rakish Regency romance" ; and Colleen Gleason, author of the Gardella Vampire Chronicles, featuring a Regency-era vampire huntress.

But who should be our headliner? Among my favorite romance writers of all time is Mary Balogh, whose many Regency-set historicals have given pleasure to millions of devoted readers. When I approached Mary, she was enthusiastic about the idea…but she had never before written a paranormal. There was no doubt in anyone's mind, however, that this fine author could write anything she put her mind to. And so she agreed, to the great delight of the rest of us.

Mary Balogh chose to reimagine Austen's novel *Persuasion*. In "Almost Persuaded," Jane Everett finally learns, after several lifetimes of trying and failing, that when it comes to love, all the advice and persuasion in the world from trusted friends and relatives are no substitute for what the heart knows.

In Janet Mullany's contemporary "Little to Hex Her," based on Austen's *Emma*, vampires populate the Hill, elves run the Pentagon and there's a witch on retainer at the White House. "Witch without a cause" Emma Woodhouse runs her family's dating agency and finds trouble and love among the paranormal population of Washington, D.C.

Colleen Gleason revisits *Northanger Abbey* in "Northanger Castle," where it's vampires instead of madmen who lock their wives away. Caroline is so highly influenced by popular Gothic novels that she sees danger and intrigue everywhere. But it's not until she comes face-to-face with a vampire that she realizes how inaccurate her instincts really are!

Whether modern or historical, the tales in *Bespelling Jane Austen* will, we hope, intrigue traditional Austen readers, as well as those who love the paranormal. If Miss Austen knew how far our love for her works would take us, how much we would want to make her world our own, I don't think she would be displeased.

Susan Krinard

ALMOST PERSUADED

Mary Balogh

Dear Reader,

Paranormal literature is something I read, not something I write. And so I told Colleen, Janet and Susan when they asked me to contribute a story to this anthology. But I loved the concept and really wished I *could* drum up a vampire or a dragon or a werewolf or two in my writer's imagination.

Susan was not willing to take no for an answer. I mentioned to her that the only paranormal topic I could handle, since it is something in which I believe, was reincarnation. That would be good enough, she said, and I realized (with some terror) that I had talked myself into being a part of this very exciting project. Of course, I still feel like a fraud when I compare my story with the other three! But you must be the judge.

Jane Austen's *Persuasion* has always been my co-favorite with *Pride and Prejudice*. There is something very poignant about Anne Elliot, who rejected the man she loved as a young, hopeful girl because her family opposed the match and her late mother's best friend, whom she respected and trusted implicitly, advised against a marriage that could not promise her financial security or the social position suited to her upbringing. And so Anne had to wait many years for Captain Wentworth to return as a successful man, though this time all her hopes, if not her dreams, have been long dead.

My story does not use the same characters. But the situation is similar. And I asked myself what if love had found my heroine many times, over numerous lifetimes, but each time she had lost it because she had not trusted her heart more than the advice and persuasions of her loved ones? What if that lesson is still to be learned and yet again she has a chance to learn it—or to be persuaded yet again to reject it?

I hope you enjoy my *slightly* paranormal story based upon the same premise as Jane Austen's classic, but with a totally different twist.

Mary Balogh

CHAPTER I

MISS JANE EVERETT, MIDDLE DAUGHTER OF SIR HORACE
Everett of Goodrich Hall in Hampshire, did not call as
often as she ought at the vicarage in the village nearby.
She called everywhere else—on tenants and laborers and
others, on those who were sick or elderly or in need of
any sort. She took her duties very seriously.

Mrs. Mitford—the elder Mrs. Mitford, that was, great-
aunt of the vicar—was definitely in need since severe
rheumatics prevented her from going much farther from
the vicarage than the garden, and even that was a great
effort on most days. And she liked company. Perhaps she
would have liked more of Jane's.

Louisa, Jane's elder sister, called at the vicarage far
more often, though her visits elsewhere were rare and
were always accompanied by such condescending pomp
that Jane doubted anyone regretted their infrequency. But
she went to the vicarage to see the younger Mrs. Mitford,
the vicar's wife. Amelia Mitford was quite happy to pay
obsequious homage to the eldest daughter of a baronet,
and since Louisa was always delighted to be worshiped
and adored, it was in many ways a friendship made in
heaven.

Edna, Jane's younger sister, almost never called at the vicarage or anywhere else unless it was to attend an evening party that promised lively entertainment, preferably dancing. Social calls were nothing but a dead bore, she always declared, when they must perforce be made on the same people, who invariably talked on and on about the same old things. Charitable calls were even more tedious because all the recipients wanted to talk about was their health, or rather their ill health.

Edna positively lived for the day when she would be married and have her own home and could expect other people to call upon *her*. However, the only really eligible gentleman in the neighborhood was William Burton, eldest son of Mr. Edward Burton of Highfield House, and William was far more interested in Jane than in Edna. He would not, of course, even consider Louisa since Sir Horace had always made it plain that he expected his eldest daughter to ally herself with no gentleman lower on the social scale than a baron. Louisa herself aspired to an earl at the least.

On this particular August afternoon, however, all three sisters were on their way to the vicarage, squeezed together on the seat of the gig. Jane would have preferred to walk, but she was outvoted by her sisters, the elder of whom did not wish to arrive with a reddened complexion and bedraggled hem, the younger of whom conveniently fancied that she had turned her ankle while strolling down by the lily pond the previous afternoon.

Jane sat in the middle, the least preferred seat, her arms pinioned against her sides. They were on their way to offer formal congratulations to elderly Mrs. Mitford on the occasion of her seventy-fifth birthday.

It was strange, Jane reflected as the carriage bowled along the driveway between sweeping lawns of the park, how the events of seventeen years ago could still embarrass her and make her reluctant either to call at the vicarage or to come face-to-face with elderly Mrs. Mitford.

She had been only four years old at the time.

Her mother, now deceased, had been returning an afternoon call made upon her two days before, and she was taking Louisa and Jane with her. Mrs. Mitford had been recently widowed, though she had remained at the vicarage, her husband's living having been granted to his son. She was a tragic figure nevertheless, Jane had overheard her mother tell her father before they left home, having suffered a great deal of trouble and loss in her life.

Jane's father had just succeeded to his title on the passing of his uncle. They had moved to Goodrich Hall only a week earlier, in fact. Jane had never seen either the vicarage or Mrs. Mitford before that afternoon. Though she was to disgrace herself horribly over both when she finally did see them.

She could remember it clearly now, though she had been very young then—and had tried her best ever since to block the memory from her mind.

She did not, after all, want to burn as a witch. Or be snatched away by gypsies.

"Oh, look," she had cried to her mother and Louisa, pointing excitedly at the vicarage as they approached in the carriage. "I used to live there."

Louisa had tutted and tossed her glance at the roof of the carriage.

"You *are* strange, Jane," she had said. "Why would you even *want* to live *there?*"

"You are mistaken, Jane," her mother had said kindly but firmly. "Of course we have never lived in such a small cottage. You really must learn to confine your imagination to the nursery and your dolls."

Jane had forever been suffering scolds for the vividness of her imaginings, which at the time she had called real and her father had called falsehoods and her mother had called inappropriate. Her nurse had occasionally made her stand in a corner to reflect upon her fibs.

After the housekeeper had admitted them to the house, Jane had looked about at the familiar scene with wide-eyed interest, noticing what was still the same and what had changed. And then, before she could say anything about her observations to her mother, a straight-backed, sweet-faced but sad-looking lady dressed all in black had stepped into the hallway to greet them. Jane had smiled brightly at her and committed the horrible social error of speaking up before any of the adults had had a chance to do so and before anyone had spoken to *her*.

"Oh!" she had cried—and she had laughed aloud with glee. "You used to be my mother."

Mrs. Mitford had looked mystified, Jane's mother had looked mortified and Louisa had smirked, because *she* was behaving with perfect six-year-old manners.

Jane had made matters worse before anyone could stop her.

"I fell in the river and drowneded," she had said, eager to explain. "The water wasn't *terribly* deep, and it wasn't *terribly* cold, either. But it took me by surprise and I drowneded. You need not have been dreadfully unhappy, though, and I would have told you so afterward if I could, but I couldn't. I went down and down into the water until I came to the light, and it was the most lovely light in the world. And he called me with his hands and I went and everything was—oh, so *lovely* that I didn't really want to come back after all. Not just then, anyway. But you can see now that you need not have worried. Here I am, safe and sound."

She had been beaming with happiness, her arms outspread, waiting to be recognized and embraced, when Mrs. Mitford crumpled into an insensible heap on the floor.

Back at Goodrich Hall a short time later, Jane had spent a few hours alone in the nursery, seated on a hard chair, before being fetched down to her father in the library and informed in a long speech, most of which she did not understand, what it meant to be Miss Jane Everett of Goodrich Hall, daughter of Sir Horace Everett, upon whose head she must never *ever* again bring down such shame. If she persisted in her wicked untruths, it was altogether probable the gypsies would come one night and take her away.

And back in the nursery she had faced what had seemed worse to her—her mother's sorrow. She had shed a few tears as she questioned Jane about how she knew the story of Mary Mitford, who had been abandoned by her lover and had then thrown herself into the river to drown. Though the *official* version was that she had slipped and fallen in and drowned by accident. Only so could she be granted Christian burial in the churchyard where her father was vicar.

"But it really *was* an accident, Mama," Jane had whispered. "I did not *mean* to fall in, and I did not mean to drown. Maybe I could have fought harder, but the light was so lovely. And he was there waiting for me, calling me with his hands. And then I was very happy. I had been sad before that."

Her mother had looked more troubled than convinced. She had taken Jane's hands and held them tightly while entreating her to curb her imagination in future.

Jane had promised. By then she was thoroughly frightened and did not wish to keep having the memories everyone called lies. She was afraid gypsies really would come for her one night when she was all alone in her bed and nurse far away in the next room.

That was not quite the end of the matter. The following day Jane's father had made mention of the burning of witches, whose numbers included those who lied and pretended to be dead people come back to life.

Her memories could not be memories, Jane had told herself, if everyone said they were not. The vicarage must look like a house she had once made up in her imagination. Mrs. Mitford must look like a mother she had invented for one of her games. She must have overheard some of the servants talking about the poor dead Mary Mitford, though she certainly could not remember doing so and she had only been at Goodrich for a week. Her mother said that was what must have happened, though.

And so Jane had suppressed all memories from that time on—or all memories that were unlike everyone else's anyway. She became a quiet, solemn, obedient child.

Her sisters had been talking all the way to the vicarage while Jane was lost in uncomfortable reverie.

"I do not know why our father could not spare the carriage," Edna was saying when Jane took notice. "There is not enough room in the gig. If Jane would move her arms forward instead of insisting upon keeping them at her sides, there would be more room for the rest of us, but it is ever her way to be selfish. I daresay I shall have a sore side all the rest of the day."

"I wonder," Louisa said, "if Captain Mitford has arrived at the vicarage yet. He is expected this week, according to Amelia, and it would be a courtesy to arrive on his great-aunt's birthday, would it not?"

"Who is Captain Mitford?" Edna asked, all sudden interest.

Louisa looked triumphant. She was fully aware, of course, that they did not know of whom she spoke.

"The Reverend Mitford's brother is coming to stay for a few weeks," she said. "He was in India with his regiment, but he was wounded a year or two ago and has only recently been well enough to come home to England to finish recuperating before rejoining his regiment in Portugal. I daresay he will be fighting the forces of that dreadful monster Napoleon Bonaparte before the winter is over."

"The Reverend Mitford's *younger* brother?" Edna asked hopefully.

"No," Louisa said. "He is the elder. And do not, pray, Edna, proceed to ask me if he is also handsome. I do not know the answer and would not be interested if I did. Rank and fortune are of far more lasting significance than good looks. The Mitfords are not a wealthy family nor a distinguished one. It is said they were in trade until two or three generations ago. It would not do for a Miss Everett of Goodrich Hall, even a younger sister, to fall in love with Captain Mitford."

"Oh," Edna said crossly, "you say that, Louisa, only because you intend to fall in love with him yourself."

Louisa's eyebrows arched upward.

"I have a better sense of my own worth," she said, "than to consider falling in love of any importance when I turn my mind to matrimony, Edna."

While the two of them argued, Jane looked ahead along the village street to the church and the vicarage beyond it. There was some activity outside the latter. Two gentlemen, one of them the vicar, were dismounting from horseback and handing the horses over to a servant's care.

The other gentleman was young, too, and taller than the vicar. He took a cane from the servant's hand and leaned his weight on it, his back to the approaching gig.

But her sisters had seen the gentlemen, too, and both of them leaned forward, releasing the pressure on Jane's arms but completely blocking her view ahead.

There was a chorus of greetings as the vicar handed first Louisa and then Edna out of the gig. At the same time he introduced them to Captain Mitford, his brother, and they exchanged bows and curtsies.

Then the vicar turned and extended a hand for Jane's.

"And Miss Jane," he said. "Last but by no means least."

He helped her down. The door of the house was opening to reveal Amelia Mitford. She curtsied and beamed at Louisa, who swept through the gateway toward her, followed by Edna.

"Miss Jane," the vicar said as they moved out of the way, "may I have the pleasure of presenting my brother, Captain Mitford? Miss *Jane* Everett, Robert."

As Jane had her first look at the captain, she prepared to curtsy and murmur what was proper to the occasion.

She forgot to do either.

She had never set eyes upon him before. Of that she was quite certain. And yet she knew just as certainly that she *knew* him. Deeply. Intimately. Her breath caught. Her stomach muscles clenched. Her knees turned weak.

Had she been able to think rationally, she would have assured herself that her temporary paralysis was *not* occasioned by his looks, though he was certainly a handsome man. He was tall with dark hair and smiling blue eyes and a sun-bronzed complexion. He was broad-shouldered and narrow-hipped, his long, shapely legs accentuated by the close fit of his riding breeches and supple leather boots.

He was also leaning upon his cane as if he needed it to support his weight.

She would also have told herself that she had *not* fallen instantly in love with him. She had never been in love, and she was far too sensible to fall for a complete stranger even if he *was* a splendid figure of a man. She would even have said that it was not any real attraction that had bowled her over. Attraction ought never to be a purely physical thing. It was something that must grow gradually between a man and a woman as they became familiar with each other's character.

She did not know Captain Mitford's character.

She did not know Captain Mitford.

And yet she *knew* him. In the depths of her being she knew him.

As if she had known him for all eternity.

As the real world fell into place about her again and she completed her curtsy and her polite "How do you do, sir?" she did not know how long had passed. Probably not even half a minute. Although he had raised his eyebrows, no one else seemed to show any awareness that the world had stopped on its axis for some indeterminate length of time before lurching into motion again.

She felt disoriented and inexplicably frightened.

"Miss Jane Everett," he said in a voice that was unfamiliar to her ears, though it rang a familiar chord somewhere in the region of her heart. "My pleasure. Shall we follow the others indoors?"

She might as well have walked after all. She felt breathless.

Captain Robert Mitford looked at the neat little figure of Miss Jane Everett as she preceded him into the vicarage and tried to imagine that he knew her, that somewhere deep inside him there was a spark of recognition.

There was none.

Which did not necessarily mean that she was *not* the one.

The thing was that his soul mate never looked the same in any two lifetimes. He had seen that with some fascination when revisiting some of those lifetimes under the guidance of his guru in India. In one lifetime she had been a lean, dark-complexioned washerwoman for a noble family in ancient Egypt, and he had been a priest at one of the royal temples—far above her in station. In another life she had been the lithe, black-haired daughter of an aboriginal chief in the Americas, and he had been a captive from another tribe. She had been the daughter of a Russian landowner once, he a serf on the man's land. And she had been a nun in medieval Italy, he a papal guard. It had been a forbidden love that time.

There had always been some impediment, of course—and always a chance to overcome that impediment, to conquer all with the power of their love for each other.

They had never made that conquest.

Not yet. But they would.

And so they were fated to meet again and again through countless lifetimes until they found the courage to choose love above all the forces, petty or otherwise, that so often appeared of more importance. This particular lesson related to romantic love, but there was more awaiting them once they had mastered it. If they could learn to choose love in its romantic guise, they could eventually learn—together—to choose it in all its many guises and to move beyond any guise to an understanding of the vast, unending breadth and height and depth of love itself.

Of the one love.

Of the one.

It had all seemed perfectly clear to Robert while he was in India recovering from his wounds. He had been able to see other lifetimes and how each time courage had failed him, or her, or both of them. He had been able to see the spirit world between lifetimes and what he and she together had discussed, with the help of their spirit guides, what they had planned and hoped to accomplish during their next incarnation.

In India he had come to understand that each time its purpose was to meet his soul mate again and try once more to unite in perfect love with her.

The catch was, though, that he had never been allowed any glimpse into the future. He had been given no clue as to the identity of his soul mate in this lifetime or how he would recognize her when he met her. Forgetfulness was a condition of human life—forgetfulness of all that had passed before physical birth. He was one of the privileged few in that he had been allowed glimpses into the vast past he had forgotten when he was born Robert Vaughan Mitford twenty-seven years ago.

But the privilege extended only so far.

Although he had had a healthy interest in women since about the age of sixteen, Robert had never really looked upon any of them as the potential one-and-only love of his life. He had certainly never thought of any as a possible soul mate. He would have laughed at the very idea with a mingling of derision and embarrassment if anyone had mentioned such a thing before his battle wounds changed his life.

He found himself now looking closely at every woman who was even vaguely eligible.

Inside the vicarage the three Everett sisters paid their

respects to Great-aunt Dinah and took their seats while Amelia sat behind the tea tray and poured the tea.

Robert observed each sister in turn. Miss Louisa Everett was beautiful with her perfect posture, dark, glossy hair and flawless complexion. She inclined her head graciously to his great-aunt and looked as if she expected some obeisance in return. She was an arrogant young lady, he decided. Not very likable. Which might be an unfair judgment since he did not really know her at all.

He hoped she was not the one.

Miss Edna Everett was pretty in a youthful, rosy-cheeked, flighty sort of way. She bobbed a curtsy to his great-aunt, spoke a few words and took a seat as far away as she could. There was a hint of petulance about her mouth. Surely she was not the one.

And then there was Miss Jane Everett. Who had inexplicably frozen into immobility for a few seconds after Gerald had introduced him to her. And who had thus caught his attention more than her sisters had done.

She was small and slender, fair-haired and blue-eyed. She was pretty without being beautiful and bore herself proudly but without arrogance. She was neatly but unostentatiously dressed in a high-waisted gown of sprigged muslin and a straw bonnet that looked as if it had survived a rain shower or two in its time. She curtsied to his great-aunt, bade her a happy birthday, hesitated and then hurried closer to draw her into a hug. Great-aunt Dinah looked a little startled and then pleased. She smiled as she took Miss Jane's hand in her gnarled, arthritic fingers, and drew her to sit on the chair beside her own. The younger woman smiled sweetly and bent her head closer to listen to what Great-aunt Dinah was saying.

She was attractive in an understated way, Robert thought. No! She was attractive plain and simple. He must be careful not to give in to wishful thinking, though, and convince himself that she was the one. She looked *nothing* like the Egyptian washerwoman or the Indian maiden or the Russian noblewoman or any of the others. But they had not looked anything like one another, either.

How he wished he could *know!*

Miss Louisa talked almost exclusively with Amelia. Miss Edna spoke mainly of her health. It was generally poor, Robert learned, though she never complained and no one ever took notice of her ailments anyway. She looked perfectly healthy to him.

Miss Jane gave most of her attention to Great-aunt Dinah, who still held her hand and gazed at her with eyes that seemed filled with affection. But Miss Jane, alone among her sisters, made an effort to be agreeable to everyone else, too. She commended Gerald on last Sunday's sermon and Amelia on the tastiness of the little cakes that were served with tea. And eventually she spoke to Robert, her cheeks coloring slightly as she did so.

"I trust, Captain Mitford," she said, "you have recovered from your wounds."

"Thank you." He inclined his head. "I must not complain. An army surgeon wanted to saw off my leg and assured me when I refused that I would never walk again. I have hopes of casting aside my cane before the summer is out. Perhaps even of dancing a jig."

He smiled at her, and she smiled back.

"You must have great fortitude, then," she said. "You are to be congratulated."

"Thank you," he said again.

Why had she paused so significantly outside the gate when she first set eyes on him, rather as if she had seen a ghost?

The visit had not yet lasted half an hour, but it was

over. Miss Louisa, doing nothing to hide her impatience to be gone, was on her feet.

"Amelia is coming to Goodrich Hall with me for an hour or two," she said, addressing her sisters. "She will need a seat in the gig, but there is not room for all four of us. One of you must walk."

"Well, it cannot be me, Louisa," Miss Edna cried. "You know I turned my ankle yesterday and it is worse today because I felt obliged to dance at the Burtons' soiree last evening. It will have to be Jane."

Robert glanced at that young lady, who did not look at all chagrined, as she might well have done.

"I do not mind walking," she said. "Indeed, I would prefer to walk than to ride on such a lovely day."

"If you will permit me," Robert said impulsively, "I will walk with you, Miss Jane."

"Oh, that is quite unnecessary," she said, turning her eyes on him again. "But if you would welcome some exercise on your own account, I will be pleased with your company."

"You will be able to escort Amelia home later, Rob," Gerald said, rubbing his hands together and looking pleased.

"And it is only right that a young lady have an escort," Great-aunt Dinah added.

Miss Jane smiled sweetly at her.

"You will all come to Goodrich Hall tomorrow evening," Miss Louisa said. It was a command more than an invitation. "Father and I will honor Mrs. Mitford's birthday with a gathering of our neighbors."

She looked about her with condescension as though she were conferring a great honor—as, Robert supposed, she was. Her mother must be dead, since there had been no mention of her. Miss Louisa, then, was mistress of the hall, and her father was a baronet. She was a great lady.

So was Miss Jane Everett.

And he was a mere army captain. It would quite possibly put something of a strain upon his father's purse to secure his promotion to major, though his father was quite insistent that it must be done.

Ah. Robert had a sudden thought and smiled inwardly. There was an impediment. Miss Jane Everett was his social superior, and if the father was anything like the eldest daughter, that fact would be of some significance.

Perhaps she really was the one.

Gerald bowed Miss Louisa Everett out of the house. Amelia followed, looking rather pathetically gratified, and Miss Edna Everett followed *her,* looking aggrieved that she had not been given due precedence.

"Shall we?" Robert asked Miss Jane Everett, and she turned to hug his great-aunt once more before stepping out of the cottage ahead of him.

Could this *possibly* be she, he wondered as they walked along the street past the church. The one he had loved and lost through life after life? The one he had loved through an eternity of between-lives? The one he must learn to love without condition through a human lifetime so that they could return to the between-time with their souls one significant step closer to the union of perfect love?

It seemed impossible. That was so grandiose an idea. She was just a quiet slip of a woman.

Whom he found curiously attractive.

But surely if she *were* the one, he would have known it instantly. How could he have known her and loved her through eternity and numerous lives and not recognize her immediately now?

How could he possibly not *know?*

"I beg your pardon," she said as the gig bowled by and Amelia waved to him, "but is it possible, Captain Mitford, that we have met before? I am quite sure we have not, but you seem so familiar to me that I feel I *must* have seen you somewhere."

Ah.

He turned his head sharply to look at her, and she turned hers to look at *him*.

The breath caught in his throat.

Was this she?

"I do beg your pardon," she said again, flushing. "Of course we have never met. How could we? The Reverend Mitford has been here only three years, and I know you have not visited him in that time."

"Your instinct is right and your logic is wrong, Miss Everett," he said. "We have known each other for a lifetime or ten. For an eternity, in fact."

His voice sounded breathless to his own ears. But he managed to smile and speak lightly, as though jokingly.

Could this be she?

"We have never met, have we?" she said, laughing.

"Not until today," he said. "Will you take my arm?"

She hesitated for a moment, but then placed her hand lightly through his arm and rested it in the crook of his elbow.

His breath seemed suspended altogether.

He was so suffused with familiarity that he felt quite dizzy. *He knew that touch.*

He made more deliberate use of his cane for a few steps until he had recovered his wits and his equilibrium.

They were together again, then.

It began again.

They were to have yet another chance at love. The dizziness threatened to overwhelm him. *Could this be?*

CHAPTER 2

JANE FELT FOOLISH FOR ASKING THAT QUESTION OUT LOUD when she knew perfectly well that they had never met. He would think she was flirting with him.

Though he had been kind enough to make a joke of it.

We have known each other for a lifetime or ten. For an eternity, in fact.

His eyes crinkled attractively at the corners when he smiled.

The visit to the vicarage had been a little strange altogether. Because elderly Mrs. Mitford had been dressed in her Sunday best and had been looking bright and happy to have visitors on her birthday, and because both Louisa and Edna had virtually ignored her after speaking the obligatory greetings, Jane had done something she had never done before. She had stepped close to Mrs. Mitford and hugged her, and instead of recoiling, the lady had caught hold of her hand and held it tightly all the time they sat together.

Did she still remember that long-ago afternoon when Jane was four? Clearly, she did not bear a grudge if she did. But why would she? Jane had been little more than a baby.

But *Jane* had remembered.

She had once been absolutely convinced, with no shadow of doubt, that Mrs. Mitford had once been her mother. With her child's logic, she had not stopped to ask herself *when* that might have been or how she could possibly have *two* mothers.

All she could remember now was that it had been a powerful conviction.

This afternoon she had sat hand-in-hand with Mrs. Mitford. And she had felt a strange welling of affection, bordering upon grief.

As if Mrs. Mitford really had been her mother once upon a time.

Perhaps she ought to try remembering more of what she had so ruthlessly suppressed all those years ago.

Or perhaps not.

At this precise moment all her attention was focused upon the man with whom she walked. She wished she had not taken his arm. She had walked thus with any number of gentlemen, but she had never before felt this…this *awareness,* this heat, this difficulty in breathing normally, this frantic need to *say* something to break the terrible tension which no doubt she was the only one feeling.

She did not like the feeling at all. She could actually *hear* her heart beating, as if it were lodged in her eardrums.

"It is a lovely day," she said with bright cheerfulness as they passed between the gates into the park.

"It is," he agreed.

"It has been a lovely summer."

"It has."

"I suppose," she said desperately, "it does not compare favorably to India, though."

"If you refer merely to degree of temperature," he said,

"you are quite right. I love India, but there is nothing lovelier than a fine summer day in England. It is where my heart belongs, for this lifetime at least."

"You are expecting more than one lifetime, then?" she asked him, relieved to feel amusement.

"Oh, certainly," he said, sounding equally amused. "How else are we to learn all there is to learn from life? And how else can life be fair, as we all feel it ought to be but as it seems so often to be decidedly *not?*"

"These are strange beliefs," she said, "for a man whose brother is a clergyman."

"Perhaps," he said, "they can remain our secret."

They both laughed.

She could feel the warmth of his arm through the sleeve of his coat. She could smell his cologne. She felt ever so slightly dizzy.

Surely she knew him.

But how could she?

"This appears to be a lovely park," he said as they proceeded along the wooded driveway.

"It is," she agreed.

"I daresay," he said, "it is at its loveliest now at the height of summer."

"It is," she said and could think of nothing else to say to prolong the conversation.

"It will be a long and tedious walk to the hall, Miss Everett," he said, "if we maintain such a polite, *lovely* conversation."

"Is the walk too far for you?" she asked half chagrined, half hopeful. "Please do not feel obliged to accompany me all the way if you would rather return to the vicarage. I walk alone in the park all the time."

"I have neither the wish nor the need to return so soon," he said. "It is, as we have agreed, both a lovely day and a lovely park. What is the very loveliest part of it?"

"The lake," she said. "But my favorite feature is the small summer pavilion. It has a wooden bench outside it overhung with roses. There I can sit and saturate my senses with beauty. Or simply dream."

"You enjoy solitude, then?" he asked her.

"And company, too," she said. "I like people who are genuinely cheerful and kind. I like them even better if they have interesting conversation and informed opinions on matters of general concern. But yes, I enjoy my own company, too."

"Because you are genuinely cheerful and kind and interesting and informed?" he said.

She laughed.

"Are you imagining," she said, "that the pavilion and bench are close enough to the water that I can gaze admiringly down at my own reflection as I sit there?"

"Perhaps," he said, "you will take me there, Miss Everett, so that we may sit together on that bench, which you have made sound so idyllic. And perhaps I may be permitted to gaze upon you even if the water is not close enough to throw back your reflection."

She darted a startled glance at him.

"Now?" she asked.

"It may be raining tomorrow," he said.

"We would have to walk across the lawn," she said, "or through these trees and then along a rough, narrow path around the far side of the lake."

"Is it too rough for you?" he asked her. "Should I carry you?"

She answered his smile with one of her own.

Louisa and Edna would wonder what had become of her. But no, of course they would not. They would not even miss her. Neither would her father. And if Amelia Mitford missed her, it would surely be with some gratification, as Jane's absence with Captain Mitford would give her more time to spend at Goodrich with Louisa.

Suddenly Jane wanted very much to take Captain Mitford to the summer pavilion, to prolong this time with him. She was… Oh, of course she was not falling in love with him. That would be more than absurd. But she was very much attracted to him. It was such an unfamiliar feeling that she felt quite dizzy again.

"It is quicker to go through the trees," she said. "But it is rougher."

He turned them off the driveway without further ado, and they were soon deep in the shade of tall, ancient trees. The silence and seclusion seemed deeper here than on the driveway.

"Tell me about Miss Jane Everett," he said.

"Oh," she said, "there is no question better designed to tie my tongue. What can I tell you about myself? I am the middle sister of three—but you already know that. We are not close, alas, even though I believe we have a sisterly regard for one another. Louisa is interested more than anything else in rank and fortune and what is her due as the eldest daughter of a baronet. Edna is interested more than anything else in making a good marriage and achieving the sort of importance it will give her in society."

"And Miss Jane Everett?" he said as they drew clear of the trees and the lake water sparkled below them, at the foot of a sloping lawn. "What interests her more than anything else? Neither fortune nor marriage?"

"Any sensible lady has a regard for both," she said as she drew him in the direction of the south side of the lake. It was wooded to the bank and was scarcely used, despite the existence of the summer pavilion. "But either or both in themselves would not bring total satisfaction or happiness. Not to me, anyway."

"What would, then?" he asked, stopping for a moment to admire the view. "Love?"

"It is a word that has so many uses and so many of them trivial," she said, "that it has become largely meaningless. And it is a sentiment at which men tend to scoff, I know."

"I am to be lumped in with all men, then?" he said. "Are you sure you do not do me an injustice, Miss Everett?"

"I long for...*meaning* in my life," she said. "For something that will make it worth living. Something like spending my life in search of a great pearl and knowing that there can be no true happiness until I have found it. Except that it is not a pearl for which I seek or indeed any material possession. I do not know *what* it is. Love, perhaps? But I do not really know what that means."

"The search," he said softly, "is always about love."

It should have sounded absurd but did not. Somehow it sent shivers along her spine and made her feel weak at the knees. It caught at her breath.

"We must go single file from here. Captain Mitford," she said, sliding her hand free of his arm. "The path is narrow."

She walked ahead of him, and they no longer talked.

The search is always about love.

What did he mean? The words had not been trivially spoken—or flirtatiously.

And yet she felt somehow caressed.

What was happening to her?

She turned her attention determinedly to her surroundings. She loved this place. She had come here a number of times with her mother, and had continued to come after her death, at first to remember her, and then mostly to sit and dream. This was almost the only place where she allowed her imagination to roam—that imagination that really had nothing to do with making up stories for her dolls in the nursery. Here she dreamed of two lovers—one of them herself—meeting and loving. And parting. It was the inevitable ending, try as she would to give the story a happy conclusion. But hope always brought her back to dream again of those lovers.

Who always seemed very real.

As did the ending of their story.

Which needed to be changed.

"This is lovely," Captain Mitford said as they came up to the pavilion and stepped around to the front of it. He laughed. "That word again. There ought to be more words to describe extraordinary beauty. This scene is… well, it is lovely. And it is *you*."

"*Me?*" she said, her eyebrows raised.

"Small and secluded and peaceful and mysterious and lovely beyond words," he said.

"Then it is certainly not me," she said with a laugh, though the outrageous compliment pleased her.

…*lovely beyond words*.

"You do not see yourself through my eyes, it would seem, Miss Everett," he said.

She felt herself blushing and turned her back in order to sit on the wooden bench to one side of the door of the little house. The walls were covered with ivy. Pink roses grew in an arch over the lintel and over a trellis above the bench. Their fragrance filled the air.

"In what way am I mysterious?" she asked as he seated himself beside her and propped his cane against the end of the bench.

"Only in that you are quiet and reserved," he said, "and I wonder who you are. I wonder if you are who I believe you very well might be."

She turned her head and looked at him for some time in silence. She was not sure she wanted to ask the obvious question. She felt a little afraid again. This was all quite beyond anything she had experienced before.

She felt as if floodgates were about to be opened on her life, ones she had kept determinedly closed for a long time. Or perhaps it was merely that she had met a handsome man and was falling into a foolish infatuation.

"You know who I am," she said.

He rubbed his leg absently and gazed out over the lake.

"Was it very badly injured?" she asked him.

"My leg?" He stopped rubbing. "Most of my injuries came from a sword and a dagger when two enemy soldiers attacked me in battle, one from the front and one from the rear. According to the army surgeon, any one of those wounds ought to have killed me. But I also had the misfortune to fall from my horse and land on my head. My horse crashed down on my leg and crushed it beneath his body until I was rescued an hour or two later. My concussion should have killed me. So should my leg, especially after I refused to have it off."

"The army surgeon must have been very skilled," she said, "despite his gloomy predictions."

"The army had to move on," he said. "I was far too badly hurt to go with it. I had to be left behind in the care of an Indian family who were related to my batman. It was they who nursed me back to health. I was with them for longer than a year. Despite all the fever and pain, it was in many ways the happiest year of my life."

"But you did not want to stay forever?" she asked.

"I was not meant to remain there," he said, "though

I believe I could have been happy there. I was meant to return here."

"By your family?" she asked. "Your regiment?"

"Those, too, I suppose," he said. "But I meant by life. This is where I am intended to live my life."

"In England?" she asked. "But to what purpose? What is it you need to find here?"

He hesitated a moment.

"Do you believe," he asked her, "in soul mates?"

He turned on the bench to look directly into her face as he asked the question. His eyes looked very intense and very blue.

Jane felt a sudden coldness in the head as though she were going to faint. The floodgates creaked.

"Soul mates?" she asked, almost in a whisper. She had never heard the term, and yet she *knew*.

"Two souls that were created to belong with each other from eternity to eternity," he said. "Two souls that seek each other out lifetime after lifetime until the time is right for them and they can love each other totally and unconditionally and move onward together to the next phase of their eternal growth."

"From eternity to eternity?" she said. "Do our souls not begin with human birth and proceed to a permanent eternal home after human death? It is what our religion teaches."

"Do you really believe that?" he asked her. "Why should a human man and a human woman have the power to give birth to an eternal soul when they have a child? Is it not far more believable that the soul in a human body comes from eternity and returns to eternity at death?"

"Is this," she asked him, "what you learned in India?"

"Part of what I learned there, yes," he said.

"That we all have a soul mate?" she asked him. "And you have come home from India to find yours?"

"Yes," He had not removed his eyes from hers, and she found it impossible to look away. There was a buzzing in her ears. This should all sound utterly alien to her. And surely it *did*.

And bone-weakeningly familiar. Where had she heard it before? How did she know it?

"And have you found her?" she asked. She forgot to breathe.

"I believe so," he said, still gazing directly at her.

She opened her mouth to speak, found words impossible, licked her lips and turned her head jerkily to gaze sightlessly at the lake.

"Me?" she asked.

"Yes," he said. "I believe so, Jane."

She got abruptly to her feet, her hands grasping the sides of her dress.

"May I ask you something?" he said. He did not wait for her permission. "When Gerald handed you down from the gig outside the vicarage earlier and introduced us, you paused before curtsying and speaking to me. Why did you pause?"

"I…I thought I knew you," she said.

"You asked me as we were leaving the vicarage," he said, "if we had met before. By then you must have known beyond all doubt that we had not. Why did you still believe that somehow you knew me?"

"I do not know," she said.

"Jane," he said softly, "are you afraid?"

"I am not afraid," she said quickly. "Why would I be?"

"Jane," he said again.

He ought not to be calling her that. She had not granted

him permission. He was a stranger. Three hours ago she had not even met him.

But he had always known her by name. She had always known him.

"Yes, I am afraid," she said, whirling on him. "I am afraid because if you speak the truth, then the last time we met I was the daughter of your great-aunt and you were the son of a duke, who had come to visit with her son, my brother. And you left me because your rank would not permit you to marry the daughter of a mere country vicar. You left me brokenhearted. And then a mere two weeks later you died when you crashed your curricle and I died a few days afterward when I cast myself into the river in a despairing search for oblivion."

"Jane—" He reached out a hand toward her, his face pale and troubled.

She took a step back from him. She had never spoken those details aloud until now. She had not even realized she remembered them.

Remembered?

He was on his feet now, too, supporting himself on his cane.

"I have upset you," he said. "I am so sorry. In India I saw a number of lives in which we loved and lost each other because we would not reach out across the barriers that held us apart. But I did not see that particular life, the last. It was not imagination, though, Jane. All that really did happen to my great-aunt's daughter and the man who deserted her."

"I must have overheard the servants talk," she said. "Servants *do* talk."

"Forgive me," he said, reaching out a hand for hers. "I *have* upset you."

He had. She, who never suffered from the vapors, felt very close to fainting now.

She looked at his hand and drew a few calming breaths before setting her own in it. She watched his fingers close about hers and felt his touch all the way down through her body to her toes.

And it felt so very right, this stranger's touch.

"Was that *you?*" she whispered, closing her eyes. "Was it really you?"

"I believe so," he said, his voice low. "Miserable coward that I was."

She opened her eyes and looked at him. Oh, he was so handsome. And he was a stranger. Except for his eyes. If she kept gazing into his eyes, she could see all the way to…

"And there were other times?" she asked him. "Other lives?"

He nodded.

"We have known each other for a long, long time, then?" she said. "Forever?"

She did not know whether she wanted him to say yes or no. Terror warred with exultation.

He did not say, either. He looked at her with those fathomless, blue eyes.

"And how will it end this time?" she asked.

"That," he said, "is up to us."

And he raised her hand and held it against his lips.

She closed her eyes, and with a rush of sensation she felt an overwhelming sense of homecoming.

And terror.

And exultation.

ROBERT TURNED HER HAND and rested it, palm in, against his heart. He rubbed his own hand over the back of it and gazed into her eyes.

This really was she.

She looked so very different from what he had expected, though he did not know what he *had* expected. Not this dainty, pretty lady, certainly, with her light muslin dress and straw bonnet. Yet here she was, known consciously for the first time in human form.

His soul mate from eternity to eternity.

He took her other hand in his, raised it briefly to his lips, and held it against the right side of his chest.

He sought out her mouth with his own, touched his lips to hers, and gave himself to the kiss. For the moment there was no sexual passion, only a yearning gratitude that he had found her at last, that they had the rest of a lifetime to be together if they chose, the rest of a lifetime in which to love.

Her lips trembled against his and then withdrew. She took half a step back, though her hands remained spread over his chest.

"This is madness," she said. "We are strangers. A few hours ago we had not even met."

"Yes, we had," he said.

"But that is absurd," she said, her eyes searching his. "It has to be. This is England in the nineteenth century. The land of sanity. The age of reason. This talk of soul mates seeking each other out over centuries of lives is nothing more than insanity. A century or two ago we would have been burned at the stake for such talk."

"Perhaps that is why," he said, "we were not allowed a glimpse beyond the veil until now. Why is it we have both been given that glimpse this time if it is not true? And why the coincidence of our both doing so and then meeting today if it was not meant to be, if we do not belong together?"

"There is no veil," she said. "And I have had no glimpse beyond something that does not even exist."

"How did you know the story of Mary Mitford?" he asked her.

"As I said, I must have heard the servants at Goodrich Hall talking," she told him.

"How old were you?" he asked.

"Four," she said. "I went with my mother to meet Mrs. Mitford, and I was delighted to announce that I had used to live at the vicarage and that she used to be my mother. I expected everyone to rejoice with me."

"And instead," he said, "they all persuaded you that your words were the product of an overactive imagination, fueled by something overheard from the servants."

"And they were right," she said firmly.

He curled his fingers about the palms of her hands and moved them down to rest against their sides. He laced his fingers with hers. He could feel her thighs warm against his. He could feel the tips of her breasts brush lightly against his coat. He could smell the slightly floral scent of her soap. He breathed it in, the essence of her human form.

His mind was still trying to cope with the reality of it all. *He had found her.* He knew it was not wishful thinking. She was the one.

"There is nothing to fear, Jane," he said, lowering his head to place featherlight kisses along her jaw. "Life cannot harm us. Nothing can. We are immortal beings, encased in flesh for the purpose of educating ourselves and learning to saturate ourselves with the wisdom of love. Even if—yet again—we do not get this specific lesson right this time, we will have another chance. Endless chances. The spirit world is eternally patient."

"I am not afraid," she protested.

But he knew she was. He had had many months to ac-
custom himself to the knowledge that had revealed itself
to him in India through long sessions of meditation and
counseling by his guru. She had had a lifetime—since the
age of four, anyway—to shut down and deny the intuitive
knowledge of eternity that had somehow come with her
through the passage of forgetfulness to her birth. She had
been frightened into forgetting, and now she was frightened at being forced to remember.

The spirit world had endless patience. He was of that
world. He must be patient, too.

He released one of her hands, took a step back and
smiled at her.

"We are strangers, then," he said. He clasped her hand
a little more tightly. "Or rather we are new acquaintances
who are strangely attracted to each other. Are you willing to grant this much, Jane?"

"Y-yes," she said hesitantly.

"Then let us walk down closer to the water and admire the view," he said. "Let us talk about anything that
comes to mind, shall we, except eternity?"

"Yes," she said a little more firmly.

They went to stand on the bank of the lake, below
the level of the pavilion, and she pointed out to him the
house—Goodrich Hall—just visible on the far side of
the water among the trees, and the jetty, where the boats
from the boathouse would be moored if they were ever
allowed to be taken out. She showed him the little island
in the lake, where she could remember picnicking with
her mother, though not since her mother's death.

"Your father does not enjoy the outdoors?" he asked.

"It would coarsen his complexion and ours," she said.
"But I believe a coarsened complexion is a risk worth tak-

ing when the alternative is to remain indoors on a sunny day."

"You are encouraged to step out only when it rains, then?" he asked.

"Then we will ruin our clothes," she said with a chuckle, "and redden our complexions and give ourselves the ague. Perversely, I like walking in the rain. I am not a very dutiful daughter, am I?"

He was not conceiving a particularly favorable impression of Sir Horace Everett.

"Is the water very deep here?" he asked.

"It is," she said. "At the far end it is shallow, so that one could bathe if one were allowed to do so."

"I suppose," he said, "you do not swim, and I have not done so since before my injuries. We had better not dive in. We will have to sit sedately on the bank and dangle our feet in the water instead."

Her head turned quickly toward his.

"Are you serious?" she asked him. "We would have to remove our shoes and stockings."

"They would get horribly wet if we did not," he said.

She was blushing rosily, he could see. She was prim. She was also charming. It was still a dizzying thought that he knew her so little and yet knew her intimately to the depths of her soul.

He sat down and tugged off his boots. After a short hesitation, she sat beside him, her legs folded neatly to one side of her and completely covered by her skirt.

He reached out a hand.

"One foot, please," he said.

"It would be very improper," she said, but he could see desire and hesitation war within her.

"And very pleasant on a hot day," he said. "One foot, please."

"I can remove my own shoe and stocking," she said, but she did not put up any fight when he took her foot in his palm, removed her shoe and then slowly edged down her stocking until he could pull it off.

Her bare foot was small and prettily shaped and sat on the palm of his hand, soft and warm. He set it on the grass and held out his hand for the other.

"This is very improper," she said again when he was finished, but her eyes were laughing when he looked into her face.

Suddenly, she looked vividly, startlingly pretty.

He grinned back at her and removed his own stockings. Apart from the faded scars about his right ankle, his foot was not too unsightly. His leg was another matter, but that was well hidden beneath his riding breeches.

When she set first one foot and then the other in the water, she laughed out loud—a happy, girlish sound.

"Oh," she said, "it is cold."

It was. It also felt delicious against his heated flesh.

He took her hand as they bathed their feet, and they talked with an ease usually indicative of a long acquaintance. They talked about school and books and childhood and religion and music and dancing and... Well, Robert did not keep tally of the subjects they covered during the half hour or so they sat there.

And eventually they fell silent, and that was most remarkable of all. Because there was no element of strain in it. They sat as though they were a couple long acquainted and thoroughly comfortable with each other.

He felt as though he had loved her forever. As, of course, he had.

He released her hand and lay back on the grass, his feet still in the water, one arm draped over his eyes to protect them from the sun. He sighed deeply.

"Do you ever feel so thoroughly happy," he asked, "that you might well burst with it?"

"Is that how you feel now?" she asked, laughing softly.

"Yes." He removed his arm, turned his head and squinted up at her.

She gazed gravely back down at him.

"So do I," she said.

He reached up one hand to tuck an errant curl of hair behind her ear, and cupped the side of her face lightly with his palm. She leaned her cheek against it.

She was all warm and soft and human. And feminine.

She was part of himself.

"Come," he said softly and wondered if he was just being impatient again, if he was pushing her too hard.

But she leaned over him and lowered her face until her lips were against his.

They were soft and warm and ever so slightly parted. He cupped her face with both palms and kissed her softly, parting his lips over hers, touching them with his tongue, curling it up to stroke the tender, moist flesh within, and then pressing it slowly past her teeth into the warm cavity beyond.

His mind burst into a happiness too intense for words.

And he wanted her. Wanted her in every way there was to want.

But he *must not* rush her.

He lifted her face away from his and held it above him while he gazed up at her with half-closed lids and smiling lips. Her own lips looked full and rosy. Her eyes were a deep, dark blue in the shade of her bonnet brim. Her hands were splayed across his chest for balance.

"This is very improper," she said—predictably.

"Must I know you for *two* eternities, then," he asked her, "before I can venture to embrace you?"

"We agreed not to talk of eternity," she said.

"And so we did," he conceded. "And why should we? For now this lifetime is enough, Jane. This *moment* is enough. I am in love with you—head over heels."

It was true, too.

"But you have known me only a few hours," she protested.

"If you will." He smiled more fully, to lessen the tension she was feeling. "But I have fallen in love with you anyway. Deeply and irretrievably. Marry me."

"Do you always offer marriage to women you have known for three or four hours?" she asked him.

"No," he said. "Only to those with whom I fall irrevocably in love. And that has happened only once in my life. Now, in fact."

"You are absurd." She sat up and proceeded to dry her feet on the hem of her dress. "When you fell from your horse, you must have addled your brain."

"I fear you are right," he said meekly.

She looked at him suspiciously before turning away to pull on first one stocking and then the other.

"Do you *really* believe all that nonsense about being born again and again into different lives?" she asked.

"Reincarnation," he said. "Yes, I do."

"But why, if it is true," she asked him, "do we not remember? It makes no sense unless we remember."

"We easily fall into the trap of habit," he said. "It is very difficult within one lifetime to change the course of our ways. We make progress and we make mistakes. We need the chance to carry the progress forward and put right those mistakes without the baggage of memory. We need to start again with a clean slate. A new life with no memory of the ones before is a brilliant answer."

"Is it?" She sounded unconvinced. "Let us suppose for

one moment that it is true. What if you had decided not to come to stay with your brother? What if I had not come to the vicarage with my sisters? What if we had simply greeted each other and gone our separate ways?"

"We would have met again some other time or in some other place," he said. "We would have been given other chances. Life recognizes the unpredictability of our movements in any given life. Somehow we would have met, Jane. We were determined that it would be so before we entered this life."

She got abruptly to her feet while he was still pulling on his boots, and brushed grass and creases from her skirt with quick, nervous-looking hands. He watched her when he was on his feet again, leaning on his cane.

"It is all absurd," she said breathlessly. "But I would be less than truthful if I did not confess that I am infected, just as you are. I have fallen in love, too, this afternoon."

Her eyes did not waver as they looked into his, but her cheeks flamed.

"But not because of any other imagined lifetimes," she said. "Because of *this* one. This is all we need. Why can we not meet for the very first time and fall in love all within one afternoon? It can surely happen. It *has* happened."

He smiled at her. For two pins he would snatch her up and spin her around in circles until they were both dizzy and pitched into the water. Or his leg would collapse ignominiously before he had completed even half a rotation.

"Your brother called you Robert?" she said.

"Yes."

"I have fallen in love with you, Robert," she said with quiet gravity. "And it seems quite mad and rather improper and certainly indiscreet and will doubtless appear all three to me by tomorrow."

And she turned without another word to lead the way back up to the summer pavilion and around the side of it to the narrow path back to the lawn and the house.

He watched her go for a few moments before going after her.

This time, he vowed silently, he would get things right. *They* would. This time they would love for a lifetime. Happily ever after—with the emphasis on the *ever after*.

This time they would be together and remain together for all eternity.

She did not have to believe it. She only had to love him for the rest of this lifetime. She would learn the glorious truth when it was over.

CHAPTER 3

BY THE NEXT DAY JANE DID INDEED WONDER WHAT ON EARTH had come over her the day before. She had wandered alone to the lake with a strange gentleman. She had sat with him, dangling her bare feet in the lake water. She had let him *kiss* her. No, *she* had kissed *him*. She had told him she loved him. She had used his given name—Robert. She had allowed him to call her Jane without reprimanding him for such familiarity.

And she had been almost convinced by his strange, alien theory of reincarnation. She had almost believed that they had lived and loved before—numerous times. She had almost believed that in their last lifetime together they had been Mary Mitford and her faithless lover.

She felt incredulous now, embarrassed.

Doubtful.

Very doubtful.

And yet it felt as if the floodgates of memory really had creaked ajar. She kept remembering a girl and a young man sitting by the lake where she had sat with Captain Mitford. Lying there, their arms wrapped about each other, talking, laughing, loving. And it was as if she *was* that girl. She could feel what it was like to love that young man.

Who was not Robert Mitford, and yet was.

Just as the girl was not Jane Everett, but was.

And she kept knowing something about the two of them apart from the fact that if they were Mary Mitford and her lover, then they were trespassing on Goodrich land. She kept knowing something that contradicted what her mother had told her all those years ago and she had mistaken for memory ever since.

The trouble was, though, that just when that knowledge was nipping at the edges of her consciousness, it slipped free like water through cupped hands and she could not recapture it.

She kept hoping he would call during the day, and hoping he would not. She kept hoping he would come with his family to the evening entertainment, and hoping he would not.

She was not at all her usual calm, sensible self.

Lady Percy was the first guest to arrive, for the simple reason that she alone had been invited to dine. All the other guests were deemed worthy enough to take tea and play a hand or two of cards in the drawing room during the evening, but not nearly grand enough to take their places around the dining-room table with Sir Horace Everett.

"They would not expect such a distinction," he said when Jane suggested that at least Mrs. Mitford and the vicar and his wife might have been invited to dine since the whole evening had been planned in honor of Mrs. Mitford's birthday.

She did not mention Captain Mitford.

"And they would merely be uncomfortable if we *did*

invite them," Louisa added. "They never serve more than five courses at the vicarage."

And so only Lady Percy joined them for dinner—as she often did. The widow of a baronet of considerable means, she had moved to a manor nearby after the early death of her husband in order to be near her dearest friend, Lady Everett, Jane's mother. After the passing of that lady, she had become a close friend and advisor to Jane, of whom she was inordinately fond. Jane alone of her sisters, according to Lady Percy, had the superior qualities of mind and character that her mother had possessed. Her family was quite unworthy of her, in fact, fond as Lady Percy was of them all. They were, after all, her only real social equals for miles around.

Social position was of some importance to Lady Percy.

Jane longed to tell her what had happened the day before. But for some reason she could not pluck up the courage to do so when they were alone together before dinner while her father and sisters were still dressing. Lady Percy would surely think she had taken leave of her senses. And she might be right.

Jane might have said something after dinner if by then Lady Percy had not already leveled a sort of criticism upon Captain Mitford, though she had not met him.

Edna had mentioned him during dinner and had waxed mildly enthusiastic about his good looks and distinguished bearing.

"Though he *does* limp," she had added. "And he must be thirty years old. He is sadly old."

"I have heard," Lady Percy had said, "that his limp was acquired when he was fighting bravely with his regiment in India, Edna. And the vicar mentioned last week that his brother is two years his senior. The Reverend Mitford is twenty-five. I daresay the captain's severe wounds have aged him prematurely."

"He *does* have an engaging smile," Edna had conceded with a sigh. "But he turned it upon Jane more than upon either Louisa or me. And he walked home with her from the vicarage because Louisa insisted that a seat be found in the gig for Amelia Mitford. They were *ages* getting home. They must have walked very slowly indeed."

"If you were to walk a little more often," Lady Percy had said, "you would discover, Edna, that it takes far longer to walk two miles than it does to travel the same distance in the gig. Jane would be far too sensible to loiter unnecessarily with a gentleman who is quite ineligible."

Quite ineligible?

Lady Percy did not explain her meaning or pursue the subject further, and Jane did not question her judgment. But she hesitated after dinner about telling her mother's friend of that walk home yesterday, when she had indeed loitered. And been considerably less than sensible.

Captain Mitford—Robert—came.

When his party was announced at the drawing-room door, he had elderly Mrs. Mitford leaning heavily upon his arm. The vicar and his wife were behind them.

Jane smiled at Mrs. Mitford while her father and Louisa greeted them with their characteristic pomp and condescension. Mrs. Mitford returned her look and her smile and Jane stepped forward to take her hand and lead her to a comfortable chair close to the fireplace.

Like a gauche girl, she had not been able to summon the courage to look at the captain.

It was strange how yesterday seemed to have obliterated seventeen years of awkwardness—on Jane's side, anyway. She felt a welling of fondness for Mrs. Mitford.

"Thank you, my dear," that lady said as Jane positioned

a stool for her feet. "You are kindness itself. I have looked forward to seeing you again this evening."

Jane sat down beside her.

Her father and Louisa were greeting Mr. and Mrs. Burton with their eldest son and their two eldest daughters. Edna was telling Amelia that she was suffering from a sore side today after having been forced to ride three abreast in the gig yesterday when it was a conveyance intended to seat only two. Not that Mrs. Mitford had taken more than her fair share of the seat on the way home, but *Jane* certainly had on the way to the vicarage. Edna was not complaining, of course. That was not her way, and no one paid her ailments any attention anyway, so there was no point in complaining, was there?

Captain Mitford was standing with his brother.

"Robert admires you greatly," Mrs. Mitford said, patting her hand as if she sensed Jane's awareness.

"That is very kind of him," Jane said, and finally she risked a glance in his direction. He and the vicar were speaking with Mr. Burton and William—and he was looking at her with a very direct gaze.

She looked hastily away. But not before her stomach turned a complete somersault—or felt as if it did—and her heart leaped into her throat. She had held his hand yesterday, their fingers laced together. She had kissed him. She had listened to his protestations of love. She had fallen in love with *him*.

He had asked her to marry him.

She glanced at him again. Could all that possibly have happened? He was gazing just as directly at her as before. He smiled slowly—a private, almost intimate smile.

Jane turned sharply away to say something to Mrs. Mitford, hoping that her cheeks did not look as hot as they felt.

"He has always been a favorite with me," Mrs. Mitford said, making it obvious that *she* had seen. "As have you, Miss Jane."

Jane felt ashamed. She had always kept as much distance between herself and Mrs. Mitford as possible, even though they lived in the same village and attended much the same social events.

Edna spoke up loudly for dancing. But Sir Horace Everett of Goodrich Hall was far too genteel to allow an informal dance in his drawing room with a mere pianoforte for music. After half an hour of conversation following everyone's arrival, the card tables were set up and everyone was assigned a partner and a group. Except, that was, for one person, since the group was not divisible by four. Jane was quite happy to be assigned to play the pianoforte instead.

She wondered as she played if their neighbors were as excited by the infrequent invitations to Goodrich Hall as her father and Louisa always believed they were. Or did they sigh and search about in their heads for some excuse to avoid the inevitable?

The playing of cards was serious business to her father, who did not encourage conversation during the games. Jane looked about several times during the next two hours but could see no real sign of enjoyment on any of the faces of the players, with the possible exception of elderly Mrs. Mitford, who enjoyed company but had all too little of it.

Captain Mitford had Helena Burton for a partner and was giving her his undivided attention. Helena was clearly smitten by his attentions.

Jane was *not* jealous. Gracious heaven!

Finally, Louisa rose, signaling the end of play and the

arrival of the tea tray. Jane folded her music and rose to her feet.

And discovered that Captain Mitford was standing at her shoulder.

"Alas," he said. "I am too late to turn the pages of your music."

"You are indeed," she said. "Did you win your games?"

"All but half of them," he said.

She laughed and gathered enough courage to look fully into his eyes at last. They were smiling back into hers. She felt that knee-weakening sense of familiarity and attraction again. Oh, *why* did she feel so strongly that she knew him? His own explanation could not possibly be true.

"Is it permitted," he asked her, "to seek out cooler air by walking outside on the terrace?"

"It is warm in here, is it not?" she said, and she turned toward the French windows, opened them back and stepped through ahead of him without stopping to fetch a shawl or consult anyone else. She had to be alone with him for just a little while. Oh, she *had* to. She would have died if he had not come tonight—or if he had come and made no move to seek out her exclusive company.

"I hope," she said, "you *enjoy* playing cards."

"I do," he said, "when there is good music to listen to. You play well."

"Thank you," she said. "But I lay no claim to anything greater than competence at the keyboard."

She turned her head to smile at him. He was walking with his cane, but she could tell that he was making an effort not to limp too noticeably.

"Great-aunt Dinah is fond of you," he said, "though she did remark yesterday after I returned to the vicarage that she fears she frightened you away a long time ago when you were a small child, after something you said caused her to faint. She wishes now she had had the courage to come and see you a day or two after. I suppose she was referring to the incident you mentioned yesterday."

"Yes," she said. "I shall start calling upon her more often. I—Well, even if she was not once as dear to me as my own mother, I still feel a fondness for her. And she just told me that I have always been a favorite of hers. I felt very ashamed that I have always avoided being close to her."

"There is always time to make up for lost opportunities," he said.

"In the next life if not in this?" she said, smiling.

"Or in the life after that." He chuckled softly.

They had crossed the wide, cobbled terrace and stood for a few silent moments at the top of the flight of stone steps that led down to the formal parterre gardens. Moonlight bathed everything below them in soft light.

They turned their heads to look at each other again.

"Lovely," they both said together and laughed like a couple of old friends—or lovers—who were so familiar with each other that they even thought and spoke alike.

It was all very disconcerting—and quite breathtaking.

Was it possible after all…

"I would have found some excuse to call upon you earlier today," he said, "if I had not been coming this evening. The day has seemed endless."

Yes. Ah, yes, it had.

"Perhaps," she said, "we ought to forget about the strange events of yesterday afternoon. They really were quite…bizarre."

"Agreed," he said, still gazing into her eyes. "It *is* bizarre to sit beneath a trellis of roses on a summer afternoon and gaze through trees and across a lake and feel one's senses almost overwhelmed by the intense beauty of it all. It is certainly bizarre to enjoy dipping one's feet in the cool water of a lake on a hot afternoon. And to enjoy the company of someone similarly employed. Yes, we must forget. It is already done on my part. *What* is it I am not to remember?"

She smiled down at the garden. It had been a foolish suggestion on her part. She knew she would always treasure her memories of yesterday afternoon. It had been the most wonderful of her life so far.

She *was* in love.

There was a swell of voices and laughter behind them, and Jane turned her head to see Caroline Burton standing between the open French windows with Edna and William.

"Shall we stroll through the parterres?" Captain Mitford suggested, offering her his free arm.

She ought to refuse. She ought to suggest joining the others so that they could all converse and enjoy the air together. It was what Jane Everett would normally do.

Instead, she slipped her hand beneath his elbow and descended the steps with him. They walked silently between neatly clipped box hedges in the garden below as if they both feared drawing the attention of the young people above if they spoke.

He broke the silence first.

"I love you," he said softly.

They were surely the most magical words in the English language, Jane thought, closing her eyes briefly and reveling in their after-echo in her heart.

"You do not know me, Captain Mitford," she said. "How can you love me? And please do not talk about other lifetimes and forever. Consider only this lifetime, which in reality is all we have. You cannot possibly love me. If it is attraction you feel, I am flattered. But it cannot be more than that. You cannot possibly know if attraction will bloom into something deeper."

But I love you, too.

"And yet yesterday," he said, "you spoke the same words to me. You told me you had fallen in love with me."

"I must have been affected by the sun," she protested.

"Or by genuine emotion," he said.

"Emotion," she told him, "is not a reliable guide for our words and actions."

"There you are wrong," he said. "Deep, true emotion is our surest guide. We make our greatest mistake when we allow our heads to rule our hearts."

She did not believe it. She had always been taught otherwise. She had always believed otherwise. Though she wished he could be proved right. She had always been ruled by reason and common sense. Her life had never been exciting—until yesterday when she had been infected by very *un*reasonable emotion.

"Emotion is our human weakness," she said, "reason our strength."

"And love," he said, "is our destiny."

It was a non sequitur. It did not settle the argument.

Except that it did. It seemed somehow like a great truth that answered all the questions of existence.

Love is our destiny.

"Is that another lake down there?" he asked when they arrived at the east side of the parterre gardens. "I did not notice it yesterday."

"Merely a lily pond," she said, "with a wrought-iron seat beneath a weeping willow tree. I like to sit there in the daytime with a book."

He led her down the sloping lawn toward the pond and

she made no protest, though perhaps it was not quite the thing to wander so far from the house when the drawing room was filled with guests.

Ah, but how could she resist? She was twenty-one years old and had never had a beau. She had never met any man whose courtship she wished to encourage, though she hoped for marriage and children one day and a home of her own. She had always hoped for affection and companionship in marriage and an equality of mind and temperament. She had never dared dream of love.

Oh, she *had,* of course. But she had always told herself she must not expect it.

She was in love now, and it surpassed all dreams.

They sat on the seat, the overhanging branches of the willow hiding them from view and shading them from the moonlight, which gleamed on the water between the lily pads.

"Let us forget reason *and* emotion," he said.

"Very well," she agreed.

"Let us simply love," he said.

She did not answer, but when he took her hand, she willingly laced her fingers with his and allowed him to rest their hands on one of his thighs.

She closed her eyes again. Surely, oh, *surely* she had known him longer than a few hours yesterday and a short while this evening. She knew the feel of him, the warmth of him, the male smell of him.

Surely she had always known him, always loved him.

But such thoughts were too dizzying.

"Tell me about India," she said softly.

He did, enchanting her with his descriptions of the land and the people. It was very obvious to her that he had been happy there.

"What are your very fondest memories?" he asked her when he was finished.

"My mother," she said.

"Tell me."

And she told him stories of her mother and things they had done together.

Their conversation, or their twin monologues, felt very like speaking to and listening to her own heart, she thought. She had never felt this comfortable with any other human being, male or female.

"I wish I had known Lady Everett," he told her.

"And I wish I knew your family in India," she said.

"But we know each other," he said, "and we are partly a product of our times with them."

She might have protested yet again that they did not know each other, that their acquaintance was still such a recent thing that they were virtually strangers. But somewhere at the heart level she knew that was not true.

She had never known anyone as well as she knew him.

He had lifted their clasped hands and was holding the back of hers against his lips. And then he released it and set his arm about her shoulders. He half turned on the seat, lifted her chin and kissed her.

She turned on the seat so that she could slide one arm behind his back and cup the other hand about the side of his face. She slid her fingers into the warmth of his hair. He drew her closer, wrapping both arms around her.

Jane had never felt desire, except for some vague, undefined yearnings on those nights when she could not sleep. She felt desire now like a raging furnace within. She opened her mouth to him and sucked his tongue deep. She pressed her bosom to his coat and reveled in the feel of his hand against the side of one breast and then moving in to her waist, out to the flair of her hip, and behind to spread over her buttocks.

What should have been shocking had her longing for more and pressing closer to him, her legs spreading on either side of one of his.

She wanted him. The startling thought presented itself with crystal clarity to her mind. And the meeting of mouths and the press of hands was not quite enough. She wanted him *there,* where she was throbbing and aching.

She had had him once upon a time. They had been together. It had been heaven.

It would be heaven again.

Someone was making sounds of longing, and it struck her that it must be she.

"Ah, my love," he murmured against her lips.

"Robert," she whispered back.

She could scarcely see him, but she knew that he smiled.

"Jane," he said, "you must tell me that—"

But he stopped abruptly and turned his head to one side, listening. She looked beyond him. She had heard it, too, the sound of carriage wheels crunching on the cobbles of the terrace. The party was ending. The carriages had been summoned. The guests were leaving.

They both stood up, and he took hold of his cane while she brushed her hands over her skirt.

"I hope for your sake," he said, "our long absence has not been remarked upon."

She clasped her hands behind her and walked beside him up the lawn to the terrace and along it to join the chattering throng of guests who were finding their carriages and bidding one another goodnight and calling thanks to Jane's father and Louisa, who were standing side by side in the doorway. No one seemed to notice Jane come up with Captain Mitford, who stepped forward to help his great-aunt into the carriage that Sir Horace had sent to bring her from the vicarage.

She looked through the open door at Jane when she was seated.

"I hope, my dear," she said, "you will not catch your death of cold from being outside without a shawl. But blood runs warm in the veins of the young."

Her eyes twinkled and turned to include Robert in her remark.

"It is a warm night," Jane told her as Robert handed in his sister-in-law. He climbed in after them and was followed by the vicar.

And the carriage was on its way, as were all the others except Lady Percy's.

He had said only a quick good-night. He had said nothing about tomorrow.

"It is after ten o'clock," her father said from the doorway behind her. "I daresay everyone was most gratified to remain so long."

"No one will talk of anything else for a week," Louisa added.

"I am quite sure," Lady Percy said, "Mrs. Mitford will remember this birthday for the rest of her life. It was kind of you to distinguish her in such a way, Sir Horace."

"This night air will cause the ague," he said. "You must be on your way without further delay, Lady Percy. I will not keep you any longer. "

"Jane will see me on my way," she said. "You must not feel obliged to stand there any longer. Go on inside, Sir Horace. And you, too, Louisa."

Her coachman handed her into the carriage as the front door closed.

"Did you have a pleasant evening, Jane?" she asked. "Captain Mitford seems a personable young man."

"He has interesting conversation," Jane said, thankful that the darkness hid her blush. Yet again she found herself unable simply to blurt out that she was in love.

"I shall see you soon," Lady Percy said, arranging her skirts about her. "Good night, Jane."

The coachman shut the door and climbed up onto the box, and Lady Percy and Jane waved to each other as the carriage rocked into motion.

Jane stood on the terrace for a few minutes before going back inside the house. She was in love. She wanted to throw back her head and shout it at the moon. It far surpassed her wildest dreams. She could never have foreseen anything as beautifully... *carnal* as the reality.

Or anything nearly as exhilarating.

She could still smell traces of his cologne on her skin. She could still taste him on her tongue and on her lips. She could still feel his hand tracing her curves, his knee and thigh wedged between her legs. She could still hear his voice—*ah, my love.*

Would he come tomorrow?

What would she do if he did not? If he never came again?

How would she live on?

But for tonight she was going to relive the memories of the past hour. One hour could have all the power of eternity.

Oh, she was in love.

She *adored* him.

And *of course* he would come tomorrow. He loved her, too.

CHAPTER 4

"I TOLD YOU," MRS. MITFORD SAID THE NEXT MORNING WHILE she and Robert were sipping tea out in the little flower garden behind the vicarage, "that something Miss Jane said when she was a child made me faint. I did not tell you *what* she said, did I?"

"No," he said. "But she did."

"Then she *does* remember," she said. "She was so very happy, Robert. Her little face was beaming with pleasure. She was not just out to make mischief, though that is what I thought at first. She really believed what she said."

"About your daughter," he said.

She sighed audibly and watched the progress of a bee as it visited several flowers with a businesslike buzz.

"She did not just speak *of* poor Mary," she said. "She spoke *as* her. It is absurd, I suppose, what comfort I took from her words days after she had spoken them. She told me that she—that *Mary* had fallen into the river, that she had not deliberately thrown herself in. A child said *that*. Do you believe it is possible she was right, Robert?"

"I do," he said.

She reached out to squeeze his hand.

"And she spoke of a lovely light that drew Mary into

the darkness and made her death quite painless," she said. "She told me *he* was beckoning her to the light. I suppose she meant the Marquess of Wigham. He died before she did, you know. I like to believe the story, foolish as it seems. I was fond of that young man. It hurt me deeply when he so callously abandoned Mary and broke her heart."

"Perhaps," he said, "the story Miss Jane Everett told was not foolish."

"I wish you had known Mary," she said. "She was a warm and lovely girl. Strangely, Miss Jane reminds me of her, though she looks nothing like her. And you remind me of the marquess—Peter, his name was—though I do not know why. He was very blond and only of medium height. Perhaps it is the smile and the blue eyes. Perhaps I watch the growing attachment between you and Miss Jane because I can dream that you are Mary and her Peter having a second chance at love."

"I would like to think, though," he said, "that I could never be as heartless and cowardly as Wigham was."

"I deeply resented him for a long, long time," she said. "I was even glad that he was dead. And of course I blamed him for Mary's death. But it is not in my nature to hate indefinitely. We all have reasons for what we do. I suppose he had reasons that made sense to him. And perhaps he regretted them before he died. Perhaps Mary did *not* kill herself. I wish I could know that for sure. It would make such a difference."

"Did she love you?" he asked.

"I believe so," she said. "Well, of course I *know* so. She was an affectionate girl and we enjoyed a close relationship."

"Then," he said, "I do not believe she would have done

that to you, Aunt Dinah. She would have understood how killing herself would hurt you."

"You are a good, kind boy," she said, patting his hand. "And look who has come."

Her face lit up with pleasure as she looked toward the back door, through which someone had just stepped.

Jane.

She was looking pink-cheeked and self-conscious. She also looked as pretty as any picture dressed in white muslin liberally embroidered with pink flowers and a straw hat trimmed with the same flowers and pink ribbons. Her eyes darted to Robert before she looked fully at his great-aunt and smiled.

"I have been calling upon Mrs. Hancock," she explained. "She is recovering very well from her confinement, and the baby is thriving. And since I was in the village anyway, I thought I would call here to return your handkerchief, Mrs. Mitford. You left it at the hall last evening."

"And so I did," Aunt Dinah said as Jane bent over her chair to set a cheek against hers while she handed her a folded handkerchief. "I missed it last night after we arrived home. I thought someone might be kind enough to bring it to church for me on Sunday."

But there was a certain twinkle in her eye that made Robert suspect that it had been done deliberately. Great-aunt Dinah was playing matchmaker.

He drew forward a chair for Jane.

"Oh," she said, darting him another look, "I must not stay."

"Do have a cup of tea," his aunt said. "And then perhaps Robert will walk you home. You did walk into the village, I suppose?"

"I did," she said, the color deepening in her cheeks, and

she sat and allowed Robert to pour her a cup of tea. "Actually, everything else was an excuse to bring me here. I need to tell you something. I can say it before Captain Mitford because he knows what happened all those years ago. Did I hurt you dreadfully on that occasion? I suppose I ought not to have waited seventeen years to ask, ought I?"

"When you told me I had once been your mother?" the older lady asked. "You *shocked* me by knowing so much about Mary's death when you were only three or four years old and it had happened long before your birth. And you shocked me by speaking of it as though it had happened to you. But *hurt* me? No, my dear. If anything, I took comfort from what you said. I chose to believe as much as I could. I liked to think that she was happy as she passed over, and even that she was reunited with that faithless lover of hers. Perhaps he treated her better in the afterlife."

Jane's cup rattled against the saucer as she set both down on the table, her tea untouched.

"Forgive me," she said, "if I am about to shock you again or reopen old wounds. I have wrestled with myself all morning, trying to decide if I *should* tell you or not. But I think I ought. Something has been trying to grab at my memory for the last couple of days—since your birthday, in fact. And it came to me suddenly in the middle of last night. I woke up knowing it, though tantalizingly only *part* of it. And *memory* is perhaps the wrong word. Everyone used to say it was merely an overvivid imagination."

Robert wished he could lean across the table and take both her hands in his. She was pale and agitated. Something, he knew, had started for her when he came into her life two days ago—or come *back* into her life. And it was something she could not stop.

"Tell me, Miss Jane," his aunt said.

"I was told," Jane said, frowning, "that he abandoned me. I am sorry—that he abandoned *your daughter*. I cannot even remember—I do not even know his name."

"The Marquess of Wigham," Aunt Dinah said. "Peter. He was the eldest son of a duke."

"Peter." Jane closed her eyes briefly. "I think it was my mother who told me that he abandoned me—*her*. I suppose it was what everyone believed, even you. But it is not true. I remembered that last night. He left without me, but he was coming back. He was going to speak with his father, and then he was coming back for me. But he died."

Robert glanced quickly at his great-aunt. Her mouth was formed into an O, but she said nothing.

"Perhaps," Robert said, "he was talked out of coming back. Perhaps his father—"

But she was shaking her head slowly, still frowning.

"It was not the misery of abandonment I was feeling," she said. "It was grief pure and simple. I fell into the river because I was blinded by my tears. I tried to fight the coldness and the weight of my clothes, but then there was the light and the sight of *him*—Peter—beckoning."

She spread her hands over her face.

"Perhaps it was a form of suicide, after all," she said. "I could not lose him again. Oh, but I did not *want* to die. I wanted to come home to you, Moth— I am sorry. I am so very sorry. I ought not to have said any of this. Mama was right all those years ago. I should have confined my imagination to nursery games. This cannot be *real*. And now I have shocked and hurt you all over again."

She got abruptly to her feet and Robert scrambled to his. His aunt, he could see, was gazing at her fixedly.

"Is it possible, Jane?" she asked. "Is it really possible? Are you my Mary?"

"No." Jane shook her head. "I am Jane Everett. But I think I was once Mary Mitford. I believe we are the same soul."

She bit her lower lip.

Robert took one of her cold hands in his, and his great-aunt's eyes moved to him.

"And are you Peter?" she asked. "*Were* you?"

"I have no memories of him, Aunt Dinah," he said gently. "But I *have* lived other lifetimes with Jane. I have seen them in a sort of trance an Indian guru was able to induce in me. We belong together. We always have and always will."

She looked from one to the other of them, tears brightening her eyes.

"I am glad," she said and got slowly to her feet, waving off the help Robert would have given her. "I am going inside now to lie down. You must not worry that you have said the wrong thing, Miss Jane. You have said the *right* thing. I think I may at long last be able to stop grieving for my daughter."

Robert and Jane watched her make her slow way indoors.

"*Why* is all this happening?" Jane asked when they were alone together. "What if the things I have just said are all imaginary? What if there is no truth in them at all?"

"You know," he said, "that there is."

"And she is happy," she said. "I could *not* make up my mind whether it was best to tell her or not."

"You did the right thing," he said. "She is happy."

Jane smiled rather wanly.

ROBERT DID, OF COURSE, walk home with her. She had come into the village to see Mrs. Hancock and bring her some baked goods from the hall. More important, she had come to tell Mrs. Mitford what she had remembered last night—if *remembered* was the right word.

And overriding both motives for coming was her need to see Robert again. She ought to have waited for *him* to call upon *her,* as he surely would have done at a more seemly hour of the afternoon. But, armed with two perfectly good excuses, she had come in search of him.

It was something the usual Jane Everett would *never* do. She was not a schemer. And she never ran after gentlemen. Not that she had ever before known one she would wish to run after.

As soon as they had left the village behind them and were walking along the secluded shade of the driveway inside the park, he set an arm about her shoulders.

"I love you," he said.

She had always believed men found it difficult, even impossible, to say those words. But Robert Mitford was not as other men were.

Jane rested the side of her head on his shoulder.

"Do you not find all this as dizzying as I do?" she asked.

"At least that much," he said. "We need something to clear out our heads. Let's go swimming."

"What?" She raised her head again and laughed.

"You told me yesterday," he said, "about the shallow end of the lake. I could not see it from the summer pavilion. It must be well out of sight of the house or anyone taking a stroll in the inner park, then. It must be quite private, in other words."

"I do not swim," she protested. "Besides, it would be very improper."

"Your favorite word," he said with a chuckle. He looked down into her face. "You are afraid of water?"

She was about to deny it. But it was true and had been all her life. She also realized the significance of both his question and his searching look.

Mary Mitford had died of drowning.

"Yes," she said. "I am. And that is not about to change. I do not *want* it to change."

"Coward!" He grinned at her and suddenly looked very boyish and hopelessly attractive. "I will hold your hand and not allow you to go even nearly out of your depth. I will show you what fun it can be to frolic in the water."

"Fun!" she said derisively and then surprised herself by laughing. "Swimming has never been allowed."

"How old *are* you?" he asked her. "Five?"

"Besides," she said, "we have no towels."

He grinned again and said nothing.

"Oh, very well, then," she said because she desperately wanted to prolong her time with him and to spend it doing something wild and carefree. "But it will not be fun at all."

He laughed aloud, took his arm from about her shoulders and laced his fingers with hers as they turned among the trees to find the short route to the lake.

Her father and Louisa had gone twenty miles into town in order to shop and dine at the finest hotel. Edna was spending the day with the Burton sisters. No one would miss her, Jane thought. They would not even if they were all at home. They considered her an oddity, uninterested as she was in appearance and fashion and gossip. They had become accustomed to her frequent absences visiting neighbors or simply tramping alone about the park. They rarely asked her whereabouts.

What would they *wear* into the lake? Oh, dear, this was all very… Well, improper.

Robert was moving at a smart pace despite his cane. She found herself laughing as they dodged trees. He turned a grinning face to hers, and suddenly she felt happier than she could ever remember feeling before.

It was a feeling that gave way to apprehension, though, when they reached the far bank of the lake and she looked across the wide expanse of water, sparkling in the sunshine.

"Perhaps," she said as he dropped his cane to the grass and began peeling off his coat without further ado, "I'll sit here and watch you this time."

"And perhaps next time," he said, "you can stand at the edge and watch me."

"Y-yes." She looked at him suspiciously.

"You have two minutes," he said, "to remove your dress and your shoes and stockings. After that you go in, ready or not."

She laughed nervously. And for the moment the water was forgotten. He expected her to *undress* in front of him? His coat and waistcoat were already on the grass, on top of his cane. He was pulling his shirt free of the waistband of his pantaloons.

But she could not go into the water fully clothed. Out of sheer vanity she had worn her favorite dress today to call at the vicarage. And her new silk stockings.

She kicked off her shoes.

Two minutes later she felt very naked, even though her shift covered her almost decently from above her bosom to her knees. He was wearing only a pair of drawers, which sat on his slim hips and just revealed his knees. Her eyes were drawn for a moment to the terrible scars that marred his right leg, but only for a moment. A bare male chest, well-muscled and dusted with dark hair, was a powerful distraction. The sun had surely grown hotter.

He reached out a hand for hers.

"We will wade in," he said, "and enjoy the coolness of the water. I promise not to take you out of your depth or let you fall in. Trust me?"

"I will," she said, smiling ruefully, and they stepped together into the water, which was a safe ankle-deep by the bank.

"Oh!" they both exclaimed together and danced from one foot to the other as they accustomed themselves to the coolness of the water.

They walked and then waded deeper, until the water reached almost to her shoulders and to his chest. It was beginning to feel warmer—and Jane was beginning to feel more fearful.

He stopped and turned to her and held her firmly by the waist with both hands. They were warmer than the water. So were his lips when he set them against hers.

She must be growing into a wanton. She was becoming accustomed to this—and to the rush of hot desire that came with the kiss. She wrapped her arms about his neck and then, when the kiss had ended, she braced her hands on his shoulders and jumped up and down a few times because she had too much energy simply to stand still.

He jumped with her, and after a minute or two they were both laughing helplessly as water splashed over their shoulders and up into their faces.

"Hold your breath," he said, "and duck your head under. You will be quite safe."

"No," she said.

"Watch," he said, and he did it himself without letting go of her waist.

He came up looking sleek with his hair plastered to his head and water streaming off his face and shoulders.

"I am an incurable coward," she told him.

"And with good reason," he said. "But this is a different lifetime, Jane. Let's do it together. Keep your hands on my shoulders."

She would regret her loss of courage tonight if she did not do it now, she knew.

She gripped his shoulders more firmly, sucked in a deep breath, shut her eyes tightly, and allowed herself to go under with him until she could feel the water closing over the top of her head and shutting her into a different world. A world without air. She shot back to the surface and gasped for air and scrunched her eyes more tightly closed. She was probably gripping Robert's shoulders hard enough to leave bruises.

"My brave Jane," he said, laughing and squeezing her waist.

She opened her eyes and smiled. Her coiffure, over which she had labored with far more that usual care today, must be sadly ruined.

"Try it again," he said. "But open your eyes this time."

Now he was asking the absolute impossible. But she did it again, and when they were below the surface, she opened her eyes and did not experience the terrible pain she had been expecting.

She was looking at him beneath the water, and his eyes looked back into hers with warm admiration as his hair waved in a halo about his head.

And then they were back up on their feet again, the sky stretching blue from horizon to horizon above their heads, the sun beaming down brightly on them, the lake floor firm beneath their feet, the air sweet and fresh. Back in the world.

But something had changed.

Everything.

She turned to wade back to the bank, and he came after her, no longer touching her.

"I am sorry," he said as they neared the bank. "I broke my promise and frightened you."

"No," she said. "You did not take me out of my depth, and if I *was* frightened, I also knew I was perfectly safe, Robert." She stopped walking, and they stood facing each other. She reached out one hand to cup the side of his face. "It *is* you. It really *is*. But this time, instead of beckoning me deeper into the light beyond death, you were warm and human and brought me up into the light of the sun. Oh, Robert, you are *human*. We *both* are. It is a wonderful thing to be. Love can be experienced so much more… Well, so much *more* when one is in human form."

She blinked her eyes. It was not the lake water that was blurring her vision, she realized. She turned away from him and stumbled onward, coming to a stop only when she reached the heap of their clothing on the grass. She fell to her knees beside her dress.

Robert Mitford looked nothing like Peter, Marquess of Wigham. But she had known there beneath the water that they were one and the same nevertheless and that she loved Robert with all her heart and soul, as she had loved Peter and all his other incarnations back through the ages.

Loved and lost each time, if Robert was to be believed.

And this time?

He was on his knees behind her, drying her arms and shoulders with his waistcoat, squeezing out the ruined knot of her coiffure before removing the pins and letting her hair fall about her shoulders.

"I love you with everything that is myself," he said,

his voice deep and warm. "I always have, and I always will."

And she turned on her knees, and they wrapped their arms tightly about each other and pressed their faces to each other's shoulder for long moments before raising their heads and gazing into the depths of each other's eyes.

He kissed her. And she kissed him back with equal ardor.

He was no longer a stranger. He never had been. This was no longer improper, wrong, immoral. He was the man she had loved from all eternity and would love to all eternity.

"Jane." His mouth was hot against her throat. His hands had pushed up under her shift to cup her buttocks and follow the flare of her hips to the curve of her waist and the firm weight of her breasts.

She raised her arms, and he lifted off the shift and dropped it to the grass beside them.

She felt curiously unembarrassed as his hands came back to her breasts, supporting them from beneath as one thumb pressed against a nipple, and his mouth came down to suckle the other.

She twined her fingers in the warm wetness of his hair and then lowered both hands to move along his thighs, spread on either side of hers.

He raised his head to pull his coat closer and spread it on the grass, and then he lowered her to lie on it while he peeled off his drawers. She sucked in her breath at the sight of him. She had never… Oh, it did not matter. She wanted him. She *needed* him. And this was right.

Nothing in her life had ever been more right than this.

He parted her thighs with his knees, came down onto her, slid his hands beneath her and came inside her, all long and hard and hot and hurting. And then not hurting at all, but hard and lovely.

Shockingly lovely.

He was her lover, the completion of her soul, and they had these bodies so that they could enjoy their love with all the carnality of their human senses and with the rhythmic give-and-take of this lovely act of ultimate intimacy.

She did not know how to make love. She did not know how to accept a loving. Yet she knew it all at the deepest core of herself, and she moved with him as he loved her and wanted it to go on and on forever and forever.

The one disadvantage of the human condition, of course, was that nothing was forever. Passion strove toward the crest, hovered for a moment upon the very peak of longing and pain, and then swooped into the lovely flowering of pain that turned out not to be pain after all but an exhilarating sort of peace.

A contradiction in terms.

And yet not.

Like all the dualities of human life.

"Robert," she murmured against his ear.

"My love."

She wondered as she sank deeper into lethargy if she would be sorry for this. Sanity was bound to reassert itself soon, surely.

But not yet.

Ah, not yet.

He raised his head, and they kissed each other with warm languor. She wrapped both arms about his neck.

He was warmly, deliciously human.

They were still joined at the core.

CHAPTER 5

THEIR CLOTHES HAD DRIED IN THE HEAT OF THE SUN WHILE they dozed side by side. But they were both awake again. Their hands were clasped on the grass between them.

That was something he had not intended to do, Robert thought, and ought not to have done. But he could not feel as sorry as perhaps he should. There had been an inevitability about it.

"Marry me?" he asked, squeezing her hand a little more tightly.

And then it struck him that it was hardly a memorable way in which to ask such a momentous question, though it was just the way he had asked two days ago. He turned his head toward her. She was looking back, and she was smiling. Her hair, half-dry, was a tangled mess. It somehow made her look more beautiful than ever.

"Yes," she said.

Just like that? Was it to be easy after all, then, during this lifetime?

"I ought to have spoken with your father first," he said. "Will he give his blessing?"

From what he had seen of Sir Horace Everett, the man

was vain and arrogant. He also seemed almost unaware of the existence of his two younger daughters.

"I do not know," she said.

"But you are of age," he reminded her.

"Yes."

"Will you marry me even if he disapproves?" he asked.

"Yes," she said.

"I cannot offer you a great deal, Jane," he said. "A captain's pay is no fortune, and following the drum is not always comfortable, even for an officer's wife. But my parents are kind, hospitable people, and would give you a perfectly comfortable home if you should choose not to travel with me. Eventually, of course, my father's property will be mine, though I cannot hope that will be soon. My grandmother's modest fortune will be divided among Gerald, our sister and me when she passes, but I also hope *that* will not be soon. I am scarcely a dazzling match for you."

"I do not want a dazzling match," she said. "Only a decent, sensible one that promises to bring me more happiness than I ever dreamed possible."

"Now *that*," he said, smiling, "I can bring you in abundance."

"I know," she said as she came into his arms.

And that was that. It seemed almost too easy.

"I will call on Sir Horace tomorrow morning," he said as he walked with her back to the house later. "Will that be a suitable time, do you suppose?"

"I will talk to him this evening," she said, "and prepare him."

He set an arm about her shoulders and she wrapped one about his waist.

"I ought to apologize," he said. "I ought not—"

"Don't," she said, touching a finger to his lips. "Please

don't regret it. I will not. I will always remember our one perfect afternoon."

Her words sounded a faint note of foreboding. Their *one* perfect afternoon? There would surely be others, and perfect mornings and nights, too. There would surely be a perfect lifetime together and a perfect forever.

He turned her to him just before the hall came into sight and kissed her slowly and deeply.

"I will see you tomorrow, then," he said, "after I have talked with your father. We will be officially betrothed, Jane, and soon we will be married and beginning our happily-ever-after."

"I will wait for you," she said, "down by the lily pond. Provided rain is not tipping down."

"Tomorrow." He kissed her again, and when they arrived outside the stable block, he turned down the driveway while she continued on to the house.

It struck him after he had seen her reach the front doors and turn to wave to him that, though he was using his cane, he did not really need it for every step any longer. He was healing, recovering. Soon he would be able to think about getting back to his regiment.

With a wife to comfort his days and warm his nights.

SIR HORACE EVERETT WAS very upset indeed that a daughter of his would consider besmirching the name of Everett by marrying a cavalry captain of no social significance whatsoever. It was even said that the family's *very* modest fortune had been made a few generations ago *in trade*.

Jane had sought him out in the library, where he retreated most evenings after dinner in order to enjoy his port. He was sitting by the fire, his handkerchief in one hand, his feet on a stool, a general air of distress and injured consequence about his person.

"His brother is our *vicar*," he said rather as if that fact set the Mitfords on a social par with the Everett boot boy.

"Mr. Mitford senior has a comfortable fortune, Papa," Jane explained. "And Captain Mitford is his elder son. Besides, Captain Mitford has distinguished himself in battle and has even been mentioned by name in dispatches. He is well-bred and well-educated."

And I love him.

"And a cripple," he said with clear distaste. He reached for the bottle of smelling salts on the table beside him and wafted it beneath his nostrils. "You will not do this, Jane. A Miss Everett of Goodrich Hall can do far better than a crippled army captain. You cannot aspire to a title, perhaps, as Louisa can, but you can expect a husband with £6,000 a year at the very least. No, Jane, I will not hear of such a match for you. Send the young man a letter and tell him he need not come here tomorrow. It would be too much for my nerves to receive him."

"Papa," she said, "I love him."

He looked repulsed, even shocked.

"Love?" he said. "Is a daughter of mine to behave like the vulgar masses and talk of *love?*"

"I wish to marry him," she said, clasping her hands at her waist. She had not been invited to sit down.

"You may wish again, miss," he said. "You always were a trial to me from your childhood on. Sometimes I wonder how you can possibly be mine. I wish your mother had survived. She would have talked sense into you."

"I wish she had lived, too," Jane said.

He waved the salts beneath his nose again before setting them aside.

"I will have to send for Lady Percy," he said. "She must come after breakfast tomorrow morning before this dreadful young man puts in an appearance demanding to speak with me. Lady Percy will advise you. *She* will support me. *She* will speak to this *soldier* and put him in his place. Such insolence! And to think that I condescended to receive him at Goodrich Hall just last evening."

"*This soldier* is Captain Mitford," Jane said softly.

"Write to Lady Percy," her father said. "Tell her she must come as soon after breakfast as she can. Tell her she must have an early breakfast. And tell her I will send my carriage. It is an embarrassment to have that ancient coach she rides about in seen outside my front doors. Go, Jane, but before you do pour me a glass of brandy. I am feeling quite faint. I must advise the vicar to send his brother away without further ado. I daresay he is a distraction. I did not think last Sunday's sermon quite up to the vicar's usual standard."

Jane did not point out that Captain Mitford had not even been at the vicarage last Sunday—or that her father had snored through the sermon, as he always did. She poured the brandy without another word, set it in her father's hand and left the room to carry out his instructions.

Lady Percy was her dearest friend despite the twenty-year gap in their ages. And she was sensible and intelligent and diplomatic. She had always been able to soothe Sir Horace's vapors. She would soothe them now and plead Jane's case with him. She would make him see that marriage to a cavalry captain, eldest son of a gentleman of modest means, was really not a dreadfully degrading match for the middle daughter of a baronet.

She wrote a fairly lengthy letter, explaining how she and Captain Mitford had met and fallen deeply in love, and how he had proposed marriage to her this afternoon and she had accepted. She described her father's reaction and her own reasons for holding firm. She sent the letter with a servant and imposed patience on herself until morning.

LADY PERCY ARRIVED AT GOODRICH soon after Jane had eaten breakfast. Not that she had eaten a great deal. She was feeling too agitated. Her father was still in bed. So were her sisters.

Lady Percy came hurrying into the morning room on the heels of the butler. Jane went to meet her and felt the reassurance of setting her hands in the older woman's outstretched ones. Lady Percy had stood in place of her mother since the latter's death when Jane was fifteen. It was an enormous relief that she had come promptly and had arrived before Robert.

"Jane, my dear girl," she said, "whatever is all this *about?* Has Captain Mitford been presumptuous and set his sights upon a daughter of Lady Everett? Oh, how unpardonable of him! And have you fallen prey to his charm, poor dear? I might have guessed that you would. You are young and impressionable and meet far too few eligible young gentlemen. That must change, and I shall tell Sir Horace so in no uncertain terms as soon as I see him."

It felt to Jane as if her heart had slipped downward in the direction of her slippers. And she remembered Lady Percy's saying just a few days ago that Robert was ineligible.

"I think," she said, smiling, "it is as much a case of *me* setting my sights upon a military hero. It is very presumptuous of me. But we love each other, you see, and nothing can make us happy except marriage to each other."

"Oh, my poor love." Lady Percy released her hands in order to set one arm about her shoulders and seat them both on a sofa. "I can remember falling in love once, too, when I was young. It was a delightful feeling, but of course it was not one upon which a steady future or lasting happiness might have been built. There were other far more important considerations, as there are in your case. You are such a sensible, mature young lady, Jane, that I sometimes forget you are only twenty-one. You need to be married. Oh, indeed you do, and I shall be quite firm with your father on the subject. Whenever he goes up to London for a few weeks, he thinks to take only Louisa with him. It is unpardonable when you are all of marriageable age."

Jane's heart, in the soles of her slippers, felt leaden.

"Why is Captain Mitford ineligible?" she asked. "He is a gentleman."

"And you, Jane," Lady Percy said, squeezing her shoulder, "are the daughter of Sir Horace Everett of Goodrich. It is an old, illustrious title and an old, illustrious family."

"He is *only* a baronet," Jane said. "He was not even the son of the last baronet, but a nephew. I am his middle daughter."

"Jane." Lady Percy took her arm from about Jane's shoulders and held her hands in a firm grasp again. "It is far more than that. You are very different from most other young ladies of my acquaintance. You are superior to them all. Certainly you are better than your sisters, even Louisa. You have a superior mind. You *must not* throw it away by becoming a soldier's wife and following the drum. You would be desperately unhappy once the glow of romance had faded from the relationship. And fade it would, Jane. I assure you of that. Oh, I hate to see you hurt, and there is a hurt look in your eyes now, but I must plead with you to listen to an older and a wiser mind. Listen to me as though I were your dear mother. She would hate to see you being led astray like this by an infatuation. It would break her heart."

Jane got to her feet, but before she could make any answer, the door opened to admit her father.

"Ah, Lady Percy," he said, "you have come. And not before time. I had not a wink of sleep last night and feel quite haggard this morning. It took my valet twice as long as usual to make me presentable. You have talked Jane out of her madness, I hope?"

"Oh, not madness, Sir Horace," she said, smiling. "But I believe I have convinced her to be her usual rational, sensible self again and listen to advice. She is so lovely. Lady Everett would have been proud of her. I need to talk to you about taking Jane and Edna, as well as Louisa, of course, to London with you next spring. They need to attend some of the entertainments of the Season. They need to meet eligible young gentlemen. They need to make the brilliant matches they are surely destined to make as your daughters."

"It would be a severe strain upon my nerves," he said with a sigh.

"Nevertheless," she said. "Imagine how you will be admired as the father of three such—"

Jane did not wait to hear more. Robert would surely be here soon, and she did not want to see him when he arrived. She hurried from the house without stopping to fetch a shawl or bonnet despite the fact that it was cooler outside today than it had been for the past week.

She half ran down to the lily pond so that she could sit hidden from view on the seat beneath the willow tree.

Her heart pounded in her chest, in her ears, against her temples.

She would hate to see you being led astray like this by an infatuation. It would break her heart.

Would her mother, too, have opposed this match if she had lived? Oh, surely not. But Lady Percy had been her dearest friend. They had thought alike on most issues. As she lay dying, Mama had begged Jane always to listen to Lady Percy, always to go to her for advice and comfort.

But Lady Percy did not know all the facts.

What would she say if she did?

If she knew that Jane had recognized Robert as soon as she met him as someone she had known and loved in a previous lifetime? That he had been searching for the soul mate he had loved and lost through countless lifetimes? That they had found each other and fallen passionately in love and knew beyond all doubt that they belonged together in this lifetime and for all eternity beyond it? That yesterday afternoon they had acted on their love for each other and made love on the grass by the lake?

What if Lady Percy knew those things?

She would look at Jane with considerable alarm. She would think she really had gone mad.

It *did* sound like madness.

Was it?

Had she been led astray by infatuation?

ROBERT STEPPED OUT OF Goodrich Hall an hour later. He looked up at the sky and saw without surprise that clouds had moved over while he was indoors. The breeze was cool. It looked as if it might rain later.

He was not worried about Sir Horace Everett's opposition to his marriage to Jane. The man was weak and vain and vaporish, and Jane had said yesterday that she would marry Robert even if her father disapproved.

It was Lady Percy who concerned him. She was sen-

sible and well-bred. She had been Lady Everett's friend
and had promised that she would always watch over Jane
as she would her own daughter. She had advised and
would continue to advise Jane to refuse his offer. Sir
Horace would take her to London next spring, and she,
Lady Percy, would go, too, and Jane would find a husband suited to her temperament and station in life.

Robert did not like Lady Percy, and it was clear to him
that she did not like him. He worried about her influence.

It was a relief to see as he walked down the sloping
lawn to the lily pond that someone with a yellow dress
was sitting beneath the willow tree. At least she had come.

She did not lift her head as he approached, though. She
looked down at her hands, which were tightly clasped in
her lap. She was not wearing a shawl or anything warmer.
He could see goose bumps on her arms.

"Jane?" he said.

She looked up then with calm, opaque eyes, and he
knew that all was lost.

"At first," she said, "I thought that if I told them everything, they would understand and gladly give their blessing. But I did not tell them. They would have thought I
was mad. And perhaps they would have been right."

"Perhaps?" He made no move to join her on the seat.

She spread her hands across her lap and looked down
at them again.

"They *would* be right," she said. "Lady Percy says
I have not met enough gentlemen, and she does have a
point. I have not met *any* except the neighbors with whom
I grew up. It is understandable that I fell in love with
you, and that I justified the intensity of my emotions by
convincing myself that we have always loved. Through
eternity. I am only sorry that in allowing myself to be so

deluded I led you astray. I hope I have not hurt you too deeply. But perhaps it is conceited to think I might."

How right he had been to fear Lady Percy's influence.

"Jane," he said, "you *know* it is not delusion. And even if it were… Well, socially we are not so very far apart. And if it is my nomadic existence as an army officer that is the chief impediment, I will sell out and settle down in one place and make a home for you and our children. We will never be destitute or even poor. And we will always have something of infinitely greater value than any fortune. We *love* each other."

"I must listen to those who are older and wiser than I," she said. "And I am convinced my mother would have counseled me to refuse you. She was the most important person in my life."

"More important than I am?" he said.

She looked at him again, her eyes troubled.

"My mind is clouded by emotion," she said. "I must listen to those who can think clearly. Perhaps at some time in the future…"

"I will come back?" he said when she did not complete the thought. He could not keep the bitterness from his voice. "Perhaps I will capture a fortune in spoils at some battle. Perhaps my grandmother will turn out to be far wealthier than I suppose. Perhaps my father—"

"Please," she said, lifting a staying hand. "Please don't be angry, Robert."

"Perhaps I *will* come back," he said. "My brother lives here, after all. Perhaps my circumstances will have changed by then. Perhaps your mind will have changed. Perhaps we will find that we still love each other. Perhaps we will marry and live happily after a few wasted years. But there are too many *perhapses* there, Jane, to provide any sort of comfort. Life is too full of uncertainties for us to be sure that there will be a second chance to do what we ought to do *now*."

She lowered her arm.

"I need time to think," she said.

"It seems to me," he said, "that it is when you have time to think, Jane, that you allow doubts to cloud your judgment. Your heart is clear on what you feel, what you want, what you know will bring you fulfillment and happiness for a lifetime and beyond. Your head, your thoughts, bring doubt because what you have experienced during the past few days does not appear to make rational sense."

"It does not," she agreed.

"Jane," he said, "look at me and tell me you are prepared to give up everything I represent for you just because your father and your mother's friend are opposed. Tell me that you truly believe your heart should be subordinate to your head—or rather to the heads of others."

She did look at him, and frowned.

"I need time," she said again.

But something had snapped in him. He could feel panic bunch like a cold, iron fist low in his abdomen, and he understood again the main frustration of the human condition with all its dualities. They were one soul, he and Jane, but here in this human form they were two, and it *took* two to restore the unity he craved. In the last lifetime he had forsaken her. In this lifetime it was the other way around.

"This is all the time you have," he said, and he could hear the change in his voice. Instead of being warm and pleading as it had been thus far, it had fallen flat. "This moment. I cannot promise the future. Neither can you. The future does not exist. You must decide now."

He could see an answering flash of anger in her eyes before she lowered them to her lap again.

"Then I have decided," she said. "The answer is no. Goodbye, Captain Mitford."

He did not even say goodbye. He turned on his heel and strode away in the direction of the driveway. He did not realize for a while that he was carrying his cane at his side, not using it.

JANE SAT WHERE SHE WAS for a long time, oblivious to the chill of the air and the passing of time.

She stared sightlessly at the water until at last she realized she could no longer see it clearly. She wiped away her tears with the heels of her hands, but she was sobbing too now, and the tears were coursing down her cheeks too fast to be dried with her bare hands.

She wept helplessly and painfully for several minutes before fumbling for a handkerchief in a side pocket of her dress. There was none there. She got to her feet and stumbled the few steps to the edge of the pond. She would wash off her face and dry it with the hem of her dress. Her complexion must be all red and blotched. It would not do to be seen thus when she went back to the house.

She almost lost her balance at the edge of the pond and tumbled in headfirst. She took a hasty step back to safety.

And something shifted inside her.

That had happened before. Then, too, she had been half-blinded by tears and distraught with grief. Except that then she had not been able to regain her balance but had fallen in. And the water had been swollen by heavy rains and was cold and fast-moving. She had drowned.

But before that, before she fell in, there had been a tree.

Jane turned sharply to look at the willow. But it had not been a willow tree. It had been something far more monumental. An oak. A great spreading tree with hidden clefts and hollows. And one in particular. It was why she had come there. She had had to see it again. And it had deepened her grief to such a wretched degree that she had cried until there were no more tears but only an unbearable pain in her chest as she continued to sob. She had wanted her mother. She had wanted to pour everything out to her at last. She had yearned for her mother's arms. But she must not go back looking like this. She must wash her face, smooth back her hair…

What *was* it in the tree?

Jane frowned in concentration.

And then remembered…

"Oh, God," she said aloud. "Oh, dear God."

And what was more, she knew *which* tree. There was only one oak like that one. It stood alone on the riverbank just outside the village, not far from the smithy.

She picked up the sides of her skirts and ran, forgetting all about her appearance and the chill breeze and the darkening clouds overhead.

Oh, *why* had she defied memory all these years?

And when memory had begun to return this week, and she might have redeemed herself, she had lost faith again. She had taken fright.

When she had been sent Robert, the completion of her own soul, she had recognized him, gloried in the recognition and loved him passionately and recklessly—and then denied the knowledge and sent him away.

She had made reason and common sense her gods.

She had allowed people who did not know what she knew or understand what she understood to be her mentors.

SHE CONTINUED TO RUN even when her breath came in labored gasps.

But when she reached the river and the ancient oak tree, she almost lost courage again. How absurd to believe that it might still be here. She was twenty-one years old. She had been born fourteen or fifteen years after Mary Mitford's death. That had happened thirty-five years ago or more.

Could one box survive that long hidden in a tree? Assuming no one had found it and tossed it on a rubbish heap in the meanwhile, of course.

She stood beneath the tree, catching her breath and closing her eyes and trying to concentrate. Trying to remember.

She lifted her right arm. Waist level? Above her head? Stretched upward as she stood on her toes? Perhaps she had had to climb up into the branches.

And then she held her arm at shoulder level and knew it felt right.

The great trunk divided into several huge branches at that point. There were clefts galore into which one might push something reasonably small to hide it. And, over *there* was an actual hollow, a hole that might stretch down all the way to the ground. It would be too deep to reach into.

Jane reached across the branches anyway and set her hand into the hollow and felt about. At first she thought there was nothing there, but then she felt it—the edge of a metal object wedged underneath the branch, where it would be hidden from view and sheltered from the weather.

She was breathless again by the time she had pulled it out. It was rusty and half-corroded, but it was unmis-

takably a metal box. She could still see traces of the remembered roses painted on its lid.

It was locked. But even if she had had the key she
would surely not have been able to open it.

Besides, it was not hers to open.

She clutched the box to her bosom and hurried off in
the direction of the vicarage.

CHAPTER 6

JANE WAS FORCED TO PAUSE A MOMENT AFTER SHE HAD PASSED the smithy. She had a stitch in her side and pressed a hand to it as she half doubled over and tried desperately to suck air into her lungs. The box was heavy.

She was hatless and breathless and doubtless red-faced and disheveled. Miss Jane Everett *never* stepped outdoors looking less than immaculate, even when she intended to remain in the park and did not expect that anyone would see her.

She hurried onward, past the gates that would have taken her back into the privacy of the park, and looked ahead to the church and the vicarage beyond it. There was a flurry of activity outside the latter, just as there had been a few days ago when she had approached it in the gig with her sisters. Except that this time there was only one horse and one horseman—who had just swung himself up into the saddle and was riding away. Three people stood in the gateway, their hands raised in fare-well, though he did not turn back to see them or return the gesture.

The vicar and his wife and elderly Mrs. Mitford were the people in the gateway.

The rider was Robert. And he was leaving.

"Stop!" Jane cried and broke into a run.

Her voice was breathless and not nearly as loud as she could have wished. But the three people at the gate turned their heads, as did Mrs. Pickering on the opposite side of the street as she pegged wet clothes on her line.

Horse and rider proceeded on their way.

"Stop!" Jane cried again, standing still and pressing one hand to her side. *"Robert!"*

And somehow—it seemed impossible that he could have heard her—he turned in the saddle, and then the horse turned about and stood still in the middle of the road.

Jane started running again, heedless of how she must look. She paused for a moment outside the vicarage to set the box down by the gate. Then she ran on.

Robert dismounted and stood watching her for a moment before abandoning his mount and striding and then running toward her. His arms opened as the gap between them lessened, and she ran into them, raising her own to clasp about his neck. He hugged her tightly as though to fold her right into himself.

She breathed in the warm comfort of him.

"Jane," he was murmuring against her ear, and there was a world of pain in his voice. "My love, my love."

She tipped back her head to look into his eyes.

"You did not abandon me," she said. "You did not leave me. You were coming back. You *were*. You did not leave me."

She had already told both him and Mrs. Mitford that. But she could see from the deepening light of his eyes that he knew she could offer more proof than just the words this time.

He was the only one in her whole life who had ever

fully understood her. How could she have doubted even for a single moment? How could she have allowed herself to be almost persuaded to give him up?

To give up her whole happiness, her very reason for being?

To give up *love,* the mightiest of all forces?

And in exchange for what? Duty to her elders? Cold logic? Common sense that really was not sensible at all?

"I did *not* abandon you?" he said, and he smiled at her before he looked beyond her, aware of his brother and sister-in-law and great-aunt still at the vicarage gate.

Jane turned to look at them, too, and he set an arm about her shoulders.

Elderly Mrs. Mitford was bent over the box, wailing.

"It is Mary's," she cried. "Oh, it is Mary's. I searched everywhere for it and never found it. The key was about her neck, and it has been about mine ever since they found her."

She touched the chain about her neck and looked up at Jane as she approached with Robert.

"You found it, Miss Jane?" she asked. "You *found* it?"

"It was in a hollow of the oak tree down by the river," Jane explained.

"But what made you look there, Miss Jane?" young Mrs. Mitford asked. "And—" She looked from Jane to Robert in some bewilderment.

"I believe, Amelia," the vicar said, "Robert may be staying here after all. I doubt that key will turn in the lock, Aunt Dinah. We will have to break it open."

"Let me try," Robert said, and he took the key from his aunt's trembling hand and worked it into the rusty lock.

It seemed very unlikely that it would turn, but with some persuasion it did. Robert pried open the lid and held the box out to his aunt.

She peered half fearfully inside and took out a browned and curled piece of parchment from the top. She looked beneath it.

"Her journal," she said. "And a handkerchief. His. You see? You can still make out the W embroidered on one corner."

"And the parchment?" Jane asked. She was almost holding her breath. She knew what it was, but even now she was not quite sure she could trust her memory not to have deceived her. This was no ordinary memory, after all. This was memory stretching back into another lifetime.

Mrs. Mitford looked at it. Her lips moved but no sound came out. She handed it to Robert and he read it.

"It is a marriage certificate," he said quietly. "They were married, Mary and the Marquess of Wigham. By special license."

"Two weeks before his death," Mrs. Mitford said. "Less than three before hers."

"Mary Mitford was the *Marchioness of Wigham?*" Amelia Mitford said. "Oh! Wait until I tell Miss Louisa."

"I am glad for your sake, Aunt Dinah," the vicar said. "At least they were married."

She was smiling—with tears in her eyes. She raised both gnarled hands and cupped Jane's face with them and gazed into her eyes.

"My dear," she said. "Oh, my dear. Thank you. For everything. Now I can die in peace when my time comes."

"This," the vicar said, "is all very public. We should step inside the house. Will you join us, Miss Jane? I am afraid I understand very little of what had gone on today."

"Miss Jane and Robert," Mrs. Mitford said, "need to talk in private, Gerald. They must go around to the flower garden, where they may be private together. But you must take my shawl, Miss Jane. It is not as warm today as it has been."

They did as they were told. Robert wrapped the shawl about Jane's shoulders as they went. They sat down on adjacent chairs in the back garden, and he took both her hands in his.

"You remembered?" he asked her.

"When I was standing by the lily pond after you left, I was about to wash my face because I had been weeping," she said, "and I almost fell in. I would have got uncomfortably wet if I had, but nothing worse. Unlike the last time, when I drowned. But I remembered that before falling in that time I had been looking through my box of treasures that I kept in the hollow of the oak tree. I had been looking at our marriage papers, which you had left with me."

"Why did I go?" he asked her.

"After we married," she said, "I think we both took fright. I did not know how to tell my mother and father, and you were quite sure your father would be furious and would cast you off even though he could not disinherit you. We must have decided—I cannot really remember—that it would be better for you to go alone to explain to him and then come back for me. We had probably decided, too, that in the meanwhile I would break the news to my mother and father. My father would not have been pleased with our marriage by special license when he was the vicar here. I think you must have got killed when you were hastening back to me."

"Jane." He kissed her hand. "We almost made it through, then, in our last lifetime. But a little cowardice sent me off without you and I was never able to come back."

"Yes." She clung to his hands. "It will not happen

again, Robert. I will not wait on the chance that you will come back in a few years' time and circumstances will be more conducive to our marrying. I will not wait a day longer. I want to marry you now—if you will still have me."

"If I will still have you." He carried both her hands to his lips and his eyes glowed with the intensity of love. "Gerald is going to make us wait a whole month while the banns are read, though."

"Oh, bother," she said.

"In the meantime," he said, "I will not willingly allow you out of my sight."

"Or I you," she assured him.

"I suppose," he said, "we were allowed the great privilege of a glimpse beyond the veil this lifetime, Jane, because we came so close last time."

"Yes," she said.

They sat gazing into each other's eyes for a long while, their hands clasped.

"It is really you," he said, smiling slowly.

"It really is." She smiled back.

"It is a little overwhelming, is it not?" he said.

"More than a little."

He got to his feet and drew her up with him, and they wrapped their arms about each other again and clung tightly as if daring the world or eternity to part them.

Nothing could or would.

Her father would not like it, Jane thought, but he would grow accustomed to it. Soon, no doubt, he would be slipping *my son-in-law, Captain Mitford, the hero from India* into his conversations.

Lady Percy would not like it. But she genuinely loved Jane, and she would soon come to see that Jane was happier than she had ever been, and she would relent.

Perhaps Robert's family would not like it, but they would grow accustomed to her. She had always been able to make people love her. She would not fail with them.

But even if the whole world was against them, it would not matter. They were together—again. And this time they would remain together. Until death did them part and—of course—long after that.

Forever.

"Robert." She drew back her head and gazed into his eyes. She could see her reflection in them, and she knew he was seeing his in her eyes.

Two souls.

One.

Soul mates.

Was there a lovelier word in the language?

"I love you," she said.

"I know."

And he tightened his arms about her waist and lifted her off her feet and spun her about in a full circle, whooping as he did so.

And without the aid of his cane.

Jane threw back her head and laughed out loud as the sun drew clear of the clouds overhead and beamed down upon them.

* * * * *

NORTHANGER CASTLE

Colleen Gleason

* * *

To Jane Austen, for making romance novels classics
and keepers for generations.

ACKNOWLEDGMENTS

Thanks to Janet Mullany, who thought of me for
this project—you know how much I adore you, dear
tickler. I am thrilled to be part of this group
of talent, and express my gratitude to Susan Krinard
for the brilliance of the idea. I'd also like to
thank Mary Balogh for taking a chance on
a paranormal element and for helping
to get this project off the ground.

Thanks to Harlequin for doing such a fantastic job of
packaging and putting together this anthology.
I couldn't be more delighted with
how this has all turned out!

And I'd also like to thank the fans and readers of the
Gardella Vampire Chronicles. Although Victoria's
story is complete, I hope you enjoy this story of a
different wing of the Gardella family just as much.
Thank you for your support and enthusiasm!

Dear Reader,

I grew up reading Gothic novels, and alternately rolling my eyes at the heroine who creeps up to the attic in the dead of night with a candle, and holding my breath, sitting on the edge of my seat and flipping pages as fast as I could, while she did so. And to this day, I am a sucker for the dark, brooding Gothic heroes who remained a mystery until the ends of those suspenseful books.

Thus, when I first read Jane Austen's *Northanger Abbey,* I knew I'd found a kindred spirit not only in Jane, through her tongue-in-cheek rendering of a Gothic novel, but also a heroine I could relate to in Catherine Morland. Like myself, Catherine sees stories everywhere, making up histories and Gothic tales in her mind. As a writer, I do that every day.

When I was invited to be part of this group for *Bespelling Jane Austen,* it was a no-brainer for me to choose *Northanger Abbey* as the Austen novel I wanted to work with. Since I had already written a series about a female vampire hunter who lived during Austen's time, I thought it would be fun to take the history of the Gardella vampire hunters and weave them into a summer at Bath with a dramatic young woman.

Thus, Caroline Merrill was born—a counterpart to Catherine Morland. A young woman who not only devours Gothic novels as Catherine Morland did, she also sees stories everywhere and in everyone. She's not always correct in her assessments (nor was Miss Morland), but she rises to the occasion when necessary.

I hope you enjoy Caroline Merrill's adventures and my tribute to Jane Austen's *Northanger Abbey.* Perhaps you'll even see a bit of yourself in a young woman who loves her books and finds people to cast as those characters. I know I did!

Happy reading!

Colleen Gleason

CHAPTER I

1845 Bath, England

MISS CAROLINE MERRILL SMOOTHED HER RUFFLED-HEM SKIRT
as she settled into the chair against the wall. She quickly
tucked her feet under the seat to keep them from being
stepped upon or tripped over, and confirmed that the
heavy, bulky reticule still dangled from her wrist. One
never knew when one might need one of the accoutre-
ments from within.

And then she had her first chance to look around, to
really see all of the excitement. The Pump Room was just
as thrilling—and packed—as Almack's had been, filled
with people meant to see and be seen.

Unfortunately, Miss Merrill was one of the former—
for other than dear, *dear* Mrs. Argenot, by whose good
graces and generosity had Miss Merrill come to be here
in Bath, the young woman knew not a soul. It was only
because Mrs. Argenot was a distant cousin and old friend
of Miss Merrill's mother, and that she had been desir-
ous of a companion, that the younger woman had been
invited to come. An event for which she still gave daily
thanks.

"My stars," Mrs. Argenot said, leaning toward Caroline with an effusive wave of rosewater, "I declare, it's cooler outside in the noonday sun than it is here in this room."

"And I would suspect the lemonade would be chillier, as well," Caroline replied, eyeing the beads of sweat on Mrs. Argenot's upper lip…and hoping she didn't sport the same decoration. "Though not by much," she added, recalling how warm the lemonade was at Almack's, which, to her recollection, had never been this uncomfortably warm. At least, it hadn't been, the single time she'd been there as a guest of Lady Jane Merriwether.

"Why do they not open some of the doors and windows? Then we could have a bit of a breeze, at least," said her companion over the roar of the music, laughter and voices pitched loudly around them. She was a tiny woman, who made Caroline feel like a large and bulky footman next to her, even though Caroline herself was the shortest member of her family.

Granted, it was no surprise that her three brothers should be taller than her, but even her mother, the elegant Mrs. Evangeline Merrill, rose three fingers' width above her daughter. "I do believe all the doors and windows are open, Mrs. Argenot," Caroline told her. "It simply makes no difference when it has been so warm outside all day, and there are so many people in here tonight."

Caroline flattened her upper lip so as to determine whether she did have those glistening dots above it, and then, surrendering to her obsession, began to dig in her reticule.

"I declare, Caro, that is the largest bag I've ever seen," Mrs. Argenot told her. "You could fit one of your precious books in there, couldn't you? Whatever do you carry around in such a thing?"

"A variety of implements," Caroline replied, rummaging past her reading spectacles and the palm-size silver cross in favor of the muslin handkerchief she'd been seeking. "One never can tell when one might be in need of a pair of scissors or a magnifying glass." Among other things that she'd managed to stuff into the bag. Which, she could not deny, really was of an awkward size, especially as an accessory for a ball.

Adding the wooden stake had been the biggest problem and, even now, she wasn't certain that the one she'd managed to fit within the bag was large and sturdy enough to do the job.

If, indeed, she ever did come face-to-face with a Lord Ruthven, or, worse, a Lord Tyndale–type. Which, heaven forbid she should ever do. But since Caroline was a practical girl, she felt it important to be prepared for any eventuality, hence the silver cross that was simply too large and bulky to wear with her gown. Nevertheless, it would certainly be a deterrent to a vampire.

Handkerchief successfully retrieved, Caroline dabbed unobtrusively at her upper lip as she scanned the room. There was no doubt in her mind that if there was a vampire lurking about Bath, he would be here in the Pump Room tonight.

After all, according to Dr. Polidori's fantastically horrid novel, the Lord Ruthvens of the world preyed on the innocent, rich-blooded young girls of the *ton*. What better place than Bath in the summer to stalk his victims?

Caroline tucked the handkerchief back into her bag and scanned the room, searching for a likely candidate. She was not about to be taken unawares, even if the rest of the attendees had nothing to worry about but treading upon the hems of their gowns or finding a dance partner.

"I vow, I've never been so exhausted in all my *life!*"

exclaimed a shrill voice. Its owner collapsed onto the chair next to Caroline in a wave of pink ruffles and rose-colored flounces and began to fan herself enthusiastically.

Caroline turned to the newcomer, who was a pretty young woman about her age with wheat-colored hair and a heart-shaped face. She looked exactly like a heroine in Mrs. Radcliffe's novels: pretty and innocent and lively. "It is quite a trial to make one's way through all of the crush and keep from getting one's toes trod upon," she agreed.

"And my slippers! They're ruined!" wailed the girl, lifting up her skirts just enough to show toes of pale pink silk. Which, as far as Caroline could see, were unblemished by scuffs, dirt or anything else.

"Er," she said, "I think they look lovely." Perhaps she wasn't the sort of girl who would sneak up to the attic to investigate a locked door during a thunderstorm…no, she would most likely be the Gothic heroine's best friend and confidante. The one who had exquisite taste in fashion.

The girl glanced at Caroline for the first time. "Oh, my word, can you not *see* the stains on them? Why, they no longer look the *least bit* pink! They've become as brown as mud!" She fussed for a few moments, adjusting her flounces and smoothing her already smooth skirt.

Caroline watched in fascination, for the newcomer was quite a lovely young woman and her costume was just as pretty. She wondered if the girl was an orphan who'd found a kindly woman guardian, a member of the *haute ton,* perhaps a very distant cousin, childless, of course, to take her in and sponsor her into Society, and that was why she was so conscientious about her clothing.

"Have you come here before tonight?" Caroline asked, in an effort to begin a conversation that had to do with something other than the state of the girl's slippers and that might lead into more information about her history.

Or perhaps she would have some information about the very proper-looking older man who lurked in the corner, his dark eyes scanning the room. He seemed just the type to have locked his mad wife away in a tower room and come searching for a new, younger bride. His nose was so sharp and his chin weak…and there was something furtive about him.

"Oh, I have been here many times before," the girl replied airily. "But as we have just arrived in town yesterday, this is the first visit we've made this summer." Again, she looked up as if she'd just noticed Caroline. "We must find someone to properly introduce us, but until then… I am Isobel Thornton," she said, still brushing at her skirts.

"What a pleasure to meet you," Caroline said. "My name is Caroline Merrill."

"Indeed," Miss Thornton said, still fussing with her flounces. Then she turned to patting her hair, which had been swept into a smooth, moonbeam-colored twist with perfect little curls framing her pretty face.

Caroline didn't want to consider what her own honey-colored hair might look like, after the stifling heat and pushing through the crowd. She was certain it didn't look nearly as fresh as Miss Thornton's.

"I do not know what's to come of this visit," Miss Thornton said. Now she was smoothing her gloves, first the left hand, all along to the elbow and then the right. "I have heard of *no one* in town at this time. It's sure to be such a *bore,* but what can one do? My dear brother, James, must have his way and visit Bath in July." She shook her head, curls bouncing charmingly. "He can be ever so frustrating, thinking only of his hounds and horses, and his club, and never once thinking of me."

Caroline forbore to point out that with the number of people crowded into the Pump Room, it could hardly be considered that "no one" was in town. And apparently Miss Thornton didn't need a kindly sponsor if her brother was taking her under his wing. Perhaps it was his wife who'd stepped in to raise his younger sister....

Then suddenly Miss Thornton was looking at her with interest. "Miss *Merrill,* you say?" Her eyes narrowed thoughtfully. "I recently had the pleasure of meeting a young man, a Mr. Robert Merrill."

"Oh," Caroline said, delight coursing through her. "Why, that would be my brother!"

"Your *brother!*" Miss Thornton's eyes widened, and a great smile erupted on her face. "Why, I just *knew* the minute I saw you that we were bound to become bosom friends!" She clasped Caroline's hand, squeezing it tightly. "And Mr. Merrill... Why, he was such a lovely man. So kind and charming and very handsome."

Caroline flushed with pleasure. "Robbie is my eldest brother, and I confess that he is my favorite of the three of them. I am so glad that you found him pleasing, Miss Thornton."

"Oh, indeed! He was the kindest, most *charming,* and most handsome man I have ever had the pleasure of walking with!" Miss Thornton said, squeezing Caroline's hand even tighter. "And you must call me Isobel. I just know we are meant to be intimate, *intimate* friends!"

Caroline responded in kind, "And you must call me Caroline, or Caro if you like. I am so pleased to have met you."

"And we shall walk tomorrow. And we must visit the Roman baths, too, of course. Oh, I am so delighted to have found such a *bosom* friend here, when it was *sure* to be such a bore! And my brother, you must meet my brother, Mr. James Thornton. He is— Why, there he is now!" She waved rather more energetically than Caroline would have, and apparently the gesture was effective, for moments later, an elegant gentleman stood before them. He wasn't much older than Miss Thornton, and as Caroline looked up at him, she thought he could very well be one of the heroes in Mrs. Radcliffe's novels. Very smartly dressed, he was, with his dark blond hair brushed back neatly from a high forehead.

"Mr. Thornton, may I present to you my dear, *dear* friend, Miss Caroline Merrill. The sister of Mr. Robert Merrill," she added.

"My pleasure," Mr. Thornton said, sweeping a deep bow in front of Caroline. "Have you filled your dance card tonight, Miss Merrill?"

"Why— Oh—" Caroline heard the squeak of surprise in her voice and took a deep breath before continuing. "Why, no, I have not." She produced her card, which was, at the moment, completely bereft of any markings, due to the fact that neither she nor Mrs. Argenot had seen anyone with whom they were acquainted.

"Then I am most privileged to have the first dance, Miss Merrill." With a great flourish, Mr. Thornton marked off one of the spaces and handed the card back to her.

Caroline glanced at Mrs. Argenot, realizing that she hadn't been properly introduced to the gentleman before her. The heat seemed to affect him, as well, for his forehead and cheeks shone. But his thick hair was neat and smooth, his brownish whiskers were well trimmed, and he dressed quite elegantly. He appeared more than capable of riding to the rescue of an endangered heroine.

Mrs. Argenot, as if pulled by a string, turned to look at her at that moment, and Caroline ventured to present Isobel and her brother to her own chaperone, who was her mother's cousin. Upon hearing their names, the older woman's face lit up. "Thornton? Of the Bayleston Thorntons in Derbyshire?"

"Why, yes, indeed," Mr. Thornton agreed with a little bow. Caroline couldn't help but notice how his hair gleamed and shone in the lamplight…almost as if it were slicked wet. If he had to rescue the heroine in a rainstorm, he would look quite handsome…although his hair would likely not be as neat as it was now. "Our family seat is Northanger Castle in Yorkshire, but we have a small estate in Derbyshire, as well."

Caroline's ears fairly twitched. Northanger *Castle?* What an intriguing name for a family home! How fascinating it must be to live in such a place, with its secret passages and enigmas from years gone by.

"How fortuitous," Mrs. Argenot crowed, continuing the conversation. Her narrow little shoulders shifted as her hands flapped in delight. "Are you then acquainted with Maybelle Thornton?"

"Our mother," Isobel said gladly, putting to rest Caroline's fears that her new friend was an orphan. But no, she lived in a castle! That was even more exciting. "You must know her, then?"

"I schooled with her many years ago," replied Caroline's companion. "Do say she is here in Bath!"

"But she is!" Isobel confirmed, quite delighted. "How happy this day is!"

Caroline could not disagree, for now she had a friend, and a partner with whom to dance, and it was all most proper because Mrs. Argenot knew their mother. Delighted with the entire situation, she fairly sprang to her feet when Mr. Thornton turned to her and said, "I do believe our set is come up."

"I simply love the country dances," Caroline said, resting her gloved hand on his arm.

Whatever his reply, it was lost in the sounds of clapping and conversation. As they walked to the dance floor, she noticed that he was just a bit taller than she was, and that his shoulders were broad. He filled out his waistcoat rather handily. Although the buttons were not strained, the brocaded fabric hadn't much room to expand. He was a very solid, square-shaped man. Very capable of saving the day if need be.

As they stepped into their positions and the orchestra began to play, Caroline felt her cheeks flush and her heart quicken.

This was why she'd begged her mother to allow her to come to Bath. To have escaped the boredom of the summer at their small estate and come here, where there was so much to see and do... Caroline was nearly as giddy now as she had been when Mrs. Argenot had secured her mother's permission for her to join them on their visit.

The only thing that would make this visit even more perfect, besides confirming Mr. Thornton as a serious beau, would be if she actually uncovered some sort of Gothic plot and rescued a hapless prisoner, locked away in a dark cellar or tall, round tower...or if she espied a vampire.

Not that she *wanted* to see a vampire, of course. But after reading Dr. Polidori's story, and the even more disturbing novel by Mr. Starcasset, she was certain that the undead mingled, unrecognized, within Society...just as evil husbands locked up their poor, dear wives or grandmothers or sons like they did in those horrid Gothic novels by Mrs. Radcliffe or Mrs. Tenet.

And Caroline was not about to be taken by surprise.

As she lifted the hem of her skirt, twirled away from Mr. Thornton and took three hop-skip steps, she saw him.

A tall, dark-haired man with fair skin...very fair skin, as if he didn't go out in the sunlight...standing in the corner.

Watching.

Watching *her*.

CHAPTER 2

"What a lovely day it is," Isobel Thornton trilled as she linked her arm through Caroline's. She held an umbrella in her hand, and it bumped against Caroline's own parasol as they walked.

Despite gray drizzle, the streets of Bath were filled with gaily dressed ladies, escorted by nattily dressed men or plainly garbed maids. They carried bags and boxes from shopping trips and skirted the dirt and puddles in the street.

Caroline looked at her new friend and barely contained a smile. A lovely day? The only thing that would make it worse would be if the overcast sky opened up and turned the drizzle into a full downpour. Which it had done late last night and into the morning.

"At least the rain has eased up a bit," she said to Isobel. "I was certain we would have to cancel our walk if it didn't stop." She glanced down at the ground, noticing the damp edges of her hem. She wasn't going to look at her slippers, for she knew what state they would be in.

Surprising that Isobel hadn't commented on what must be another pair of ruined footwear.

"Mr. Merrill was such a delight," Isobel said. "Your

brother carried my umbrella for me when we walked in the rain one day. I am *so* happy that you and I are finally acquainted! He spoke so kindly of you, Caroline, *dear* Caroline. I felt like I already knew you when we at last met! And I have been wanting to meet you for so long!"

Caroline skirted a rather ominous-looking puddle. "He is a very kind man," she replied. "Very—"

"And now we are inseparable, you and I," Isobel continued. "We have the same interests and thoughts about *everything!* And what a lovely frock you are wearing today. It reminds me of the one I was wearing the very first time I met Mr. Merrill. It was yellow, splashed with tiny purple flowers and three rows of flounces at the hem. He complimented me on it, and of course, I demurred… but secretly, I was overcome that he even noticed it!"

They had walked all along Pulteney Street and were now coming to the old Roman baths. "Shall we stop in and see them?" asked Caroline when Isobel paused for breath. "I haven't had the occasion, as we just arrived two days ago."

"Oh, no, I don't fancy going in there. I've been so many times before, and it is so warm and close, and the air simply smells like sulfur and heat. It's very unpleasant. My hair will flatten out into long strips and I will look a terrible fright!"

Despite the fact that Caroline yearned to see what had been public baths for the ancient Romans, and that Isobel herself had insisted only the night before that they would visit them, she was more loath to quit Isobel's companionship. So, despite her interest in investigating the baths, she adjusted her umbrella so that the little drips didn't dampen her shoulders and continued to stroll along with her new friend.

"Do you like to read?" she asked as Isobel paused from

her discourse on the first walk she took with Robbie…up the street and around the corner, beyond the baker's—where Robbie bought her a little cake—and on to the milliner's, where he was kind enough to wait while she tried on several smart little spring hats….

"Read?" Isobel said in surprise. "But of course."

Caroline smiled in delight. Happy day! "I am so glad that we share that interest. My mother claims I'm never to be found without a book in hand, and although that isn't strictly true—"

"Oh, indeed! My mother says exactly the same. I just love books."

"My favorites are those horrid Gothic novels by Mrs. Radcliffe," Caroline confessed. "And those by Mrs. Tenet, as well."

"Oh, yes, indeed! I love those books, as well. I'm certain Mr. Merrill knows what a great reader you are, and that we have so much in common."

But Caroline, having embarked on her favorite subject of all, had more to say. "I have read them all so many times, but my favorite is *Udolpho.* Did you see the man last night, in the corner? He looked just as I pictured Montoni would be."

"Oh, my gracious, I couldn't agree more!" Isobel trilled. "He was so handsome and charming."

"I am speaking of the one with the hooked nose. He had such dark brows, and a way of looking at people… I was sure he was Montoni, that horrible man. He looks just the type to lock his wife away in a tower."

"Oh," Isobel said. "Oh, indeed. I couldn't agree more. And, look! Oh, look, Caroline! There is my own brother. Why, he could not stop talking about you last night, and here he is. He has found us. I rather suspected he might. You," she said, looking at Caroline hard enough that she felt a warm flush over her cheeks, "have acquired an admirer."

Hardly had the words settled in and Caroline's attention flew to the smart barouche that trundled along the street than Isobel raised her hand and waved. "James! James!"

The mud-spattered conveyance rolled up and Mr. Thornton tipped his hat. "What a pleasant surprise, Miss Merrill. It is such a dreary day, without a ray of sun in sight, but I thought perhaps you might wish a bit of a drive."

"Indeed she does! If for no other reason than to save her hems," Isobel said with a vivacious smile. "I shall come on as chaperone, of course, but come now, Caro! Let us go for a ride."

Caroline could hardly believe her fortune, for it was eminently obvious that Mr. Thornton had indeed sought them out...and dare she hope that it was she in particular?

Mr. Thornton clambered down from his perch, holding the reins looped over his hand, and helped Caroline climb into the high seat. Isobel followed, and then Mr. Thornton walked over to the other side and regained his place, putting Caroline in the middle.

The light carriage started off with a bit of a jolt, sending a trickle of rain careening off the edge of the roof behind them.

"We have been walking all morning, James," Isobel announced. "What a delight that you found us." She adjusted her skirt again. "We walked all along Pulteney and then went to the milliner's, but it's a small shop and didn't have anything worth looking at. We had no wish to go into that awful dark and close bath spa, did we, Caroline? Even though it's so wet. But now you've come along, dear James, and we can see the sights without mussing our slippers."

"Mmph," he replied as he navigated the horses down the center of the street. "Had to see to some business before I came out."

"I declare, the smell on this street is simply revolting," exclaimed Isobel. "Whatever have they dumped in the mews? Hurry on, James, get us past this horrible place."

"Are you fond of hounds, Miss Merrill?" Mr. Thornton asked.

Caroline jumped, for she hadn't expected him to direct a comment at her, and her attention had been caught by a tall, darkly garbed figure. He'd been walking along briskly, the drizzle gathering at the curling edges of his hat and sparkling on the shoulders of his cloak. She recognized him straight away from the dance last night.

Not the man with the hooked nose, who brought to mind Montoni, but the one who'd been watching her and Mr. Thornton as they made their way through the steps of the quadrille. The pale-visaged one who looked just as Caroline had imagined the vampire Lord Ruthven to look.

"Er," she said, turning to gaze at the man as their carriage passed by. "Hounds? I cannot say that I know much about them." Other than the fact that they jumped all over one's gowns and employed their tongues in quite a sloppy manner.

The man on the street glanced up for a moment and their eyes met, his dark and steady beneath the brim of his hat. Even from a distance, she recognized disdain in his expression. She shivered and pulled her eyes away, her heart beating as shock buzzed through her.

If he were indeed a vampire, she must take care not to look directly at him. According to what she'd learned, the undead were known for being able to enthrall a mortal being with their eyes alone. But it was also well-known—to anyone who'd read Dr. Polidori's or Mr. Starcasset's stories, at any rate—that vampires were only able to come out at night. Exposure to the sun was…

Caroline blinked. But of course. There was no sun today; or at least, what little light shone was buffered, filtered through heavy clouds and rain. Perhaps with a hat to protect one from the direct sun, and gloves, of course, even the undead could walk the streets of Bath during the day.

"—do you not, Miss Merrill?"

With a start, Caroline realized that Mr. Thornton had been discoursing on some subject… What was it? Her mind scrambled to recall, and quickly settled on hounds. However, she hadn't any idea what he had just asked her.

So Caroline responded, "Mmm…indeed, Mr. Thornton, what do you think?" hoping that he hadn't just spent the last few moments telling her just that.

But even if he had, she'd learned from watching her mother manage conversations with her father, uncles and brothers that men never seemed to tire giving their opinions about anything. Even if they had just given them. This propensity thus enabled a woman to retreat to her own thoughts whilst they sermonized.

She sighed as Mr. Thornton launched into a treatise on the proper color of a hound. Not that Caroline had ever heard of a white-spotted beagle being a better hunter than a brown-spotted one, but, apparently, it made a difference to Mr. Thornton.

If her own family, and her limited experience with young men—and now Mr. Thornton—were to be any indication, it appeared that Caroline was doomed to a life of listening.

The rest of the carriage ride included Mr. Thornton's opinions on new boots and Isobel's classification of each dress shop that they passed as worthy of being patronized or not.

Despite her lack of participation in the conversation, Caroline enjoyed the opportunity to ride with her new friend and her potential beau, and realized that it was her own fault that she had been left out of the discussions because her mind had continued to drift to that gentleman she'd seen on the street.

She shivered just as the barouche stopped in front of the house that the Argenots had let.

"Oh, dear, I do hope you aren't getting a chill, my *dearest* Caro," Isobel said. "I would hate for anything to disrupt our going to the theater tomorrow night. You will join us, won't you?"

"Oh," Caroline replied in specious delight. "I should so love to, but of course, I must acquire permission from Mr. and Mrs. Argenot before I accept your invitation."

"But they must join us," said Mr. Thornton immediately. "Of course, there is room enough in our box."

Thus, Caroline could not have been happier when she entered the little bungalow and told Mrs. Argenot about the invitation.

"But of course we shall attend! How kind of them. Mr. Argenot will make his excuses, but you and I will of course accept. I shall send word around right away."

And so it was arranged that the next night, Caroline and Mrs. Argenot would be called for by the Thorntons in their carriage.

Mrs. Argenot, however, had a bit of the headache that night, which kept Caroline home from the Upper Assembly Rooms, which was another place to go, dance and be seen. "But I am certain I shall be right as rain in the morning," her older cousin told her. "And we shall go to visit the bath spa before luncheon, as it is a shame you did not get there today."

Caroline didn't mind missing the evening at the Upper Rooms anyway, for Mr. Thornton had already indicated that he was otherwise engaged. Instead, she stayed up much too late and read the entirety of one of her favorite novels by Mrs. Radcliffe.

And that night, she dreamt of the man with the hooked nose laughing as he locked her into a room with barred windows... and the dark-haired man from the street slipping through the bars like tendrils of smoke and bending over her bare neck in the night. Fangs gleamed and his eyes burned red and he still wore the same curly-brimmed hat as he laughed and laughed.

CHAPTER 3

THE NEXT MORNING DAWNED BRIGHT AND SUNNY. OF COURSE, Caroline did not actually see that event, for she was long abed after her late-night reading and the ensuing dreams. But when she actually awoke and dressed and joined Mrs. Argenot in the dining room for a late breakfast, the yellow sun gave such a cheer to the room that Caroline nearly laughed with joy.

Only three days in Bath, and she had already made a friend and had met a handsome, well-appointed young man who seemed more than passingly interested in her. And she had an invitation to the theater this very night. As well, Caroline was certain that there was an adventure to be had, or a mystery to be solved, with the hooknosed man (whose wife was locked in the tower) or the man from the street and his obvious vampiric tendencies.

All in all, even if it were the cloudiest of days, Caroline would have been in high spirits.

Less than an hour after breaking their fast, Caroline and Mrs. Argenot strolled along the street toward the ruins of the Roman bath spa. Feeling quite the thing in a pale blue lawn with a single white flounce and the most cunning little butterflies embroidered on her sleeves, Caro had a matching spring in her step.

Inside the spa, which was underground, she found it crowded with visitors, dark and close, and endlessly fascinating. The brick walls had long been colored rust from the iron in the water, and the steam did indeed make the air muggy and smell of sulfur—as Isobel had claimed—but Caroline didn't find it as unappealing as her friend.

"I do think I must get a bit of air," Mrs. Argenot said, fanning her face, which looked alarmingly pink. Of necessity, she leaned closer than normal, for the low rumble of constant conversation, along with the tumbling water, was picked up by the cavernous space, making the sounds expand and echo.

"May I stay for a bit longer?" Caroline asked. "I wanted to look at the Sacred Temple again."

"Oh, I shouldn't want to spoil your fun," the older woman told her with a smile. "Stay as long as you like. I shall sit in the garden under the rose pergola and enjoy the butterflies."

Thus Caroline was sitting on one of the stone benches along the edge of the bath, quite out of the way and in shadow, watching the parades of visitors streaming by, when she saw him.

Him. The man from the street, the man with the curly-brimmed hat and the pale skin.

A strange prickle went over her shoulders and Caroline found herself pressing more deeply into the alcove in which she sat. He couldn't see her from his position, but she had an excellent view of him as he strode through with great purpose. He was very tall, and today a dark coat covered his broad shoulders, but he was without a hat or gloves.

Rather than taking his time to admire the work of the

ancient Romans, he seemed to be intent on something else, for he walked through quickly, glancing only cursorily at the other tourists as he wove between and around them.

Was he stalking his prey? Was there a young woman who had become separated from her party that he had homed in on, with his superior undead powers? Was he now hurrying to lure her into a dark corner before her companions missed her?

Caroline felt a shiver cast over her shoulders, quite ignoring the fact that she herself met that basic description. Instead, she dug into her impossibly large reticule, feeling around for the wooden stake…but then she recalled that she'd removed it before embarking on her walk with Isobel the day before. Out in daylight, she hadn't expected to need such a weapon. And she'd forgotten to return it to its place. Fiddlesticks.

It was sunny today, but the spa was dark. How long had he been lurking here, under cover of the shadows, waiting for his opportunity? Perhaps he even slept here, hiding when the doors were locked for the evening. This would be a most convenient place for a vampire to live if he did not have his coffin nearby.

She was ready to close her reticule in disgust when her fingers brushed the silver cross. Yanking it from the bag, Caroline stood and, heart pounding, she slunk from the dark alcove and began to follow in the footsteps of the man.

Skirting around clusters of people, she gripped the cross and hurried as quickly as she dared. But a new influx of tourists had arrived, and of course they had all settled in a deep crowd in the very spot through which she must pass in order to follow her quarry.

Caroline found it nearly impossible to be polite as she

edged her way into the mass of people. No sooner had she inserted herself halfway into the group than the crowd, in its entirety, seemed to move like a large lumbering cow along the very pathway through which she had just walked, and Caroline was jostled along with them in the opposite direction to which she desired to go.

It was several moments later, and more than a few minutes since her prey had disappeared that Caroline emerged from the other side of the cluster of sheeplike people. She hadn't the barest notion what had caught the interest of such a large number of tourists at that very moment that she needed to pass through, and she didn't care to find out.

Instead, still gripping the silver cross—which had become a bit slick from the dampness of her palm—she hurried on through the doorway through which the man had passed.

Suddenly, she came around a corner and there he was, walking briskly toward her. He seemed to be brushing something off the upper sleeve of his coat, and he had a satisfied expression on a face that might have been handsome if it weren't so forbidding.

Caroline stopped in her tracks, startled to have come upon him so expediently.

"Where are you going? This area is not open to the public," he said, his glance sweeping over her. It lingered for a moment on the hand clutching the cross, but then returned to meet her gaze. "And as such, it could be quite dangerous for a young woman alone." Menace tinged his voice.

She was struck by how cool and dark his eyes were, and she tightened her fingers on the silver object. Of course, he couldn't tell what she was holding in her hand. That was her intent, for if she needed to employ the item as a shield, it was best to take the vampire by surprise. Instead of being cowed, and fully aware that there was a crowd of people within screaming distance, she returned his look boldly.

Caroline felt the weight of his gaze—now much more potent than it had ever been before because of its proximity—and steeled herself against the warmth that tempted to shiver inside her. She would not fall prey to his thrall. Instead, she replied, "If that is the case, I wonder why *you* were skulking about back there."

Was it her imagination or did his eyes flare a bit in surprise? She was certain she'd seen it. Now perhaps it was a glint of humor that lit his dark expression as he returned, "Skulking about? Whoever speaks like a Gothic novel but one who has read many of them, I suspect."

"I have indeed, and I've found horrid novels not only very entertaining, but also quite enlightening. Particularly the latest one by Dr. Polidori." As soon as she spoke those last words, Caroline wished she could take them back. She drew in a steadying breath and reminded herself of the comforting weight in her hand. She could hardly believe she'd been so bold. Not only had she fairly accused him of a nefarious purpose, but she'd also exposed her own knowledge and intent. *Foolish, Caro! Now he will be suspicious of you.*

"Indeed?" he replied, his voice cool. "So you consider yourself an expert on haunted castles and ghostly moors? You can distinguish an innocent tower from that in which the crazed madwoman of a wife is locked away? And perhaps you think you might be able to identify a Lord Ruthven, should you come face-to-face with him?" The man's black eyes lit with mockery.

Was he deliberately baiting her? Telling her that she had indeed come face-to-face with a vampire?

"Not at all," she replied, once again assuring herself privately that she was within easy distance of assistance should he make any threatening move toward her. In fact, the chatter of the crowd beyond filtered quite readily to her ears, giving her the confidence to continue her conversation. "I've found well-written books to be quite instructive with regard to the private characters of people I chance to meet. How well true character can be hidden by a facade or other subterfuge."

He gave an impolite snort. "I shall take that under advisement the next time I embark on a character study. Surely you know that Dr. Polidori's novel, while immensely entertaining and possibly informative in the way of characterization, is pure fabrication," he continued. "And if it weren't, it certainly wouldn't do for a young lady like yourself to be skulking about into dark, shadowy, lonely places. Something terrible might happen to her."

He leaned toward her and Caroline felt her breath catch, but she refused to move back a whole step. Just a shuffle of her feet…because the stone wall was right behind her.

"Or, instead, she might be the only one to witness a horrible event and come to the aid of a woman in distress," she replied. Her voice sounded breathless and unsteady, and she was aware of how difficult it was to continue to hold his gaze. Yet she forced herself to look up at him.

"Don't be a foolish chit," he said, his voice sharp. "You'd do best to stay out of things which you do not understand—and dark corners and abandoned rooms where danger lurks. I should hate to see anything happen to that lovely white neck of yours."

Caroline snatched in her breath at his effrontery and

the gleam of—dear goodness, what *was* that in his eyes? She felt warm suddenly and, once again, that tug of his thrall. "I assure you, I am not as foolish as those silly heroines who go to investigate the attic alone at night," she managed to say.

"But if they did not go into the attic at night alone," he said, a wicked smile suddenly curving his lips, "there would be no story, would there?"

She barely suppressed a surprised laugh; instead, she smothered the instinct into a sort of gasp as the heat of his quick grin jolted her. But before she could open her mouth to respond, the smile disappeared from his face and he moved even closer toward her. Her heart slammed in her chest and it became difficult to swallow.

"Enough of this," he said as she became aware of the scent of rosemary balm. "I have other matters to attend to than to stand here and exchange repartee with a foolish chit. Take yourself off, madam, and I strongly encourage you to deny your natural curiosities—and your obvious penchant to be your own Gothic heroine—and keep to the public areas of the bath spa. And other places. Or the next time you might find yourself in greater trouble than having to hold your own in a bout of wordplay."

She drew in her breath to reply, but the black expression on his face, and the peremptory gesture he made back toward the public area compelled her to move. As long as he followed her, she would leave…and then perhaps sneak back once he was gone to see if there was any sign of disturbance. Or worse.

Caroline turned and started back toward the buzzing crowd, fully aware of the weight of his surveillance settling over the back of her bare neck. But she refused to hurry, to allow him to think he'd rattled her. He had not.

He'd merely given her even more reason to be suspicious of him by warning her off.

She returned to the gathering of other tourists, noting that it had thinned out a bit. But that the smell of sulfur and too many women wearing rosewater clung to the air even more strongly than before. Once she slipped beyond the crowd and behind one of the cornices, she turned to watch. Sure enough…the man emerged from the shadowy hall, scanned the room sharply, then turned down another corridor and disappeared.

As soon as he did so, Caroline pushed her way back toward the area he'd deemed as not open to the public, and this time she did see the notice tacked to the wall. Closed for Restoration.

But she ignored the sign and hurried along the dimly lit hallway. If he'd lured his prey back into the empty, unrestored area, the poor girl could be lying injured and bleeding. Or worse.

Yet Caroline found nothing untoward but a few piles of dirt and dust among the flickering torches hung high on the wall. Clearly, whoever was doing the restoration was not at work today…or recently. And, even more clearly, she had interrupted whatever plans the man had had to entrap his victim.

Disappointed, yet satisfied that she'd at least disrupted his villainous purpose, Caroline strolled back out to find Mrs. Argenot in the gardens. Her companion was not sitting beneath the rose pergola, which was not a surprise to Caro. She'd learned that her distant cousin was prone to distraction when it came to flower gardens, and had most likely been lured from her seat by an unusual specimen of butterfly or a unique arrangement of bushes.

Grateful for the fresh summer air after the rotten-egg

and heavy rose perfume of the baths, Caroline settled on the bench to await her friend's return.

She had been sitting for only a moment, wishing that she had slipped a book into her bulky reticule, when a young woman passing by paused to admire the spray of pink-tipped ivory tea roses.

"How lovely," she said, pausing to remove her glove. She reached to touch a petal.

"They smell much better than the ones inside," Caroline said before she caught herself. Whatever had got hold of her tongue today? "Oh, dear," she began.

To her relief, the young woman laughed and said, "I cannot but agree. Much as I appreciate the scent of roses, I must admit I cannot admire it when there is quite so much of it in such a small area."

Caroline nodded, also smiling. "Although my favorite scent is that of gardenia, my cousin prefers roses. In fact, I thought she would be waiting for me here, but she has obviously found something else of interest whilst passing the time."

The other woman released the rose petal, and the blossom shifted back into place. "And I was supposed to meet my party here, as well, but, apparently, they have not yet arrived. Or else I am too late and they have walked along."

"Perhaps you would like to sit and wait for them?" Caroline asked, making a show of moving her skirts. "Surely they will return in search of you."

"How kind of you." The other woman took advantage of her hospitality and settled next to her on the bench, removing her other glove. She appeared to be Caroline's age, although she was a bit more petite than Isobel, which gave the impression that she might be a bit younger. With rich chestnut-colored hair and laughing blue eyes, she was very pretty and seemed to be full of life. "My name is Ellen Henry."

"I am pleased to make your acquaintance," replied Caroline, giving her own name. "Have you been in Bath long?"

Miss Henry shook her head. "No, we have only just arrived this last day. My guardian and I have joined my aunt and her two daughters—that is the party whom I am waiting for." She smiled a bit abashedly. "I confess, though I have been to Bath thrice now, I never tire of wandering through the bathhouse, imagining the way it was centuries ago. My aunt and cousins find it a bit of a bore after only a short time, so they have learned to leave me to my imagination so that I'm not rushed."

A rush of kindred spirit flooded Caroline, and she smiled. "That is the precise reason I am waiting here for my companion, Mrs. Argenot. She found herself bored while I could not pull myself away."

"They claim there is little to see but a few large rooms with warm water, and that it takes but a few moments to admire it…but to me, there is so much to think about and to imagine." She giggled, her nose wrinkling prettily. "And there is the smell, of course. They complain that it smells like foul eggs."

"The aroma surprised me at first," Caroline said, "but I found I got used to it readily, and it didn't detract from my enjoyment of the area. Oh, and there is Mrs. Argenot now." She stood, suddenly reluctant to leave her new friend.

Miss Henry appeared to have similar compunctions. "Perhaps I shall see you at the Upper Rooms tonight?" she said, also standing.

Caroline felt a sincere wave of disappointment when she recalled her engagement with the Thorntons for this evening. But whyever should she do so? "I'm afraid not, for I shall be at the theater, but perhaps we could walk tomorrow? And then we could come back to the bathhouse and wander through to our hearts' content?"

"That would be most enjoyable," Miss Henry replied enthusiastically. "I'm certain my aunt would approve, Miss Merrill, if for no other reason than that she would not have to take me back here."

Caroline smiled with equal delight, and upon Mrs. Argenot's arrival, she obtained her companion's permission for the outing, and they settled on a time and place to meet the next day. Then she and Mrs. Argenot bid their farewells, and as they strolled back to their house to prepare for the evening at the theater, Caroline found her step to be quite light and merry once again.

Indeed, this visit to Bath was turning into a more pleasurable one than she could ever have imagined.

CHAPTER 4

CAROLINE LOOKED DOWN AT THE STAGE, WHERE THE ACTORS and actresses filled the space with their bright costumes, then across the small theater to the other boxes. Enough light remained to illuminate the house almost as well as the stage, for, just as in London, the attendees wished to see and be seen more than they meant to watch the entertainment below.

Of course, she didn't expect to recognize any of the other spectators, but she certainly could admire their frocks and observe their interactions. And there was the possibility that she might espy her Lord Ruthven look-alike from the spa earlier today, or the hook-nosed man with the imprisoned wife. Or any number of other mysterious figures.

There had to be at least one scheming woman in Bath who was poisoning her innocent husband's tea.

"It is *such* a *delight* to have you sitting next to me tonight," Isobel gushed, leaning close enough that Caroline got a strong whiff of powder and tea rose. "Mr. Merrill was so kind as to escort me to five theatrical performances. Three of them were by Mr. Shakespeare, and he was such a gentleman when I was overcome at the tragic ending! Poor, *poor* Juliet! He offered me a handkerchief, and he patted my hand until I was able to cease my waterworks."

"Mr. Shakespeare patted your hand?" Caroline asked ironically.

"No, no, goose," Isobel trilled, patting Caroline's own gloved hand. "I was speaking of Mr. Merrill. Your brother. He was so very kind and considerate. And…I recall, that night he was wearing the *smartest* dark blue waistcoat with a sable coat and pantaloons. I had chosen, with the help of Misry, my maid, of course, a dark blue frock with pale blue trimmings. And we looked delightful together. *Everyone* commented on how well we looked. It was quite a topic of conversation."

Caroline nodded and made automatic murmuring noises, for her attention had been seized by a familiar figure. Instead of sitting in one of the two short rows of chairs in his box, the Lord Ruthven look-alike stood near the front of the small balcony. Leaning against the wall, his arms crossed over his middle, he appeared not so much bored as watchful.

Not that the actors onstage seemed to draw his attention. Like most of the other theatergoers, the brooding man seemed less interested in the play below than other goings-on.

Intrigued, Caroline examined the other members of his party. Three women, all of whom were older than Caroline herself, and four other gentlemen. One of the women seemed to wish to draw Lord Ruthven—she really *should* come up with a different name for the man if she was going to keep seeing him about—into conversation, but while he appeared to respond politely, he declined to sit in the chair next to her and continued to remain watchful over the other boxes.

Then, suddenly, he seemed to notice her. His gaze fixed on her from halfway across the theater and, for a moment, she fancied her heart stopped beating. Then it started up again, pounding harder. Her mouth dried, and she found it difficult to pull her own gaze away from his dark, intense one.

Ruthven lifted his chin in an arrogant pose and made a brief bow in her direction. She did not miss the sardonic expression that flickered across his countenance. At last, she was able to pull her attention from his, and commenced with what she hoped was a casual glance around the theater as her cheeks felt warm and her breath rushed.

He must know she suspected him, and he'd attempted to enthrall her right then, right *here,* as a warning. The next thing that would happen was that his eyes would turn red and begin to glow. Then his fangs would extend…

Her palms dampened beneath their gloves and she was aware of the nervous churning in her belly, yet she could not keep the mental images away. He would bend to her, his mouth warm and his fingers strong and sturdy around her arms…he would kiss her first, gently, at the side of her mouth. And then he would move to the edge of her jaw, then to her bare neck—

With a little gasp, Caroline was jerked back into reality by Mr. Thornton, who'd leaned forward from the seat behind and spoke behind her. Heart pounding, skin still prickling, she turned in her chair in time to hear Isobel respond to her brother, who'd leaned forward between the two of them. "Of course not, James," she said. "We've only just arrived. There's been no chance for anyone to even *notice* us yet, dear brother."

Caroline realized that Mr. Thornton had been inquiring as to whether they would like to take a turn about the galley or get some refreshments, and she was relieved that Isobel had declined. Despite the fact that the man had caught her looking at him, she intended to keep a close watch on Ruthven.

She turned back to her task of observing the handsome—she supposed he was handsome—pale-visaged man. When he tensed and straightened, Caroline noticed, though it was a subtle movement. He seemed to come to attention, his sharp eyes fixated on a box two away from hers. His gaze appeared to have been engaged by a new arrival. A woman with a cloud of dark hair, in a rose-colored frock. She was some years older than Caroline, but still seemed delicate and demure.

A prickle tingled up her spine. Was she Lord Ruthven's latest target? She had arrived in the box without escort, although its other occupants greeted her with delight.

A woman alone. Caroline's heart began to beat faster. A perfect target for a Lord Ruthven.

Perhaps she should think of him as Lord Brooding. Lord Gloomy? Then she recalled his short, clipped conversation with her today and revised: Lord Rude.

Isobel suddenly clamped her fingers around Caroline's arm and gave a sharp tug. "Do you see that?"

"Yes, yes, I see it, too. He's looking at—"

"What a *cunning* little wrap Mrs. Erthwistle is wearing! Why, it's nearly as smart as the one I nearly lost on the first day I met Mr. Merrill. I left it behind on a park bench and he kindly returned it to me. Of course, we had already been introduced, otherwise it might have been rather awkward, but he was so *very* kind. And so polite."

Caroline, having been jolted from her observations when Isobel's fingernails dug into her gloved arm, mur-

mured something appropriate and returned her attention
to the box where Lord Ruthven had been sitting.

He was gone.

Fiddlesticks and ferndots.

Caroline half rose in her seat, leaning forward to peer
toward Lord Rude's box in the event that he'd simply
moved to the back of the space. But she could see no
sign of a tall, dark figure lurking in the back, and she
settled back in her seat, frowning worriedly. Something
was wrong. He was up to something nefarious.

She *knew* it.

And she was the only person here who suspected.

Then she looked over at the box with the delicate brunette woman. The woman had taken a seat in the second
row of chairs, leaving Caroline to wonder how such a
small figure meant to see over the other occupants of
her box. But she didn't appear to be discouraged by her
view, for the woman leaned near the man next to her as
if to exchange some comment.

When the young man responded, the brunette smiled
demurely, then accepted a handkerchief offered her. The
gentleman was clearly besotted, and she seemed quite as
delighted to be in his presence. Yet...Caroline caught a
certain angle of her expression, and something seemed
odd. As if it were not as innocent as it appeared.

And that was when the prickling became stronger over
her bare shoulders. Perhaps the woman was married...
and she'd fallen in love with this younger man. Yes, that
made sense. She was much older than the smart dandy
next to her.

But if the woman was married, she must, of course,
find a way to dispose of her husband. The prickling became stronger. So delicate, so demure and innocent-look-
ing...but Caroline was not fooled. Just like the villainess

in Mrs. Tenet's novel *The Iron Gate,* the woman seemed all innocence…but she was slowly poisoning her husband to death so that she could be with her younger lover.

Of course, the villainess in Mrs. Tenet's novel had different motives that involved a chest of family jewels, but that didn't matter. She was the same sort. Caroline had seen it in that brief flash of her eyes.

She jumped when Isobel grabbed her again. "You simply *must* come with us," Isobel demanded. Her voice was pitched with excitement.

Caroline firmly withdrew her limb, certain that in the morning her skin would be decorated with small bruises. Isobel had no sense of how her excitement manifested itself.

"May she, Mrs. Argenot?" Isobel had turned to the older woman, who, despite the activity going on around the theater, seemed to have been quite engrossed in the play below. "May she indeed?"

Caroline smiled at Isobel's enthusiasm. The girl's blue eyes sparkled, and she looked so pretty and alive that any lingering annoyance about her propensity for inflicting bruises faded. "And what is this great plan?" she asked, glancing briefly at the boxes.

Lord Rude had not yet returned, and Mistress Poison remained in tête-à-tête with her younger companion. Perhaps it wasn't she who'd garnered Rude's attention after all.

Yet Caroline was certain that if Rude had left the box, he must have done so for some nefarious purpose. He *must* have.

"Why, James has concocted a scheme to take us on an evening picnic to the abbey ruins tomorrow," Isobel said. "Come, James, will you not tell Caroline about it?"

"Would be my pleasure, Miss Merrill," Mr. Thornton said, leaning forward from his seat behind Caroline. "Could show you my new pair. Just bought them today, and a fine step they have, if I do say." His smile showed a wide expanse of very white teeth and a charming dimple in his left cheek.

Her first response to the invitation had been a leap of delight, but then Caroline recalled her engagement to meet Miss Henry tomorrow afternoon at the old bath spa. She feared that would not give her enough time to return home, change and be ready to join the Thorntons for an early evening. "Oh, dear," she said with great apology. "I am afraid I have already been engaged for tomorrow. I should very much love to go to the ruins," she added quite truthfully. "But I must decline. Unless it could be arranged for another day."

Ruins, whether they be bathhouses or abbeys or castles could only be filled with fascinating finds. Ghosts, remains, hidden secrets and old passageways—and under the moonlight of an evening picnic? What more thrilling adventure, she could not conceive.

Though Caroline's disappointment was acute, she was in no way inclined to cancel her arrangements with Miss Henry, even if she must let the opportunity pass.

"But you must come with us," Isobel cajoled. "Whatever can be more exciting than to visit the old abbey? And James will drive us, and we shall have a splendid picnic! You must cancel your engagement and plan it another day, Caroline! You must, for I vow I shall not allow you to miss the day."

"Perhaps if Mr. Thornton's schedule permits," Mrs. Argenot, who sat on the other side of Caroline, said gently, "you might arrange it for a different day? I would not be surprised if the day turned rainy tomorrow, for the clouds this evening were heavy and dark. If it does not rain tomorrow, it looks as if it will be quite stormy tonight, leaving it very wet tomorrow."

"But with whom do you have an engagement tomorrow that you are abandoning us?" Isobel demanded, speaking over Mrs. Argenot's quite sensible suggestion. "I simply cannot accept that we should go without you, Caroline! Can you, James? It just cannot be. We must convince her to come with, dear brother. We must go tomorrow evening! The scheme has been made up already!"

Caroline imagined that if Isobel had been standing, she would have stomped her foot and perhaps even crossed her arms petulantly over her middle. And, as this was the first mention of such an adventure, she suspected its inception had been only moments ago. Hardly a disruption in any plans.

"I should very much love to attend," she said appeasingly. "But earlier today I made arrangements with my friend Miss Henry for an afternoon engagement, and if it is to be wet again, as Mrs. Argenot suggests, I do not think it would be all the thing to go tomorrow."

She glanced back over to the boxes and noticed with a start that Mistress Poison had left her seat, and so had her young gentleman friend. Caroline straightened, her heart thumping, scanning the interior of the box. No, indeed. They had left.

Could they be bent on putting Mistress Poison's husband out of his misery this very night? Was it possible that he was waiting at home, ill in bed from his rancid tea, and she was too impatient to wait for his death any longer? She meant to hurry it along, perhaps with a well-placed pillow, held by her young lover?

Or did they merely plan to take a stroll about the gallery, perhaps to finalize the details of Mistress Poison's husband's demise? What better place to discuss such a topic than in a public, yet private place?

And had Lord Rude indeed been watching Mistress Poison for his own purposes? Even if she planned her husband's death, one could not sit back and allow her to fall into the hands of a vampire.

Yet, Caroline told herself she should not worry, for if the woman had a companion with her, certainly she would be safe from any attempt by Rude to lure her into the dark.

But, then again…Caroline pursed her lips. The man seemed rather young and a bit flimsy, like the foolish dandy in Mr. Starcasset's novel who was lured to a gentleman's club by Lord Tyndale, only to find that it was populated with vampires like Tyndale himself. The poor fop became Tyndale's latest victim and was left for dead, bleeding into the cobblestones of Baker Street.

She tried to settle in her seat and even to watch the play, but Caroline could not keep her thoughts from wandering hither and yon. She must investigate, if only to ease her own mind.

Gathering up her skirt, which happened to be an unusual lavender color that Mrs. Argenot claimed looked particularly well with her honey-colored hair, Caroline bent to her friend's ear and said, "I must excuse myself for a moment."

"Oh, indeed," Isobel said. "Dear James will escort you, and he must convince you to join our party tomorrow." Her smile seemed complacent, as if certain that her brother would succeed.

Caroline tried to think of a manner in which to decline his presence, but there was no polite way to do so. To her chagrin, Mr. Thornton offered his arm and led her out of the box.

"I confess, you might find it to be a bit of a bore," she told him as they started along the long room that served as gallery for the theater patrons. "I merely wished to walk a bit and to…uh…admire the murals and statues."

She realized belatedly that the majority of the murals and statues were little more than cherubic angels playing harps and lyres, with long, faded red scarves streaming out behind them. Not particularly imaginative, nor worth a second glance. As she warned him: boring.

They were not the only couple strolling through the gallery, she noted. But none of the other random visitors were Madame Poison, her young lover or Lord Rude.

"It is my deepest pleasure, Miss Merrill, to accompany you," he told her, patting her gloved fingers, which had curled lightly around his forearm. "I could have wished for nothing more than to have a few moments of your time, in which I might express my sincere admiration for you and your person."

He gave her that smile again, wide and white, and with the deep-cut dimple, and Caroline formed her lips into a responding one. "Why, thank you, Mr. Thornton," she replied.

"I do hope," he said a bit pompously, "that you would give me the great honor of addressing me by my given name, James."

"Oh," Caroline said, and felt the swarm of heat over her cheeks. How forward of him, after knowing her for only two days! But she was fully aware of the honor he did her by the request and, feeling a bit like one of those wooden toy men her brothers had played with, bobbed her head. "How kind of you, Mr.…er, James."

How odd, how *foreign,* to be speaking a man's Christian name. Of course, she spoke of her brothers in such a manner, but never had she done so before to any other adult man. As her mind raced and bobbed along, and she was aware that Mr. Thornton—James—had led her to the end of the gallery, she reminded herself of her purpose for coming out of the theater box and Caroline gathered back her thoughts.

"Mr....er, James," she said, "I wonder if you might be so kind as to fetch a refreshment? Did I see that they offered lemonade?"

"But of course, Miss Merrill," he said. "Whatever you wish. Come along, I do believe I saw a table in this direction."

"Oh," she said, stopping. She gave him her most charming smile. "I wonder...would you perhaps bring it back for me? I am simply enamored of this...uhm," she fumbled for something to say, then continued, "this lovely painting. The detail of the cherub's wings! I must admire it, and learn how the artist's technique was applied."

"Of course, Miss Merrill," he replied. "I did not know you were a painter." Was it her imagination that he continued to use her name as a reminder that she had not yet given him leave to call her by her Christian name? "With your permission, I shall return in haste."

Oh, please do not. "Thank you, James," she said. "And...I would be honored if you felt familiar enough to call me by my Christian name, as well."

"Caroline. Such a lovely name," he told her. James gave a bow and he started off, leaving Caroline in her contemplation of the cherub's wings until he was safely out of sight.

"I cannot see what you find so admirable about *that* painting," came a familiar sardonic voice behind her.

Caroline nearly leaped out of her skin, barely controlling herself from clasping a hand to her chest and gasping like one of Mrs. Radcliffe's heroines. Instead, she curled her fingers into her palms and willed her heart to stop its frightened pounding.

"It looks as if a child had done it," continued Lord Rude.

While she privately agreed, she couldn't exactly divulge that her reason for admiring the work was so that she would have a private moment to try and find the man standing in front of her. "And what brings you from your theater box this evening?" she asked boldly, thinking that if she detained him with some conversation, he might also be foiled in his plan of coaxing Mistress Poison—or which other victim he'd identified—into his clutches.

Caroline could not help but notice how crisp and snowy white was his shirtwaist, and how intricately his burgundy and black cravat had been tied. Yet, he seemed to have a bit of dust or ashes on an otherwise pristine costume, gray and clinging to his right sleeve as well as the same side of his coat.

His dark hair, which would be described as being the color of a raven's wing in one of Mrs. Radcliffe's thrilling novels, had been brushed neatly back from his high forehead and chiseled cheekbones. As was the fashion, his sideburns grew long, but they were neatly trimmed and did not threaten to swallow his face. The rest of his strong features had been carved by the same bold sculptor—a straight, prominent nose, large deep-set eyes and a solid, square chin.

Imposing and arrogant, and truly quite handsome, Lord Rude nevertheless seemed to have an air of suppressed energy simmering beneath his well-cut coat. He reminded her of one of her father's stallions—Teton, a black, muscular monster that barely restrained himself while bridled, and even then allowed only Caroline's father and her brother, Robbie, to ride him.

Rude was definitely more of a Lord Tyndale type of vampire than a Lord Ruthven, she decided at that moment. She felt her palms dampen beneath her gloves. Very attractive and very dangerous.

Lord Rude lifted his eyebrow and fixed his gaze on her. Caroline felt that little tremor shiver through her when their eyes met, and she yanked hers away.

"I had business to attend to," he replied to the question that she'd already forgotten she'd asked. "But I need not inquire what has drawn you from your seat."

Surprised, she forgot herself and her attention flew back to his dark eyes. "What do you mean?" Could he have realized her purpose?

His lips, thin with mockery, curved up on one side. "Whether it was your excuse or that of your companion, the result is the same: a few stolen moments of privacy whereupon he might wax rhapsodic about your freckled, button nose or your cornflower-blue eyes."

Caroline clapped her hand over her nose. How much powder had she applied to cover that horrid wash of freckles? Apparently, not enough. And at least she didn't have dirty smudges on her clothing. "I do not have a button nose," she retorted. She'd always thought of her proboscis as being larger than it need be. "It's much too large to be considered *buttony*."

He gave a short laugh. "It is all a matter of perspective, I do believe." He gestured to his own prominent feature. "But I find it interesting that you do not deny the presence of freckles, yet argue the size of your nose."

"I cannot change the size of my nose," Caroline replied, wondering how she'd come to be engaged in such a conversation with a suspected vampire. "But I can attempt to obliterate my freckles. And it would be much more polite if you were not to mention them."

Lord Rude gave a short bow. "I shall leave that to your companion."

"Have you been digging in a fireplace?" she asked, unable to keep from mentioning the ashes. "Your coat is a bit dusty. Just… there," she added with a little gesture.

"Ah," he said, and brushed at it. "My apologies if it offended you." The ash filtered into the air, pungent and musty, like nothing she'd ever smelled before.

But when he returned his attention to her, she saw that his expression had changed. "You and Mr. Thornton seem to have become quite familiar with each other. Dare I presume that the man has taken your fancy?"

Caroline could hardly believe the effrontery of his question. "Mr. Thornton is very kind," she said, with a pointed emphasis on this last word. "And I cannot imagine why our relationship should be of interest to you, Lo—" She caught herself before speaking the moniker she'd given him privately.

Rude cocked that eyebrow again. "I was merely attempting to make conversation, Miss…?"

"We have not been properly introduced," she reminded him. And lifted her so-called button nose.

"You state the obvious," he replied dryly. "And since we have commenced with discussing the others' appendages as well as flaws in dress, I had thought to rectify the situation. But apparently that is not to be so."

"If there is ever a reason for us to be formally introduced, I am certain that instance shall occur."

"Indeed." Then his expression became even more forbidding. "I should like to remind you once more, madam, that young attractive women like yourself ought to take care in walking about alone. I can't think what Mr. Thornton—is it?—thought to leave you unattended."

"It was at my own request," she replied. Glancing about, she reassured herself that they were not the only occupants of the gallery, and that she could summon assistance if she needed it.

"How convenient," he murmured, his ironic gaze sweeping over her, "that you have so quickly enthralled Mr. Thornton."

Enthralled? Caroline caught her breath. For him to use such a word…the term used to describe the vampire's power over his victim. Her suspicions solidified. "Mr. Thornton is no Lord Tyndale," she retorted meaningfully. "I am certain of that."

"Tyndale?" Lord Rude stilled, and suddenly Caroline felt very aware…and perhaps a bit frightened by the black expression that came over his face. "What do you mean mentioning Lord Tyndale? Do not tell me you have read Starcasset's book?"

"Why, I have indeed," she replied, taking a very small step backward. She felt a statue's pedestal behind her. "And I have found it to be quite enlightening." It was an effort to keep her voice steady in the face of such a response.

"Enlightening? You *would* find it so, wouldn't you?" He appeared quite angry. "However did you come by a copy of that ridiculous tale? It was never supposed to have—" He caught himself, and for the first time, Caroline felt as if Lord Rude were tipped a bit off balance.

"It was not easy to obtain a copy," she told him, feeling a bit more sure of herself in the face of his obvious discomfiture. "But my brother is a friend of the publisher's son, and managed to gift me with an early copy because I had enjoyed Dr. Polidori's story so well. And then," she added, frowning in remembrance, "I did hear that the rest of the books were destroyed in a fire." She looked up at him. "And the publisher decided not to print any more of them. I cannot understand why, for it was quite a thrilling tale."

Lord Rude said something under his breath that she was certain should not have been uttered in the hearing of a gently bred woman like herself, but he made no attempt to apologize. Then he fixed his dark gaze on her once more. "So that is why you continue to gad about, spying on people. It is a dangerous occupation."

Caroline swallowed. So he had figured it out. But before she could respond, he continued, "I'll warn you again, madam, not to poke that pert little nose of yours into business that you don't understand, and things that could endanger your slender, delicate neck. Starcasset's book is a fairy tale, the figment of an overactive imagination. Do not allow it to mislead you into ridiculous assumptions."

Perhaps he might have continued his lecture if Mr. Thornton—James—had not appeared at that moment from the other end of the gallery. He was dutifully carrying two small cups, and recognition must have shown in Caroline's expression, for Lord Rude was facing the opposite direction and would not have seen him.

"So your companion has returned," Rude said, beginning to ease away. "Do not take my warning lightly, madam," he said as he stalked off.

Moments later, Caroline realized her fingers were still shaking a bit as she gratefully accepted the cup of lemonade from James.

"My apologies that it took much longer than I'd hoped," James told her, glancing beyond her shoulder at Rude's disappearing figure. "The first cup they offered me was too warm, and the second I thought tasted much too sweet. I made certain they prepared it correctly. Who was that you were chatting with, Miss…er, Caroline?"

Having sipped the lemonade, and finding herself agreeing that the beverage was neither too warm nor too sweet, she swallowed and replied, "A gentleman passing by who stopped to ask for directions to the upper boxes." How quick she was on her feet with James! Why could she not be quite as snappy when she spoke with Lord Rude?

James nodded, and offered her his arm, then peered at one of the murals. "What a ridiculous rendition of a hound," he said. "Why would one ever portray a hunting dog with a snout of that length? It's much too short, and shallow, to be of any use running down a fox or hare."

Caroline glanced at the image in question, noting that the hound seemed to be running happily alongside cherubs, hares, cats, and the like. She forbore to point out that it looked nothing like a hunting dog, and more like a pup frolicking with friends. Not that James would have heard her response, for he was still waxing on about not only the size of the snout, but also about the unfortunate pup's haunches.

Apparently, they were too curved.

"Perhaps we should return to our seats," Caroline at last managed to insert when he paused to sip his lemonade. "I'm certain Isobel is wondering what has befallen us."

"And I must return with you and your agreement to accompany us on our adventure tomorrow evening," James said. "I shall not take your declination, my dear Caroline, without being grievously offended."

"But I cannot cancel my previous engagement," she replied as they began to walk back to their box. "Surely you understand it would not be seemly for me to do so. I am meeting my friend Miss Henry late in the afternoon, and I do not believe there will be time to—"

"Why do you not invite her to join our party," James suggested. "That will solve the problem, and we shall be able to go as planned."

Oh, that was a splendid idea, and one which Caroline seized upon readily. If Miss Henry were as intrigued by the old spa as she seemed, then she would no doubt be even more delighted to take part in their other adventure.

"I shall put the invitation to her," she told James. "But if she does not wish to join us, I am afraid I must keep my engagement with her."

"Of course," James replied, opening the door to their box. "But I trust that you will be greatly persuasive so that I am not to be deprived of your company…under the moonlight."

Caroline felt her face heat and she ducked her head as she slipped past him into the box. "Indeed" was all she replied as she did so, taking her seat.

"Has he succeeded?" Isobel asked, swooping down on her as soon as she sat. "You will be attending with us tomorrow, will you not? James, tell me you did convince my dear Caroline to come with."

Isobel's question to her brother saved Caroline from having to answer, leaving her free to glance out over the other spectators. Immediately, she found herself meeting the dark, intense stare of Lord Rude from across the way. This time, he didn't attempt to be casual about it; he caught her gaze, nodded and even made a subtle bow.

Caroline pulled her attention from him, refusing to acknowledge his mockery. But as she scanned over the other boxes, she noted that, while Mistress Poison's young lover had returned to his seat in the balcony, he sat alone.

Mistress Poison was nowhere to be seen, and, although Caroline watched during the remainder of the performance, the tiny brunette never reappeared.

CHAPTER 5

CAROLINE HAD JUST FINISHED BREAKING HER FAST THE NEXT morning and was still sitting in the dining room with Mrs. Argenot when the butler announced a visitor.

"Mr. Robert Merrill," he said.

"Robbie!" Caroline was out of her chair in a flurry of skirts, throwing her arms around the eldest, and favorite, of her three brothers. "What on earth are you doing in Bath?"

"Mama mentioned you were here with Cousin Hilda," he said, bowing to Mrs. Argenot, who had risen when he entered, "and when I happened to be in town for a time, I knew that I must come to call." He returned her hug and dropped a quick peck on her cheek.

"Indeed you had must," Caroline said, ignoring proper grammar in the light of this lovely surprise. "For if I had heard you were here and that you did not visit me, I should never have let you live through it."

"More frogs in my bed?" he said, taking a seat now that the ladies had also taken theirs. "But you know that my only recourse would then be to fill yours with spiders."

Caroline rang for the butler to bring another place setting (for their staff in Bath was small), and replied with a wave, "Ah, pish. I am no longer afraid of spiders. So you would have gone to the trouble of catching the crawly creatures in vain."

"I am glad to hear that," Robbie said with a smile. He was a handsome fellow, with the Merrill dimples that graced all the siblings, courtesy of their mother. He had the same dark hair as their father, while Caroline and the other brothers had honey-colored curls. "For I confess, it was nearly as traumatic for me to catch them as it was for you to find them in your bedwarming pan."

"Oh!" Caroline squealed, suddenly remembering her good news. "I am ever so pleased you are here. I have a wondrous surprise for you."

"And what might that be?" Robbie asked, helping himself to a rasher of bacon.

"I have made the acquaintance of one of your friends. A Miss Isobel Thornton."

"Isobel is here?" He seemed sincerely surprised, and just as delighted. "That is a grand bit of news."

"And we are going on a twilight picnic tonight at the ruins of an old abbey," she told him. "You must come with us, Robbie! Isobel will be inconsolable if you don't. Say you haven't any other engagements."

"I haven't any other engagements," he told her with a fond smile. "And I can only imagine how Isobel would stomp her foot if she learned that her plans were turned awry. I shall indeed accompany you." He dabbed at a spot of grease from the bacon. "A ruined abbey by twilight, hmm? You must be in your great glory, kitten," he added. "I do believe the clouds might have dissipated by then, for they have been rolling in frightfully dark. But you wouldn't mind that at all, would you? It makes the day all the more gloomy—the better for an intriguing adventure."

"I do anticipate it to be a fascinating excursion, clouds or no clouds. At least it hasn't rained, as Mrs. Argenot suggested it might. And I am so happy you will join our party. I'll send word round to Isobel that we have another guest attending. Shall I tell her it's you, or shall we surprise her?"

"Oh, I think you'd best tell her that I'm here," Robbie replied. "Isobel puts such effort into her dress for any occasion that I suspect a surprise might disrupt her planning."

Caroline laughed. How well her brother knew her friend. "Indeed. I'll send word around straight away, and then I must beg your leave, dear Robbie. For I have another engagement myself. Unless you wish to walk me to the Baths?"

"No, thank you, kitten," he said. "Since I am now engaged this evening, I have other matters to attend to. I will be here tonight, though, and be well ready to see Isobel again. Now I am even more delighted that I made the point of seeing you while I am here." His teasing smile told her that he was purely joking.

"I must be off after I dash off the message," Caroline told him. "I will see you tonight."

So quickly and with such delight did Isobel receive the message that Robbie was to accompany them that her response came back before Caroline left to meet Miss Henry. And when she read the message, which stated, *"What a happy surprise! I am most pleased that your brother will join us along with three more of our acquaintances. And if there are any others who might wish to make up our party, tell them they are welcome to attend, as well."*

Miss Henry, or Ellen, as she insisted that Caroline call her, was as enthusiastic about the twilight picnic as she was about the old spa. "I must gain permission from my guardian for the adventure, but I am certain he will approve, provided my cousins are invited to attend, as well."

Caroline linked her arm through Ellen's as they walked through the crowded bathhouse. "I am almost tempted to cut our visit short so that you might obtain permission immediately!"

Ellen's pretty bow lips smiled. "You have just spoken my own thoughts, but let us at least walk through the spa for a bit. My aunt and cousins are shopping for some new ribbons, and they won't be back to fetch me for another hour."

"Very well. But tell me, do you think your guardian will allow you to come tonight?"

"Mr. Blanchard is rather strict, but he is not unreasonable," Ellen told her. "I have great hope that he will allow the adventure, especially if Aunt Lou chaperones."

"Then we shall fix our thoughts on such an outcome and enjoy the rest of our visit here." As they came around the corner into the main bath area, Caroline saw the hook-nosed man from the Pump Room.

Her arm must have tensed against Ellen, for her friend said, "Is something amiss?"

Caroline tugged her friend to the side and spoke quietly. "That man there, standing next to the very tall woman. Do you see him? He has dark hair, with the nose like a knife blade?"

"Oh, I do," Ellen replied in a hushed voice—although such prudence wasn't strictly necessary, as the cavernous room echoed with laughter and conversation. "He looks frightfully dangerous." Then her eyes widened. "Oh, I do hope I have not offended you and that he isn't Mr. Thornton. Or your brother, Mr. Merrill." Even in the dim light, Caroline recognized the flush of pink over her friend's cheeks.

"Oh, no indeed," she replied. "I had thought the same thing. Does he not bring to mind the evil Melantrott from *The Iron Gate?* I am certain he has a lonely, frightened wife locked away in a tower somewhere. Does he not look the type?"

Ellen gasped an unladylike snort of laughter, then clapped a hand over her mouth, her eyes wide above it. "Caroline, you ought to be ashamed!"

But mirth crinkled her face and she kept looking back at the hook-nosed man. "I cannot deny that he does have a certain look about him." Ellen burst into giggles again. "And I suppose you look at that young woman there, in the yellow frock," she said, gesturing subtly with her pinkie finger whilst her hand was still covering her mouth, "and suspect that she is an orphan girl who has been taken into the home of the kindly man and woman walking with her."

Caroline stepped back and leaned against the wall so that she could have a better look at the girl in question. "Yes, indeed, and of course she has a horrid secret that she dare not allow to be exposed. Is there not a certain look about her eyes?"

"Of course. For if the secret is brought into the daylight, she'll find herself in the same situation as Miss Harriet Leavenworth in *The Dark Blade of Hawthorne Castle*," Ellen finished.

"And there may not be a Laird Blade to save her," added Caroline. "Though he was so dark and unpleasant at first, I sensed there was more to him than simply villainy."

"He ended up being so dashing and heroic," Ellen sighed.

"I do believe Laird Blade is my favorite villain-turned-hero in all the books I have read," Caroline agreed.

They looked at each other and giggled. "I vow," Ellen said as she wiped away the tears from her eyes, "I never believed I could have so much fun at the hot springs."

"Nor I," Caroline added, once again linking her arm through Ellen's. "Oh." She stopped suddenly, a flush rushing over her face. "Oh, my, Ellen," she said from the side of her mouth, and tightened her fingers on her friend's arm. "Do you see that man over there? Oh, dear, he is gone."

It had indeed been Lord Rude who seemed to have appeared from nowhere, walking briskly through the bath ruins, pushing past the throngs with ease and aplomb. But he hadn't seen Caroline, for she and Ellen were tucked into a dark corner as they watched the people go by. And then he disappeared, his face settled in its familiar frown.

"Who was it? Your brother? Mr. Thornton? You cannot know how intrigued I am to meet this Mr. Thornton, who seems to have taken quite a fix to you."

Caroline stood on her tiptoes, the better to peer over the other tourists' heads. "No, no. Neither of them. It was… I believe he might be a Lord Tyndale type," she said with a meaningful nod.

"Lord Tyndale?" Ellen frowned. "I don't know to what book you are referring, Caro."

"Oh, it is the most exciting book," Caroline said. "*The Venator,* by Mr. George Starcasset. It's better than *The Vampyre* by Dr. Polidori, and it's much longer, too."

Ellen was shaking her head, smiling. "I haven't even heard of *The Venator*. But I was reading *The Vampyre* and Mr. Blanchard became quite annoyed. Normally he doesn't care what books I read—he claims that reading anything is better than reading nothing (although he is careful not to say that in front of Aunt Lou). I once caught him reading one of Mrs. Radcliffe's novels, and he seemed to be enjoying it. Though he would not admit to it."

Caroline had the picture of a very proper, portly gentleman with plump white fingers sitting in his chair and reading with a glass of whatever it was men drank when they were reading horrid novels. She said, "I am not surprised that you haven't read the book, dearest Ellen, for there were only a few copies made. I begin to wonder if there isn't a reason for it. But, I digress. What I meant to say is, Lord Tyndale is a most frightening vampire. His eyes turn red when his fangs appear, and he lures young women—or men!—out into the darkness, where he feeds upon them. There is nothing of the romantic about him at all."

Ellen's eyes had grown wide. "How horrifying!"

Caroline nodded soberly. "It is nothing as titillating as *The Vampyre.* And Tyndale has humans who serve him because he is an undead and cannot go about in the sunlight. They belong to a secret society called the Tutela."

"What a terrible tale! I must read it," Ellen said, her eyes sparkling. "Will it keep me awake, listening to every odd sound?"

"It is a most horrid book that had me locking my window at night! But there are vampire hunters," Caroline added in a whisper. "A whole family of them, for generations. They work in secret to keep humans safe from the horrible creatures, hunting and killing them with wooden stakes. When they stab at a vampire, it explodes into the dust its body would have turned to if it had remained dead and in its grave."

"In the book?" Ellen whispered back.

"Yes. The Venators—that is what they are called, and hence the title of the book—are quite heroic. But...I begin to wonder if the book isn't purely fiction. And if that's why there weren't many copies made of it."

"Because it revealed too many se—"

"At last I have found you, Ellen. I have been searching for you these last thirty minutes."

Caroline's neck prickled and she turned at the familiar voice.

Ellen had straightened up at the sound of Lord Rude's words, as if loath to be caught whispering conspiratorially. But she didn't appear to be upset at his presence, and instead replied, "I'm sorry to worry you, but I didn't expect to see you here, Mr. Blanchard. Aunt Lou and the cousins are shopping and intended to retrieve me at half-past three."

Mr. Blanchard? Caroline felt her face grow fiery red as she looked up and met the eyes of none other than Lord Rude... who was also, apparently, Ellen's guardian. And possibly, quite possibly, a vampire. She swallowed and tried to appear unmoved. But inside, her heart was pounding mercilessly.

His dark eyes skated over her, dismissing quite rapidly Caroline's mental image of the portly gentleman with the pudgy fingers reading a horrid novel. "Well, now, Ellen, my dear," he murmured. "I do hope you will properly introduce me to your companion."

"Of course," the girl replied. "Mr. Thaddeus Blanchard, may I present you to my dear friend Miss Caroline Merrill."

Caroline gave a brief curtsy and nodded when Mr. Blanchard executed a correct bow. "The pleasure is mine, Miss Merrill," he said. When he raised his face and looked at her, she had the distinct impression he was laughing inside. At her.

Beastly man.

Then she realized what this could mean. Her dear friend Ellen was living with a vampire!

However was she going to tell her? Caroline swallowed hard and refrained, with difficulty, from biting her lip. She would say nothing until she confirmed her suspicions, and then she would carefully divulge the news. Poor, dear Ellen!

She realized suddenly that Lord Rude—Mr. Blanchard— was looking at her, along with Ellen. "Pardon me," Caroline said, her face heating again. "I was woolgathering for a moment."

"Mr. Blanchard is considering my request to accompany you on the twilight picnic tonight," Ellen said, her eyes excited with the possibility.

"But I would like to know exactly who is making up the party," added Lord Rude.

"It will be myself, along with Miss Isobel Thornton and her brother, Mr. James Thornton, as well as my brother, Mr. Robert Merrill, and perhaps three other friends of the Thorntons," Caroline told him.

After a moment, Lord—Mr. Blanchard—nodded briefly. "Then I should be quite remiss in withholding my permission, Ellen, dear. You may attend with my blessings."

The young woman clapped her hands and smiled in delight and, for a moment, Caroline thought she meant to bound into her guardian's arms in appreciation. "Thank you, Mr. Blanchard."

"But perhaps I should join the party, as well," he suggested, his attention sliding over Caroline and then back to Ellen. "It sounds as if it is to be quite the adventure."

No! Oh, no!

Caroline's eyes flew to his and she saw the mirth lighting them. "I do believe I shall," he added blandly, looking at Ellen. "If you do not mind that an old man should join you."

"Why, Mr. Blanchard, you are not an old man," Ellen said with the same sort of familiarity Caroline used when she spoke to her brothers. "Why, you cannot have attained more than thirty years! And there is not a speck of a gray hair in your entire head. You must certainly join us if you wish." She looked at Caroline. "My guardian always seems to have the most interesting bits of information to share about any excursion on which we embark."

"Of course," Caroline said, trying to keep her expression blank. Vampires were indeed ageless, and would never get gray hair no matter how long they lived. "But are you certain you will be able to attend? You must be very busy, Mr. Blanchard, and I do believe we intend to leave just before sundown."

She looked meaningfully at him with this last statement.

"Before sundown?" he repeated. And then a flash of something shone in his eyes.

He knows that I know. A rush of prickles swept over Caroline, but she maintained a calm expression. Her palms dampened beneath her gloves.

"But you are quite correct, Miss Merrill," he said, "I am rather busy this afternoon. Perhaps I shall not make it after all. Or perhaps," he added, looking directly at Caroline, "I shall simply join your party later."

After the sun goes down.

The words were unspoken, but Caroline heard them as if they had truly been uttered. Her breath became shorter and now she was more certain than ever that poor, dear Ellen's guardian was a vampire.

But then it occurred to her that, here he was, out in the daylight. How could he be a vampire—oh, of course. Robbie had mentioned the dark clouds, and Caroline well knew that a well-curtained carriage could shield one from whatever sun might filter through clouds, and one could alight beneath the cover of an awning. And if one remained inside dark buildings, such as these dank ruins, a vampire could indeed move about during the day if he took care.

What was she going to do?

"With your permission," Mr. Blanchard said suddenly, glancing toward a cluster of people that included the orphan girl in the yellow frock, as well as her adoptive parents. "I shall take my leave. Ellen," he added, drawing his attention away from the spectators and back to his ward, "I meant to tell you that your aunt was required to bring one of your cousins home for the headache, and she has asked me to escort you back. I will return for you in," he glanced over again, "no longer than ten minutes."

"Oh," Ellen said, seeming a bit crestfallen that their meeting should end so early. "But of course, Mr. Blanchard. And we will have plenty of time this evening, Caro, won't we?"

Before Caroline could reply, Mr. Blanchard walked off as if intent on meeting someone. She watched as he appeared to wander, but with a sense of direction nevertheless.

Was he following the orphan girl in the yellow dress?

But before Caroline could turn to watch him, Ellen tugged on her arm and said, "Come, Caro, let us finish looking at the Sacred Spring again before Mr. Blanchard returns."

Caroline bit her lip, but allowed herself to be directed off. Perhaps she was wrong. Perhaps the girl in the yellow dress would remain safely with her adoptive parents.

But she could not put the young woman out of her mind and worried about her the rest of the day.

CHAPTER 6

As it turned out, the Thorntons' carriage did not call for Caroline, Ellen and Robbie until the sun had actually set.

Caroline had not really known whether the sun would be down when they left, but she felt not a bit of guilt that she had misled Mr. Blanchard. She simply did not want to have to worry about vampires tonight when she was exploring the moonlit ruins of Blaize Abbey, although she managed to fit a slender wooden stake and a bulb of garlic into her largest reticule. Despite her precautions, she was relieved when Ellen arrived at the Argenots' home without her guardians.

"Mr. Blanchard decided not to attend?" Caroline asked innocently.

"Oh, he was much too busy. Although he said he might join us later, I do believe he was merely teasing me," Ellen said.

Privately, Caroline disagreed that Mr. Blanchard might do anything at all resembling teasing, but she said nothing to her friend and commenced with introducing her to Robbie. Shortly thereafter, the Thorntons arrived, and along with them, a second carriage, for by now the party had grown to eight.

Isobel was delighted beyond words—quite a feat for her—to see Robbie again, and Caroline could see that he was quite attached to the young woman as well. Isobel arranged it so that she and Robbie rode in the same carriage as Caroline and Mr. Thornton, leaving poor Ellen to ride with the other three young people—the Misses Wren, and their cousin Mr. Yarmouth.

Despite her efforts to include Ellen in their carriage, Isobel would have none of it. "It will throw the balance off," she said in a fierce undertone to Caroline, and she settled herself next to Robbie. This left Caroline in the front with Mr. Thornton, who was driving the rig.

"Let us be off!" Isobel crowed. Then she leaned forward to speak to Caroline. "You look very fine tonight, my dearest, *darling* Caroline! I do not think I've ever seen you so well."

"Thank you, Isobel," she replied. "I confess, I—"

"And do you not notice the *cunning* little beading on the edges of my gloves? I declare I've not seen anything to *compare* to it, and they look so lovely with my slippers. I do hope they don't get ruined in the dirt," she added with a sidewise glance at Robbie. "I can only imagine that the ruins will be *frightfully* messy. I may have to impose upon someone to assist me getting through the mud and over the dirt."

Caroline forbore to point out that it was foolish to wear such ornate and dainty footwear when one was going to explore ruins—she herself had donned her riding boots— but before she could open her mouth, Isobel had turned to Robbie and commenced a discussion about her pretty blue slippers and the beauty of the sunset beneath heavy gray clouds, and a variety of other things.

This left Caroline to listen to Mr. Thornton's discourse on whether one ought to eat one's toast with strawberry preserves or eggs. And aside from making her feel rather hungry, she found it one of the least interesting one-sided conversations ever.

But less than thirty minutes after leaving the outskirts of Bath, Blaize Abbey rose on a low hillock above them and Caroline's spirits picked up considerably. No sooner had she alighted from the carriage than she found Ellen. The two bosom friends clasped hands, looking about at the ragged stonework of the old abbey and the way it sprawled in a long, low area. The clouds had indeed gone, and the full moon cast a broad swath of light, almost as if it were day.

"Shall we eat first?" suggested Isobel, who had taken no more than two mincing steps away from the carriage until Robbie gallantly spread his coat for her to walk upon.

Noting that the grass was thick and full, and the waste of a good coat, Caroline said nothing to Robbie, but instead smiled to herself. He must be quite attached to Isobel if he would ruin his coat.

Caroline and Ellen ate as quickly as they dared, planning their excursion through the grounds as they conversed with the twin Misses Wrens—who had little to recommend themselves as conversationalists except that they finished each others' sentences. Mr. Thornton seated himself next to Caroline and endeavored to redirect the topic of discussion to classic Greek architecture, but even that fascinating subject failed to interest Caroline when led by Isobel's brother.

As soon as the meal was finished, she and Ellen started off on their explorations. Mr. Thornton insisted upon joining them. At first, he remained in their company, but when his suggestions for which direction to explore were ignored, he excused himself and wandered off along a different path.

Caroline and Ellen were delighted to find dark and hidden cubbyholes, exposed by the small torches they'd lit from the carriage lanterns, and even a hollow stone bench in what appeared to be a sitting room that could have belonged to the abbess. It took great effort for them to move the heavy top, but Caroline went into raptures when her torch exposed an old string of prayer beads inside. She pulled them out to show Ellen.

"This must have belonged to a poor young woman, sent away from the man she loved when her father refused to allow her to wed him," Caroline guessed.

"And she spent her days in prayer, lonely and sad, until she died an old woman," agreed Ellen. "The beads are lovely! They look like opals."

"Such a fancy string of beads for a poor sister. She must have come from a rich family," said Caroline. "Perhaps she became a powerful abbess herself, and this was her sitting room."

Just then, they heard their names being called. "Miss Henry! Caro! Where are you?"

"That's Robbie," said Caroline.

"There you are," her brother said, coming around the corner. "I have been looking for you." He spoke to Ellen, "Your guardian has just arrived and there was an unfortunate accident."

"What is it? Is Mr. Blanchard injured?" Ellen's face paled in the torchlight and Caroline realized how fond she must be of her warden. What a tragedy it would be for her to learn the truth about him!

"He is not injured, but Miss Thornton appears to have

turned her ankle," Robbie explained. "The party is to return to Bath now, and I have come to fetch you."

Caroline clamped her mouth shut over the disappointment that the excursion was to end so soon. And that the fault lay with Isobel, once again. Of course, it wasn't Isobel's fault she'd turned her ankle, although if she had worn more appropriate footwear, she may not have done so.

Working to hide her disappointment, Caroline followed her brother from the ruins, feeling Ellen's own discouragement as well. "Look here, Robbie," she said, producing the prayer beads. "We found this in the abbess's sitting room."

He took the beads and was examining them as they reached the rest of the group. Caroline's eyes went immediately to Mr. Blanchard, who looked even more forbidding tonight, dressed all in black. The silvery moonlight gilded his austere face, making him appear even more the way she'd pictured Lord Tyndale. He turned to look at her, as if feeling her attention on him, producing a deep shiver down Caroline's spine.

Isobel sat on a blanket on the ground, and when Robbie went to kneel next to her, Caroline noticed that her friend hardly acknowledged his presence. She was more intent on describing her injury, in the most delicate terms, of course, to Mr. Blanchard.

"Perhaps you might assist me to the carriage," Isobel asked, offering her hand to Ellen's guardian.

Caroline watched in confusion as Lord Rude smoothly assisted Isobel to her feet, and when it appeared that the young woman could not stand on her own, he swept her into his arms and carried her to his rig.

She glanced at Robbie, who'd passed the prayer beads

to Mr. Thornton, and saw that he'd turned away from the little tableau. What had happened?

Before she could pursue that thought, Caroline realized that Mr. Blanchard was about to drive off with Isobel—alone.

"I must get back and have my ankle seen to," Isobel was explaining to the Misses Wren. "Mr. Blanchard has offered to drive me."

"I shall ride along, too," Caroline said quickly, hurrying to the rig. She could not allow Isobel to be alone with the vampire, and at least she had her stake to protect her if the need arose.

"But of course, we must be properly chaperoned," Lord Rude said, a faint smile twitching the corners of his mouth. "I was about to suggest that my ward might wish to ride with us, but if you would prefer to do the honors, Miss Merrill, I would not decline." He gave a little bow that seemed more mocking than polite.

"Oh," Caroline said. "Of course Ellen must ride with you." Surely the vampire wouldn't do anything untoward with his ward in the carriage. And this would give her the chance to speak with Robbie about Isobel. They seemed to have been getting on quite well earlier. Perhaps they had had an argument.

"What a lovely string of beads," Mr. Thornton said, drawing Caro's attention away as Ellen was helped into her guardian's carriage. "Where did you find them?"

Caroline explained, and even went so far as to show him the place in the old sitting room. That was when he tried to kiss her.

"Miss Merrill," he said, walking toward her so that her back bumped the stony wall. "I must proclaim my deepest regard for you."

Fearing that her face expressed three *O*s of surprise—

her mouth and two eyes—Caroline struggled to find something to say. But Mr. Thornton glided closer, and she could not move when his hands settled on her shoulders and drew her close for a kiss.

His lips settled over hers, light and warm…and chilly, too, from the night air…and she felt her heart pounding in her breast as he pressed them harder against hers. And then, to her great relief, he pulled away.

"I do not wish to frighten you, Miss Merrill," he said. "But I could not contain myself. You, here in the moonlight, are a sight to behold. My heart stirs when I look at you."

"Caro!"

Thank heavens! "I'm here, Robbie," Caroline called back.

Moments later, Robbie appeared, looking a bit forlorn. "Are you ready to leave now, kitten?" he asked.

"Yes, I am feeling quite weary," she said.

"I shall be along in a moment," Mr. Thornton said, but Caroline hardly heard his words, for she was off so quickly with Robbie.

"Whatever happened with you and Isobel?" she hissed as they exited the ruins. The Misses Wren and their cousin were still waiting, having climbed into their carriage.

"I don't know," her brother replied. "One moment, she was delightfully Isobel, and the next, she had turned her ankle and could see only Mr. Blanchard."

He looked miserable and Caroline's heart went out to him. "I am certain that Mr. Blanchard will provide no further competition for you after this night, darling," she said. "Isobel could speak of nothing but you for the last week that I have known her. Perhaps she felt as if she were showing you too much attention and wished to be more prudent."

Robbie seemed to lighten up after that, and Caroline was left to mull those very thoughts on the way home that night.

But the next day her worries resurfaced, for she received a message—with an intriguing invitation—from Isobel and Mr. Thornton.

We are returning to our family home, Northanger Castle, and request your presence at a weekend house party. Mr. Blanchard and Miss Henry have already accepted our invitation, and we should like you to make up the other guests. Regards, Miss Isobel and Mr. John Thornton.

Although Robbie's name wasn't specifically mentioned in the invitation, Caroline responded with an acceptance for both of them, knowing that her parents' permission would be more readily obtained if she were accompanied by her brother. And aside from that, she was certain that whatever had happened with Isobel was a misunderstanding that would easily be addressed when they were all together again.

She did not miss the fact that the invitation was not given in person, nor did it have the same enthusiasm as Isobel's previous schemes.

Perhaps Mr. Thornton had insisted his sister extend the request.

Regardless, Caroline was determined to go—for she must set things right with Isobel and Robbie, and she was the only person who realized the danger in the person of Mr. Blanchard. Above all, she must keep Ellen *and* Isobel safe from him.

CHAPTER 7

CAROLINE'S FIRST GLIMPSE OF NORTHANGER CASTLE WAS enough to set her heart to thumping in anticipation. Dark and gloomy, set atop a hill and surrounded by an iron-gated fence, the Thorntons' homestead jutted with spires and odd-shaped additions. Trees grew nearby, ivy clung to the gray stone, and Caroline swore she saw a window curtain move in one of the high towers.

She could not have imagined a more Gothic, secret-ridden structure had she tried.

Oh, there must be hidden passages and locked-door towers throughout. Mysteries to solve, enigmas to uncover. Danger and perhaps even ghosts!

One thing was certain: there was a vampire in residence, in the form of Mr. Blanchard, who had presumably arrived earlier that day with Ellen.

Caroline had had to wait until Robbie put his affairs in order before they could leave Bath, having already received her parents' permission to accompany her brother. They had embarked later in the day than had the Thorntons, Ellen and Mr. Blanchard, and were just arriving as evening approached.

Even the weather cooperated with Caroline's imagination, for just as Robbie turned on the road that led to the forbidding castle, a boom of thunder shook the air. Lightning flashed, sudden and spindly in the darkening sky. By the time they entered the iron gates, the rain had begun to pelt in large, furious drops.

Thankfully, the butler greeted them at the front door with a large umbrella, and Caroline managed her entry into the vestibule without a single drop of rain marring her clothing.

"Dinner will be served momentarily," the gaunt-faced butler—the perfect servant for such a Gothic home—intoned. "Perhaps you wish to freshen up after Mrs. Humpton shows you to your chamber."

The last was more of a command than a suggestion, and Caroline hurried to comply. As she and Robbie followed Mrs. Humpton to the second floor, they passed the sitting room, where the other guests had gathered for little glasses of sherry. Aside from Ellen, her guardian and the Thorntons, the room contained several other people unknown to Caroline. Mr. Blanchard happened to look up as she walked by, and he raised the dainty glass to her in a mocking salute. His dark eyes followed her, fastening on her person in such a way that it made her stomach flutter.

"Seems like a fine fellow," Robbie commented, obviously having seen the gesture, but not comprehending the intensity of his stare.

Caroline declined to respond. The truth would come out soon enough—perhaps even as early as tonight. She shivered in anticipation as well as nervousness as she imagined slipping through the dark warren of hallways in the dead of night, in search of the vampire himself.

Not that she would be so foolish as to attempt to hunt him down, à la the Venators in the Starcasset book, but if she could foil his plan to lure anyone into a dark corner, she would do so, armed with stake, holy cross and garlic—along with a powerful set of lungs that could scream to shake the rafters.

The storm whipped itself up as the evening meal approached, and the dinner, served in a long, red room, was punctuated by ferocious thunder that rattled the silver.

Despite the delicious meal of minted lamb chops and new potatoes, Caroline could hardly enjoy it, for her brother's misery seemed hardly subtle. Isobel had seated Mr. Blanchard next to her vivacious self, and her dinner companion seemed intent on keeping her entertained.

Caroline, positioned across the table from Robbie and next to Mr. Thornton, attempted to divide her attention between her conversation with them while angling to hear just what was so particularly amusing between Isobel and Lord Rude. She could scarcely comprehend him having anything to say that might be witty or charming.

Ellen had been seated next to Robbie, which gave her ample opportunity to exchange glances with Caroline. As the wind howled and the rain battered the windows, the two young friends sent each other private messages with the lift of an eyebrow or a gesture of the chin.

In this manner, they agreed that meeting in the library while the gentlemen had their port would be a good place to start their exploration of this fascinating place.

But those plans were to be ruined, for as the meal broke up, Mr. Thornton suggested that the gentlemen forgo their cigars and port to join the ladies for cards and a bit of music.

Isobel could not have been more delighted, in Caroline's eyes, for she edged next to Mr. Blanchard until he offered her his arm as escort into the large parlor. As they passed by, she heard Isobel discussing the particular color of her frock in comparison to the ribbons edging it.

Poor Robbie was left to escort Ellen into the parlor, watching the beacon-headed Isobel disappear ahead of him, her laughter trilling behind. Caroline's jaw hurt from gritting her teeth.

"Miss Merrill," said a deep voice at her shoulder.

Caroline turned, a bit startled, and found Mr. Thornton—she still could not think of him as James—standing behind her.

He offered his arm. "I was hoping you might join me for a little walk through the portrait gallery of the Thornton family ancestors."

Unable to find a polite way to refuse, Caroline slid her fingers around his arm and allowed him to lead her away. "How kind of you, Mr. Thornton," she said. Despite the fact that she wanted to keep an eye on Mr. Blanchard, she was intrigued to have a bit of a tour of the castle.

"And I confess, Caroline, that I had hoped to find a few moments alone with you," he told her, glancing down as they walked along a dimly lit corridor. "I have not had the opportunity to express my delight at your presence here in Northanger. I do hope you find the estate to your liking."

Caroline felt her heart begin to pound harder. Why should he care if she approved of his estate, unless he anticipated her spending a great amount of time here? Her mouth had dried and she looked up at the gentleman next to her. He was a fine-looking fellow, polite, if a bit dry in his conversations. Isobel could be genuinely amusing, but only in small amounts.

"Here is the portrait of my great-great-great-grandfather," James told her, pausing in front of a very large painting.

Caroline listened to his voice, which had become the most animated she had ever heard it, as he gave her brief histories of grandparents and uncles. When they reached the end of the gallery, he paused, turning her to stand in a pool of moonlight.

"Miss Merrill—Caroline—I know that this may come as a bit sudden," he said, and to her mortification, dropped onto one knee in front of her. "But my affection for you has taken hold of my sensibilities, and I find that I must wait no longer in expressing my very deep attachment to you."

"Mr. Thornton," she began, aware that her palms had become damp and that her heart was pounding.

"Please, Caroline, I wish to offer you a token of my great fondness—and dare I say love—as an indication of my serious intentions to you. Until I can speak with your father, I hope that you will keep this—" and at that, he pulled a small metal object from his pocket and pressed it into her hand "—near your heart, as I shall keep thoughts of you near mine."

Caroline hardly knew what to say, so she focused her attention on the item he laid in her glove. "It's quite unique," she said, looking at what appeared to be a brooch wrought of some old metal, perhaps bronze. A lion's face, its mane writhing about it in darker bronze, and two chips of garnet glinting as the feline's eyes. "It appears very old."

"It is," he told her. "I found it at Blaize Abbey, not so far from where you found those prayer beads. Perhaps they belonged to the same person."

Caroline looked up at him, for the first time fully appreciating the fact that James Thornton seemed to understand her affinity for the mysterious. "How kind of you," she said. "I shall treasure it."

He pulled back to his feet, and offered her his arm again. "Is it possible that my intentions might be welcomed by you, then, Miss Merrill?"

She felt an odd heaviness in her middle, but the weight of the brooch overruled it. "I do believe they would be."

After all, she would be mistress of this estate. Of a *castle,* with rooms for her to explore to her heart's content! She could never have imagined such an outcome.

"You have made me a most happy man," James told her.

He seemed as if he might bend toward her for a kiss again, and Caroline felt just a bit unsettled, so she spoke quickly, "Perhaps we ought to return."

James nodded, and suggested, "And you will want to put that brooch away somewhere safely, I am certain. Perhaps in your room? In a pocket of your trunk or deep in a small reticule?"

Caroline agreed. "You are correct. I shall stop in my chamber and do just that, then I will join you belowstairs."

A crash of thunder set a glass chandelier to clinking, and a great spear of lightning lit the room as if it were midday.

"What a horrid storm," she said as they parted ways at the staircase. "Do you have them often here at Northanger?"

James looked up at her. "Indeed, but I hope not too often for your taste."

"No indeed," she replied, starting up the steps.

The storms, she decided, would be the best part of living here.

CHAPTER 8

CAROLINE DID AS JAMES SUGGESTED AND WRAPPED UP THE lion brooch in her least favorite reticule, then tucked it in the deepest part of her trunk.

When she finished, she slipped from her room and, hearing the chatter and laughter wafting up from below, decided that she simply could not miss the opportunity to do a bit of exploring. As she came down the flight of stairs to the main floor, she stayed to the right and in the shadows, sneaking off toward the older wing of the castle.

If there was anything curious or sinister to find, it would certainly be there, where James had mentioned that the household rarely ventured. He claimed it was left uninhabited because it was too cold and damp, but Caroline could not resist the chance to check that sensation for herself.

She hadn't gone far when she heard the soft brush of a footstep behind her.

Starting, she whirled and found Lord Rude—Mr. Blanchard—emerging from the shadows. Her heart thumping madly, Caroline began to dig in her reticule for the stake.

"So there you are." Was there a tinge of relief in his voice? "We'd begun to miss you," he said, walking toward her. "You left with Thornton, but he returned without you."

"I had something to put away," she said, pleased that her voice was calm despite the fact that her fingers didn't seem to be able to grasp the stake.

"In the deserted area of the castle?" he asked, his voice tinged with mockery. "Or are you playing at being Emily St. Aubert, intending to get yourself into trouble?"

"So you have read *Udolpho*," she said.

"And a variety of other novels in which a young woman, at great risk to herself, foolishly goes harking about dark and dangerous castles or abbeys when she knows that danger lurks about. Or she gets herself involved with unsavory people."

Caroline lifted her chin. "It is not a foolish thing to do if nothing untoward happens." But her throat turned dry, for she realized she may have just proved her point. For it certainly appeared as if something unpleasant was about to happen.

"I thought it would be in your best interest if I came looking for you. In the event you got lost." He was standing very close to her now, and his dark eyes had fixed on hers.

Caroline found it difficult to breathe, and knew she was sinking into his thrall. But she could not look away, and, as the moment stretched on, she felt less endangered and more…warm, and tingly. Back in the deepest part of her mind, she knew he was doing it purposely, and she tried to fight it…but she could not. His eyes were about to turn red, and those sharp fangs would appear.

Mr. Blanchard stepped even closer, and she felt his hands settle on her upper arms. She was powerless to pull away. "Do you not know how much danger you are in, here in this very house?" he murmured.

At that moment, deep in the pouch, her fingers closed over the smooth wood of the stake. But before she could yank it free, he bent toward her.

Caroline's heart seized and her breath clogged in her throat, but instead of a sharp pain in the side of her neck, she felt the soft warmth of lips closing over hers. Shock trammeled through her as their lips met, her own mouth parting slightly as if to allow his to fit just right.

She very much feared she might faint at the range of sensations that suddenly burst over her. Warmth and pleasure, solidness and curiosity, and a desire for more. Her heart began to function again and she realized that his lips had moved gently over hers, brushing against them in a tingling, whisper-soft caress, over and over. Gentle, tender, coaxing…and that she had been moving her own mouth against his in the same manner.

When he pulled his face away, and looked down at her, the expression in his eyes made her feel weak in the knees. Caroline realized, foggily, that she still grasped the stake, and she closed her eyes, fighting back the thrall that seemed to have snagged her.

Just as he bent toward her again, she struggled to pull her hand free from where it was trapped between them. But as she moved, clumsily, he bumped her and the stake fell from her nervous hand, clattering to the floor.

It rolled loudly on the marble floor and came to rest at the edge of a rug.

Mr. Blanchard pulled farther away from her now, still holding on to her arms, and looked at the spindle lying on the ground. "What in the blazes is that?"

"I—" Caroline tried to speak, but no words would come from her dry mouth. Her heart still raced and her knees felt as though they might buckle at any moment so that she was relieved he still held on to her as she dug once more in her reticule.

"Is that a *stake?*" he said, incredulously.

"Yes, I am afraid I know your secret, Mr. Blanchard," Caroline managed to say, pulling the silver cross triumphantly from her pouch. She brandished it in his face as he released her arms.

But instead of cowering in fear, or even wincing at the sight of the holy article, Mr. Blanchard took one look at the cross, then his attention went to the stake on the floor. And he began to laugh.

Caroline seized the moment to rush over to the stake and swipe it up into her hand, so that when she turned back to him, she wielded the cross in one hand and the stake in the other. He might laugh at her, but he would be surprised at her boldness. She would not be frightened into the corner, not when the life of her friend Ellen was at stake.

"Miss Merrill," he said, his laughter having ebbed into seriousness, "or perhaps I should be granted permission to call you Caroline, after that most pleasant interlude a moment ago. Caroline, did you mean to stake *me?*"

"Yes, indeed," she replied, feeling much more powerful now that he didn't seem to have the ability to enthrall her, and now that she was armed with her two weapons. "I told you, I know your secret. I have been observing you and following you for days."

His lips twitched in a way that annoyed her, because it made him appear even more handsome and charming—which wasn't saying much, for she hadn't nicknamed him Lord Rude for naught.

"And my secret is…that I am a vampire?" he said.

"You cannot deny it. I saw you at the Roman spa, and

you lured that young lady to her death back in the area that was closed to the public. You must have disposed of her body when you were finished. And that woman in pink, with the dark hair, at the theater. I realized she was poisoning her husband, but that was no excuse for you to coax her into the darkness and—and—"

By now he was looking at her so incredulously that her voice trailed off. "The woman in pink? The older woman, who was with the younger man at the theater? Was poisoning her husband?"

"Yes, and then just after that, you accosted me in the gallery, Mr. Blanchard. I daresay if James hadn't appeared at that moment, you would have done the same to me."

"My dear Caroline," he said, his voice filtering over the syllables of her name most tenderly. Yet, there was a bit of humor lying beneath. "Do you mean to say that you saw that young lady and knew something was amiss? And the woman at the theater—you noticed her maliciousness?" His eyes narrowed. "I suppose then that you noticed the young girl in the yellow dress, just the other day at the spa when I came upon you and Ellen?"

"The orphan girl with a devastating secret," Caroline said, nodding. "Never say you were after her, as well!"

"I was indeed hunting all three of those women. But not for the reason you seem to think," he said. His eyes, usually so dark and annoyed, had lit with appreciation. "They were the vampires, and I did indeed lure them away so that I could—er—dispose of them. But how could you know that?"

Caroline felt her eyes widen. *Impossible.* Mr. Blanchard—should she call him Thaddeus now?—was a vampire *hunter?* "And why should I believe you?" she asked. "How do I know you have not simply made up such a story to hide your true deviltry?"

He spread his hands. "Stake me if you wish, then, Caroline. If I am a vampire, I will explode into a pile of ash. If not, then I shall bleed quite profusely and you shall have to nurse me back to health." He smiled suddenly, a very wicked smile that had her stomach pitching and dropping to her knees. "I do believe I should like very much to know a woman besides Miss Pesaro, who is altogether too full of herself thanks to her father, who can sense the presence of a vampire."

Caroline blinked. "Who is Miss Pesaro?"

"Oh, she is a hunter of vampires like myself, and a bit of an annoying chit if one must know—all because of who her parents are. Well, then, are you going to stake me?" Thaddeus (yes, indeed, she had given herself permission to call him by his Christian name) asked, offering his rather broad chest, suitably covered in shirtwaist and waistcoat, but impressive nevertheless.

She raised her stake, aiming it at that wide expanse of white linen, and he stopped her. "No, darling Caro, you mustn't hold it like that. See how easy it is for me to stop the blow?"

He adjusted the wooden pike in her hand so that she had a better grip and a more formidable angle to her strike, and once again opened his arms for her target. "There, now, take a blow. Right in the heart."

"I know it must go into the heart," she said, suddenly very unsure of herself. "But is there not another way to prove whether you are a vampire or not?"

He smiled. "You may simply believe me when I tell you I am not. I am a Venator myself, a member of the famous Gardella family—which I trust you have read about in that ridiculous novel by George Starcasset. Pesaro is going to be more than a bit livid to find that there are still some copies of it going about. I daresay Starcasset will have to disappear somewhere permanently, or Pesaro will do the honors himself."

"A *Venator?*" Caroline drew in her breath. "You are a Venator? A vampire hunter? Truly?"

"Of course. But it is not something I rush about telling people. We do keep that sort of information to ourselves for obvious reasons."

"What sort of obvious reasons?"

He spread his hand to encompass herself, her stake and the cross. "So that we do not have untrained, inexperienced people like yourself getting in our way when we attempt to do our jobs." Despite his words, the tone to his voice was light. "I have a confession to make now, my dear Caroline, and I hope that you will find it as amusing as I do."

"What is that?" she asked suspiciously.

"Until you tried to stake me, it occurred to me that you might be a member of the Tutela."

"The secret society of vampire protectors?" Caroline said. She was aghast. "Why on earth would you think that?"

And so was that the only reason he had kissed her? For some reason, she felt as though her whole world had turned dark.

He stepped closer to her again, and brushed his fingers along her chin. She allowed him to do it—after all, she'd assumed he was a vampire, and she considered that that made them even.

"Because I have been watching James Thornton— who, my dear, *does* happen to be a vampire—for some time now. I knew he was about to pass a very important artifact on to a member of the Tutela. All I knew was that she was a woman. After a bit of observation, I came to the conclusion that it was either you or Miss Thornton."

"Well, it certainly isn't me," Caroline said, feeling more than a bit huffy for a variety of reasons she didn't dare to examine.

"I cannot tell you how delighted I am to learn that," Thaddeus said. And he drew her into his arms. The moonlight shone through the window, falling over her arms and bosom. "How lovely you look, dressed in the silver gilt of moon," he said, bending to kiss her again.

Caroline found her arms moving up and around his neck as their mouths met. She tumbled into a realm of pleasure—of warmth and comfort, a delicious tingling and sleek, languorous movements. And in the back of her mind, she realized she was not being kissed because she was a member of the Tutela, but because she *wasn't* a member of the Tutela, which caused her to smile against his mouth.

When she at last extricated herself from him, something that he was reluctant to allow, she looked up at him. "So do you believe that Miss Thornton is the member of the Tutela? But she is his sister."

"Indeed. I no longer suspect her—for a variety of reasons, one of which is that I cannot endure another moment of listening to a discourse upon which ribbon goes with which slipper, and how she searched for a week for a particular hat with a—what is the word? *cunning*—little feather. I don't believe she has a space in her head for anything other than such nonsense," he said. "So she is not a member of the Tutela."

"But if it isn't her and it isn't me," Caroline said, "to whom is Mr. Thornton giving the artifact?"

"I don't know yet. And that is the only reason I have not introduced him to the pointed end of my stake." As if to prove his point, he slipped a wicked-looking black spindle from beneath his coat. Caroline shivered, realizing at once that he must be quite formidable as a vampire hunter.

"But perhaps we shall find out over the rest of this house party," he said. Thaddeus offered her his arm. "Although nothing would give me greater pleasure than to remain here with you in the moonlight, sharing perhaps another kiss...or helping you to explore the abandoned wing of the castle, I suppose we must be prudent and return before we are missed."

Caroline, suddenly feeling light of foot and heart, curled her fingers around the solid musculature of his arm. Such a difference from the softness under James's coat sleeve. Then a thought struck her. "You knew that James was a vampire, but you allowed me to go about with him? Why, how could you allow such a thing? I might have been lured into a dark alcove and torn apart!"

Thaddeus smiled down at her and, for the first time, she realized that it wasn't a vampiric thrall that made her heart stutter and her breath stop—it was something much more pleasant.

"I knew you were in no danger from James, at least now. He is much more cunning, to use his sister's word, than that. It would be too obvious if he were squiring you about and you suddenly disappeared or were attacked. In fact, being the object of his affection made you as safe as you could be from him at this time." Then his muscles flexed beneath her fingers. "At least, as safe as you could be when not under my protection. Which you will be from this moment forward, Caroline...if you will allow it. And welcome my intentions."

Caroline realized that this was the second proposal of sorts she'd received this evening. But for some reason, this proposal made her feel billowy and warm inside, while the statement of James's intentions had merely made her feel upset. "I believe I do welcome your intentions, Thaddeus."

"I am quite relieved to hear it, for it has been quite a struggle for me. Either you had fallen under Thornton's spell, or you were a member of the Tutela—and in either case, it was becoming more difficult for me to ignore your lovely button nose, that sassy smattering of freckles you try so hard to hide, your quick wit and the fascinating conversations we seem to have."

They began to stroll back through the corridor. "And," he added, "it appears you have the uncanny ability to identify vampires, without actually realizing you are doing so. Quite intriguing."

"But don't you have that same skill, as a Venator? They seemed to in the book."

"I do, of course. It's part of the family legacy. But for a non-Venator to have that sense, well," he said, once more smiling at her, "it's rather fascinating."

Caroline bloomed warm again beneath his attention and realized why Ellen seemed so fond of her guardian. Although sharp with his words, and often rude and intense, he had a right to be when doing such a dangerous job. But he also had a more pleasant aspect to his personality, and one that she intended to see much more of.

"I shall have to return the gift Mr. Thornton gave me tonight," she murmured, thinking to herself as they strolled along. And then she stopped suddenly. "Oh my!"

"What is it?" Thaddeus asked.

"The artifact... Oh, I am so stupid!"

He raised his brows. "Now, I have never said such a thing, even when lecturing you about going into the empty areas by yourself. Or being wooed by a vampire."

"Is it a lion's head?" she asked. "A pin?"

Thaddeus's eyes narrowed and his face became serious. "Have you seen it?"

"He gave it to me. Tonight! And he told me to hide it."

"He must know that I—or someone—is after it. Where did you put it, Caroline? Take me there immediately."

Without giving a second thought to the idea of bringing a gentleman to her bedchamber, Caroline led him to that very place and burst into the room.

James Thornton stood there, his hands deep in her clothing trunk. He spun, and there before her eyes, his irises turned a burning red. "So!" he said, and the fangs erupted from his mouth. "Where have you hidden it? I must have it back now!"

He lunged for Caroline, who, in her excitement, had preceded Thaddeus into the room. James's fingers closed around her arm and he yanked her toward him.

Everything happened so fast after that. Thaddeus moved, there was a flash of his arm as he leaped toward them, slamming the stake down into the vampire's chest. James Thornton froze, his mouth open wide in shock.

The grip on Caroline's arm released, and as she turned, James disintegrated into a puff of ash, filtering all over the room.

The smell was foul, and the dust clung to her, and, as she brushed it away with shaking fingers, Caroline realized she had seen Thaddeus do exactly the same thing that first day in the bath spa. And when she'd seen him at the theater, she'd pointed out the dust speckling his coat.

"He's gone," she said when she found her voice. "You—you did that so quickly."

"Of course," Thaddeus said matter-of-factly, slipping

the stake back into his inner pocket. "Now where is the lion's brooch?"

Caroline dug it from the depths of her trunk and handed it to him.

"Thank you, my dear," he said, once more pulling her flush against his body for a long, thorough kiss. "You have made my task much easier and more enjoyable this time."

"I am delighted to be of help," she replied.

"Now, we had best return to the rest of the party," he told her.

"But what will we do about James?" she asked.

Thaddeus shrugged. "There is nothing we can do. But there is no body to be found, so everyone will simply believe he disappeared."

She slipped her hand once more around his arm. "What a fascinating life you must lead, Thaddeus."

He looked down at her, his eyes warm and velvety. "I have a feeling, my dear Caroline, that with you involved, it's about to get even more fascinating."

She smiled up at him. "Well, I certainly hope so, for after this, I don't believe I'll be satisfied simply reading about Gothic adventures."

"No, my dear, I shouldn't think so." And with that, he dropped a quick kiss onto her freckled, buttony nose and took her back to the party.

THREE MONTHS LATER, they were married.

Two months after that, with the effusive blessings of her guardian, Miss Ellen Henry wed Mr. Robbie Merrill.

And six months later, Miss Isobel Thornton found a wealthy earl to wed, and to keep her in ribbons and cunning hats and embroidered slippers.

* * * * *

BLOOD AND PREJUDICE

Susan Krinard

Dear Reader,

I have never been a purist. I'm willing to consider all kinds of adaptations of my favorite stories, including those that are a little offbeat. I love Shakespeare plays set in modern times, and science-fiction treatments of classic novels.

For me, Jane Austen's works have an appeal that extends beyond the traditional Regency-era milieu. I've loved her stories for many years…particularly *Pride and Prejudice,* which I have enjoyed not only in the original novel form, but also in three distinct television and movie versions. Each, for me, has its own charms, though none can be considered strictly "perfect" adaptations.

So it was no stretch at all when, well before the current interest in Austen "mash-ups," I became intrigued by the idea of combining the paranormal with *Pride and Prejudice.* I saw Darcy as a perfect vampire, definitely of the honorable variety, and a modern-day Lizzy as his perfect foil. I even had the perfect title— "Blood and Prejudice."

The story came to me more quickly than any other I'd ever written. I submitted an anthology idea to my agent, which I called *Bespelling Jane Austen.* We collected three other terrific authors, each of whom chose a different Austen novel to adapt, and the anthology found a home at HQN Books.

I've been thrilled to be a part of *Bespelling Jane Austen.* I hope that readers, be they fans of Austen or paranormal or both, will enjoy this collection as much as we enjoyed writing it.

Susan Krinard

CHAPTER I

Present Day New Haven, Connecticut

IT IS A TRUTH UNIVERSALLY ACKNOWLEDGED, THAT EVERY decent straight guy who isn't dead broke, is in want of a good woman.

As my dear Grandpa Bennet used to say... Bull.

I should know. Not that *I've* been looking, mind you. My two younger sisters make up for the rest of us ten times over. But Jane...why no one has snapped her up yet is incomprehensible. Of course, no ordinary guy would deserve her. Not my sweet, adorable Jane.

I was thinking about the perfect husband for my big sister when the family gathered for Dad's annual office birthday party at Bennet Laboratories. Dad, BL's president and founder; Jane, head of Personnel; and Mary, assistant accountant, were already at the office. Mom had come in from my parents' house in Branford, Kitty and Lydia from their "closet" in Manhattan, and I put up my out-to-lunch sign at Longbourn Books and walked the six blocks to BL's modest headquarters and research facility.

Not that I'd lose many customers; Dad said it was only my natural stubbornness that kept me firmly planted in the struggling independent bookstore business. The same way he kept fighting to preserve some small bit of pride as he watched Bennet Laboratories facing a complete takeover by a company that didn't give a damn about what he'd accomplished.

But I was thinking about Jane that early afternoon, wondering what would happen to her if BL went under. Not that she couldn't find another job…at least so long as she stuck up for herself a little. Of course I was worried about Dad and Mom and Mary, too. I couldn't imagine a world without BL—*my* world, at least. It had been at the center of my family for almost as long as I could remember.

If Dad hadn't been so reckless with his investments, if he hadn't taken a few too many risks in his eternal quest for new discoveries…

I tried to put BL's problems out of my mind as I took the stairs to the second floor. The employees were standing around in nervous groups, trying to appear cheerful for Dad's sake. Jane was beaming at everyone; even if she were nervous, she wouldn't show it. She'd put up balloons and streamers and had laid out a feast of finger foods, sandwiches and drinks. Mary looked as if she'd much rather be at her desk buried in her account books, though that couldn't be a very pleasant job these days.

As for Mom, she was chattering at an unfortunate lab tech who had wandered a little too close to her web. His face collapsed in pathetic gratitude when Mom saw me.

"Lizzy!" She held out her hands, grabbed mine and kissed me noisily on the cheek. "Have you heard? Mr. Bingley is coming!"

I was so surprised by her announcement that I was momentarily speechless. Mom didn't waste any time filling the silence.

"Can you imagine?" she went on in a tone made up of one part indignation and two parts satisfaction. "Your *father* invited him. Mr. Bennet said that we should show that we're not worried about the acquisition."

"He's right," I said, though my thoughts were anything but calm. "So much of this depends on how you play the game. Putting up a confident front is—"

"I know that very well, Lizzy," she said irritably. She leaned closer, as if the whole room couldn't already hear her. "I haven't met Mr. Bingley. You know how your father refuses to tell me *anything* that's going on here… but I've been told that he's a very handsome man. And extraordinarily rich."

Trust Mom to think that was the most important thing, not the fact that BL was on the verge of going under. "What does *that* have to do with anything, Mom?" I asked.

"It must be obvious even to you, Lizzy. I'm counting on him marrying one of you girls. Then, if Mr. Bingley does take over, we won't have anything to worry about!"

I'd been annoyed at Mom plenty of times in my life, but I'd learned how to hide it at a very young age. "Who did you have in mind?" I asked dryly.

"Well, Jane is the eldest, and she really ought to have first shot."

"Did I hear my name?" Jane said, coming to join us. She smiled at Mom and at me with that unfeigned warmth I'd never been able to match.

"You've heard that Mr. Bingley is coming to the party?" Mom asked.

"No, I didn't. But it seems like a good idea."

"Why?" I asked bluntly.

"Well, he only inherited BP a few months ago. He's never attended the negotiations himself, but I've heard

good things about him. I'm sure he'll want to recon-
sider some of his representatives' more stringent demands
when he really knows us."

I shook my head. "Your faith in people never ceases
to amaze me, Jane."

"Oh, Izba," she said, using the nickname she'd given
me when I was a baby. "You only have to look a little
harder. The good is always there."

"How right you are, darling," Mom said. "I'm sure
that Mr. Bingley will be perfectly charming."

I rolled my eyes. "Where's Dad?"

Jane's forehead wrinkled. "He had some last-minute
call. I don't think it was good news."

Is it ever? I thought. But I smiled and squeezed her
hand. "This is supposed to be a celebration, remember?"

She brightened. No one could keep Jane down for long.
"Yes. Everything is ready. I have the champagne on ice,
and—"

The absolute quiet in the room was so sudden that Jane
stopped in midsentence. Mom turned around. Everyone
was staring toward the door to the hallway as two men
walked in, and I knew that Mr. Bingley had arrived.

Handsome. Okay, I'd give him that, though he wasn't
my type. Blond, blue-eyed, average height and smiling
in a way that seemed almost as sincere as Jane on one
of her happy binges. His suit was a little rumpled, as if
he didn't much care if he looked like the extremely rich
president of a major pharmaceutical company.

He held my attention for about five seconds before his
friend stalked in.

Now, I'm not the girly type. I don't fall all over myself
when a good-looking guy looks my way. But this time I
held my breath and just stared.

Tall, dark and handsome. Check, check and check. He

moved like a dancer, or maybe just a guy who was used to being noticed wherever he went. His athletic build and broad shoulders were admirably displayed in his impeccable custom-made suit, as faultlessly pressed as Bingley's was rumpled.

And there was something else about him. Something dangerous. It radiated from him, casting everyone and everything else in shadow. When he glanced in my direction, I saw more than arrogance and self-assurance in his eyes. There was a glint to them that reminded me of a wolf strolling into a pen full of fat sheep.

Mom rushed over to Bingley and his looming shadow with a grin that would have frightened any man with brains. "Mr. Bingley! How very delightful!"

Jane sidled up next to me. "I didn't expect Mr. Bingley to be so…" She trailed off and bit her lip, but I noticed that her eyes were very bright. "I mean, doesn't he look like a nice person?"

My poor, naive Jane. He did look "nice," our Mr. Bingley. Just the kind of guy who'd let others do his dirty work so that he could maintain his facade of "niceness."

But maybe Jane was right. She often was. And if *I'd* had to pick the guy most likely to eliminate the competition by tossing out a life raft with a slow leak in it, it would be Mr. Tall-Dark-and-Handsome.

"Who is the guy with Bingley?" I asked Jane.

"Oh, that must be Mr. Darcy. He's on the Bingley Pharmaceuticals Board of Directors."

Figured. "He looks like Bingley's bodyguard."

"I've heard they're good friends."

Well, I thought, *they do say opposites attract.*

I was about to reflect further on the subject when Dad came into the room. He looked a little like a mad scientist with his wisps of white hair sticking out at all angles and his preoccupied air. Like Mary, he'd rather have been back at his desk than partying, and I couldn't believe he was thrilled about Bingley being there, even if he'd felt the need to invite him.

Dad greeted Bingley and Darcy with a smile and outstretched hands, introducing them to the other employees and to Kitty and Lydia, who had joined Mom in a froth of giggles and flirtatious glances. I stood well out of the way, watching Jane gravitate ever nearer to Bingley while Darcy hovered behind his "friend," treating everyone who came within spitting distance to a sneer worthy of Edward G. Robinson.

Maybe they're gay, I thought. That would certainly throw a wrench in Mom's plans. But Bingley seemed to ignore Darcy completely, greeting everyone with the kind of friendliness that was hard to fake. He came to a dead stop when Dad introduced Jane. He looked at her, and she looked at him, a pair of angels heading for a fall.

Now, I've never believed in love at first sight. It makes for good movies and bad novels, but it really comes down to sex. And Jane just wasn't that kind of girl.

I decided I'd spent enough time watching. I grabbed a couple of champagnes, served up in fancy plastic flutes, and joined them.

Jane turned to me with the most radiant smile I'd ever seen. "Lizzy!" she said. "Mr. Bingley, Mr. Darcy, this is my sister, Elizabeth."

I raised one flute in salute. "Nice to meet you," I lied. "Care for some champagne?"

Bingley grinned, showing a mouthful of gleaming white teeth. "Thank you, Ms. Bennet," he said in a pleasant tenor. "I think I will. But please call me Charles."

"Charles." I glanced at the formidable Mr. Darcy. "Would you like one, Mr. Darcy?"

For the first time our eyes met, and it was like walking into a metaphor describing brick walls and immovable objects. I'd taken a step back before I even realized it, and the champagne sloshed over my blouse.

Darcy didn't seem to notice. He was staring at me with his piercing indigo eyes as if we were the only two people in the room and he was about to eat me for lunch.

The picture that idea put into my mind made me feel... well, let's just say it's been a while since I had quite that reaction on meeting a guy for the first time. And I couldn't figure out what the hell was wrong with me. I'd met other tall, handsome guys before.

But not like him.

I wanted to run screaming out of the room. Instead, I tipped back the plastic flute and drank the remaining champagne in one swallow, then promptly fell into a fit of coughing.

Two seconds later Charles was pounding me on the back while Jane's face swam in front of me like an old VCR tape copied one too many times.

"Lizzy! Are you all right?"

I straightened, blinking tears from my eyes. "Completely."

Except I could feel Darcy's eyes skewering me, haughty and contemptuous.

"How clumsy of me," I said with a sharp smile. "You should have taken the champagne, Mr. Darcy."

"I don't care for any, thank you."

His voice was crisp, formal and very English. My heart started to flutter like Marilyn Monroe's white dress in *The Seven Year Itch*.

"I think I'd better clean up," I said, pushing the empty flute into Jane's hand. "Excuse me."

I rushed out and ducked into the bathroom, as rattled

as if I'd just woken up from one of those dreams where you're walking around your old high school in your underwear. I skidded to a stop in front of a mirror and leaned over the sink.

Lydia used to tease me about not caring how I looked. For her, looks are everything; for me, not so much. But now I was thinking of Darcy staring at me, and I noticed that my hair was curling in all the wrong places, I had dark circles under my eyes from staying up late reading the latest Sue Grafton and the subtle lipstick I'd put on was smeared.

I hit the sink with my fist and instantly regretted it. I shook my hand until it stopped buzzing, combed my hair with my fingers, repaired my lipstick and examined my blouse. No help there, unless I ran back to the store and grabbed a T-shirt.

To hell with Darcy. I didn't give a damn what he thought.

Did I?

In spite of my determination to pretend I hadn't made a fool of myself, I hesitated outside the door to the meeting room. I could hear two men talking very quietly just inside, and immediately recognized the voice of my nemesis.

"You know how I detest such gatherings, Bingley," he said. "I have no interest in the affairs of this company's employees, least of all those of the family."

"You can be such a jerk at times, Darcy," Bingley said. "You didn't exactly refuse when I asked you to come. And anyway, these people should have your sympathy."

"Bingley Pharmaceuticals belongs to *you,* I believe."

"And I should have been paying more attention to how it's being run."

"You have carried on your father's work in seeking

cures for obscure diseases that no other company will touch," Darcy said. "You need feel no qualms about acquiring a business that is on the verge of collapse."

"Your business advice is usually sound, but in this case—"

"If you wish to succeed in the work you support, you cannot be sentimental in such matters."

"I know how much you want Bingley Laboratories, Darcy, but this isn't the place for one of your lectures." He cleared his throat. "What do you think about her?"

"To whom are you referring?"

"Didn't you *see* her? She's so beautiful."

"Tolerable."

"What do you mean, tolerable? All that beautiful blond hair…"

"Ah. I fear I misunderstood. You refer to the elder sister."

"Of course. What did you think I…" A chuckle. "Oh, I get it. You thought I meant Elizabeth. I should have known she'd be more your type."

"Hardly. Unlike you, Charles, I am more particular in my choices. You can scarcely expect me to be engaged by a woman incapable of drinking a simple glass of champagne."

CHAPTER 2

MY FACE WAS SO HOT THAT I KNEW I'D SCARE JANE HALF TO
death if she saw me now. Who did he think he was? *No
interest in the affairs...* He was worse than I'd thought.
Much worse. And where had he learned to talk, anyway?
His speech was like something out of a Victorian novel.

"I am more particular in my choices." It wasn't just
an insult to me, but to my whole family. He'd made very
clear what he thought of us.

Girding my loins, I charged into the room, nearly
knocking Bingley off his feet. I paused to apologize and
batted my eyelashes at Darcy, who actually looked a little
perturbed.

"Are you all right, Elizabeth?" Charles asked with a
look of genuine concern.

"Fine, thanks. Would you like more champagne?"

Charles patted his stomach. "No, thank you. You have
so much good food here that I couldn't eat another bite."

"You can thank Jane for that." I glared at Darcy—who
subjected me to a cool, cynical stare that consigned me to
the ranks of scurrying, pestiferous hexapods—and walked
away with my head high and my heart playing hopscotch
under my ribs.

I went directly to Jane, who took one look at my face and pulled me into a corner. I proceeded to tell her what Bingley had said about her—winning a blush and a shy smile—and then filled her in on Darcy's judgment of me and our family.

"He didn't mean it, I'm sure. Though he does seem a little serious."

"Serious!" I laughed. "'You cannot be sentimental in such matters.' He's a creep, and you know it. But Charles…"

"Oh, Lizzy. He's perfect. Bingley Pharma can't be as bad as some of the others if he's researching cures for rare diseases. It isn't so different from what we've been doing for years." She lowered her voice. "From from what you've said, Charles obviously *hasn't* known what's going on with the negotiations."

"You may be right," I said. "Darcy, on the other hand…"

"He can't be as bad as he seems, Lizzy. Listen… Charles will be at the next meeting. I believe Mr. Darcy will be there, too. I'll tell you what I observe."

Through the most shocking pink of rose-colored glasses. If I hadn't been heading off to the Frankfurt Book Fair—a trip for which I'd been saving for the past two years—I would have asked to be in on the meetings, too.

If Darcy were the real brains behind the takeover, Dad needed all the backup he could get. How could I blame my quiet, unassuming father for failing to stand up to such a…

Since this story is rated for general audiences, I won't say what I *really* thought of Darcy. I tried to ignore him completely as I rejoined the party, pretending I didn't notice him watching me when I offered a toast to my dear old dad and joined in the general conversation and good-natured ribbing. Once or twice I managed to watch *him* glaring at Jane and Charles, who were showing no signs of losing interest in one another.

Given the conversation I'd overheard, it didn't seem unreasonable to assume that Darcy didn't want his friend spending personal time with the daughter of the man whose company he intended to devour. I was almost tempted to go right up to him and challenge him on exactly that point—and a couple of others—but before I could get him alone, the party was over and he was striding out of the office, Charles trailing after him with mournful puppy-dog eyes.

"Did you *see* how much Mr. Bingley liked Jane?" Mom said, breaking into my thoughts with all the subtlety of a charging rhinoceros. "Exactly as I suspected. I knew she couldn't be so pretty for nothing!"

"Yes, but—"

"But oh, my *poor* Lizzy-girl! Jane told me what that awful man said about you. Let me tell you, my heart would be broken if he *did* like you. Everyone agrees that he is a conceited so-and-so who thinks he's better than everyone else."

For once Mom wasn't exaggerating.

I saw Jane one more time. She was walking on air, a radiant Venus with Cupid's arrow firmly stuck between her arched blond eyebrows. I didn't see much point in warning her that she might be jumping the gun; I'd have to rely on the common sense that usually prevented her from making serious mistakes when her naturally trusting and gentle nature led her astray.

You'd better not let her down, Bingley.

And as for Darcy...the next time we met, I'd let him know exactly what I thought of his attitude. If I didn't,

I might actually become afraid of him. And that was a situation not to be tolerated for an instant.

THE WEATHER WAS FINE IN Frankfurt, and I'd managed to forget about Mr. Darcy for a whole twenty-four hours before I opened my inbox and found Jane's email.

Dearest Izba,

I'm more certain than ever that I was right. We have had two meetings since you left, and it's clear that Charles had no idea what was really going on in the negotiations. He treats Dad with respect, and he's already backed away from the other negotiators' more unreasonable conditions.

Good, I thought. Maybe he could be trusted after all.

I have a very good feeling about all this, Lizzy. I've spoken to Charles privately after both meetings, and I only like him more each time.

"Of course," I muttered.

On the other hand, I really don't understand Mr. Darcy at all. He is quite an imposing person, even a bit frightening at times. I think he believes that Charles can't take care of himself. Charles certainly listens to him whenever he actually has something to say, and I do think that Mr. Darcy would prefer to return to the previous way of doing business.

"Bastard," I said loudly, earning the censorious glance of the English bibliophile sitting next to me in the *Kaffeestube*.

Still, I don't dislike him, Lizzy. How can he be all bad if he's Charles's friend?

"Ha!" I exclaimed.

The bibliophile stabbed at his keyboard, closed the laptop and stalked away. I managed to finish reading the email in silence. When I'd finished, I sat at my table until the coffee was cold.

There's something else... You won't believe this, Izba. Charles has invited me to come for a weekend at his mansion, Netherfield, in Westchester County. Oh, I know you'd say it's too soon. But you also know that I won't do anything stupid... Charles's sister will be there, too. Both Mom and Dad think I should go, and I really don't see the harm in it.

I forced myself to drink the coffee and swallow it. Dad must really feel they were making progress in the negotiations if he was willing to send Jane off to Charles Bingley's estate. Mom must be thrilled that her scheme to catch a rich bachelor for one of her daughters was working out so well.

It did seem a bit soon. But could I object if Jane really cared about Charles, especially if Charles's liking for her might be encouraging him to be more liberal with his terms? Jane could end up being the family's salvation, which would delight her no end.

I sighed, closed my laptop and returned to the book fair. I salivated over first editions I couldn't afford to purchase, attended fascinating lectures and mingled with eccentrics, collectors and aficionados who provided me with endless opportunities for study. Two days later, just as I was packing up for my Rhine River cruise, I got another email from Jane.

Dearest Izba,

First, let me tell you how incredible Charles's estate is, and what a wonderful host he's been. I'd barely arrived when he introduced me to his sister, Caroline Bingley. What a beautiful woman! She must buy all her clothes from the top New York designers, and she wears them like a queen. But she's very friendly, and made me feel right at home.

I have a little bad news. The evening after I got here, I slipped on the stairs (how embarrassing!) and sprained my ankle. Now Charles insists that I stay a few more days, until I can walk again.

Oh, my poor Jane! She was normally far from clumsy, but I guess that's what love does to a girl.

You might be interested to know that Mr. Darcy is staying with Charles. He's polite, but I think he'd rather not have me here. Can you believe that I still haven't learned his first name?

Without giving it any more than a moment's thought, I called the cruise line, canceled my trip and booked a flight straight home. Twenty-four hours after I arrived in New York I was on my way to Westchester County.

Charles Bingley's mansion was every bit as amazing as Jane had suggested. It was a Gothic monstrosity made out like a European estate, suggestive of excess and the kind of money even the Depression hadn't touched. It had its own miniature lake, a wood blazing with color and tennis courts.

I rang the buzzer at the gate, waited a few minutes and gave my name to the man who eventually answered. The gates swung open and I followed the curving drive up to the forbidding front entrance.

A man wearing an impeccable formal suit greeted me at the door. I guessed he was the butler or some kind of servant, hard as that is to believe in the twenty-first century.

"Miss Bennet?" he asked with an inclination of his graying head. "Mr. Bingley is expecting you in the grand salon. May I take your coat?"

I shrugged out of it and handed it to him, suddenly conscious of my jeans and baggy sweater. I hadn't been thinking about my clothes when I'd raced out of my apartment. My mind had been full of Jane…and Mr. Darcy.

Now I realized that I'd made a strategic mistake.

"Thank you," I said with a smile I hoped didn't seem too nervous. I clutched my handbag tighter under my arm and followed the butler into a hallway adorned with marble floors and oak paneling so polished that it reflected me like a mirror. The driving rhythm of fast jazz echoed in the corridor.

As soon as I entered what I guessed was the "salon," Charles Bingley shot up from the sofa near the huge flagstone fireplace and strode toward me, hand extended, smiling so infectiously that I felt myself grinning in return.

"How are you, Elizabeth?" he asked, pumping my hand. "It's great to see you again. I know Jane will be very glad that you've come."

I cleared my throat, more than a little overwhelmed by his enthusiasm. "I'm sorry I didn't call ahead of time."

"Don't worry about that." He tugged on my hand, pulling me toward the arrangement of handsome antique sofas and chairs that I knew weren't just fine reproductions. "Caroline, look who's here!"

My first glimpse of Caroline Bingley told me that Jane hadn't been exaggerating. *Elegant* isn't a word you hear often these days, but Miss Bingley wore it as easily as I did my favorite jeans. The dress alone must have cost several thousand dollars, and it fit her model's figure like the proverbial glove. She wore a very tasteful pair of diamond earrings and a matching choker that could probably have bought a small country.

"Elizabeth, this is my sister, Caroline," Charles said. "Caroline, Elizabeth."

Caroline extended a languid hand and smiled just enough to look sincere without disturbing her flawless makeup. "How nice to meet you, Elizabeth. I've heard so much about you."

I hadn't heard much about *her,* but I disliked her instantly. I took her hand and squeezed just enough to let her know that her superior air didn't scare me. "Jane has told me how kind you've been," I said. "Thanks so much for taking care of her."

"It's no trouble, really," Caroline said in that upper-class East Coast accent affected in the '30s by the likes of Bette Davis, Norma Shearer and Katharine Hepburn. Her gaze fell to my slightly scuffed oxfords and slowly rose to take in the rest of my casual ensemble. "Would you like something to drink? A Shirley Temple, perhaps?"

She might as well have asked me if I'd like to take a good wallow with the pigs. "Water, if it's not too much trouble," I said.

"Champagne," Charles said. "We're celebrating Jane's recovery."

"Is she walking again?" I asked eagerly.

"The swelling has really gone down. She's getting dressed right now."

"If you don't mind, I'll go up and see her."

"Please don't deprive us of your company so soon," Caroline purred. "Jane will be down at any moment."

I couldn't think of a good way to get out of it, so I took one of the chairs and accepted a glass of champagne from the butler.

"How is your family?" Charles asked, leaning forward with his hands dangling between his knees.

"Fine, thanks. A little worried about Jane."

"There's absolutely no reason to be. She'll stay here until she can walk easily again."

"That's very nice of you, but—"

"I would advise you, Miss Bennet, not to contradict Charles," a deep voice said. "He is accustomed to getting his way, in spite of all advice to the contrary."

I crawled back into my skin and turned to look behind me. There, big as life and twice as aggravating, stood Mr. Darcy.

CHAPTER 3

"DARCY," CHARLES SAID, HIS USUAL GOOD HUMOR SOUNDING a bit strained, "why do you always have to sneak up on everyone like that?"

The older man strolled into the room and stopped beside the fireplace, his hands folded behind his back. Once again he wore what could only be the finest workmanship of the best European tailors, as crisp and formal as if he'd just come from a gathering of New York's most high-powered financiers.

"Can I be blamed," he said coolly, "if you prefer to surround yourself with so much noise that you are unable to hear anything less cacophonous than a chorus of jackhammers?"

"Darcy," Charles said, addressing me, "doesn't like jazz. I've had to drag him kicking and screaming into the twentieth century."

"Don't you mean the twenty-first century?" I asked, sliding a glance at the subject of our conversation.

"They *had* jazz in the twentieth century," he said dryly.

"You shouldn't make fun of Darcy just because he has better taste than you do," Caroline said, easing her way toward Darcy with all the subtlety of a hockey puck slamming into a goal. "Mendelssohn still has many more admirers than Miles Davis."

"I don't think even Mendelssohn was around when Darcy was born," Charles said.

Darcy seemed completely immune to Charles's quips and continued to look down his nose at the room in general. Caroline was practically in his lap, but he didn't pay her any attention—a fact that obviously ticked her off no end. You'd have to be as clueless as a bachelor at a baby shower not to see that she had a thing for him.

They deserve each other, I thought. But then Darcy looked straight at me with those dark, penetrating eyes, and I forgot my sarcasm. I knew he didn't like me any more than I liked him, so I could only figure that he was trying to scare me off.

That, of course, was the surest way to make me stay.

"What kind of music do you prefer, Miss Bennet?" he asked.

If I hadn't known better, I'd have said that Darcy was being polite. "I like all kinds, Mr. Darcy," I said. "You could say I'm eclectic in my tastes."

"Yes, dear," Caroline said, staring pointedly at my clothes again. "That's quite obvious."

Darcy cast her a glance that made her go a little pale under her artfully applied blush. "A wide range of interests is scarcely to be sneered at," he said.

I goggled. Why was he defending *me?* "Mr. Darcy—" I began, and promptly forgot what I was going to say. "Do you have a first name?"

"He does," Charles said, "but he doesn't like to use it."

"It's not Egbert, is it?" I whispered.

"Worse," he whispered back. "It's Fitzwilliam."

It would have been very rude to laugh. I risked a glance

at Darcy and knew immediately that he'd heard the exchange. Charles noticed, as well.

"He's been Darcy as long as I've known him," he said aloud.

"How long have you been friends?" I asked, including both Darcy and Charles in my question.

"He was on the Board years before my father died," Bingley said in a sober voice.

"The late Mr. Bingley requested that I continue to advise his son," Darcy said.

You'd have thought that Darcy was twenty years older than Charles, when he looked about five at most. "I'm sure he's lucky to have a mentor like you," I said with more than a touch of sarcasm.

"He has worked miracles for Bingley Pharmaceuticals," Caroline said sharply. "He is admired for his philanthropy, as well. I understand that you might not regard him quite as favorably, given your…situation."

Darcy gave Caroline a black look. Charles stood abruptly and had opened his mouth to speak when Jane appeared at the top of the grand staircase, pale but smiling. Charles bounded up the stairs to support her as she began to descend.

"Lizzy!" she called. "I'm so glad you've come!"

I watched her anxiously, noting her slight limp as she reached the bottom of the stairs. "Are you all right?" I asked, hurrying toward her. "Sit down and let me look at that ankle."

She complied, though her eyes were all for Charles. I knelt in front of her and pulled up the leg of her soft wool trousers.

"It's still swollen," I said. "Are you sure it's only a sprain?"

"That was the opinion of the doctor," Charles said, his

fair eyebrows drawn in a frown, "but I don't think she should leave until all the swelling is gone."

I glanced at Darcy and Caroline. Darcy's expression was neutral, but I caught Caroline in a strained and very fake smile.

"Of course you must stay," she said sweetly. "And you, too, Elizabeth."

"Thanks, but I didn't bring much with me...."

"I'm sure we can find something...appropriate for you."

"That's decided, then," Charles said, oblivious to his sister's catty remark.

For a while, the rest of us stood or sat around awkwardly while Charles and Jane smiled idiotically at one another. I couldn't say I was unhappy about it. Jane was delirious, and if Charles was sincere, I had nothing to worry about. Unless someone *else* chose to interfere.

Darcy moved in my direction and took a large leather armchair not far from mine. Caroline quickly pulled another chair close to his.

"And how is Georgiana?" she cooed to the object of her affections, all but batting her lashes as she took her seat. "I can't wait to see her again."

"She is very well," Darcy said, though he was looking at me instead of Caroline. "Georgiana, Miss Elizabeth, is my sister."

"And so very talented," Caroline said with a glare in my direction. "Such exquisite taste. I've never known such a young girl to be as bright and gifted as she is." She leaned over the arm of her chair so that the neckline of her dress gaped open. "If you met her, Elizabeth, you'd understand why Darcy is so particular in his choice of women friends."

"Oh, does he have any?" I asked. I wanted to take the

snide comment back as soon as I said it, but Darcy only stared at me intently, an almost puzzled look in his eyes. I wanted to sink deep into my chair, but sat up straighter instead.

Caroline laid her hand on Darcy's sleeve. "Georgiana has impeccable manners," she said to me waspishly. "A pity you didn't have the benefit of her education."

Well, I *had* deserved that. I decided on the better part of valor. "Charles," I said, "I noticed that you have beautiful grounds behind the house. Do you mind if I take a look?"

"Hmmm? Oh, please be my guest. Darcy, would you mind showing her around?"

I sat frozen, my mouth dry as a quote from Oscar Wilde. "Uh, that won't be necessary, really."

"I would be delighted," Darcy said, rising. Caroline clung to him like a boa constrictor.

"Please don't interrupt your conversation on my account," I said, sidling toward the French doors that looked over the sloping lawn. Darcy didn't come after me.

Once I was outside I ran down the hill to the wood of ash and maple that had already turned bright shades of yellow, orange and red. I came up against one of the trunks, breathless and slightly dizzy.

I'd managed to insult Darcy almost as much as he'd insulted me and my family at the party, but he hadn't taken the bait. To the contrary, he'd been downright courteous. And what had Caroline said about his philanthropic work?

Had I been wrong about him?

I was still chewing over the possibility after I'd made a complete inspection of the grounds and gardens and returned to the house. Low voices stopped me just outside the doors. For the second time in two weeks I held a brief internal debate about the propriety of eavesdropping. As always, curiosity beat good manners by a mile. I pressed my back against the wall.

"Well, Darcy," Caroline was saying, "I can see now why you have such a low opinion of the Bennets. Jane is charming, but her sister…" She chuckled. "I suppose, working in a bookstore, she doesn't have any reason to care about her looks. Still, you'd think she'd want to buy new clothes every once in a while."

Darcy's reply was too soft for me to hear. Caroline wasn't finished. "And her hair! She must have had it styled with a cleaver. Well, what can you expect from someone whose father started out as a hospital janitor?"

"I was not thinking about her origins," Darcy said, loud enough for me to hear. "Or her choice of clothing."

"Oh? Do tell me. Have I missed some of her faults?"

"You have apparently failed to notice the beauty of her eyes."

"Her *eyes?* If that's all you can find to praise—"

"Shall I enumerate the other qualities I admire?"

"How can you admire anything about her? She's been nothing but crass and rude since she walked in the door."

"She is obviously concerned for the welfare of her family. One cannot but respect such loyalty in the face of one's opponents."

"How sentimental of you, Darcy. You have never previously had any qualms about acquiring any other failing company, regardless of the disadvantages to them. The Bennets were about to lose the business in any case. You're doing them a favor!"

"You cannot expect Miss Bennet to share our views."

"I see. Then I presume you intend to advise Charles to obtain the company at a loss for BP?"

"I do not. My concern is for the success of Bingley

Pharmaceuticals. I am capable, nevertheless, of regarding Elizabeth Bennet with a certain forbearance."

Caroline was silent so long that I thought they'd both left the room. When she spoke again, it was in a tone halfway between a whine and a snarl.

"So when do you plan to convert her, Darcy?" she asked.

"Why would you assume I have any such scheme in mind?"

"You don't need *her*. You know I've wanted it for years. I won't be a burden on you, Darcy. I—"

That was the last I heard from her. When I peeked through the windows, she and Darcy were gone.

I stayed where I was for a few minutes longer, trying to figure out what Caroline had meant. Convert me? To what? Darcy didn't seem religious. Maybe he belonged to one of those crazy cults that pass as religion these days.

That was certainly a puzzle, but I was just as struck by his ongoing defense of me in response to Caroline's insults. Beautiful eyes? Respecting my loyalty? *Forbearance.*

But he'd as good as admitted that he still didn't care what happened to my family, as long as *he* got his way. *"My only concern is for the success of Bingley Pharmaceuticals."*

I strode through the French doors, looked around for the bottle of champagne the butler had left in a free-standing wine chiller beside the sofa, and poured myself a glass. Maybe Darcy had a few nice things to say about me, but I'd be an idiot to feel flattered by the good opinion of someone like him. Let him "convert" Caroline, since she wanted it so much.

But as I finished the rest of my champagne, I kept seeing his dark blue eyes watching me, the firm jaw and aristocratic nose and thick, black hair...not to mention the lean, broad-shouldered body and perfect poise. And that something more I couldn't name, that dangerous something that went beyond his plan to gobble up Bennet Laboratories and spit out the bones.

I still didn't like him. But I was beginning to *feel* him in a way that made my feet itch to run and keep on running. Part of me wanted to kill him. The other part wanted him to kiss me.

As I started up the stairs to look for Jane, I began to believe there really was such a thing as the Devil.

CHAPTER 4

THE YOUNG LAWYER CLASPED BOTH MY HANDS IN HIS, leaning toward me with mischief in his eyes and a grin that rivaled Charles's in sheer voltage.

"Please, call me George," he said, finally releasing his grip. "I'll be aiding Mr. Mason in the negotiations from now on, so you'll be seeing a lot of me."

I was charmed, I have to admit. I'd barely arrived at my parents' home for our family's monthly Sunday dinner together, and I hadn't expected other guests. George Wickham had already proven to be a very pleasant surprise. Not only was he handsome, but he had a spark of danger about him…not as sinister as Darcy's but far more interesting than Charles's transparent "niceness."

"Glad to meet you, George," I said, grinning back. "I don't know if you'll be seeing a lot of me, since I don't work at BL—"

"Oh, I'm sure there will be many occasions," George said with a wink. "I would be distraught if we were to be kept apart."

Normally I would have found that kind of talk ridiculous, but somehow it worked with George, maybe because

I knew that our old family lawyer, Mr. Mason, must trust him implicitly to take him on.

"My store is only a few blocks from the office," I said. "You're certainly welcome to drop in, if you—"

"Don't keep him all to yourself, Lizzy!" Lydia said, bumping into me as she maneuvered her way closer to George. She smiled dazzlingly at the lawyer, and his attention shifted to her—and no wonder. She was wearing a high-end cropped T-shirt that showed off her toned midriff, a short, tight skirt and boots that might have belonged to a dominatrix.

Not that Lydia cared what anyone thought. She dressed as she pleased and acted as she pleased; apparently her chutzpah—and choice of fashion, if it could be called that—was an advantage in her job at a trendy New York boutique. Too bad she had been living far beyond her means and probably had credit-card debt to match her extravagant lifestyle.

"Hey, Georgie," Lydia said, striking a pose with one hand on her outthrust hip. "Has Lizzy been boring you talking about her books?"

"Boring me?" George said, managing to keep his eyes on her face. "Not at all." He smiled at me. "Any man would be overwhelmed by all the beauty and intelligence in the Bennet family."

Lydia pouted. "Elizabeth has no taste in clothes." She looked George up and down. "I'll bet you'd look hot in a red leather Ferragamo jacket."

"That's quite a compliment, coming from you," George said. "But I'm just a simple country lawyer. I'm afraid I'm a little behind on the latest fashions."

"I can take care of that," Lydia said, grabbing his hand.

"Come visit me in Manhattan, and I'll take you shopping anytime."

"I can help, too," Kitty said, creeping up behind Lydia.

Lydia glared at my second-youngest sister. "I thought Mom wanted you in the kitchen, Kitty."

"Not anymore." Kitty sniffled and simpered at George. "Dinner's ready."

"The same old turkey and potatoes," Lydia complained, rolling her eyes. "It's like we're still stuck in the '80s."

"I'm sure it will be delicious." George caught my eye, and I could tell he found Lydia and Kitty just as empty-headed as I did. It was as if he and I shared a conspiracy, though about what I didn't know. I had a feeling we were definitely going to get to know each other better. And *that* would certainly be an improvement over my "relationship" with Fitzwilliam Darcy.

The meal was pretty much the same as always, though I didn't share Lydia's distaste for turkey and potatoes. George seduced Mom with a few compliments on her cooking and the table decorations; I was pretty sure by the time dinner was over that she was calculating which of her daughters *he* should marry.

Jane, thank God, was out of the running. She'd been pretty far gone since we'd come back from Charles's house, and I knew the two of them were emailing and texting every few hours. If the man didn't propose to Jane in less than a month, I'd trade in my copy of *Casablanca*, with all the extras, for the latest teenage-kids-find-an-abandoned-house-in-the-woods-and-die-horribly-one-by-one slasher flick.

At least Darcy—if he did indeed have any concerns about Jane's potential, if unwitting, influence on Charles's decisions—hadn't come between them.

Why couldn't he stay out of *my* mind?

"Lizzy!"

Lydia, in one of her typical rapid changes of mood, had grabbed hold of my arm and was bouncing up and down so energetically that I was afraid her huge, dangling earrings would poke out my eye. "You have to come this time. George won't if you don't agree!"

"Agree to what?" I asked, prying her fingers from my arm.

"Come to New York, of course. This weekend. You can stay with me and Kitty…we'll find room for you somehow."

"And why would I want to come to New York?"

Lydia gave me an incredulous look. "Because Wickham has promised to take us to Brighton."

"What does a city in England have to do with New York?"

My youngest sister had eye-rolling down to an art form. "Brighton Palace! The new Club in the East Village. It's almost impossible to get in unless you know somebody, but George—"

"I thought George was just a simple country lawyer."

"Oh, God. Can't you tell when someone's joking?"

So there was more to George than met the eye. "I'm no clubber. Why would George want me to come?"

"Don't ask me. He'd have a lot more fun with just me and Kitty." She grinned slyly. "Or just me."

If George was interested in having "fun" with Lydia, I'd take back everything good I'd thought about him. But the fact that he wanted me along suggested that he didn't find my sisters adequate company.

Going with them would give me a chance to see George in another environment, which wouldn't be a bad idea. I hadn't danced in a long time, but I wasn't dead yet. It might even be fun.

"I'll think about it," I said.

"Good! I'll tell Georgie. Come on Thursday, and we'll have time to find you something to wear."

"That's not necessary. I have a couple of—"

"I've already looked through your closet. I wouldn't be caught dead wearing any of your stuff."

Right back atcha, I thought. But I knew this was a battle I couldn't win. "I don't have a lot of money to spare, Lydia."

"Oh," she said airily. "I can get you discounts."

And that was that.

I spent the next few days going over my accounts and inventory, assisting my handful of customers—one of whom, fortunately, bought a very expensive first edition—and then did an online search for a special order. When I was closing up on Wednesday night, I saw the shadow of a man just outside the window, silhouetted against the light of the streetlamp. I knew without even thinking about it that this guy, in his long black trench coat, was no last-minute customer.

Instinctively, I reached for the can of pepper spray I kept in my desk drawer.

"We're closed!" I yelled.

He didn't answer. He didn't leave. He looked in the window, and there was just enough glow from my desk lamp to reveal his features and a strange reddish reflection in his eyes.

Darcy.

I slammed the can down on the desk and charged for the door, my stomach bubbling with an uncomfortable stew of fear, anger and excitement. When I yanked the door open, he was gone. There were several people on the street, hunched against the drizzle, but no sign of a tall, brooding guy in a black trench coat.

I closed the door and leaned against it, breathing fast. What in hell had *he* been doing here? Why had he been hanging around my window like some…some deviant, instead of coming in?

Shaken as I was, I finished locking up and walked as fast as I could to BL. Everyone except the janitor had already gone; Dad had taken to sending everyone home early—just more proof of his dejection at the prospect of losing the company he'd worked so hard to build.

Making my bad mood worse, the bus was late and crammed full, forcing me to sit next to a guy whose idea of cleanliness would have made a fourteenth-century privy-cleaner proud. It was pouring by the time I reached my stop. When I finally got to sleep, Darcy insisted on slinking through my dreams with a mustachio-twirling leer on his face. He was leaning over my bed, grinning maniacally with a mouth full of pointed teeth when my alarm went off.

I sat straight up, reaching for my neck. I didn't know why, but I was sure something had bitten me. A spider maybe, or even a hardy mosquito.

But when I stumbled out of bed and into the bathroom, I couldn't find so much as a red spot. I groaned, splashed water over my face and wandered into the kitchen to make a pot of coffee. I jumped at every sound, half expecting Darcy to sneak up behind me with a swirling cape, tall black hat and subtitles.

Damn. Apparently, I really did need a night out, dancing myself senseless with cute, nonthreatening guys who never thought about anything but their hair and abs.

I arrived at Lydia and Kitty's tiny apartment at two-thirty that afternoon. Kitty seemed genuinely glad to see me, but Lydia was furiously texting and barely looked up when I set my bag down on the sofa. I'd just finished my glass of water when she came roaring into the kitchenette, made a scathing comment about my cords and oxford shirt and hauled me out the door.

At least she hadn't been exaggerating about the discounts. I managed to get out of the last store with a total bill under $250, though I couldn't believe that I, Elizabeth-the-boring, would be wearing such a short dress or such high heels. Lydia pronounced me acceptable, and we spent that evening and the next day catching up, though Lydia did most of the talking. On Saturday, after dinner at one of Lydia's favorite sushi bars, we went to meet George at the club.

The line stretched around the block. The muscular guy whose job it was to pronounce sentence on the cowering supplicants didn't so much as glance at us as we waited outside the rope.

"Where is Georgie?" Lydia asked irritably as Kitty shivered in her thin, cropped jacket. "He said he'd be here by—"

"There you are!" George appeared before us, arms spread as if he planned to embrace us all together. "Lydia, Kitty…you look fantastic." His gaze settled on me, and I smiled weakly. "But Elizabeth…you're gorgeous!"

So was he. I had the feeling that his jeans, jacket and silk shirt had cost multiples of what I'd spent on my dress and shoes, but I couldn't really blame him; he wanted to make the most of his good looks, which was only natural, and I had a feeling he had a bright future ahead of him.

I expected him to escort us to the back of the line, but he herded us right to the front and spoke quietly to the bouncer. The man nodded, and—much to the obvious displeasure of the people on line—let us in.

The place was as noisy and garish as I would have expected. Lydia was in her element; she grabbed George
and ran into the very thick of the crowd, gyrating wildly.
Kitty, unwilling to be left behind, followed more diffi-
dently. I wandered to the bar and ordered a light drink,
content to observe the tribal mating rituals of twenty-
first-century *Homo sapiens Manhattansis.*

Fifteen minutes later, as my eardrums were explod-
ing, Lydia joined me at the bar, red and breathless. "Why
aren't you dancing, Lizzy?" she asked, waving to the
handsome bartender.

"I'll get to it eventually," I said. By which I meant one
more drink and I wouldn't care if I made a fool of myself. The seething crowd opened up for a moment, and
George emerged like a butterfly from a neon cocoon.

"Elizabeth!" he said, plopping down on the vacant
stool between Lydia and me. "Why aren't you dancing?"

"I was waiting for you," I said with a smile.

Lydia, anxious to be included in the conversation,
made a face of eloquent distaste. "Darcy would be the
perfect partner for *you,* Lizzy," she said. "He probably
can't even—"

"Darcy?" George repeated. "God, no. He probably
hasn't danced since the gavotte was all the rage."

"What's a gavotte?" Kitty asked, joining us.

I didn't answer. I thought it was interesting that both
Charles and George had made reference to Darcy's being
not only old-fashioned, but actually from another century.

"You sound as if you know Darcy pretty well," I said,
"but you've just started working for Mr. Mason's firm.
Have you met before?"

George picked up his whiskey and soda. "I've had that
misfortune," he said.

"Do you mind my asking…"

The whiskey was gone in a swallow, and George ordered another. "It's a long story. I'll tell it to you sometime."

And that was that. George knocked back his second drink, seized my hand and pulled me onto the dance floor.

For the next couple of hours I actually forgot to be self-conscious about my very short dress. Lydia flirted with anything in pants; Kitty followed her lead, as always; and I found plenty of willing partners, one of whom made a suggestion that sent me scurrying into the adjoining alley for air.

I found clouds of smoke instead, the stench of rotting garbage and a half-dozen sullen kids sucking on cigarettes. I pushed through them and discovered a very small area where some trick of the atmosphere provided the means to breathe. I was enjoying the respite when the kids suddenly disappeared, leaving the alley deserted.

All the little hairs on the back of my neck stood on end. I'm not exactly the most streetwise girl in the world, but even I could tell that something was wrong.

Wrong turned out to be three unpleasant-looking guys of indeterminate age wearing hoodies and low-slung jeans. They definitely weren't clubbers; in fact, they looked like they'd rather do some "clubbing" in the more traditional sense of the word. What they were doing in the alley I didn't know, and I was much less interested in speculating than in escape.

I was halfway to the door when they saw me. They didn't say anything. They didn't need to. One of them grinned, showing a wide gap between his two front teeth. The other two were chillingly casual as they strolled toward me.

They wouldn't try anything here, I told myself. They'd be crazy if they did. As I backed away, kicking off one shoe and grabbing the other to use as a rather pitiful weapon, the door burst open and George walked into the alley.

Suddenly I was in one of those old movies where they would speed up the film to make fights look faster than was humanly possible. I blinked, and George was on the nasty guys like a spider on a juicy fly. He sent the grinning gangbanger spinning away like a Frisbee. Another landed at the other end of the alley, and I heard the crack of breaking bones.

The last one was pinned to the opposite wall about two feet off the ground, George's fists clenched in his hoodie. There was real terror in the kid's eyes, and I knew George was going to hurt him. Badly.

"George!" I yelled. "It's all right. I'll call the police. You don't have to—"

Without letting the kid down, George twisted to face me. His eyes were swallowed up in black like someone on heavy drugs, and his teeth…

They were pointed. And red.

CHAPTER 5

IT WAS A MOVIE. A VERY *BAD* MOVIE.

I scrambled back against the wall, sucking garbage-scented air through my nose. George snarled and dropped the kid, who fell in a heap at his feet. He glared at the grinner, who scuttled crabwise toward the mouth of the alley, grabbing his moaning friend on the way.

The third gangbanger crawled on hands and knees until he was out from under George's feet and staggered after his homies. A dreamlike silence settled over the alley.

"Elizabeth?"

Going by the usual script, I should have screamed and flailed helplessly as the monster ripped open my chest and tore out my throat. But I was too stunned to move, and George looked more sheepish than batlike.

"I'm sorry, Elizabeth," he said, holding out very ordinary-looking hands in a gesture of apology. "I didn't mean for this to happen."

The rational part of me noted that his eyes were back to normal, and he didn't have any blood on his mouth.

But I'd seen what I'd seen. A crimson smear on the kid's neck. And George with his teeth sinking into flesh...

"Tell me I'm dreaming," I gasped.

"I'm afraid not." He sighed, and I got another glimpse of his...fangs. "You have every reason to doubt your senses, but in this case they did not deceive you. I am not human."

"Did you just...drink that kid's blood?"

He hung his head. "I did. But I assure you he was not hurt as a result of *that*."

At times like these, all you can do is pretend you're still sane. "You're a...vampire?"

"*Strigoi* is the preferred term. Most vampires—"

"Most?" I squeaked. "You mean there are more like you?"

He became more serious than I'd ever seen him. "Not all are like me. *I* would never harm you, Elizabeth, or any human who did not attempt to harm me first."

That's very comforting, I thought, clinging frantically to my sarcasm as if it were the last lifeboat from the *Titanic*. "Well," I said aloud, "I guess I should thank you."

He glanced up, a convincingly contrite look on his face. "I'm ashamed that I resorted to such violence, but I could not let them attack you." His eyes caught mine, sincere and full of pain. "You can't imagine what it's like, Elizabeth. I would give anything not to be what I am."

I gulped. "You, uh...drink blood regularly?"

"Unfortunately, it is necessary for my survival."

"But you said you don't hurt anyone."

"The process is not normally harmful for the donor, and can actually be very pleasurable for both parties."

Donor. What a civilized word. It hadn't been very pleasurable for the homeboy.

I touched my neck. "You aren't thinking of... I mean—"

"No, Elizabeth. Never without permission." He took another step toward me, and I saw something a little less benign in his gaze. "My control over this curse is the only thing that keeps me from ending my life."

"It's literally a curse?"

"I wish it were that simple."

It was hard, in spite of my dazed state of mind, not to feel sympathy for his obvious distress. My world had turned upside down, but *his*...

"How did it happen?" I whispered. "Is it like the legends say?"

He looked up into the glare of the Manhattan night, and his shoulders sagged. "You asked how I knew Darcy," he said. "It was he who did this to me. He converted me against my will."

A dozen thoughts bounced around inside my head, whipping my brain to the consistency of strawberry Jell-O. *Converted.* That was the word I'd heard Caroline Bingley use when she'd been dissing me to Darcy. Something about when he planned to convert...

Me.

I have to admit that I got a little dizzy then, and might have fallen if George hadn't caught me. His touch felt warm and safe, not dangerous at all.

"Yes," he said, "Darcy is also *strigoi.* But he delights in what he is." He shook his head sorrowfully. "Some *strigoi* wield unusual influence over mortals and even other *strigoi.* Darcy possesses such abilities. That power, in addition to virtual immortality and greater strength and speed, are features of this condition he exploits to the fullest."

That explained a great deal, but certainly didn't ease my mind, especially when I thought about my own unwilling obsession with him. Charles *seemed* to be defying Darcy's wishes, but he clearly considered Darcy a good friend as well as an advisor. What had Charles said? "I don't think even Mendelssohn was around when Darcy was born."

He'd meant it literally. He *knew*.

"Whatever you may believe, I care about you, Elizabeth," George said into my silence. "Being *strigoi* does not destroy all emotion or loyalty. I know Darcy wishes you only ill. I do not think it likely that he will take any direct action against your family, but I will do everything I can to protect you."

Direct action. I didn't even want to think what that could mean. But now I had an immediate choice: trust George, or not. I chose trust...for the time being. I had a thousand questions, but I knew this wasn't the time or the place to ask them. I had to get Lydia and Kitty home first.

By unspoken agreement, George and I returned to the club. I could see right away that Lydia had drunk far too much, and it took some effort to pry her away from the bar. She complained loudly when George and I dragged her out of the building, Kitty trailing in her wake.

Lydia was still whining when we bustled her and Kitty into their walk-up and deposited her on the sofa. I asked George if he wouldn't mind waiting outside while I sat with Lydia and made sure she wouldn't go out again. The very ordinariness of the activities, and the knowledge that George had done no harm to anyone but the bad guys, gradually calmed my apprehension.

Once both Lydia and Kitty were asleep, I went outside to join George. He was pacing back and forth on the landing and looked up as I closed the apartment door.

"Is she all right?" he asked.

"She'll get over it," I said. I wondered if I would. "I think we should talk."

"By all means...if you feel able to accept what you've seen."

"I don't know if I'm *able* to, but I don't think I have any choice."

He flashed me the old-George grin, and I wondered why I hadn't noticed the pointed incisors before. It was really true what they said: you don't look for something out of the ordinary unless you have reason to.

Did I ever have reason to now.

"We haven't much time," George said, walking toward me as if he planned to take my arm. At the last minute he must have seen me flinch, because he backed off. "*Strigoi* are not fond of sunlight."

I imagined him burning to a crisp and felt a little sick. "What does it do to you?"

"Some exposure is acceptable, but too much—"

I remembered that I'd never seen Darcy actually walking outside in daylight. "Does it take a stake through the heart to kill you?" I joked.

I immediately regretted it, but George took it well. "More than that, I'm afraid," he said.

Warning duly noted. "Where should we go?"

"I know a place," he said, and turned for the stairs.

After we'd gone a few blocks, I began to really accept that George didn't intend to waylay me and suck me dry. He led me into a twenty-four-hour coffee bar and found a small table in the back. I ordered an espresso, figuring I wasn't likely to get any sleep for what remained of the night. George ordered one, as well.

He didn't wait for me to begin asking questions. He became very serious again. "What I tell you now must remain between the two of us."

"Of course," I said. "No one would believe me, anyway."

He didn't fall for my attempt at lightness. "First, you must know that we are not undead, as the stories claim. Conversion is not a mythical curse, but a biological process. We are every bit as alive as any mortal. We can eat and drink. Our hearts beat just as yours do."

That was a relief. "But you said you're virtually immortal."

"Yes. It requires that we occasionally disappear in order to avoid dangerous questions. I have been many men in many times, though I always return to the name with which I was born."

I could see the difficulty in such a life. "How often do you have to drink blood?"

"Regularly. But, as I said, donors are seldom unwilling."

"They know what's happening? How can you be sure they won't tell?"

"As you said, no one would believe them. And most have no desire to expose us."

Even if they did, I thought with a shiver, a man faster and stronger than any "mortal" could easily stop them.

George brooded over his coffee. "You wanted to know how I became the way I am," he said.

"Darcy," I murmured.

"Indeed. We grew up together, he and I."

I hadn't believed the night could hold any more surprises for me. "You're kidding."

"Unfortunately, I am not. We were both born in Derbyshire, in the northern part of England, in the late eighteenth century."

I managed to get my natural skepticism under control, since it was pretty useless at this point. "And he did this against your will."

His lips twisted. "Generally, converts seek the transformation. Darcy, like those of his ilk, offers no such choice. This is why I have dedicated my life to opposing such evildoers, that cohort of *strigoi* who treat humans as prey and are not above using violence."

He went on to tell a story about growing up as a steward's son on a large estate, loved by Darcy's aristocratic father and granted an education equal to the younger Mr. Darcy's. Fitzwilliam had been jealous enough to wish George ill from childhood. He'd seen to it that George had lost the inheritance intended for him by the former Mr. Darcy, and when they had grown to manhood and George had fallen in love with a woman "above his station," Darcy had plotted his rival's downfall. "He separated me from my betrothed, and then set about destroying my life, financially and physically."

"Was he already a vampire?" I asked, obliviously gulping my cold coffee.

"He was converted by his aunt, Lady Catherine de Bourgh, at his own request. He has been driven by greed from childhood; he wanted even more power than his fortune and position already gave him. His ambition was, and is, limitless. He has accumulated vast wealth over the decades by the most ruthless tactics, including blackmail and forcible conversion. For Darcy, power and cruelty are the greatest aphrodisiacs."

All the vampire legends I'd ever heard filled my head with visions of bloodless corpses and mouths gaping in silent screams. "Would he…has he killed anyone?"

"Most *strigoi* recognize the dangers of murder, but I would put nothing past Darcy."

I shivered again and went back over everything I'd heard Darcy say since I'd met him, every conversation I'd been party to or overheard. He hadn't sounded like a killer. And Caroline Bingley had known about conversion and what it entailed. She'd said she'd *wanted* it…

A sudden and alarming thought brought the coffee back up the wrong way. I coughed until tears spilled over my face.

"Is *Charles* a vampire, too?" I choked out.

George shook his head. "He is not, though he might as well be. You see, a man once converted becomes the virtual property of his patron, bound to his will."

"But you…" Another terrible thought came into my head. "*You* aren't—"

"No. I was one of the fortunate few able to escape that fate through a trick of the conversion process."

"And Darcy…is he controlled by his aunt?"

"That I do not know." He reached out to cover my hand with his. "I only know what *I* must do since I am free, which is to thwart Darcy's plots whenever I can."

"Did you join Mason and Associates to fight him?"

"That was a large factor in my seeking the position." He touched my cheek. "I tell you all this to warn you, Elizabeth. Be wary. Never turn your back on Darcy."

"But why is he so eager to get Bennet Labs?"

"He doubtless has some nefarious purpose. It seems unlikely that he will take the risk of exposing himself, and will first attempt to get his way by the usual means."

"What about Charles? He knows Darcy's a vampire, doesn't he?"

"Yes."

"But he's in love with Jane!"

"That will protect you, as well, since Darcy is unlikely to alienate Charles by openly forbidding such a relationship. Charles is a tool to be used, and a very useful one."

"Wouldn't it just be *easier* to convert him?"

"As a human, Bingley can move in places Darcy cannot. That is a benefit."

"But what does Charles get out of this…'friendship' with Darcy? Does Darcy drink Charles's blood? Does he…do they—"

"I do not believe so. Darcy's advice has doubtless helped Charles increase his own fortune. And he can make most humans greatly desire his goodwill. But Charles is not entirely ruled by him. Yet."

I was beginning to develop a splitting headache. "Where *does* Darcy get his blood?"

"In the usual way. I have no doubt that he takes from the unwilling, but he also has a harem of women who are flattered by his attentions and hope to become his protégées."

"Uh…does he…does he do other things with them? I mean—"

"Vampires can have sex," Charles said with the ghost of a smile.

It was way past time for embarrassment. "Jane was staying at Charles's estate," I said, my voice rising high enough to attract the attention of the slacker sprawled on the couch against the opposite wall. "What if Darcy drank her blood?"

Get yourself under control, woman. I swallowed and spoke more softly, though I couldn't keep my voice from shaking. "Could he have converted her?"

George gazed at me with gentle sympathy. "I'm afraid I wasn't very clear. A *strigoi* may take blood from any donor he chooses, but conversion is a matter of deliberate will. You would see if she had changed."

Oh, my God. "Would he go that far to keep her and Charles apart?" I asked in a deadly monotone.

"He certainly would disapprove of any relationship between them for any number of reasons."

That was it. "I've got to get home right away."

"Of course. But there's something else I'd like you to see first."

I was pretty sure he'd have let me go if I'd insisted on it. But I had to know everything I could about my enemy. And I had few doubts by now that Darcy *was* the enemy. The more I learned about vampires, the better equipped I'd be to stop him from hurting my family to get his way.

I pulled on my coat and charged out of the coffee bar, only a little surprised to find George at the door ahead of me.

"You must stay behind me at all times," he said.

"Okay. Let's go."

I had come to realize that George could move faster than I could think, but he kept an easy pace to accommodate my heels. I chewed my lip to a pulp while we rode the subway back to the East Village. The streets were still alive with casual strollers and partygoers enjoying the unseasonably warm late October night; I noticed that they tended to step out of George's way without seeming to realize they were doing it.

Did they sense that George wasn't quite "normal"? I'd felt that about Darcy from our first meeting without understanding why, but George had done a very good job of blending in. In a way, that was as scary a thought as any I'd had since we'd left the club.

After we'd gone about four blocks from the station and turned several corners, we reached a narrow side street so dimly lit that I could barely discern the people congregating around the door halfway down the alley.

"Where are we?" I demanded, pulling my coat more tightly around my shoulders.

George took my arm and pushed me behind him. "Do you see those people?" he asked.

My vision had begun to adjust and I could finally make out the individual figures in the clump: three young, very pretty women and an equally handsome young man, all dressed to the nines.

"Are they vampires?" I whispered.

"The male is," George said in an equally low tone. "The women are his—shall we say, his 'groupies.' They enjoy exchanging their blood for the sexual pleasure his bite—and other skills—gives them."

Normally I wouldn't care how consenting adults got their kicks, as long as it didn't hurt anybody. But the idea of willingly becoming a vampire's sex slave…

"Just inside that alley is a club frequented by *strigoi* and their human adherents," George said. "Any mortal may enter Rosings, at his or her own risk. Darcy is a frequent guest."

"You said he has a…a 'harem.'"

"As he is among the most powerful *strigoi* in Manhattan, he draws many admirers."

"And how many…how many besides you…has he converted?"

"Who can say? He believes himself to be discreet, and would keep his protégées under strict control."

"Do you think we should go in?" I asked in a small voice.

He smiled, lips closed. "Ah, my brave Elizabeth. I would not subject you to such an ordeal. I will see you back to the apartment to collect your things, and then—"

His sudden silence grabbed my attention, and I followed his stare. A man was looking back at him: tall, dark, his features unmistakable and unforgettable. A trio of women were clustered around him, and in the dim light I thought I could see the darkness of blood on his mouth.

I wanted to run. Instead, I yanked George's arm and pulled him to safety. "Are you all right?" I gasped.

"I'm fine." He frowned. "I do not know if he saw you, Elizabeth. Be very careful."

Neither of us spoke as we took the subway back to Washington Heights. Only when we were nearly to Lydia's apartment did George speak again.

"Darcy would kill me if he could," he said.

I tried, and failed, to imagine what a fight between two vampires would be like. "He wouldn't dare attack you openly," I said. "Would he?"

He took my hand in both of his and gazed into my eyes. "Don't worry. I shall carry on the fight regardless of what he threatens to do to me."

His words not only increased my admiration for him, but also gave me the feeling that even *I* could stand up to Darcy. Elizabeth Bennet, Fearless Vampire Hunter.

Until I remembered Darcy lurking outside the window of my bookshop, gliding away into the darkness before I could confront him.

What had he wanted from me? Was it really possible that he *did* want to convert me? In heaven's name, why? Was it another way to get hold of BL? Was the "admiration" he'd expressed for me strong enough to make him want to drink my blood…or worse?

Maybe Jane wasn't the only one in danger.

I ran up the stairs and let myself into Lydia's apartment. She and Kitty were asleep, so I grabbed my things and called a taxi to take me to the train station. George saw me off, and I turned to watch him recede into the distance, thinking about how much had changed in just a few hours.

I was still looking over my shoulder when I arrived at my apartment door.

CHAPTER 6

I TRIED TO TELL JANE. I REALLY DID.

I caught her at BL during her break the very next morning and locked us into the small meeting room, where we could talk in private. But as soon as we sat down, Jane started in on Charles.

"You can't believe how happy I am, Lizzy," she said, taking my hands. "It's like a miracle!"

While I'd been away in New York, Charles had called on Jane twice, once with Caroline and once by himself. He'd taken Jane on a picnic at East Rock Park, had dinner with Mom and Dad and sent a half-dozen bouquets of roses to Jane's apartment just before he returned to Westchester. The latest negotiations had gone spectacularly well, and it appeared that a deal was about to be struck…a deal outstandingly favorable for BL.

"It's so wonderful," Jane said, her eyes tearing up. "To think that everything is working out so well for our family—I feel as if I'm living in a dream."

You are, I thought. I smiled and gave her a long, hard hug, examining her neck for any signs of bite marks.

Nothing, not even a freckle. How was I supposed to explain to Jane that I was afraid she might be in danger…

that the man she loved, who seemed to love *her* so passionately, might be in the thrall of a two-hundred-year-old vampire?

Or was he? George had said that Charles wasn't entirely "ruled by Darcy. Yet." If Bingley Pharma had offered such favorable terms, didn't that mean that Charles was getting his way?

Was it possible that Darcy had some respect for Charles's obviously genuine feelings? Could he have changed his mind so quickly about Bennet Labs if he was as ruthless—as *evil*—as George had made him out to be?

No. I'd seen and heard enough of Darcy to believe that he wouldn't give up control once he had it. Maybe it was all some sort of game, letting Charles have a little freedom and then yanking back on the chain. Maybe he'd convert Jane and use her like a puppet to force Charles to—

I dropped my head into my hands and groaned. If I hadn't thought I was going crazy before, now I was sure of it.

"What's wrong, Lizzy?" Jane asked.

This was my chance. Jane would believe me. She tended to trust everyone anyway, and she'd never suspect *me* of—

"Is it Darcy?"

She'd always known me far too well. "Why should you think that?"

"I don't know. Sometimes it almost seems as if he likes you."

I laughed. "I don't *think* so." I recognized the note of hysteria in my voice and deliberately softened it. "I've been talking to George Wickham."

"Really?" She leaned toward me. "He is nice, isn't he? Do you like him, Lizzy?"

Like was a loaded word. "He's pretty likable."

"And handsome," she said with a sly smile.

"But that's not what I wanted to talk about." I took a deep breath. "Did you know that George and Darcy used to know each other when they were kids?"

"You're kidding!"

"I wish I were. According to George, Darcy isn't a very nice guy. In fact, he's a lot worse than we suspected."

"But Lizzy, *I* never thought—"

"All right, worse than *I* expected."

"In what way?"

She was really listening now, her eyes serious and her expression thoughtful. I forged ahead, explaining about their mutual past, Darcy's jealousy and his malicious interference in George's life without mentioning how long ago the events had taken place...or that the principals weren't human.

"This is very hard to believe," Jane said, leaning back.

"If you'd heard George talk about it, you wouldn't be so skeptical."

Jane digested all this in silence, rubbing her hands over her arms as if she'd taken a sudden chill. "It doesn't seem as if George would lie about something so important. But isn't it just as likely that there's been some kind of misunderstanding?"

"The truth doesn't always lie in the middle, Jane. It's a lot more likely that Charles has been fooled than that George made it all up."

"Still..."

This was the moment when I should have told Jane about vampires. But my throat clogged up, and I couldn't get the words out.

I had to have proof, though I had no idea how I was going to get it. I reached for her hands and held them tightly.

"Promise me that you'll stay away from Darcy," I said.

"You can't really think he'd bother *me*, Lizzy! We barely know each other!"

"He's a control freak. If he thinks you have more influence over Charles than *he* does…"

"Even if Darcy is as bad as George says, he'd never see someone like me as any kind of threat."

I knew then that nothing was going to convince her. Nothing short of the truth.

"Okay. Then promise me that you'll keep an eye out, and try not to be alone with him."

"Oh, Lizzy." She hugged me, drew back and looked into my eyes. "You've always had such a vivid imagination." She pushed a stray strand of hair away from my forehead. "You'll be seeing Darcy as soon as I will, anyway. The Halloween party, remember?"

Oh God. I *had* forgotten about it. Halloween was this Saturday, and everyone in my family, and from the office, had been invited to Netherfield.

"You're white as a ghost, Lizzy!" Jane exclaimed. "Are you *that* worried about seeing Darcy again?"

"I'm not worried." I grinned crookedly. "I just haven't figured out what to wear."

AS IT HAPPENED, I FOUND the ideal costume at a local community theater. When I walked into Netherfield's "grand salon" with Jane, Mom, Dad, Lydia, Kitty and Mary, we found it festooned with garlands of autumn leaves and lavishly supplied with crystal vases of orange and yellow chrysanthemums, dahlias and zinnias, all very tastefully arranged. Not a hinged paper skeleton, plastic pumpkin or animated ghost in sight.

Immediately, I looked for Darcy, but he wasn't to be found. I was pretty sure that George had been invited, along with Mr. Mason, but would he show up?

"Elizabeth!" Caroline Bingley came gliding up, dressed in a silver lace gown that skimmed over her slender figure from a high waist below a neckline that emphasized her swanlike neck. She looked me up and down with a barely disguised sneer.

"I see that we had the same idea," she said. "Bullseye must have a wider selection of costumes than I would have imagined."

I curtsied. "Thanks for the compliment, Caroline. You've done a wonderful job with your own costume. Did Darcy dig it up in his attic?"

Her perfectly controlled features slackened as she considered how much she should be insulted and then wondered what other meaning I might have intended. I sailed away before she could respond, looking for Jane or Charles or both.

Of course, they were already together, Jane radiant in a Marie Antoinette getup and Charles wearing very authentic-looking cowboy duds. Their heads were together, and they were laughing. Clearly, Jane wasn't taking my warnings about Darcy seriously.

There were a number of guests I didn't know, including several very good-looking guys. My first thought was that they might be vampires, but there was no indication that they were any different than anyone else—nothing of that weird charisma Darcy, and, to a lesser extent George, possessed. I finally acknowledged that I was on the verge of becoming paranoid.

Lydia and Kitty, both dressed in variations of Gothmedieval dresses, were running from one potential victim to another, evidently trying to decide which man was most worthy of Lydia's attention. Mom, in a 1920s gown much too small for her, was quivering with excitement and Dad—as usual—was looking a bit bemused in his Roman centurion's armor.

After a while I was sure that George wasn't there. I didn't know whether to be relieved or disappointed. I wandered over to the open bar and chose a glass of expensive chardonnay.

"Good evening, Miss Elizabeth."

My stomach made another attempt to jump out of my throat. Darcy was beside me; I hadn't even heard him coming, and in light of what I'd learned I knew I shouldn't be surprised.

But I was. And I was already wondering if he was going to admit he saw me outside of Rosings, or pretend he hadn't.

"Hello," I said casually, sipping my wine. I eyed his costume… a fantastically detailed, early-nineteenth-century coat, waistcoat and breeches that showed off his physique superbly and made my plain Regency dress look shabby.

He definitely got that *out of his attic,* I thought. "What made you pick that particular costume, Mr. Darcy?" I asked.

"I might ask the same of you." He settled on the stool beside me, every motion grace itself. I risked a sideways glance at his face. I kept forgetting how stunningly handsome he was. But it was his eyes I was drawn to. I couldn't mistake the predatory gleam in them, or the faintest trace of red.

"Oh," I said airily, "it's all they had left at Bullseye." My joke must have gone over his head, because he didn't show any sign of amusement. "It suits you very well," he said.

He was being nice again. *Too* nice. Was that the way vampires—evil ones, that is—set up their victims?

"Another glass of wine?" he asked, signaling the bartender.

He's trying to get me drunk. I shook my head.

"Thanks, but not right now." I fell silent, trying to think of something to say. Should I come right out and confront him? The very thought—which I had considered seriously for the past several days—made my mouth feel like the inside of a vacuum-cleaner bag.

"It's your turn to say something, Mr. Darcy," I said stupidly.

"What would you like me to say?"

I laughed, hoping he wouldn't hear my incipient panic. "I guess we're alike in one way. Neither one of us much cares to talk unless we can think of some bit of wit or wisdom to impart."

He frowned. "I doubt that is a very accurate representation of yourself."

"You mean I talk too much?"

"You put words into my mouth, Miss Elizabeth."

For some strange reason I found myself looking at that part of his body. His mouth. His firm, masculine lips. And what they hid beneath them.

What would it be like to be kissed by that mouth? What had George said about vampire groupies? *"They enjoy exchanging their blood for the sexual pleasure his bite...gives them."*

What would it be like to make love with a vampire?

The room had begun to feel like a sauna. The stool was definitely rubbing me the wrong way. I had thoughts in my head that would have made Lydia blush. And Darcy was staring at me as if he knew exactly what my mind and body were up to.

My only hope now was to go on the attack.

"I've been talking to an acquaintance of yours, Mr. Darcy," I said, deliberately meeting his indigo gaze.

"Indeed?"

I knew he knew what I was going to say. "It's funny that you never mentioned knowing him when he came to work for Bennet Laboratories."

"You refer to George Wickham."

His voice had gone cold enough to turn the sauna into an ice bath. "You were with him in Manhattan, were you not?" he asked.

So he *had* seen me with George in the alley. Well, George had warned me. Darcy must realize I knew what he and George were. What in hell was I getting myself into?

There was nothing to do but keep bluffing my way through to the end. "George had some interesting things to say about your mutual past," I said lightly, circling my finger around a ring of condensation on the marble counter.

"I have no doubt."

I glanced up again. Darcy was no longer just handsome and remote and dangerously sexy. He looked the same way George had just after he'd thrashed those guys outside Brighton: implacable, savage and deadly.

"Wickham has a glib tongue, Miss Elizabeth," he said, "and a certain skill in convincing new acquaintances of his honesty. Whether he can keep their good opinion is another matter entirely."

"He certainly lost a lot more than just your *good opinion,* Mr. Darcy."

"Yes," he said. "Wickham is always the innocent victim."

Oh, I badly wanted that second drink now. "I think *victim* is a very appropriate word."

His hand came down over mine with all the leashed fury of a tiger deciding to play with its prey before dispatching it. "You had better take care," he said very softly, "that you do not become his next one."

CHAPTER 7

MY BODY WENT BONELESS, AND IT TOOK ALL MY WILLPOWER to stay upright on my stool.

"Funny thing about me," I said, shaping each word with the greatest care. "The more someone tries to scare me, the braver I get."

His fingers curled over mine. "It is not my intention to frighten you, Miss Elizabeth, but to warn you."

My eyelids were getting heavy, and I wondered if vampires used some kind of hypnosis as one of their hunting techniques.

"You don't have to warn *me*, Mr. Darcy," my voice sounding slurred and very far away,

Darcy's was sharp and clear. "You would be well advised to remove Wickham from your employ, madam."

Madam. I giggled. "Now *that's* funny." I rolled my head around to look into his eyes. "Why were you hanging around outside my window the other night?"

I wasn't so far gone not to take some satisfaction in Darcy's expression. For a second he actually seemed taken aback.

"Oh, yes, I saw you," I drawled. I poked him in the center of his white brocade waistcoat. "I didn't know you

liked bookstores, Mr. Darcy. You should have come in…
I'd have picked out something just right for you."

His expression changed again. Not deadly this time, or
surprised. Just intense enough to fry the sun to a cinder.

"And do you know what is just right for me, Elizabeth?" he asked.

Sanity was beginning to return. I tried to wiggle my
hand from under his. "I…um…don't suppose you're a
fan of the romantic poets? Byron, Shelley, those guys?"

"I am not averse to poetry," he said. "What else can
you offer me?"

Oh, boy. *"Frankenstein?"*

He leaned closer. His breath didn't smell the way
you'd expect the breath of a blood drinker to smell. It
was actually very nice. So was the warmth that washed
over me, and the steady sound of his breathing, and the
way his thumb rubbed up and down over the back of my
hand. Oh, so *not*-undead.

"I did not come to your shop for a book," he said.

I wasn't imagining the change in his tone, or fooled
by the coolness of his expression. Just as I wasn't imagining the crazy drumming of my heart or the chemical
reactions tearing my willpower to shreds.

"What did you have in mind?" I murmured.

"Darcy!"

Caroline Bingley jostled into my shoulder, nearly
knocking me off the stool. Darcy let go of my hand, and
I snapped to full alertness. For once I had reason to be
grateful to the wench.

"I've been looking all over for you," Caroline said,
ignoring me completely. "You can't just sit here when
everyone else is having a good time."

The woman really was blind if she couldn't recognize

the contempt in Darcy's gaze. "I am having a good time," he said.

"Oh?" She gave me a vicious, dismissive glance. "Do you enjoy talking about George Wickham, Darcy?"

So she'd been eavesdropping. I should have known, since I'd become so good at it myself. Darcy stared at the counter for a moment and then slid from his stool.

"If you will forgive me, ladies, I have business to attend to."

Caroline stared after him as he strode away, her skin flushed. When she turned back to me, her smile had become a blunt instrument.

"Elizabeth, dear," she said, "you should know that Wickham is a very bad man. You won't get anywhere with Darcy by mentioning him."

"I'm not trying to get anywhere with Darcy. I leave that to you."

She opened her mouth to respond, but I was already on my way to find Jane. I hadn't expected Charles to leave her side for a second, but at the moment she was alone, beaming at the room in general.

I rushed over to her. "How's it going?" I whispered.

"Oh, Lizzy."

"I guess that means Charles is as much in love with you as ever."

She laughed out of sheer happiness, took my arm and pulled me around a corner. "What about you? I saw you talking with Darcy. What did he want?"

I made a face. "I don't know, but he didn't exactly defend himself when I brought up George Wickham."

"You didn't! What did he say?"

"Some stuff about George having a 'glib tongue' and not being honest."

"I don't know what to think," Jane said with a frown.

"I mentioned it to Charles, and he seemed to believe that George had done something bad enough to warrant Darcy's dislike."

"Does he know what happened?"

"I don't think so."

"Then all he's doing is defending a man he considers a friend. That's only natural."

"Maybe, but..." She bit her lip. "I guess we'll have to withhold judgment until we have more facts."

"Fair enough," I said. The small band in the corner of the grand salon was tuning up; people were gathering in the central area that had been cleared of furniture. "Here comes the dancing. I think I'll make myself scarce."

"Why? I'm sure a lot of the guys here would like to dance with you."

I didn't tell her that I'd had enough of dancing at Brighton. "I'd rather watch. You go on and have fun."

Just then Charles came to claim my sister. So I was spared further arguments for a little while as Jane danced with Charles, the two of them grinning at each other with the vacuous expressions of people in love. The only thing that clouded the picture was Darcy, who stood on the sidelines and stared at the couple with a grim look on his face. It was all I could do not to charge up to him and demand to know what his problem was.

Hadn't George made that clear enough? I turned around, thinking that what I really needed right now was time to myself. Time to get my messy feelings under control and figure out just what I had to do.

The "ladies' room" was a huge bathroom with scads of imported marble and fixtures, conveniently situated at the end of the wide corridor. I was halfway there when Darcy literally appeared in front of me. Again.

He bowed. "Miss Elizabeth," he said formally, "Are you not in the mood for dancing?"

The band had struck up a slow jazz tune for its second number, and the back of my neck began to prickle. "I wouldn't take you for the dancing type, Mr. Darcy."

He came closer. "It depends upon the partner."

"I, uh…" I backed away. "I really have to—"

"Surely you can spare a few minutes."

Darcy was gazing at me in that scary way, reminding me that I refused on principle to be intimidated by guys like him. Even if the guy could snap my neck like a wishbone. And he wouldn't dare bite me in such a public place.

Would he?

Risk or not, if he focused on me, Jane was sure to be safe from his resentment. I let him take my hand. I let him pull me into his arms. I tried to keep my body stiff enough to keep him from holding me too close, but it was a useless defense. He was strong. I could feel the strength in the muscles of his shoulders and biceps and pecs through his shirt, waistcoat and jacket. He rested his hand on my back just above my waist, sending shock waves all the way to the virtually nonexistent heels of my ballet flats. When he moved, guiding me in a slow, hypnotic circle, it was like being carried out to sea by a riptide.

We didn't talk. I couldn't think of a single impertinent thing to say. Especially when Darcy lowered his head and rested his cheek against mine, breathing softly in my ear. His mouth was very close to the base of my neck.

And I wasn't afraid. I was too busy experiencing the exquisite ache in parts of my body that hadn't been active in a pretty long time. I couldn't *really* be sexually attracted to him. All this was just more proof that he had some superhuman skill to drive women wild. Look at those women at the vampire club. Look at Caroline, making herself a fool over him, wanting him to...

Darcy's hand stroked my back. I wanted him to move it a little lower. I wanted to escape. I closed my eyes, aware that he was aroused under his close-fitting breeches. Aroused and very large.

A chasm was opening up under my feet. Another step and I'd be dragging him into an empty bedroom.

"Darcy? Darcy, are you down here?"

We jumped apart. For the second time that evening I owed Caroline a big favor. I didn't wait to see what Darcy thought of the interruption; I ran into the bathroom and locked the door. My lungs felt like deflated balloons, and I had to lean against the door until I could breathe again.

Someone knocked on the door. I glanced at my watch. Twenty minutes had passed, and I'd been standing in the same place the whole time.

Not daring to look in the mirror, I opened the door and let the woman in. She gave me an odd look. "Are you all right?" she asked.

I mumbled some kind of answer and beat a hasty retreat. The music had stopped. I didn't search for Darcy but went straight to Mom, who was chatting loudly with Dad's secretary, Mrs. Lucas.

"I'm sure Jane will be picking out a wedding gown any day now," Mom was saying. "Can you imagine? She'll be rich, and Bennet Laboratories will be safe. Jane will make sure of that."

Even I, never known for my reticence, was embarrassed at Mom's public gloating. "Mom," I said, smiling at Mrs. Lucas, "I think a button on the back of my dress is coming loose. Can you help me fix it?"

Mom gave me a blank look, blinked and smiled beatifically. "Of course, Lizzy. Will you excuse me, Gladys?"

I flashed Mrs. Lucas an apologetic grin—though I was pretty sure she wouldn't be *too* disappointed at being relieved of Mom's incessant gossip—and dragged Mom off to the bathroom. Out of the corner of my eye, I saw Mr. Darcy staring after us.

FOR THE NEXT FEW DAYS after the party, time seemed suspended. I went through the motions at the bookstore, absurdly grateful that business was a little off. I found myself reaching for Gaiman instead of Grisham and shelved Geometry in with Gardening. I waltzed in the narrow spaces between the shelves, enfolded in imaginary arms.

Then I'd snap out of it again, and remember everything George Wickham had said. The deadly look in Darcy's eye when I'd mentioned him. The way he'd watched Charles and Jane.

But his voice had been so gentle when he'd asked me to dance. He hadn't hurt me. He hadn't hurt Jane. He hadn't hurt anyone that I knew of. And he'd let Charles come up with an acquisition plan that wasn't going to cripple my family and my dad's employees.

How could I have such starkly opposite feelings about him? My head said one thing, my heart another. At closing time I was staring blankly at my computer screen, trying not to look out the window. He hadn't shown up last night or the night before, and he wasn't coming tonight. I didn't *want* him to come.

The computer chimed, letting me know that I'd received an email. I almost let it go until tomorrow, but at the last minute clicked it open.

Dearest Izba,
I don't know what to think. Charles has left for England with Caroline. She just emailed me from the airport; they're off to

London on some business for the company, and she doesn't
know when they're coming back.

Oh, Lizzy... I can't believe this is happening! Why would
he go without saying anything to me?

I'll be at Mom and Dad's tonight. Please come!

Love,

Your Jane.

CHAPTER 8

I GAPED AT THE WORDS UNTIL THEY BEGAN TO MAKE SENSE, shut down the laptop and grabbed my coat and handbag. My hands were shaking as I locked the door.

Left for England? With no word to Jane? It was unbelievable. There was no comfort in reminding myself that vampires had once seemed unbelievable, too.

Without stopping by my apartment, I drove straight to my parents'. Jane was sitting in the living room with Mom and Dad, both of whom wore long faces…though Dad was a lot more subtle about it than Mom, who looked as though she'd lost her credit line at Saks. Even Mary had apparently dropped by to provide her own idea of moral support.

"No woman," she said gravely, "should ever rely on the consistency of a man's heart. It's always a mistake to assume that just because a man seems to like you he plans to marry you."

"Oh, stuff it, Mary," I said, throwing my coat over the back of a chair and sitting beside Jane on the love seat. It was pretty obvious that she'd been crying, though she tried to smile in her usual way.

"I'm all right, Lizzy," she said with a very soft sniff. "I was disappointed at first, but now—"

"Disappointed!" Mom shrieked. "You are heartbroken, darling, and no wonder! He led you on. Oh, I can't bear it!"

I put my arm around Jane's shoulders. "Was there more in the email from Caroline you didn't tell me?" I asked.

"Oh, yes." She glanced at Mom, who was too busy with her own frustration to pay any attention to us. "She said several times that she and Charles had no intention of returning this year. In fact, she made it pretty clear that they might not come back at all."

"But that's ridiculous! Isn't his business in the U.S.?"

"He lived for quite a while in England before he inherited the company. Darcy has many business interests in London. Caroline said that they'd be staying at Charles's London flat and at Darcy's estate in Derbyshire."

Darcy. I growled, and Jane patted my hand.

"Really, Izba, it's not necessary—"

"Not necessary! What is going on with these people?" I looked at Dad. "What about the acquisition?"

"On hold," Dad said, removing his glasses and wiping them with his handkerchief. "There is no guarantee that the same deal will be offered again."

"That's the worst of it," Jane said. "I just hate to think that everyone at BL will suffer because—"

"Because Charles is a heel?"

"Don't say that." She dabbed at her nose with a tissue. "There must be some good reason."

Somehow I controlled myself. "What else did Caroline say?"

Jane rose suddenly. "Come with me."

"Jane!" Mom cried, sitting up. "Where are you going?"

"We'll be right back, Mom," I said as Jane pulled me down the hall and into her old bedroom. It was still unchanged from years ago, pink and frilly and neat as a pin.

"See for yourself," Jane said, pushing a printed sheet into my hand.

It didn't take long for me to understand why Jane hadn't wanted Mom around. The email was a lot more explicit than Jane had hinted to me.

Caroline spent a few paragraphs saying how much she'd miss Jane, and then got to the meat of it. She said that she was looking forward to seeing Georgiana, Darcy's younger sister, at the Derbyshire estate, and went on to rhapsodize about Georgiana's manifold charms and accomplishments.

I don't know if I've ever mentioned this, but I've always thought that Georgie would make a wonderful sister. It seems more likely than ever that I'll get my wish. Charles has always adored her; he'll be seeing so much of her that I'm sure he'll realize how happy they'd be together.

I sat down on the bed. "That little—"

"Keep reading, Izba."

My brother's marriage to Georgie will make everyone they know very happy and join two prominent and honorable families across the Atlantic. Think how much the combination of these fortunes can achieve. With this money and Charles's good heart, our company will be able to continue with our cutting-edge research and create the advances that will change the lives of so many people for the better.

"Ha!" I said. "As if *she* gives a damn about making anyone's life better. Except her own, that is."

"Charles told me about Georgie," Jane said, looking away. "She does sound wonderful."

"But Charles isn't in love with her!"

"We don't know that, Izba."

"We only have Caroline's word for any of this. It's obvious that she didn't want to see you and Charles together, no matter how much she pretended to be your 'friend.' We're— You're—not rich or high-class enough for her. But that doesn't mean Charles's feelings have changed. If she nags him as much as she nags Darcy, he probably went with her just to shut her up for a while."

"Maybe you're right, Lizzy."

"I *am* right." I crumpled the paper and stood up. "This is all talk right now. The woman's clearly a shrew, and you can trust her just about as much as you can trust a piranha to pass up a succulent set of toes. In a few weeks Charles will be back, and all this will be forgotten."

I WAS WRONG. A FEW WEEKS later, Jane got another email that made it very clear that a wedding between Charles and Darcy's sister was imminent. I'd tried to convince myself that the mastermind behind this separation had to be Caroline, but I couldn't fool myself any longer.

Darcy had to be at least partly responsible. Whether it was because he wanted to undermine the negotiations, to simply keep Charles under his heel or to see his friend marry his sister, he had more than a little to do with it.

It occurred to me that I knew next to nothing about Georgiana. Was she a vampire, too? I presumed that her parents—and Darcy's—were long dead, and she wouldn't still be alive if she weren't the same as her brother. It was the most logical explanation.

Apparently, vampires married just like normal people. For eternity. In that case, wouldn't Charles have to be converted, too?

Maybe that was another reason for Darcy's interference...if he let Charles and Jane get together, a lot more people would know, sooner or later, that vampires existed. If Mom found out, there would be no shutting her up on such a juicy subject.

On the other hand, it wasn't as if the vampires I'd seen at the club seemed particularly nervous about being exposed. According to what George had said, there was an entire subculture of *strigoi* and their followers in New York.

What if I'd found the courage to confront Darcy outright and make him own up to what he was? Would he have denied it? Would he have felt the need to take some action to silence me?

There wasn't much point in brooding about that now. Darcy was in England with the others, no longer an immediate source of danger. Jane was safe, too.

But while the rest of the world might have been fooled by Jane's stiff upper lip, I wasn't. Mom gnashed her teeth, Mary offered unwanted advice, Kitty and Lydia urged Jane to come to Manhattan and find a "real" man. Jane bore it all like a champion, and in time even the rest of my family conceded that Jane had gotten over Charles.

"Everything will go back to normal now," Jane said, her eyes shadowed by dark circles like bruises. "I'll remember Charles as the nicest guy I've ever met, but that's all."

I smiled and nodded and pretended I didn't see her pain. Charles had proved to be a huge disappointment; if he couldn't stand up to Darcy—or his own sister, for that matter—as far as his own happiness was concerned, Jane was well rid of him.

As for George Wickham, I'd hardly exchanged more than a few words with him when he announced that he'd been offered a senior position in a friend's Los Angeles law firm, an offer he couldn't refuse. I can't say that Mr. Mason seemed that sorry to let him go.

I still liked George, vampire or not, and was sorry that I couldn't continue to quiz him about *strigoi* life and habits—anything that might give me a basis for fighting Darcy if it ever came to that. George promised me that he'd answer my questions by mail (not email, he said, because he didn't want that kind of information floating around the internet) and assured me that he hadn't forgotten his commitment to the battle against Darcy's kind.

He'd told me the day he left that Darcy would do anything to destroy him. And that he wouldn't have me or my family suffer because of his history with the man.

I thought that was a very noble attitude, and felt a definite regret after he was gone. I couldn't really blame him when my letters went unanswered after the first two I wrote. He was incredibly busy, he said, and while vampires didn't have much need for sleep and had stamina beyond that of the most talented human athlete, even he was beginning to feel the heat of living up to expectations. I knew I had to let him get settled, and managed to turn my attention to other things. Just as I managed, by the end of every day, to stop thinking about Darcy. Until I started all over again.

I finally recognized that I had to take some action, no matter how pointless it might seem. I began to research Darcy's public background, finances and business interests, hoping to turn up something useful. Everything I could find was rock-solid and completely aboveboard.

Jane and I both had a welcome distraction when our aunt, Sally Gardiner, came over from England to visit. She was a smart, sensible woman who saw things as they were, and her brisk, warm good nature cheered Jane considerably. When she invited Jane to go back with her to London and stay in her and Uncle Edward's flat until New Year's, Jane quickly agreed.

If the Bingleys and Darcy were really on a country estate in Derbyshire, it didn't seem likely that they'd meet Jane or the Gardiners in London. They didn't exactly run in the same circles, anyway. And though I told myself that Charles would never break ranks to see her on his own, even if he somehow found out she was there, part of me hoped he would.

I didn't know that Jane had already emailed Caroline, telling her she'd be in London. Jane, of course, still hadn't been able to blame the woman for encouraging Charles into leaving the States. She was bound and determined to give the harpy another chance.

So, for the first few days after Jane and my aunt and uncle arrived at Heathrow, I haunted my computer from five in the morning until midnight. The first few emails were all about how much she loved Aunt Sally's flat, London and England. There was a long stretch when I didn't hear from her at all. Then, at the end of the third week, she gave me the bad news.

Dearest Izba,
Please don't tell me, "I told you so." I know you've been trying to warn me about Caroline, but I just couldn't believe she was as bad as you implied.

Well, I was wrong. Caroline had written back after my first email, mentioning that she'd love to see me. I didn't hear from her after that—she never came to visit me—so I went to see her at Charles's flat. Charles was still at Pemberley, but Caroline answered the door.

She was polite. She made it very clear that I wasn't likely to see Charles anytime soon...he was busy with Mr. Darcy and their business interests in England. She didn't invite me to stay long; she was off to dinner with friends.

Still, I thought she might finally come to visit me before Christmas. And she did, but it was a disaster. She didn't even try to be polite. She kept talking about Charles's forthcoming wedding to Georgiana Darcy, hinted that Charles knew I was in town and made it very clear without actually saying so that she didn't expect to see much more of me.

So now we know. I don't understand why Caroline was so friendly with me when I was recuperating at Netherfield, but any friendship we might have had is over. I haven't seen Charles once, and now I know I never will.

But don't worry about me. I'm having a great time with Aunt Sally, and Christmas in London is wonderful. I can't wait to see you again on the second.

Write soon.

Love,

Your Jane

I shoved my chair away from the desk and made a few choice comments that would have made a Hell's Angel blush. Nothing Jane had said about Caroline had surprised me, but my opinion of Charles had sunk beyond recovery. Jane was better off without him.

And I, as it turned out, was better off without George. Lydia, who had gone to L.A. to spend Christmas with our other aunt, Daisy Phillips, sent a newspaper clipping announcing George's engagement to one Mary King.

If I felt any regret, it didn't last long. I was more interested in wondering if Mary King was a vampire, too, and how many laws would be passed against vampire marriage if people knew *strigoi* existed.

But there was still precious little *I* knew about vampires. Maybe we'd never see Darcy again. I could only hope so. Still, I was presumably one of a select few "mortals" who realized that such nonhuman creatures haunted our world. Wasn't it still my duty to learn more as long as there was the slightest chance that Darcy wasn't through with Bennet Labs?

My resolve hardened when I received another brief email from Jane.

Dearest Izba,

I don't know what to make of it. Today I saw Mr. Darcy at Harrods. It seemed like a coincidence until I saw him again at the British Museum the next day.

What does he want? He didn't talk to me…in fact, he disappeared both times when I saw him. I can't think of any reason he'd be spying on me, can you?

I'd worried that Darcy had some kind of evil interest in Jane, and now I was sure of it. If he'd just wanted to keep her away from Charles, well, he'd already succeeded in that, hadn't he?

I could think of only one thing to do. If the vampires wouldn't come to me, I'd have to go to the vampires.

CHAPTER 9

I HAD BOOKED A HOTEL IN MANHATTAN TO BEGIN MY QUEST, and from the looks of things, Rosings was hopping tonight.

I pulled my shawl around my shoulders, shivering in the frigid December air. Thank God it hadn't snowed; I'd have fallen in my spike heels. As it was, I'd had to leave my puffy down coat behind; I didn't think it would make a very good accessory to my little black dress.

Most of the women I saw hanging around the alley were just as inappropriately dressed as I was. Some were wearing a lot less than a skimpy dress. A few milled around in nervous-looking groups, as if they weren't sure they should be there. The rest were fawning over the guys—and one woman—who obviously regarded the human's abject worship as their due.

I swallowed, twice, and reminded myself why I was here. George had said that most vampires didn't hurt humans when they fed—too risky—and preferred willing partners—of whom there were clearly plenty available. I realized there was a chance that one of the "bad" *strigoi* would be present, but I'd already resolved that gaining knowledge was more important than practicing caution.

I took a step, stumbled, found my footing again and started for the door.

"Hello, beautiful."

The guy wasn't handsome. At that point I'd come to believe that being attractive was a requirement for any self-respecting *strigoi,* George and Darcy being prime examples. This guy was homely at best—short, chubby and balding—and he was so lacking in the charisma of the vampires I knew that I wondered for a minute if he was a vampire at all.

"You're new here, aren't you?" he asked.

I smiled in what I hoped was a simpering fashion. "Yes." I leaned toward him, letting him have a look at my cleavage. "Are you really a vampire?"

He showed his teeth and licked them sensuously. I couldn't mistake the pointed canines.

"Oh!" I said with a shiver that wasn't completely faked. "I'm so glad to meet you!"

"The pleasure is mutual." He preened, brushing off the sleeves of his tux. "Do you want to go inside, or have a quickie here?"

My hands had begun to tremble. I buried them in the shawl.

"Inside, if you don't mind," I said. "I promise you won't regret it."

He grabbed my arm. "Not everyone gets in, you know," he said. "Especially new donors. But since you're with me…"

"Thank you *so* much," I purred. "What's your name?"

"William Collins, at your service."

"I'm Elizabeth. Elizabeth Barrett."

"I think we're about to become very good friends, Elizabeth."

I sincerely hoped not, but I didn't really have much

choice at the moment. I went with him, concentrating on each step. We got up to the door, and the doorman—a beefy guy who didn't look any more like a vampire than Collins did—passed us through with hardly a glance in my direction.

The place was like one of those grand drawing rooms in nineteenth-century novels, complete with mirrored walls (which reflected everyone in the room, thank you very much), a high ceiling painted with cherubs and classical figures, portraits of glaring ancestors, and intimate arrangements of overstuffed chairs and sofas. Red doors running along two of the walls indicated the presence of other rooms, and I formed a picture of vampires and their groupies enjoying a little bite in blissful solitude. Did Darcy take his entire "harem" with him at once?

There were about a hundred people in the room, but it wasn't as noisy as you'd expect. In fact, the quiet was downright creepy. Presumably mortal women—and men—draped themselves over *strigoi* of both sexes (who definitely could *not*, among so many humans, be mistaken for anything but vampires). There were no orgiastic revels that I could see, no blood on the floor or furniture. None of the groupies seemed to have been hurt in any way. It was all supremely civilized.

"What do you think?" Collins asked, his chest puffed out with pride.

"It's…it's incredible."

"All the doing of my patroness, Lady Catherine de Bourgh."

If I hadn't been firmly planted on my towering heels, I might have fallen on my posterior. George's words leaped into my mind: *"He was converted by his aunt, Lady Catherine de Bourgh, at his own request."*

The woman who had changed Darcy into a vampire was here, in this very room.

"There she is, Elizabeth," Collins said, gesturing toward the head of the room. "Behold!"

I followed his pointing finger. A middle-aged woman with a long, haughty face sat in a high-backed chair raised on a stagelike platform. A smaller chair beside hers was occupied by a sallow younger woman, and several gorgeous young men stood behind the chairs. I noticed right away that the women were dressed in the same kind of high-waisted, Regency-style gowns that Caroline Bingley and I had worn to the Halloween party.

"Is she not the very height of elegance and beauty?" Collins said rapturously. I noted with half my mind that his language had suddenly changed, becoming more formal and accented very much like Mr. Darcy's. "My patroness," Collins had said. Were he and Darcy literally blood brothers?

Somehow I managed to gasp out an answer. "She's... very impressive," I said in what I hoped was an appropriately awestruck voice. "She runs this place?"

"*Runs* it?" Collins said, staring at me in indignation. "She does not merely run it, my dear Elizabeth. She presides over the *strigoi* assembly in Manhattan whenever her duties do not demand her presence in England. She and her daughter, Miss Anne De Bourgh, are admired, feared and loved wherever they appear."

I cast Lady Catherine de Bourgh a more searching glance. I still had almost no idea how *strigoi* interacted with each other on a daily basis. How much did conversion change a person? George had indicated that emotions didn't change afterward, and vampires could obviously hate. Could they love, as well? Did Darcy love his aunt? Could he love anyone?

"I had thought to seek privacy at once," Collins said, oblivious to my thoughts, "but I believe I shall do you the honor of presenting you to my patroness."

The last thing I wanted was to have such a woman's attention drawn to me. "Oh," I said, shuffling backward, "If you don't mind, I think—"

"Come, I insist. You need not be afraid. You will find her most obliging to those who recognize her superiority of mind and breeding."

In other words, if I groveled enough, I'd probably be okay. I let Collins grab my arm again and he pulled me toward the platform.

I expected to be intimidated by a woman who could convert a man like Darcy and lord it over a city's worth of bloodsuckers, but as I got closer to the platform I started to wonder if Collins had been exaggerating. There was nothing really remarkable about her—except maybe in the size of her nose, which she looked down very skillfully.

Collins almost crawled up to the platform, bobbing and slobbering as he made the introductions. Because I was more than a little scared, I looked straight up at Lady Catherine.

"Hello," I said, resisting the urge to curtsy.

She said something I couldn't quite hear, her eyes cold, and Collins replied obsequiously on my behalf. I was occupied with fighting off a severe sense of disorientation and looking for some resemblance between her and Darcy.

It was there, all right, though Darcy seemed to have gotten all the good looks in the family. From the way she was staring, I had a sense that Lady Catherine saw something in me she didn't like. Could she have some idea who I was? I'd changed my last name, but not by very much. It wouldn't take a great leap to figure out that *Barrett* was pretty close to *Bennet*.

But would Darcy have talked to her about me? George had said he didn't know if Darcy was under his aunt's control. Maybe he reported everything to her. Maybe I'd inadvertently walked into a trap.

At least I knew Darcy himself was in England with Charles and Caroline.

Whatever my fears, I was allowed to walk away from Lady Catherine none the worse for wear. I was so shaken, however, that when Collins led me toward one of the red doors I climbed out of the pit and walked right into the pendulum.

"Does Lady Catherine have relatives in the city?" I blurted.

Collins stopped and looked at me in surprise. "Relatives? Are you speaking of protégées?"

"Um, I meant other vam...*strigoi.*"

He gave me a thoughtful look. "She has a nephew who occasionally appears at Rosings. Why do you ask?"

"Is he called Mr. Darcy?"

"You know Mr. Darcy?"

"I met him once."

"But how extraordinary!" He frowned. "Did he invite you here?"

"*No.* No. I mean, I heard about this place after I met him, and wondered...if he comes here sometimes."

Collins took a step away from me. "You have donated to Mr. Darcy?"

I didn't know if the chill I felt came from horror or excitement. "No. Some of the girls I know...they were talking about him. He's supposed to be—"

"He is, of course, one of the most illustrious *strigoi* in

England or America," Collins said with a sniff. "But he does not bestow his favors indiscriminately."

Irritation was beginning to overcome my nervousness. "His donors must be very grateful to be chosen."

"Naturally. Mr. Darcy is known to be extremely generous with his mortal adherents. Many have benefited greatly from his condescension. Perhaps you have heard of Mr. Charles Bingley?"

"The head of that big pharmaceutical company?"

"Indeed. Bingley's success is entirely due to Mr. Darcy's guidance." He drew near me again. "Only recently, he extracted Mr. Bingley from a very infortuitous alliance."

I stiffened. "What do you mean?"

"His friend was about to offer marriage to a young lady who would have been entirely unsuitable for such a favored mortal, both in breeding and in understanding. Mr. Darcy took steps to ensure that such an alliance would not take place."

I didn't hear whatever else Collins said. I was too furious.

"I've got to go," I said, heading for the door.

"But you just arrived!"

"I'm sorry."

Collins wasn't the kind of vampire to inspire fear in anyone, and I didn't expect him to stop me. But he grabbed the trailing end of my shawl with easy strength, and I was too surprised to shrug off the shawl and keep going.

"You must not leave just yet, Elizabeth," he said in a menacing voice that reminded me of a certain decaying intergalactic emperor. "Not so soon after I introduced you to Lady Catherine. It would not be at all proper."

"Maybe some other time."

"I think not." Collins flashed his teeth at me. "This need not be unpleasant. I flatter myself that I can please my admirers."

"Believe me, Mr. Collins, I don't admire you, Lady Catherine, Mr. Darcy or anyone else in this place."

Collins's mouth fell open. Then he pulled me against him, and I was reminded that even a wimpy-looking little vampire was still a vampire.

"You will enjoy my company, I think, better than you would greater scrutiny by Lady Catherine," he whispered. His hot breath blew over my neck. I resisted, but it was like trying to break out of a straitjacket. His teeth grazed my skin.

"Let her go."

Darcy loomed behind Collins, his expression so lethal that I expected Collins to vanish in a puff of smoke.

But Collins didn't disappear. He let me go, bowed deeply and let loose a barrage of sickeningly subservient compliments and whining explanations.

I looked up at Darcy, my heart plunging to the polished parquet floor. He briefly met my gaze and then watched Collins scuttle away. Only when the smaller man was out of sight did he look at me again.

"What are you doing here, Miss Elizabeth?" he said.

If Darcy had seemed dangerous in an everyday setting, he was positively menacing here. Every instinct told me to cringe and scuttle away, just like Collins.

But not even mortals are creatures of instinct alone. "I must say, Mr. Darcy," I said with a defiant smile, "you do have a way of popping up at the most interesting moments."

CHAPTER 10

DARCY DIDN'T DIGNIFY MY QUIP WITH A RESPONSE. WHEN HE put his arm around my shoulders and steered me toward a cluster of empty seats near the side of the room, I began to understand what those Victorian females felt like just before they collapsed into a graceful swoon. Only mine wouldn't be so graceful. Darcy all but pushed me onto a sofa and sat beside me.

"Answer me," he said softly. "Why are you here?"

"I might ask the same of you," I said, edging away from him. "I thought you were in England with Mr. Bingley."

"That is of no moment. I asked you—"

"My sister was in London," I said, anger restoring my courage. "You didn't happen to see her, did you?"

He seemed surprised at my line of questioning, and some of the arrogance went out of his face. "I did not," he said.

"I'm sorry to hear it. You and Charles left so suddenly that we were a little concerned."

"You need not have been."

"Of course, you were taking very good care of Charles, weren't you?"

Maybe I was getting better at reading his feelings, or maybe he was less skilled at hiding them, but I could have sworn that he looked embarrassed. "He is often in need of care."

"How lucky he is to have you."

Darcy shifted on the sofa. "*You* are obviously in need of advice, Miss Elizabeth, or you would not have come to Rosings."

"Whose advice *should* I have listened to, Mr. Darcy?"

He released his breath and glanced around the room, his gaze briefly settling on Lady Catherine. She was staring in our direction.

"Perhaps you are not aware of the perils you may face here," he said.

"The worst thing I can lose is my blood."

Could a vampire blush? Darcy looked over my head at the mirrored wall. "You have known for some time," he said.

"Since before we met at the party. It was pretty clear that you knew I knew, and I knew you knew I knew." I smiled defiantly. "I'll admit it was a bit of a shock at first, but I've learned to deal with it."

He looked straight into my eyes, and I knew what gave him so much power over people. Including me. So much so that my body was beginning to react in the same way it had at the Halloween party. If he touched me…

"Why are you here, Elizabeth?" he asked again, his voice gentle and hypnotic. I felt the overwhelming desire to answer honestly, to spill my guts without any thought to the consequences.

"I…I wanted to learn more about vampires."

"You have chosen the most dangerous way of going about it."

"I don't think Collins could have forced me to do anything I didn't want to do."

"You deceive yourself. Even he is capable of compelling your cooperation."

"I guess he's like you in that respect."

His eyes narrowed. "I have never compelled anyone to do my will."

"No? You've resisted every temptation to use your vampire influence to make people do what you want?"

He was about to answer—with some heat, I thought—when Lady Catherine de Bourgh came up behind him. I hadn't heard her approach, but Darcy was thoroughly composed by the time the woman joined us.

"What are you speaking of, Darcy?" she demanded. "I must know what you're talking about."

Darcy half turned toward her, emotionless and controlled. "The subject would not be of interest to you, Aunt."

"Everything that occurs here is of interest to me." She gave me a calculating, distinctly unfriendly glance. "I did not know this girl was of *interest* to you."

"I was just leaving," I said, popping out of my seat. "Thanks for your hospitality, Lady Catherine."

Darcy rose with me. "She is most assuredly of interest to me," he said, meeting his aunt's stare. "If you will forgive us." He bowed, ignoring the lady's obvious outrage, and grabbed my poor, abused arm. Striding at such a fast pace that I had to run to keep up with him, he led me to one of the red doors, opened it and ushered me through.

I won't lie and say I wasn't scared. There was good reason to be. The room looked like a bordello, all red velvet, huge bed and very low light. Darcy released me as soon as the door was closed and kept his distance, but I didn't feel reassured.

Giving the bed a wide berth, I edged toward the door, trying to think of some subject completely unrelated to blood drinking. I didn't quite succeed.

"I'm surprised you didn't need Lady Catherine's permission to bring me in here," I said.

He seemed distracted, and his voice was sharp when he answered. "She has no control over me," he said.

"Didn't she convert you?"

"There are ways to overcome…" He stopped, turning his darkest frown in my direction.

"I really do need to go," I said.

"You are afraid of me."

"Not at all. But I prefer to make my own decisions about who I hang out with."

He moved his shoulders in a gesture I couldn't interpret and began to pace from one side of the room to the other. "You must not judge all of us according to Collins's behavior."

"You just warned me that I might be in danger here, so there must be more where he came from," I said pointedly.

"How is your family?"

Aha. A sudden change of subject. "They're well for the most part, though my father is concerned about the family business. You know, the one Charles was about to acquire on terms favorable to Bennet Labs and its employees."

Darcy paused in front of the far wall and took an audible breath. "Miss Elizabeth—"

"Mr. Darcy, I—"

He spun around so quickly that I was already running for the door before I'd even had a chance to think about it. He was there first.

"It will not do," he said, his expression shockingly anguished. "My feelings will not be repressed." He grabbed me, lifted me off my feet and kissed me.

Now, I've been kissed before. Several times. Sometimes I enjoyed it, sometimes I didn't. But this time…

Oh, this time I shot straight to the moon, made a few orbits and crash-landed in the Sea of Euphoria. I tangled my fingers in his thick black hair, opening my mouth to welcome his thrusting tongue and meeting it with my own.

At some point we came up for air, and that was when I remembered where I was. Darcy loosened his hold just enough to let me wriggle free. I stumbled back until I reached the wall and tried to catch my breath, astonished and mortified.

"Elizabeth," he said, hoarse and breathing just as fast as I was. "You must make me the happiest of men and allow me to take you under my protection."

They say laughter is the best medicine. All that came out was a squeak. "Under your protection? Is that what you call it?"

I had meant to provoke him, but he actually seemed bewildered. It was a moment of weakness that almost—almost—made me sympathize with him.

He seemed to take my silence for encouragement. "I have admired you since we were first acquainted," he said. "I have never met a woman like you in my two centuries of life. I offer you everything you could possibly desire: every comfort, every luxury and my complete devotion."

It wasn't easy, but I maintained my defenses. "In exchange for what? My blood? My body? My eternal obedience?"

His voice softened. "Not obedience, my dear Elizabeth. I shall never force you in any way." He took up his agitated pacing again, his fists curling and uncurling at his sides. "It is not a request that I make lightly. I have fought my own feelings every day since our introduction. I am very discriminating in my choice of human companionship. I am well aware that you are from a common family of limited understanding, despite your many admirable qualities. Our association will require great circumspection on my part. My aunt will be deeply disturbed by such an alliance, and will frequently make her feelings known." He turned to face me. "Nevertheless, I am willing to make such sacrifices if you will consent to my request."

His *request.* I still wasn't sure if he was offering to make me his mistress or his convert, but it didn't matter. I'd heard enough.

"How many times have you made such a 'request'?" I asked hanging on to my courage by a thread of panic at my own embarrassing instinct to accept him. "What about your harem of devoted fans? Do you plan to give them up, too?"

"My harem? What—"

"How many women—and men—have you converted, with or without their consent?"

He had been moving toward me, but now he stopped again and searched my face as if he were really seeing me for the first time. His eyes took on a cast I could only describe as feral, and his lip curled.

"Who has been telling you these lies?" he demanded. "Was it Wickham?"

"Are they lies? Isn't it true that you converted George against his will?"

"You take an eager interest in that gentleman's concerns," he snapped.

"Anyone who knew about what happened to him would be interested," I retorted.

A vampire's contempt was a terrible thing. "Oh, yes. What happened to him was terrible indeed."

I moved a step away from the wall, my own fists clenched. "I'm glad you can joke about ruining a man's life."

He made a sound of disgust. "Then you choose to believe his story."

"Maybe if that were the only strike against you, I might be more skeptical. But you've deliberately hurt my family, 'common' as it is, by separating Jane from the man who loves her. You've undermined Charles's intentions for letting Bennet Laboratories keep some independence under Bingley Pharmaceutical's ownership. Then you tell me that you want me against your better judgment. That's a pretty strange way of showing affection!"

He looked away, his profile stark and his body rigid. "So this is your opinion of me," he said quietly. "By this light my faults must seem egregious indeed. Yet I believe you would not have judged me so harshly if your own feelings had not been wounded."

I edged toward the door again. "You're wrong, Mr. Darcy. From the very beginning I've been aware of your belief in your own superiority, even before I knew you were a vampire. You've never given a damn about anyone else's feelings. You pretend to be a gentleman, but your arrogance has just made it easier for me to turn you down."

Without waiting for his answer, I opened the door and walked out. He didn't try to stop me. I headed straight for the entrance, aware of Lady Catherine's stare burning into my back, and practically ran all the way to the street.

I've never been a crier, but once I was in my hotel room, I threw myself on the bed and sobbed until my nose was stuffed up like a Thanksgiving turkey.

Even when I was looking at my puffy eyes and flushed face in the bathroom mirror, I was thinking that I was glad Darcy would never see me like this. Never again tell me that he'd admired me from the day we'd met. Never again ask to "protect me." Never kiss me. Never make love to me.

There really wasn't any other answer I could have given. I knew that. Darcy hadn't denied that he'd worked to separate Jane and Charles. He'd made fun of George.

But he'd also accused me of "choosing to believe" George's story. He was, in effect, calling George a liar.

Just another attack, I told myself. But I lay awake in bed, watching one of those endless thigh-buster infomercials, and wished I could order up a nice, all-consuming black hole from room service.

CHAPTER II

By morning I was my usual self, determined to put last night's fiasco out of my mind. But when I pulled on my robe and stumbled toward the bathroom, there was an envelope lying just inside the door. I opened it to find expensive-looking stationery painstakingly covered in an elegant cursive.

> Be not alarmed, madam, that this letter contains any repetition of those sentiments, or renewal of those offers, which were last night so disgusting to you. I write without any intention of paining you, or humbling myself, by dwelling on wishes, which, for the happiness of both, cannot be too soon forgotten.

I nearly tossed the letter on the floor, but an obsessive curiosity kept me reading. I won't repeat everything he said here; let's just say that when I was finished, I was very tempted to throw myself on the bed and cry for a couple more hours.

It wasn't an apology. It was a calm, cool recitation of facts laying out what Darcy had felt and done since we'd met. He talked about observing Charles with Jane, and noting that Charles had never showed such "partiality" for a woman before. He'd learned that there was an expectation of marriage and had watched even more closely.

Instead of concluding that Jane and Charles were in love, he became certain that Jane, open and friendly as she was, didn't have the same regard for Charles as he did for her. He'd concluded that her heart "was not likely to be easily touched."

That alone would have been enough for me to tear the letter into tiny pieces and flush it down the toilet, but he went on to admit that there was even more behind his objection to the potential marriage. He had come to believe that Charles's generous concessions in the negotiations with BL were the result of a deliberate attempt by my family to influence him by getting him to fall in love with Jane. Because of this conviction, Darcy had persuaded Charles to leave America, avoid Jane in England and give up all idea of marriage to her.

I was seconds away from raiding the mini-bar for every tiny bottle of alcohol it contained when I read the bit where he admitted that he might have been wrong in his suspicions and his judgment of Jane—that, in fact, he should have known that any sister of *mine* would never consent to such deception. From a guy like Darcy, this was a major confession.

So I kept on reading. About George Wickham…almost the same story George had told me, but from a very different perspective. Darcy's father had loved George as a son, put him through school and given him everything he could want. When Darcy had inherited the estate, George had lived in "idleness and dissipation" and thrown his money into gambling, chasing women and flitting from one career to another.

There was more about a "living" Darcy's father had

meant George to have, and George's demand that he be given the worth of the living in cash. Sometime while he was off in London wasting the money, George had been turned into a vampire. Darcy later learned that he'd acquired a bevy of women followers and had converted more than a few against their will.

Once George had gone through all the money in his usual way, he'd returned to Pemberley to demand the living as his due. When Darcy had refused, George had decided to take revenge and had begun to work on seducing Darcy's sister, Georgiana, who was only sixteen years old at the time.

That wasn't the worst of it. When Wickham found out that Darcy had discovered what he was up to, he'd run off with Georgiana and forcibly converted her. Not only had Georgiana become a vampire like her elder brother, but she had nearly died as a result, falling prey to some rare disease that affects only one in a hundred converts.

This, madam, is a faithful narrative of every event in which we have been concerned together. If you accept any part of it as truth, I hope you will acquit me of any cruelty toward Mr. Wickham. I do not know how he convinced you of his lies, but considering how little you knew of him, and his natural ability to charm, I can hardly be surprised that you believed him.

My eyes were getting blurry by the time I read the last line. Maybe I should have been more skeptical of the things Darcy had revealed in his letter. He hadn't said anything about how *he* had become a vampire, or why Georgiana wasn't still under Wickham's power. But

Darcy didn't want me anymore; he had no earthly reason to lie about anything.

I sat on the edge of the bed and let the letter fall from my hands. I had every reason to be furious with Darcy over his opinion of my family, his belief that Jane had conspired against Charles and his assumption that I'd be thrilled to offer my neck to him.

But Charles had told Jane that Darcy might have reason to dislike George, and I remembered that Wickham, for all his pretty words, had made promises he hadn't kept. He'd run away rather than face Darcy as he'd claimed he intended to do. He'd dropped me, and my family, like a stone.

Darcy was far from perfect; he'd improve considerably if someone would take him down a few pegs. And at least he was sincere. He hadn't forced me when I'd refused him, when he could easily have done so.

I fell back on the bed and covered my face with a pillow. I wasn't fooling myself. There was one more reason I didn't crumple the letter into a ball and consign it to the trash can.

I was in love. In love with a vampire.

I laughed until my throat was sore and my chest ached. The joke was on me. I barely knew the guy, and what I *did* know about him wasn't exactly reassuring.

But that was why I couldn't just sit here in my hotel room and wallow in emotional martyrdom, or return to New Haven and pretend none of this had happened. It *had* happened. And the only way to prove to myself that I hadn't gone stark raving mad was to face the problem head-on.

Tossing the pillow aside, I sat up and scrubbed at my face. Darcy was in New York, which meant I'd probably be safe enough for the time being. Jane would be in London for one more week. I could catch a flight first thing tomorrow; the hope of finding some sort of resolution was worth the expense.

First I'd see Jane and tell her what I should have told her weeks ago. Oh, not everything—not until I was satisfied that I had a few more answers. I'd already done the research on Darcy's public business connections in England; while in London, I'd talk to anyone I could find who was willing to be honest about his or her dealings with him. I'd scour the neighborhood around Charles's flat for any clues about Darcy's habits, behavior and treatment of the mortals he came in contact with every day. If that wasn't enough, I'd take a trip up to Derbyshire and grill the people living around Pemberley.

I'd bluff, wheedle and lie my way to the truth about Mr. Fitzwilliam Darcy—whether he was the monster George had described, or a basically good guy who'd been handed a raw deal two hundred years ago.

A guy I might actually be able to love without despising myself. Not that it would make any difference now that Darcy had made clear how much he despised me. If I had been wrong about him all along, I had only myself to blame.

JANE REACTED EXACTLY THE WAY I'd expected she would, but much more nicely than I would have done in her place.

The only thing that convinced her in the end was her absolute faith in me. Once she knew I wasn't teasing, she could only sympathize with what I'd been through.

"Oh, Izba. And to think you've had to carry this secret for weeks! You should have told me right after you talked to George!"

Dear Jane. Once she was with me, she was with me all

the way. I naturally didn't tell her how Darcy had conspired to separate her and Charles, or what he'd believed
about her motives; I was deliberately vague about Darcy's
proposition to me. But I explained what George had said,
and how Darcy had refuted Wickham's claims.

"It's unbelievable!" Jane said, completely unaware
that she seemed far more shocked by George's apparent
lies than by the fact that he wasn't human. "He seemed
so nice. And you liked him, Lizzy!" She didn't let me
defend myself, but went on to sympathize with poor Mr.
Darcy.

"Just think how awful it must have been to see his sister turned into a vampire against her will. I can't believe
that any friend of Charles would punish George by doing
the same thing to him, or hurt people just for the fun of
it! And Lizzy, he couldn't possibly love you if he were
so bad."

I'd protested that he didn't love me, but she'd made
up her mind. And Jane, having made up her mind, was a
formidable opponent. She insisted on helping me in my
investigative work, but I begged her not to get involved
and promised I'd give her regular updates as to my progress.

Making progress was not as difficult as I'd feared. Not
everyone was willing to talk with me—a strange American—about Darcy. But those who did had almost entirely
good things to say about him. He was not effusive in his
behavior but was uniformly generous, kind and pleasant
with his employees, fellow businessmen and the people
who worked in the surrounding area. I saw no indication
that anyone knew what he really was.

I thought several times about visiting Charles's London flat in hopes of finding him there, but that meant I'd

probably meet Caroline, as well. I didn't want to give Jane any further cause for humiliation.

I finally decided that I had to take a shot at Pemberley. Like so many historic estates in England, the place was open part of the time for tour groups. The odds of Darcy being there were small; I hadn't heard that he'd come back to London.

I had just returned to Aunt Sally's flat from my latest interrogatory outing when Jane told me that she'd been invited to spend a few nights in Paris with one of our English cousins. She didn't want to leave me, but I convinced her that the opportunity was too good to pass up.

Once she found out that I was going to Derbyshire, Aunt Sally insisted on coming with me. She'd been born in Derbyshire—in the very area where Darcy's estate stood—and I couldn't think of a good way to refuse her.

My first sight of Pemberley gave me a thrill I hadn't expected. It was a magnificent stone structure set on a low hill amid an extensive wood of fine old trees, and I could imagine it having looked exactly the same way two hundred and more years ago, inhabited by elegant lords and ladies of the *ton*.

And vampires.

Part of me wanted to turn tail then and there. But Aunt Sally was bursting with praise and enthusiasm, so my sense had a chance to overcome my sensibility. Several tour buses were parked in a gravel lot off to the side, along with a dozen or so cars. We parked, bought tickets and joined one of the tour groups.

I could never think about that visit again without remembering how beautiful it all was, how well-proportioned and handsomely furnished the rooms were, suggesting that someone had good taste untainted by a need for ostentation. The views from the windows were astonishing. When the guide led us through a gallery filled with portraits of Darcy ancestors, I noticed right away that the last few resembled him to the point that they were almost indistinguishable except for dress and background.

"Mr. Darcy's recent ancestors," the woman guide announced with obvious pride. "His father, his grandfather and his great-grandfather. All were painted at the age of thirty years. The entire family has been blessed with longevity as well as good looks, as you can see." Some of the women in the group tittered, and I felt a spark of irrational jealousy.

"They do seem to show a remarkable resemblance to the current Mr. Darcy," my aunt said. "Of course, I've only seen his photographs in the papers, and then only once or twice. Is he really as handsome as that in person?"

The guide looked at me with interest. "Does the young lady know Mr. Darcy?"

I could feel my face turning red. "A little," I mumbled.

She looked very pleased at this admission, and quickly led the group to another portrait, this of a young girl with cascades of blond hair and a sweet expression.

"Mr. Darcy's sister, Georgiana Darcy. She was named after a distant relation, a cousin of Mr. Darcy's great-grandfather."

"She's lovely," my aunt murmured.

She was. Like Darcy, she probably hadn't changed a bit in two hundred years…perpetually sixteen, with no hope of getting any older, of having regular dates, a real boyfriend or any of the other growing pains most kids lived through before they were wise enough to know better.

"The Darcys have always had an excellent reputation in Derbyshire, and in the whole of England," the guide said. "They have been excellent employers. Many charitable institutions have benefited greatly from their generosity." She lowered her voice to whisper in my ear. "I've lived here all my life, and I've never known a better boy or man. Not like the wild young men today, who think of nothing but themselves. Some people think he's proud, but in my opinion, it's only because he doesn't speak until he has something to say."

I didn't know what to think, let alone what to say. This was exactly what I'd wanted to know, wasn't it? Didn't it confirm what I'd already been told by the people in London?

The tour group moved on, but I stayed behind, staring at the portraits. When I found myself alone, I didn't run after the others but turned straight for a door marked No Entry.

The door opened up to a corridor, and the corridor led to several rooms which I guessed must belong to the family. One of them held a huge grand piano; another was an office with bookshelf-lined walls and thick binders on a wide oak desk.

Feeling like a thief, I snuck into the room and closed the door. Some instinct drew me to the desk. It was neat, without a single random sheet of paper or loose pen anywhere in evidence. The blotter was spotless. I knew without looking any further that it must belong to Mr. Darcy.

I thought about it for a few seconds and then opened one of the binders. It was stuffed with page after page of sheets mounted behind plastic, letters and certificates that offered sincere gratitude to a man named Mr. F. Darcy. Some were honorary degrees, others formal acknowledgments, still others simple thank-you letters. Each one mentioned some liberal donation to a charitable institution or medical center, a children's hospital or human-rights organization. One letter told of the work that would be done with the money: experimental research on the blood disorders and cancers of children. The amounts received were in the tens and hundreds of thousands.

Darcy had done this. A vampire, contributing to the welfare of the mortals he had seemed to despise. Caroline had said as much, and I, in my anger, had refused to believe it. I closed the binder and opened another one, my heart filled with a terrible joy.

"Hello?" a soft voice said.

I spun around, guilt pasting a stupid smile on my face. "Um, hello!" I said brightly. "I know I shouldn't be in here, but—"

I stopped. The girl couldn't have been more than sixteen, with very pale skin and cascades of golden hair.

I'd met Georgiana Darcy at last.

CHAPTER 12

"You're Miss Darcy!" I blurted before I could think.

The girl smiled. "Yes, I am. Are you with the tour group?"

"I, uh…I'm really sorry. I wandered off and lost my way…."

"It's all right." She came nearer and laid her small, pale hand on the desk. "I don't mind."

My heart settled into a slow gallop. "I didn't know the family was here," I said.

"I'm here most of the time," she said. "Usually it's just me, Mr. Cavendish and my governess."

A governess, for God's sake. Poor kid. "Your house is beautiful," I said.

"Yes, it is. My brother always makes sure it's comfortable, too." She pushed a strand of hair away from her gentle face. "You're an American, aren't you? How I'd love to see the Grand Canyon, and the deserts, and the Pacific Ocean."

"You've never been?"

"No. I—" She lowered her head, covered her mouth and coughed. I remembered what Darcy had written about her having suffered from some kind of *strigoi* disease.

I started toward her. "Are you all right?"

She dropped her hand. "Yes, thank you for asking." She looked at me as if she could see past all the defenses and peer into my soul.

She's a vampire, idiot, I told myself. But there was no threat about her. She behaved like any ordinary teenager, except that she was a lot more polite.

And innocent. Could a vampire be innocent?

"Your brother," I said cautiously, "seems to be quite a philanthropist."

"Oh, yes." Her face lit up again, nearly blinding me with the love that shone from it. "He's such a good man."

I looked down at the binders. "I didn't know," I muttered.

"Didn't know what?"

"Um…I didn't know…that anyone could be so generous."

She cocked her head, and I had the distinct feeling that she didn't believe my answer. "My brother doesn't usually advertise it," she said. "You're very interested in him, aren't you?"

I knew my expression was much too bland. "It's always interesting to find out about the people who live in these mansions."

"But you speak as if you know him."

How she'd gathered that from what I'd said I didn't know, but I was convinced in that moment that she had guessed at least part of the truth.

"I met him once, in New York," I said.

"He goes there often on business. How did you meet him?"

"At a party." That was the truth, wasn't it?

The intensity in her blue eyes reminded me far too much of her brother. She stroked her hand over the surface of the desk. "Do you mind if I ask…what is your name?"

Someone else answered for me.

"Miss Elizabeth Bennet," Darcy said, walking into the room. I expected him to be disdainful, if not furious, but as his eyes met mine I saw only surprise and consternation. "I did not know you were in England."

"I didn't know you were at Pemberley!" I stammered.

"Elizabeth Bennet!" Georgiana cried, clapping her hands. "How wonderful!"

Darcy, dressed in an ordinary but superbly cut business suit, seemed more off balance than ever. "You have met my sister, Miss Elizabeth," he said.

"Yes." I smiled at Georgiana, not wanting her to feel the excruciating tension in the room.

"I've heard so much about you," Georgiana said, linking her arm through Darcy's.

"You have?"

"Yes. So many good things."

Darcy had been talking about me? Why? And why had I been so stupid as to risk coming here if there was any chance he'd be here, too?

Whatever Darcy was thinking, he didn't let it show. He smiled at his sister and stroked her hair. "It's time for you to rest," he said.

"Oh, but I want to visit with Miss Bennet!"

"You will have your chance." He glanced at me and quickly looked away again. "You may play for Miss Bennet after dinner."

With a sigh and a nod of acquiescence, Georgiana left the room. Darcy cleared his throat.

"If you will forgive me, Miss Elizabeth, I must see to my sister. If you would be so good as to wait in the small drawing room at the end of the corridor…"

"I shouldn't be here at all," I said. "I should get back."

He turned to face me full-on, and all the bones in my body threatened to melt. "My sister would be gratified if you would stay to dinner," he said.

"Oh. Well, thanks, but I'm with my aunt."

"She is also welcome." He didn't smile, but his eyes weren't cold. Quite the contrary. "I would not ask for myself, but Georgiana will be most disappointed if you refuse."

Not for himself. Okay, then I was safe. Just like all the other times I'd told myself I had nothing to worry about.

"In that case, my aunt and I will be honored."

He stared at me a moment longer, bowed and left the room.

I collapsed into the desk chair. Was this really happening? Hadn't Darcy made it clear he didn't want anything more to do with me?

He didn't exactly welcome you with open arms. But I didn't want him to. Did I?

Finding my strength again, I rushed into the corridor and through the door to the public area, searching frantically for Aunt Sally. She was shocked at my appearance and worried that I had taken ill. When I told her about the invitation, she shook her head in amazement.

"Jane told me about Mr. Darcy," she said, "But I was under the impression that you and he didn't like each other."

"Well, I…I don't know what to make of it, Aunt Sally, but I don't think it would be very polite to refuse, would it?"

She agreed, and so when a dignified gentleman—a Mr. Cavendish—met us at the front door to confirm that we were to attend dinner, we accepted. We returned to the bed-and-breakfast we'd booked for the night, washed and dressed (I'd brought one decent outfit with me, thank God) and were on our way to my rental car when a limousine pulled up, sent from Pemberley.

On our arrival, I clutched my aunt's arm as the driver escorted us to a side door used as the family's entrance. Mr. Cavendish led us down another hallway to a room that reminded me of Charles's grand salon at Netherfield, but much more glamorous. Sitting on one of the sofas was Caroline Bingley, and across from her in a Directoire chair was Charles.

I stopped, stock-still, and only my aunt's urgent whisper kept me going. Charles got to his feet with his usual, exuberant grin.

"Elizabeth!" he said. "I'm so glad to see you!" He pumped my hand, nearly detaching it from my arm. "You remember my sister, Caroline."

I nodded in the woman's direction, and she gave me an icy nod in return. She didn't look at all happy.

I soon began to understand why. When Darcy and Georgiana walked into the room, Darcy ignored Caroline, and Georgiana walked right past Charles with only a brief glance in his direction. Not exactly an indication of the kind of "adoration" Caroline had implied she felt for Charles. Maybe he didn't want to marry a sixteen-year-old girl (who wasn't really sixteen). Or maybe they had never intended to get married at all.

I'd been prepared to be very mad at Charles, but it wasn't possible to maintain the feeling. He asked several times about my family, and the way he skirted around any mention of Jane, in particular, told me that she was very much on his mind. He spoke ruefully of the good times we'd had together, and when I introduced him to my aunt, he seemed ready and willing to keep her entertained. Part of me was starting to hope that he was so interested because he still cared for Jane.

While Georgiana chattered gaily, pelting me with questions about America and my life there, Darcy stood by the mantelpiece and watched me. This time I didn't feel any judgment from him, only a kind of melancholy. I felt the same way myself. I'd clearly misjudged him on most counts—I'd never done anything but mock him—and yet he'd wanted me to share his life.

The dinner was incredible. A round, cheerful woman served the dishes with the help of the butler, Mr. Cavendish, and the mood was almost relaxed. Even Darcy seemed in better spirits. He and Georgiana ate along with everyone else. Neither brother nor sister seemed to feel any particular urge to run out and find some willing mortal to bite.

Does Darcy keep a harem here? I wondered, determined to torment myself into indifference. It didn't work. I was more aware of Darcy, and my attraction to him, than ever before.

Near the end of the meal Georgiana swayed in her seat, and Darcy jumped up to catch her. I helped lift her out of her chair, and Darcy's hand brushed mine.

"She must go up to bed," he said. "Please make yourself comfortable in the drawing room. Ask Cavendish for anything you require."

I could barely finish my dessert because the hand he had touched had gone numb. When we all went to the drawing room, Aunt Sally sat down next to me.

"There is something very interesting in the way Mr. Darcy is staring at you," she whispered.

"He does that," I said, flustered by her perceptiveness. "And not just to me. At home—"

"Come off it, Lizzy. He's obviously taken with you." She lowered her voice. "He must be in love with you."

I sputtered some answer, but she only gave me a knowing look and took the coffee Mr. Cavendish offered. At some point my cell phone rang; I was so discombobulated that I didn't answer. When Darcy returned, we all went for a walk in Pemberley's extensive gardens. Darcy set out to charm my aunt, smiling more than I'd ever seen him do before.

Could he be in love with me? He'd never said anything about love at Rosings. I'd wondered if vampires were even *capable* of the feeling, but Darcy and his sister clearly loved each other very much.

It wasn't until we were back at the B and B and I, in a state of total confusion, was drifting through the evening's ablutions that my cell rang again and I forced myself to pick it up.

Ten minutes later I was pounding on the bathroom door. My aunt came out, a towel wrapped around her hair.

"What in heaven's name is it, Lizzy?" she asked.

It took a few minutes, because I was crying and had to start over twice. I explained everything, from George's revelations about vampires to my own personal confirmation of their existence, finishing with the part about Wickham and his attack on Georgiana.

I didn't expect Aunt Sally to take it all in as quickly as Jane had, but she surprised me. There had apparently been legends of nightwalkers in that part of Derbyshire for centuries, which she'd believed as a child. The Darcys had always had an aura of mystery about them that had led to much speculation through the years.

"I never thought it would be real," she murmured. "But as vivid as your imagination can be, Lizzy, I know you are not insane. If you say it is true, I believe it."

After a grateful hug, I told her the worst part. She got up, went downstairs and returned with a bottle of wine and glasses supplied by the innkeepers.

"Here," she said. "We must think clearly, but first we must calm down."

I gulped the wine and told myself I wouldn't start crying again. When Mrs. Rainsford came up to tell us that we had a visitor, I dashed downstairs in a loose shirt and jeans, praying it would somehow be more news of Lydia.

Darcy was waiting in the sitting room. He jumped to his feet when I barreled in.

"Miss Elizabeth!" he said, starting toward me. "Good God! What is the matter?"

Unable to contain my worry, I repeated what Jane had told me, which she'd learned from Dad only a few hours ago. Lydia had run off with George Wickham in L.A. She'd sent an email to Kitty boasting about it, and how George had promised to show her a new way of life that would make her rich and free her from the necessity of ever working again. Dad and Mom were upset, though not really worried yet. *I* was the one who knew the truth.

"When I think that *I* might have prevented it," I said, pacing around the tiny little room. "I *knew* what he was. If only I'd told Lydia, my family—" I collapsed onto the sofa. Darcy remained where he was, and I was grateful that I couldn't see his face.

"I am grieved," he said. "Does any of your family know where she is?"

"No. Oh, God." I pushed my face into the upholstery. "Even if I tell everyone the truth, how can they possibly stop a vampire who has already destroyed at least one life?"

He was so quiet that I thought he'd left, but he wasn't quite ready to abandon me to my misery. "I am afraid you have long desired my absence," he said. "If only there were something I could do that might offer consolation."

I choked out some kind of thanks, and he drifted away. I had the feeling I'd never see him again. If it hadn't been for my fear for Lydia, I might have raided Mrs. Rainsford's kitchen for every bottle of wine she had.

But Aunt Sally was right. I had to keep my head. I ran upstairs and told Aunt Sally that I had to get to London at once, collect Jane and take the first possible flight back to New York.

We were packed and ready in half an hour. Aunt Sally went down to speak to Mrs. Rainsford while I went to get the car.

I didn't hear the footsteps coming up behind me. I wasn't prepared when a woman's voice called my name, and I turned to see Lady Catherine de Bourgh.

"Elizabeth Bennet," she said, baring her teeth. "How convenient to find you here."

And then she bit me.

CHAPTER 13

I WOKE UP IN A DAMP, DARK ROOM, MY MOUTH TASTING LIKE mothballs and my neck aching like the devil. I touched the little puncture wounds. They weren't very big, and they weren't bleeding.

But a vampire had bitten me. I didn't feel as if I'd changed, but then again I didn't know how long a conversion would take…if that was what Lady Catherine had intended.

Oddly enough, I didn't panic. I struggled to my knees and looked around. I seemed to be in some kind of cellar; the only light came from a half-blocked window set in one of the dank brick walls. From what I could see, the room was nearly empty except for a pile of rope, loose bricks and some broken pieces of wood. I heard squeaking and tried to pretend I hadn't.

Lady Catherine de Bourgh. Last time I'd seen her, she was lording it over the vampire drinking club. She hadn't shown any liking for me then. Now she was in England, and she obviously had it in for me. How she'd known where to find me, or what she wanted, wasn't as clear.

George had said she'd converted Darcy, and Darcy had pretty much confirmed that. But Darcy had also made clear that he wasn't under her control, and he hadn't behaved as if he took her very seriously.

Still, this had to have *something* to do with his relationship to Lady Catherine. Maybe she was jealous of any woman, vampire or mortal, who got near him. It was all wild speculation at this point. And all the speculation in the world wouldn't get me out of danger now. I knew in my heart that Darcy wouldn't save me this time. Lady Catherine wouldn't have done any of this if she thought I might be rescued.

Okay, Lizzy, I thought. *What will get you out?*

I got up, groaning at the stiffness in my legs. How long had I been here? Hours? A day? I had no sense of the passing of time, but my mouth was bone-dry and my stomach was growling.

Feeling my way, I explored the room. I crouched to examine the wood pieces. Several of them had been broken into sharp points. The rope, while a little mildewed, was still in one piece.

Maybe, as George said, it would take a lot more to kill a vampire than a stake through the heart, but I was willing to give it a try. Lady Catherine wouldn't leave me here indefinitely. She'd be back, and I'd be ready.

Gathering up the stakes, I hauled the rope to the back of the room. I knew Lady Catherine was twice as strong as I was, if not more; I'd have to rely on the element of surprise. If I had to go, I'd go knowing that Darcy wouldn't think I was a helpless little human female.

After a few hours the room got darker, and I guessed that night had fallen. I fell asleep, jerked myself awake and listened, my nerves stretched well past the breaking point. The door opened and a pair of hulking men came in, lifted me by my arms and dragged me out of the building. The sticks and rope stayed behind.

There weren't any streetlamps in the vicinity, and I had no hope of breaking the men's painful grip. I had the idea that I was still in the country, and I was convinced of that when the men half carried me across a field, past a tiny country road and through a wood to an estate at least as big as Pemberley.

Lady Catherine was holding court in an immense drawing room dripping with gold paint, red velvet and black drapes heavy enough to smother a dinosaur. Several young men lounged around her chair, all of them startlingly handsome. Lady Catherine's daughter sat on a smaller chair beside her.

"So, Miss Bennet," Lady Catherine said as the men threw me at her feet. "You can be at no loss to understand the reason for your being here."

"All I know is that you're guilty of kidnapping," I said, climbing to my knees.

Lady Catherine snorted. "It is much more than that, my dear."

I stuck up my chin. "You should know that people will be looking for me. My aunt—"

"Your aunt," Lady Catherine said scornfully, "has been taken care of."

I got about a half step toward her before her thugs hauled me back. "What have you done to her?" I demanded.

"She is unharmed. And you may remain so, should you give me certain assurances."

"I still don't know what you're talking about."

"You ought to know that I am not to be trifled with. Do you deny that you have, by your arts and allurements, seduced my nephew into offering you his patronage?"

I laughed weakly. "Why would he do that? He's been working against my family since we met."

"I saw you at Rosings. I observed the nature of his infatuation, which would never have come about were he in his right mind."

"You know him better than I do. *Is* he in his right mind?"

She surged to her feet. "Miss Bennet, do you know who I am? Mr. Darcy is my kind, bound to me. As he is shortly to be bound in matrimony to my daughter, Anne."

Anne de Bourgh gave me a blank look. I stared back. "How lucky for him. Are you sure *Darcy* wants it?"

"You are an ignorant mortal of no understanding. While in their cradles, his mother and I planned this union. It was meant to be for a lifetime; now it will be for eternity."

I was able, for a few seconds, to feel sorry for Darcy. "What do you want from me?" I asked, my teeth beginning to chatter.

"Tell me once and for all if Darcy has attached you."

"I'm not anyone's 'attachment,'" I said.

"And will you promise me never to enter into such an engagement?"

I was too angry to be smart. "I will not promise anything."

She descended from the platform, stretching her thin lips wide. "You have made a mistake, Miss Bennet. A very serious mistake."

There wasn't much hope of my escaping. The logical part of me knew I'd be lucky to be alive five minutes from now, and if I were, I wouldn't be much more than a slave.

The emotional part of me was stronger. I turned and ran straight for the thugs, who were too astonished to stop me. The door was only a few yards away. I could hear the whisper of feet behind me, feel hot breath on my neck, a hand reaching…

I hit a hard, warm surface. Darcy steadied me and pushed me behind him.

"Kindly stay where you are, Aunt," he said.

Lady Catherine skidded to a stop, her long skirts swirling around her legs. "Darcy!"

"Good evening, Lady Catherine. Had I known you would be inviting Miss Elizabeth to your little gathering, I would have been sure to make myself available."

"But…but my dear nephew…" I peeked around the implacable barrier of Darcy's body, and Lady Catherine smiled at me sweetly. "Miss Bennet and I were only having a pleasant tête-à-tête."

Darcy glanced at me, unmistakable worry in his eyes. "You do not deceive me, Aunt. I know you too well."

Her face hardened into a gorgon's mask. "*You* are the one deceived, Darcy. Deceived by this puny mortal who thinks herself the equal of our noble lineage. She has dared to ask *me* to make her one of us."

I could feel Darcy stiffen. "That is a lie."

"Of course it is!" I said, my voice muffled by his coat. "I don't know if she intended to convert me, but she wasn't about to crown me queen of Transylvania!"

Darcy pulled me forward and held me close to his side. "You have made a mistake, Aunt," he said softly. "Miss Bennet is under my protection."

Lady Catherine gave a squealing growl of frustration. "Can you not see, Darcy?" she demanded. "Use her if you must, slake your thirst, but do not presume to consider her more than a thing to be used and discarded like any other mortal!"

Darcy's smile was chilling. "Perhaps you have forgotten that you no longer rule me, Aunt. Nor are you, or those of your persuasion, likely to continue your forcible conversions much longer."

Lady Catherine had already been pale, but now she was almost transparent. "Your cursed experiments!" she exclaimed. "You will not succeed, Darcy!"

"I believe I will, Aunt. Just as I will find the means to negate the *strigoi* need for human blood and produce a cure for my sister."

I looked up into his face, a germ of understanding forming in my mind. How could I ever have thought this man was evil? How could I help but love him?

The few seconds of silence following his declaration didn't last. With a shriek of rage, Lady Catherine flung herself at Darcy. He tossed me back, ordered me to run and met his aunt's attack head-on.

Once I'd wondered what it would be like to see a battle between two vampires. I didn't have to wonder any longer. It was complete, utter, no-holds-barred savagery. Their movements, as graceful and intricate as those of the finest martial artists, were hardly more than a blur to my human eyes. It seemed that Darcy and his aunt were perfectly matched, neither more likely to win than the other. Darcy wasn't holding back because she was a woman; if he had, she would have destroyed him.

I was forced to stand on the sidelines with the boy toys and the handful of other people in the room. If I'd had any way of interfering, I would have gone after Lady Catherine in a flash. But I couldn't even get near them.

I thought of the pointed sticks I'd found in my prison. Maybe I wouldn't have to get near Lacy Catherine to make a difference.

One of the thugs made a halfhearted attempt to stop me as I ran for the door, but he was too absorbed in the fight to chase after me. I blundered down the steps and ran in the direction I thought the guards and I had come from. There was just enough of a moon to help me find my way.

I found the small brick building and, tripping and cursing, felt my way inside and to the rear. The stakes were still there. I gathered up as many as I could carry and ran back the way I had come. No one blocked my way as I dashed into the house.

Both the battling *strigoi* were beginning to show signs of wear and tear. Lady Catherine's movements were slowing, her dyed-blond hair falling into her face, and Darcy had begun to breathe heavily. I dropped the pile of stakes to the floor, keeping the longest in my hand. One of the boy toys glanced at me, pretty lips curved in an O of surprise, as I aimed the stake in Lady Catherine's direction and hurled it.

The first missile missed her by about a foot, the second one by a lot less. I got off the third just before the thugs tackled me. I heard Lady Catherine shriek. From under one thug's arm I could see her breaking Darcy's hold. She lunged toward me, scattering the guards, and almost had her hands around my neck when Darcy roared and leaped on her back.

It was as if some avenging fury had taken hold of him, and in seconds he had her pinned to the ground, crouching over her with teeth bared and muscles rigid.

Something happened then, an exchange I couldn't hear or understand. Darcy stayed where he was a few moments longer and then suddenly sprang to his feet. Lady Catherine didn't move; her face was slack, her body limp. She'd lost, and she knew it. The battle was over.

Darcy turned his back on her, put his arm around my shoulders and supported me as we walked through the hall and out the front door. As soon as we were outside my knees threatened to give out and I plopped onto the stairs.

"Is it really over?" I whispered.

He sat beside me. "Yes," he said. "thanks to your courage. Lady Catherine will never trouble you again."

"Are you…are you hurt?"

"I am very well."

I covered my face with my hands. Now that it was really hitting me, I wasn't sure I'd be able to stand again.

"I didn't think you'd come," I said.

"I will always come for you, Elizabeth."

"But no one knew. She said she'd…taken care of—" I started up, feeling ill. "My aunt! I have to find her!"

"She is safe, I assure you." He laid his hand lightly on my back. "We found her not far from here, under guard. Lady Catherine's minions were quickly dispatched."

"You didn't… I mean, they aren't…"

He removed his hand. "They have been temporarily incapacitated."

I realized that I'd managed to hurt his feelings, as impossible as that seemed. "I'm sorry," I sighed. "I know you wouldn't hurt them."

He leaned forward to look into my eyes. "Do you?"

I glanced down at his hands, long-fingered and strong and elegant. "Yes. I'm sorry about this. About everything that's happened. I owe you my life."

"You owe me nothing," he said grimly. "It was entirely my fault that Lady Catherine attacked you in the first place."

He was referring to his proposition at Rosings…one he'd never make again. "It wasn't anyone's fault," I said, feeling those treacherous tears gathering again. "Lady Catherine is obviously crazy."

"Nevertheless, I knew she was angry that I had… I

should have anticipated her reaction when she learned that I—" He broke off, looking away.

Unthinkingly I took his hand. "It's hard for a sane person to know what a crazy person might do."

He looked straight into my eyes in that mesmerizing way of his. I was so close to getting sucked in that I started to be afraid. I let go of his hand.

"When George Wickham told me about vampires," I murmured, "he— Oh, my God. *Lydia!*" I succeeded in standing this time, but my stomach preferred to remain sitting. I swayed, and Darcy caught me. I could feel his rapid heartbeats, his cheek against my hair.

"George Wickham has her," I gasped. "I have to get back—"

He picked me up as if I weighed as much as a goose-down pillow and strode away from Lady Catherine's mansion, walking into the wood and coming out the other side without breaking a sweat.

A pair of cars were parked by the narrow road I'd seen earlier, my rental and another I didn't recognize. Several people were standing beside them—Aunt Sally, Charles Bingley and—

"Jane!"

CHAPTER 14

DARCY PUT ME DOWN, AND I RAN TO MY SISTER. WE HUGGED until both of us were breathless.

"Lizzy! Are you all right?"

"I'm fine." I turned to my aunt and hugged her, as well. "Are *you* all right?"

She smiled, though her face looked a little haggard in the moonlight. "Thanks to Mr. Darcy."

I looked over my shoulder. Darcy was keeping his distance, the moonlight and shadow turning him into a hero from a romance-novel cover.

"We have much to thank Mr. Darcy for," Jane said, turning to smile at Charles. He looked back at her adoringly, and I knew that somehow they'd gotten back together.

Jane's expression grew serious again. "I was so worried when I returned to London and found both of you gone. I hadn't expected to return from Paris so soon, and all I could learn was that you'd left six days ago...."

"Six days? But that means I was unconscious— Oh, my God."

Jane hugged me again. "Mr. Darcy came to the flat last night," she said. "He was frantic.... I've never seen him look so upset. Charles was with him. Darcy said he had been searching for you for two days, but had finally received some information that had given him an idea as to where you might be. I insisted on coming, of course."

"But Jane…" I struggled to gather my thoughts. "What about Lydia? All this time—"

"Lydia is fine." She moved closer to Charles, who put his arm around her. "Charles told me the whole story. The evening after I called, before he knew you were missing, Darcy had his private jet fly him to Los Angeles. I'm not sure how he did it, but he tracked down George and Lydia just before they were about to fly off to South America."

I could feel the adrenaline draining out of me, leaving me limp as an overcooked noodle. "But…but was Lydia hurt?" I asked. "Was she…"

"No damage was done," Charles said, an almost dangerous gleam in his eye. "Wickham may have planned to convert her, but he didn't get around to it."

"Where is he now?"

Charles shrugged. "Gone. And not likely to show his face again, at least not anywhere Darcy can reach him."

I didn't ask how Darcy had managed that. "Where is Lydia now?"

"Home with Mom and Dad. She's not exactly sorry, but Darcy took her aside and talked some sense into her. I don't think she'll be running off with another vampire anytime soon."

I couldn't believe it. In less than a week, Darcy had saved Lydia and taken care of Wickham, then found and rescued me from a fate possibly worse than death.

"That's not all, Lizzy," Jane continued. "We don't have to worry about Bennet Labs anymore. We just received a huge anonymous grant. BL will have full independence, and all the funding it needs for the next five years at least. Charles is in full agreement."

"Should have seen it weeks ago," Charles said, blushing. "BL can do better work just as it is."

My heart was so filled with happiness that for a minute I couldn't speak. All Darcy's doing. I knew he had taken Charles to meet Jane on purpose. He'd given up his determination to keep them apart.

And as for the grant money... Maybe Charles had had something to do with it, but I was pretty sure that the funding had come straight from Darcy.

"Jane," I said, "I don't know what to say."

She laughed. "Poor Lizzy. Not your usual state, is it?" She squeezed Charles's hand. "I have one more piece of good news. Charles has asked me to marry him."

I bounced. I couldn't help myself. "Jane!" I shrieked.

Charles gave a sheepish grin, grabbed Jane and kissed her soundly. I backed away to give them a little privacy. And because there were things I needed to say to a certain gentleman vampire.

I turned to face him. He hadn't moved an inch. Those few feet between us felt like miles.

"Thank you," I said around the lump in my throat. "Lydia, Jane, BL... Your compassion and generosity..."

The sadness in his smile was very human. "Your sister should not have confided so much to you."

"I'm glad she did. Otherwise, I wouldn't have been able to tell you have grateful we are. Jane, Lydia, my family—"

He sighed. "If you will thank me, let it be for yourself alone. Much as I respect your family, I thought only of you."

My face felt as hot as a sunburned jalapeño. "I... You

must be tired. Do vampires get tired? Maybe you need a little…" I gulped. "I'd be happy to donate, if you—"

"That will not be necessary."

"But I want to do something for *you*," I burst out. "Isn't there anything—"

"Yes, Elizabeth. There is." He moved closer, gliding on silent feet. "You are too generous to trifle with me. If you feel the same as you did at Rosings, tell me so at once. *My* affections have not changed, but I will never mention it again if you say the word."

My mouth fell open. I shut it again. "Your affections?"

"My pride," he said with that same sad smile, "did not permit me to confess the fullness of my emotions. Let me do so now. I love you, Elizabeth Bennet."

My legs had gotten into a bad habit of buckling, which was getting downright embarrassing. Darcy caught me again. His lips were nearly touching mine, but he didn't kiss me.

"Do you fear me, Elizabeth?" he murmured.

I stared at his mouth. "No."

"Have I hope?" He shifted his arms so that the whole lengths of our bodies were touching, chest to chest, hip to hip, thigh to thigh. "You need do nothing that discomfits you. I ask only that you consider a life with me. You will have all the freedom you desire; I will not seek to bind you."

"You mean," I said, "you won't bite me?"

"Not unless you desire it."

"You won't convert me?"

"Never." He searched my eyes. "I would ask you to marry me, but—"

"Marry me? You'd do that?"

"If you would have me."

I stretched my neck a little and kissed him. Still he didn't kiss me back. He wanted to be sure that *I* was sure.

And I was. He could do whatever he wanted to me, and I wouldn't complain. In fact, there were certain things I very badly wanted him to do to me. "I guess vampires aren't any smarter than humans," I said. "I've loved you ever since Charles told me that your first name was Fitzwilliam."

"My dearest Elizabeth…"

This time when I kissed him, he most definitely kissed me back.

A LITTLE WHILE LATER—after we'd all returned to Pemberley, Georgiana had been told the whole story, my aunt was in bed and Charles and Jane were…occupied—Darcy and I made ourselves comfortable on one of the more welcoming sofas, my head on his shoulder and his arms wrapped around me as if he were afraid I'd change my mind.

"What made you decide to ask me again?" I asked. "I wasn't exactly polite about refusing you at Rosings."

"I hardly acted the gentleman," he said, brushing my hair with his lips. "My behavior was unpardonable. No better, in fact, than Wickham's."

I bolted upright. "Don't ever say that! You're exactly the opposite of what he told me."

"Your belief in my virtues is gratifying, but not entirely accurate. As a boy, I took my wealth and status too much for granted. When I was converted—"

"Against your will, right? George lied about that, too. You never wanted to be a vampire."

He nodded. "When my aunt took my life from me—and from her own daughter—my distress was such that my pride and conceit only increased. I was ashamed of my needs and how I was compelled to acquire nourishment. It was many years before I was able to permit myself human company again. Even then I remained proud and arrogant, as your dealings with me so amply illustrated."

"You never doubted that I'd accept your offer at Rosings."

"Never. By you I was properly humbled."

"You're making me blush."

"I intend to make you do far more than blush, dearest Elizabeth."

I snuggled into him again. "Everyone's asleep. We could go upstairs and—"

"After we are married."

"Do you have to be so blasted old-fashioned?"

"Even after two hundred years, certain habits persist."

I leaned back to better see his face. "When did you decide you loved me?"

"I was in the middle before I knew I had begun."

"I guess you were sick of those groupies who fling themselves at everything with fangs." I looked at him sideways. "Speaking of groupies... I saw you with those women outside Rosings."

Yes, vampires could definitely blush. "As I said, I am not proud of what has been necessary to keep myself alive, but for Georgiana's sake—"

I pressed my finger to his lips. "You did what you have to do, and I know you did it as gently as you could. But I'm afraid I'm not going to be able to live with a harem."

His eyes widened. "Elizabeth, I swear to you—"

"Just promise you'll tell me if you...have to *see* someone else. I'll understand."

Copper tinged his deep blue eyes. "They meant nothing to me, Elizabeth. I have already made arrangements to find nonhuman sources of blood, and my research—"

"It's all right, Darcy. I know you can't live on me

alone. I won't be jealous." I pouted. "Well, maybe just a little."

He hugged me until I cried uncle. "You will never have the slightest cause."

"Humph." I smiled to show him I wasn't angry and began playing with his fingers. "So what *did* make you ask me again after I was so nasty to you?"

"It is difficult to explain. Your manner at Pemberley… your friendliness toward my sister gave me hope."

"Your letter made me question everything I'd believed," I said. "When I met your sister, and saw the binders with all the thank-you letters, I knew I'd been wrong."

He shook his head with a wry smile. "When one has lived two centuries and possesses such considerable assets, generosity is easy."

"But you've used those assets for good." I sat up to face him, loving the strong lines of his face, the black hair that fell into his eyes, the sensuality of his lips. "You've given so much to medicine, to children."

He ran a strand of my hair through his fingers. "It was not entirely unselfish. For two hundred years, Georgiana has suffered malaise and weakness so severe that she is seldom able to leave Pemberley. I have sought a cure since medical progress has made such exploration possible. It is why I have acquired interests in so many biological research companies, including Charles's. I had already been encouraged by the discovery of a certain drug that could break the bond between a *strigoi* patron and his protégé."

"That's why Lady Catherine couldn't control you. Georgiana took the drug, too?"

"Yes."

"And Wickham?"

"He would not have known of it. I would not be sur-

prised if he found a way to kill his patron, which is another way of breaking the bond." He shook his head. "As
for my obsession with acquiring Bennet Laboratories…
I knew that your researchers had created and utilized in-
novative techniques and protocols that many larger companies would not have ventured to. I had hoped that one
day, with my guidance, BL might have found the cure for
Georgiana and perhaps even produced a blood product of
sufficient efficacy to remove *strigoi* reliance on human
donors."

"But you couldn't have told anyone what you really
wanted."

"It is possible to turn such work in certain specific directions if one is subtle."

"You're not always subtle," I murmured.

"Not where certain subjects are concerned." He kissed
me lightly. I pulled him down. Sometime later I said,
"What made you decide to give BL the grant?"

"Need you ask?"

I sighed. "You're too good to me. And Jane… You
gave your blessing to Charles, didn't you?"

"I was a fool. My misjudgment of their mutual affection was egregious. Charles never suspected my deliberate
interference. I made known to him my mistaken impres-
sions of your sister's intentions, and he was eager to go
to her again."

"If you were wrong, so was Charles. He should have
stuck with the woman he loved. I wish I could have given
him a piece of my—"

Darcy silenced me with another kiss. "That is all in
the past. It is the future that concerns us now."

The future. A future in which I would grow older, and
Darcy would stay exactly the same. I knew he'd love me
even when I couldn't walk or see or hear. But the idea of
giving him up, ever…

"I want you to bite me," I said suddenly.

He sat upright. "Now?"

"Why not? I have to get used to it sooner or later."

"I will not impose—"

"I'm marrying a vampire. 'To love, cherish and donate.' All those other women will just have to wait in line."

He pulled me around on his lap and gazed into my eyes. "There are certain dangers inherent in repeated donation."

"You mean I'll become a vampire."

"Theoretically, every *strigoi* can control the process according to his will. But instinct can be very strong, especially where affection is involved."

"Is that such a bad thing?"

"Think about what you are saying. You may not feel so sanguine once you are changed."

"Sanguine. That's a good one." I grew serious again. "I don't want to have you for one lifetime, Darcy. I want you for eternity."

He gave me a dubious look, and I quickly convinced him of my sincerity.

Darcy, Jane, Charles and I flew back to New York a week later. Jane could hardly contain herself when I told her I was to be Elizabeth Bennet-Darcy. Georgiana begged us to be married at Pemberley, and Darcy immediately offered to fly my whole family to England.

Dad had tears in his eyes when I told him about Darcy's proposal, though I wasn't yet ready to tell him just what kind of proposal it was. He seemed to sense that Darcy was behind BL's unexpected salvation. Darcy insisted on asking him for my hand, and he gladly agreed.

Mom was ecstatic. "Oh, my sweetest Lizzy! Oh, Lord, what will become of me? I think I'm going to faint!"

* * * * *

LITTLE TO HEX HER

Janet Mullany

* * *

For Pam Rosenthal, my partner-in-crime.

ACKNOWLEDGMENTS

Thanks to Susan, Mary, and Colleen;
and Tracy Farrell and Lucienne Diver.

Dear Reader,

When Susan Krinard invited me to participate in this anthology, I knew immediately which Austen I'd choose, pretty confident that no one else would want it. As Austen said, Emma really is "a heroine whom no-one but myself will much like," and therein lies both the genius of Austen and the pitfalls for a lesser writer putting her own spin on the novel. What's amazing about Emma is that everyone in the novel likes her (with the exception of Mrs. Elton), at least for some of the time. I don't mind so much that she's a provincial, meddling, busybody (oh, go on, Janet, tell us what you really think) but I knew I couldn't sustain interest—mine or yours—in a heroine who's so blissfully unaware of what's under her nose.

And then there's Mr. Knightley, the only Austen leading man who you know is going to be a massive bore in bed; even virtuous Edmund Bertram has the promise of more friskiness between the sheets (but then I love *Mansfield Park,* too).

The answer, I decided, was to give both Emma and George I-hate-my-first-name Knightley a twenty-first-century awareness of themselves and, dare I say it, some acknowledgment of their shortcomings—Emma is very conscious of her situation as the not-so-big fish in the not-so-small pond. Knightley is a success in some, but not all, areas of his life.

What I mainly took from Austen was her setting of the idiosyncratic village and its social strata, which in this case is the city of Washington, D.C. Perhaps the White House really does need a witch on retainer and we all know Capitol Hill is full of bloodsuckers....

I hope you enjoy this anthology and my take on *Emma,* which I had so much fun writing.

Best,

Janet Mullany

CHAPTER I

Present Day Washington, D.C.

Emma Woodhouse, handsome, clever and temporarily rich, with a comfortable (borrowed) apartment and happy disposition, seemed to unite some
of the best blessings of existence; and had lived
nearly twenty-nine years in the world with very
little to distress or hex her.

"SHE TURNED ME INTO A FROG."

I bit back the comment that he seemed to have recovered.

"I can't tell you how sorry I am, Elton. I know it's no
excuse, but it is almost full moon, and Harriet tends to
be…" I paused and added a description of my assistant
that seemed lame as soon as it was out of my mouth. "Difficult."

"Difficult!" Elton's shout almost drowned out the
sound of early-morning traffic on K Street.

I winced. Harriet, heading for her werewolf time of

the month, must have been an intimidating mix of horniness and ferocity.

"I'm so sorry. The agency will give you a full refund and free membership for the next year—two years. We'll also pay for any dry-cleaning costs or—"

"At least. Look at this shirt! It was blue yesterday."

"I believe it's residual frog. It will wear off. I'm pretty sure it's gotten more blue since we've been sitting here…"

Elton was staring at a fly that had landed on the table to investigate a crumb from my croissant. His tongue flickered at the corner of his mouth. He drew back, his chair clattering on the sidewalk.

"Oh, Christ!"

"Can I get you another latte?" The waitress, who had been hanging around nearby, wandered over, gazing at Elton as though she wanted to have his pointy-eared offspring then and there. She probably did; it's the traditional relationship between elves and humans. I generally cast a mild protective spell over myself when one-on-one with an elf.

Elton waved her away and dropped back into his chair, a horrified expression on his face. I thought he was about to burst into tears.

"Did you see that?" he whispered. "I nearly— I wanted to—"

I patted his hand, hoping the embarrassment of temporary frogness would prevent him from considering legal action. The last thing I needed was some sleazy vamp lawyer sharpening his canines on the agency. "It will wear off, I promise you. I'm so sorry, Elton."

"Is that all you can say?" He glared at me. "It's your fault."

"Of course I take responsibility for—"

He leaned forward, stabbing a finger for emphasis, the tips of his ears quivering. "I only dated Harriet because you wanted me to, Emma. I thought you were interested in me and you were so insistent I agreed."

"But I never date clients. I—" That's what Isabella had said. *Never, never get personally involved with clients, Emma. It gets sticky.* Right. They end up wearing frog-green polo shirts and nearly eating flies blocks from the White House.

"You'll be hearing from me," Elton said. He stood. "You're not doing very well with the agency, are you? You should have stuck to teaching jocks History of Witchcraft 101. I'm sure Isabella would be distressed by this."

I stood, too, and held out a hand which he ignored. "May I say again how very sorry I am and if the agency can make it up to you in any way—"

But he'd turned and strode away from me, while the waitress chewed her lip ring and glared at me as though I'd ruined her life, too.

My ASSISTANT CHEWED ON a piece of beef jerky and made a sound that might have been a growl as I entered the office.

I placed my laptop on the desk and was tempted to growl back. Instead, I logged on to review any new memberships that had come in overnight, and considered how best to confront Harriet in her delicate condition.

Once again, I wished that my sister, Isabella, had not left when her husband was invited to join a European magic think tank in Brussels, leaving me to run her dating agency for a year. I'd been quite happy holding down a succession of postgraduate magic lab positions ("cauldron washing," as my family referred to it) and, as Elton reminded me, teaching a few undergraduate magic courses to jocks who needed the credits. I couldn't say I was serious about an academic career, but I wasn't frivolous about it, either. I just needed…time to sort out who I was and what I wanted to do, and that's what I was still saying five years after my master's.

One thing was for sure. I absolutely didn't want to make a career of matching lovelorn paranormals and I found Washington, D.C., with its cliques and rituals and stuffiness, unwelcoming and unfriendly.

I flipped my laptop shut. "Harriet, we must talk about last night. How are you feeling?"

She slurped on a cup of some horrible werewolf brew. "Okay. He was a jerk. I thought he liked me."

"So did I. I'm sorry. But I lent you my spell book to look at, not to use. You said you were interested in going back to school."

"He said bad things to me. Like he thought I was stupid." She hung her head and mumbled something about having a photographic memory at her time of the month.

"Oh, Harriet, you know that's not true. You're very bright. But, please remember that turning a client into a frog, however rude or aggravating or insulting they are, must never happen again. I'm afraid Elton may sue us. He was very angry and unpleasant and upset, and I don't blame him. What if something had eaten him?"

She bared her teeth. "*I* would have eaten him." Then her eyes filled with tears. "He said he only dated me because you wanted him to. He liked *you,* Emma."

I patted her shoulder and handed her a tissue. "Yes, I know. That's what he told me, too, and I had no idea."

"He said he took those pictures of me with his cell because you were next to me."

I saw that she was about to analyze every episode, every conversation with Elton, and cause herself more pain. "We have to move on, Harriet. I expect Elton will leave the agency—I've offered him a full refund, and I hope he won't make trouble for us. I think he mentioned something about going on vacation soon, so at least he'll be out of town for a bit and he'll cool down."

She sniffed. "You know what elves are like. Bloodthirsty."

She was right, even if it was the pot calling the kettle black. Elves swarmed through the Pentagon and populated defense contractors; if Peter Jackson got one thing right in *The Lord of the Rings,* it was the elves, armed to the teeth and marching in military formation; so much for frolicking in the woods wearing pretty jewelry.

Harriet and I set to work, routine stuff of creating pairings on the database for our next gathering and processing new members—our clients got a five-minute "date" with each other at our mixers, at which they'd grade the people they'd met as possible friends (really a polite way of saying they weren't interested) and possible people they'd like to meet one-on-one. We, of course, would effect the introductions and make sure that compatible people, or rather beings, since the clientele consisted of more than humans, got to spend time with each other.

I wasn't terribly efficient that morning, replaying my meeting with Elton in my head. I'd missed a major vibe from Elton to myself, and wasn't my job to detect that sort of attraction? Harriet, with her werewolf nose, could sniff out pheromones (particularly at the full moon), which was particularly useful, but even she'd missed Elton's real object of desire.

And God, no, I wouldn't date an elf. All that ego, and his hair products cluttering up the bathroom, not to mention the bloodthirsty instincts and the talent for holding grudges for centuries.

Yes, I was glad Elton was out of town.

To cheer us both up, I suggested a walk along the Mall at lunchtime, and Harriet became quite puppyish at the idea. We strolled down to the Tidal Basin where the cherry trees were preparing for their big showcase of the year and said hello to a few former clients. We, or rather Isabella, had had some particularly spectacular successes with cherry tree dryads and Tidal Basin and Reflecting Pool naiads.

My cell rang. "Hartfield Dating Agency."

"Oh, Emma. Emma? Sometimes I don't—I was thinking to myself, I must call Emma and tell her the news, because I know she'll be so excited and—you'll never guess what—remember when I told you about my friend, Jane—it was when we had that thing—"

Missy Bates, I mouthed to Harriet as the flow of words on the line spilled out like beer foam down a frat boy's glass.

"—and she sent me that cute email about what cats would—I sent it to you—wasn't it darling—and the other one, I hope you sent it on to eight of your best friends for luck—"

"Missy, I'd love to chat, but I'm in the middle of something—"

"Oh, I won't keep you a moment—but I have to tell you because you've always been so interested in Jane and we—Knightley gave me a ride home after that concert at the Kennedy Center and it was so—and then there was a text on my cell saying she—but I forgot the funniest bit—and she says she'll be here in two days and I'm not sure whether she's allergic to cats or—so I thought I must introduce her to the agency and then I'll get three months, or is it four, I don't remember—because she doesn't know anyone in town and—Knightley said she was very—but when I—"

"Jane Fairfax? She's coming to D.C.?"

"Yes, oh, silly me, didn't I say? I knew you'd be excited—she's looking for a job at—I had to laugh—when I told Knightley, he—"

"Terrific. And of course you'll get your additional three months for bringing in a new client, Missy. That's wonderful. I'd better let you go—"

I stanched Missy's flood of words with firm promises to extend her membership, cursing the day that I had ever come up with what I had considered a brilliant piece of promotion. My head banged gently, the way it always did after a conversation with Missy, and I took a few deep breaths.

"Jane Fairfax is coming to town?" Harriet asked. "I didn't even think she was real."

"In some ways she's far too real." I sank into gloom, remembering disjointed tales of out-of-town gatherings and trips, my email bombarded with invitations to view photographs online or follow links to Jane's latest activities. Even worse, at events Missy pressed me into a corner to relay, word for word (embellished with many odd diversions and comments), conversations with Jane, while I bleated feebly about other clients who might feel neglected.

"Grrr," said Harriet.

As WELL AS INHERITING my sister's job for a year, I'd also inherited her apartment in a gem of an art deco building a stone's throw from the zoo at Woodley Park. At first I'd thought the strange whooping sounds that woke me at dawn were the gargoyles, until I realized they were the gibbons greeting the new day. I loved the apartment with its huge windows and elegant parquet floors.

I loved the marble and mosaics and gilding of the lobby, the wrought-iron splendor of the dignified slow elevator. I even loved the gargoyles, particularly after I'd drawn the blinds.

There was only one problem with the place, and here he was ambling across the lobby, sporting a toolbelt and carrying a toilet plunger.

"Yo, Woodhouse," said George I-hate-my-first-name Knightley. Despite his disguise as a janitor, he was the owner of the building. He enjoyed the occasional spot of maintenance as relaxation from the world of high finance—*it keeps me humble.* Humble! As though any member of that renowned and ancient family of wizards even knew the meaning of the word.

"Hi, George," I returned, and had the pleasure of seeing him scowl.

"How's matchmaking?" he asked.

"Pretty good. Mostly. Uh." Nothing had changed in the ten years since our awkward (on my part, at least) college relationship. I still lost most of my vocabulary around him.

The toolbelt, sitting low and easy on his hips, clad in snug faded denim, was giving me some inappropriate lustful thoughts.

"Was something clogged up?" I asked and wished

I hadn't. Dumb, dumb, Emma. The plunger probably wasn't a fashion accessory.

"Three-C. Their kid threw his teddy in the can. Is everything okay in Isabella's? I know she had some problems with the garbage disposal. I could come up—"

"No, no, it's fine. Really." Images of him splayed on the kitchen floor, the muscles in his bare arms flexing as he rummaged beneath the sink, flew into my head. I took a deep breath.

"Gargoyles behaving okay?" he asked.

"Yes, fine, thanks."

"You need to be firm with them."

"Right." I backed away. "I'll be— Good to see you, Knightley. I'll just, uh…"

He smirked.

I changed direction smartly and headed toward the elevator, not away from it. A vampire, dressed in fuck-me shoes and the sort of dress I wouldn't dare bend over while wearing, if I dared wear it at all, joined me.

"Sex on a stick," she said as the door closed.

"I dated him in college."

She raised her eyebrows and eyed my neck. "Lucky you."

Not really. Not really lucky at all.

CHAPTER 2

THE PROBLEM WITH ME AND KNIGHTLEY WAS, IN A WORD, ME.

If I'd met him later, say, now, for the first time, I could have handled him, after working with, and particularly teaching, other insecure snotty Ivy League brats from rich, influential families. That's what he was then, only I couldn't see it. I was intimidated by his good looks—lanky, slightly scruffy, with the occasional spot, but still breathtaking—his scarily sophisticated family, his horrible frat house, the casual magic tricks. Never pass someone the box of pizza if you could make it float around the room, loop the loop, release the pepperoni to form their own cute little constellations before burrowing back into the cheese—you get the idea. Our relationship didn't have a chance. I bailed out at the first opportunity and felt elated and slightly shocked at the expression on his face when I told him we were over. I don't think Knightley had ever been dumped before.

But after that he was always around. I'd gone to Europe and bumped into him in Rome. And Paris. London, too. I'd run into him on the campuses where I had my cauldron-washing jobs—just visiting friends, of course. Was it coincidence, as he claimed, or something else?

"Guess who owns our apartment!" my sister had cried in absolute joy. She liked Knightley. Everyone did. (And what was all that about Missy Bates getting a ride home with him from the Kennedy Center? Surely he wasn't dating her. His ear would have fallen off.) Scowling, I tossed my purse onto a chair as I entered the apartment.

"Bite me," I said to a gargoyle waggling its tongue at me outside the window and snapped the blind down.

I flopped onto the sofa and stared at the photo of me and Isabella shortly before she'd gone abroad, when we'd visited the Washington Monument. She'd insisted that her last weekend in town consist of touristy activities, because when you live in Washington you never go to any of the spots the tourists visit. It's as unhip as standing on the wrong side of the escalator on the Metro. It was her way of saying goodbye to the city. So there we were, squinting into the sun and wind, big smiles and wavy chestnut hair and blue eyes, two pretty witches on a girls' day out. (And that was another thing that screwed up things with me and Knightley. Because I was young and dumb, two years behind Isabella and playing ugly duckling to the princess, to mix my fairy-tale metaphors, I didn't think much of my looks then. At the back of my mind hovered the unworthy thought, *What does* he *see in me?*)

The phone rang.

"Emma? Isabella and Jim said I should give you a call when I get into town. This is Frank. Frank Churchill."

I assessed the voice. Rich, deep, seductive—almost definitely a vamp, something Isabella hadn't mentioned.

"Oh, yeah. Hi. Isabella said you'd probably call. How are you?"

"Good." There was a moment's hesitation. A shy vampire! How cute. "I don't want to be forward, but I was wondering if you and I could get together for a drink."

"Sure." Already I was scrabbling at my daytimer. Now! Tonight! I'll wear a thong! I took a deep breath and calmed myself. He was a vampire, I reminded myself. Even on a phone call he could assess my pulse and send me into a stupor of lust. "I have an appointment tomorrow afternoon that should end about six, so why don't you meet me after?" I gave him the name of the bar and he assured me he could find it.

I was being kind to Isabella's husband's friend, nothing more. He might even become a client—in which case my interest in him should cease immediately. So he might not become a client after all.

JANE FAIRFAX STIRRED her ginger ale. We sat at a table in a courtyard that was part of a restaurant converted from a Foggy Bottom carriage house. Above us a vine curled new tendrils on a trellis and geraniums and ivy tumbled from a hanging basket.

Jane was gorgeous, as unlike plain, dumpy Missy as I could imagine, tall and slender with a yard of long, dark, rippling hair and huge violet eyes. Her ice cubes gave off small sparks and she blushed.

"Sorry."

"That's okay." Interesting. Only a witch who was upset about something would spontaneously leak magic.

"You see, Emma…" she fiddled with her straw some more. "I'm not into dating at the moment. It was Missy's idea."

Most people who are given a free trial membership

said that, so I nodded encouragingly. Who wants to admit that they're hard up for company of the opposite sex?

"I'm here to explore some job possibilities and I have to find an apartment, and…well, I'm busy."

"Of course." I went into my standard spiel. Since everybody here claimed to be busy, or too important, to think of dating, that really didn't mean anything, either. "But because you're new in town this is such a great opportunity for you in terms of networking and establishing a social circle. You can make some valuable friendships and professional connections with Hartfield Dating Agency. And for a busy professional like yourself it can be very hard to find the time or resources to do that on your own."

"I guess so." She sighed. "I've just ended a fairly serious relationship. I'm not sure I'm ready…."

"Oh, absolutely. I understand." I beckoned to a waiter who was standing nearby staring at Jane to bring us fresh drinks. "This might be a good time to have some fun, Jane. Find some people to hang out with. We're not in the business of pairing people up who don't want to be paired up—we'd lose all our clients that way!"

She smiled for the first time at my pathetic joke.

"So," I continued, flipping through my daytimer, "let's see what we can do for you. The first thing I'd suggest is that you and Missy come to our next mixer. It's very low key and you'll have a fabulous time even if you don't meet any males you're interested in. We hold our mixers in the private room here; it has a great atmosphere and our clients always enjoy themselves. Strictly between the two of us, Jane, is there any being you wouldn't consider dating, or hanging out with?"

She pushed her glass away, the ice cubes giving a pale green flash. "No vampires."

"Okay. I'll keep that in mind. They're not everyone's cup of tea, I know." I felt a mild fizzing excitement at the thought of my six o'clock cup of tea. "And you're welcome to attend as an observer and not participate in the timed meetings; in fact, I'd recommend it for the first time. You can see how things work. Some clients like to go straight to a lunch date and skip the mixer, but usually they're people who have a very clear idea of their ideal mate."

We talked a little more business—she agreed to fill out our online survey in the next few days, where she'd give the agency more information on her interests and background, but since she had been referred by an existing client, that was more of a formality than anything else.

Generally at this point clients, particularly female ones, would open up, feeling more relaxed with the process. I asked about her work as an economist, and received a mind-bogglingly complicated answer at which I nodded thoughtfully and assumed an intelligent expression. I tried not to look at the display on my cell to see what time it was, while wondering if Jane's lack of personality had anything to do with her failed relationship. Finally, after she'd prodded her ice cubes with her straw a little more, she murmured that she had another appointment, we shook hands and I saw her leave with a sigh of relief.

As she headed for the exit into the main part of the restaurant, a man stepped through the doorway and held the door open for her.

He watched her leave.

"What are you doing here, Knightley?" I asked.

"Looking for my date. Wow. Who was that? One of your clients?"

"Possibly. I don't think your date is here. Try the main part of the restaurant."

"Oh. Yeah." He looked around the courtyard as though finally realizing that a couple in a corner, oblivious of everything but each other, and I were the only occupants. For a financial wizard he seemed to have trouble counting. "She was really hot. Maybe I should get you to fix me up."

"The application's online, Knightley." I ostentatiously looked at my cell. "I'd love to chat, but I have another appointment in a few minutes."

"Sure."

He held the door open for me as I made my way into the restaurant and retired to the restroom to replenish my lip gloss and fluff out my hair. For a brief moment I considered fixing Jane and Knightley up together. *She was really hot.* They'd deserve each other. She could talk economics while he described his toilet-plunging technique.

Armed with a minor spell to prevent me presenting my jugular in the first five minutes, I sauntered back out into the courtyard. To my annoyance, Knightley was still there, in conversation with someone who could only be Frank Churchill.

They both turned as I approached. "Good seeing you again, Frank," Knightley said. He looked at me and smirked. "Have a good time, sugar."

Sugar? "I think your date's in the bar, Knightley. Big chest, blonde?"

"That's her. See you."

"Bye," I said, and the word turned into a sigh as Frank Churchill bared his teeth in a smile.

My first thought was that I should have used a stronger spell, my second was that I didn't care. My third, as common sense took over, was that I'd better be careful.

He was gorgeous. More gorgeous than vamps have a right to be, with dark blue eyes and dirty blond hair, tall and lithe. He made Knightley look ordinary. He had charisma up the wazoo and he hadn't even said anything to me yet.

He pulled out a chair at a nearby table. What he did say was quite ordinary, except for his voice, which was even better than on the phone, rich and molten like a great dessert. "You look so like your sister. How's she doing?"

"Oh, good, good," I babbled, fortunately landing on the chair as my knees gave way. "I didn't know you knew Knightley."

"I met him at Iz and Jim's place. That's the funny thing about D.C. We all know each other. It's like a collection of villages." He snapped his fingers and the waiter, who'd previously ogled Jane, now seemed to have made a radical change in sexual preference. Frank murmured an order and the waiter left.

"You're ordering for me?"

"You'll like it." He leaned one arm on the table. I stared, awestruck, at the golden hairs on his forearm. Would he notice if I bent forward and licked them? "Talking of mutual acquaintances, wasn't that Jane Fairfax who was just here?"

"Yes, you know her?" White-hot jealousy shot through me. How dare he notice another woman when I was here!

"Sure. She was here visiting Missy one time. Iz and Jim had us all over to dinner."

I couldn't imagine Missy babbling away to this beautiful man; I suppose she used some sort of protection, because even the most amateur of witches knew how to do that.

"Isabella said you were her legal advisor for Hartfield," I said, attempting normal conversation, "but she didn't tell me much else about you. Where are you working now?"

He mentioned a major law firm in town and I nodded. Vamps do well as lawyers, having a natural rapaciousness and a penchant for long, billable hours, well into the dark.

"Better than driving a cab," he added, with a grin and flash of white canines, mentioning the other favored occupation of vamps.

At that point, the waiter and a colleague returned, bearing an ice bucket and a tray of food, and spent much time fussing around, staring at Frank, and making sure we had everything we needed (or everything Frank needed). Finally, having run out of napkins and cutlery to press unnecessarily upon us, they left.

"Champagne?" I squeaked.

"I thought you'd like it." He eased the cork off with barely a suggestive froth, and poured. He raised his glass to mine. "To success."

"To success," I echoed.

I stared at the plates of hors d'oeuvres. "Who do you know in the kitchen? They never cook stuff like this for the agency."

"Vamp by the name of Angelo, sous-chef," Frank said. He picked out a delectable little pastry item. "Mention my name. Open up."

Somehow I managed not to lick his fingers as they brushed against my lips.

Heaven, I thought. I'm in heaven. A vampire was gazing into my eyes, plying me with delicious food and drink, and I had enough enchantment to keep me safe (probably) while I could enjoy the nuance of danger that came with the moment.

"I've wanted to meet you for years," Frank said.

"Why?" I sprayed phyllo crumbs lightly over the table.

"Iz talked about you. Your family's so proud of you."

"They are?" I was dumbfounded. Iz was the one with the successful business, the handsome husband and the great apartment.

"Oh, yeah. And, well, I had a bit of a crush on Iz, and…"

"I seemed like the next best thing?"

There's nothing quite as comic as an embarrassed vamp. He blushed and flapped his hands in an ungraceful sort of way. "Oh, God, no. I'm sorry. No, no. I mean, that if someone like Iz said her sister was so terrific, then you had to be really something."

"I hope I live up to your expectations."

He refilled my glass and stared into my eyes. "You will."

With a great effort I stopped myself sliding under the table in a boneless heap of desire. It was only standard vamp stuff, I reminded myself, his biological destiny. In a way he couldn't help himself. He'd be coming on to the geraniums in the hanging basket if I wasn't here—and even as I thought that, petals showered onto the table like drops of blood.

"You're good," I said, "but please don't read my mind."

"Okay. Sorry." He picked out another delectable edible for me.

I knew I shouldn't. This time I let my tongue touch his fingers.

"Bad girl," he said softly, and I saw his canines touch his lips. "Bad, hungry girl."

"Can I get you anything else, sir?" Our waiter insinuated himself into our private circle of lust, effectively breaking the moment.

"No, we're fine," Frank said. "So tell me how the agency is doing, Emma. Any new clients?"

I didn't tell him about Elton, but I gave him a rosy picture of my successes, or, to be honest, near successes, hoping he was being a gentleman and not probing my mind. He nodded approvingly at my referral promotion, and laughed when I told him that so far my only success was Missy Bates.

Dusk was falling and so was I, or at least thinking about falling down with Frank on top of me. I rose, attempting a bright professionalism. I intended to walk home to clear my head before diving into a cold shower. "This has been great, Frank. I've really enjoyed meeting you, but I'd better get going."

He tossed a couple of bills onto the table. "I'll put you in a cab."

We made our way through the restaurant and onto the street, where Frank raised a finger and a cab drew up—vamp-to-vamp efficiency. I would have had to jump up and down waving both arms in the air for a good ten minutes.

His knee brushed against mine as we settled in the backseat and I feared my protective spell was wearing a little thin. He took a strand of my hair and tucked it behind my ear. "So, if I became a client, do you think Jane Fairfax and I would suit each other?"

"Oh, please, Frank, I'm not the madam of a bordello. Besides, she doesn't seem like your type."

"Ah. And what do you think my type is?"

"Once you've filled out the agency survey I could give you a better answer. For instance, I'd need to know if you wanted to date outside your subgroup."

He moved closer to me. "Definitely, and I think you know my type. Blue-eyed witches with curly hair."

"I don't date clients, Frank."

He nodded. "Then I think I'll postpone becoming a client. Sorry."

The cab drew up at my apartment building.

"I'll see you to the door," he said.

"Oh, you don't have to—" I wondered if I should invite him up for a drink, but supplies were low in the apartment. I didn't have anything nearly as good as that champagne; in fact, it was more likely that I had a half-full bottle of diet soda and some stale wine I was saving for cooking. I might as well be offering him a drink of me, which I probably was, and which might not be that good an idea.

He took my hand as we walked up the mosaic steps to the entrance. "I'll call you. Let's have dinner soon."

"Great. Yeah. I'd like that. I—"

His kiss was soft and sweet with enough of a touch of elongated canine to graze my lip and hint at danger and wildness. It stopped my babbling immediately.

"Good night." He stepped into the shadows and disappeared.

"Show-off," I muttered as I pushed open the door into the lobby.

To my surprise, Knightley emerged from the elevator, his face full of disapproval. There, I thought, was someone who didn't score tonight.

"Hi, Dad, sorry I'm late," I chirped.

"Very funny, Emma. Do you really think it's smart to mess with vampires?"

"About as smart as messing with pneumatic blondes, Knightley."

"It's hardly the same," he said with the arrogant tilt of the head I disliked so much. "You don't even know Churchill. What's that on your front?"

"You used to have a better grasp of anatomy— Oh, shit." I dabbed at the unpleasant-looking blob on my white shirt and wondering, horror-struck, how long it had been there. "Eggplant, I think."

"Hope you didn't get any on your friend the vamp," he drawled. "Good night."

CHAPTER 3

"AND THEN WHAT HAPPENED?" HARRIET ASKED AS WE SET up for the mixer, the first I'd hosted. I was nervous about it, even though I was following Isabella's instructions to the letter.

"I changed my shirt." I flipped open my laptop and turned on the wireless connection. "Can we stop this table wobbling?"

"You took your shirt off in front of Knightley?"

"No. Back in the apartment." I ducked under the table with a folded-up piece of paper and wedged it under the leg.

"You really like this Churchill guy," said Harriet in one of her rare moments of intuitive wisdom, followed by one of her normally clueless statements. "But not as much as you like Knightley."

I was saved from having to respond by the arrival of a shy, vaguely hairy person with a badly knotted tie and a copy of the *Washington Paranormal Paper* in his hand. "Uh, hi. Uh, I have the coupon."

"Great. Welcome to Hartfield Dating Agency, Mr.—" I glanced at his credit card. "Mr. Martin. If you decide to sign with us after tonight, your $20 admission will be discounted from a six-month or more membership. Now, I'll need your address and phone number, please…" My heart sank as I typed in his information. Even for a werewolf, a species not known for its social skills, he was homely and painfully shy.

Harriet beamed at him with great interest, which made him fidget and blush under his facial hair. "Here's your name badge and a drink ticket. The bar's over there, I'll show you, and snacks—"

"To your left," I interrupted her. "Have a great evening, Robert."

"Bob," he mumbled and peered at Harriet's name badge. "I…"

"Go have fun," I said, and steered him past us and into the room. I introduced him to a small group of regulars who stood in a circle discussing sports. I took a quick look around. It looked good—candles glimmered softly on tables and clients chatted happily together. The doors stood open to the courtyard where Frank and I had sat a few nights before; it was going to be warm enough again to sit outside.

Harriet scowled at me when I came back to the table. "Why did you do that? I liked him. He smelled good."

I was tempted to remind her of her last dating adventure, but didn't want to upset her. "Frankly, Harriet, I think you can do better than that, whatever his scent is like."

We both watched as a woman approached, leaving damp footprints in her wake. She wrung out her clinging wet garments, which sprang into the shape of a cute spring dress and her bare feet assumed strappy sandals. A toss of her limp greenish hair achieved a miraculous sheen and bounce. As a final touch, her minimal breasts swelled into a high, round swimsuit-issue pair. She handed us a coupon.

As I took her details, I motioned her to come closer. "You might want to lose the boobs. False advertising."

The naiad grinned and deflated her breasts. "Okay."

Some regulars came in—one pair holding hands, and I felt a swelling pride that they might be leaving us soon, for entirely all the right reasons.

"She's so hot," the male of the pair, a vampire whispered to me. "And her blood— Oh, my God, Emma, you wouldn't believe how—"

"I'm so happy for you," I said, pleased that the relationship had become serious. "Now go have fun."

That, I reminded myself, was the downside of dating a vampire. Eventually, the issue of blood, or rather my blood, would come up with me and Frank, and I wasn't sure I was ready for that sort of commitment. So far things had been casual—lots of texting and flirtatious emails. He'd sent flowers, which had made the gargoyles hoot with laughter. We'd talked on the phone. A lot. And to-night…well, after our mixer, Frank and I had plans.

"Hi, Emma." I was jolted out of my pleasant reverie by a familiar voice.

I met the gaze of a pair of hard, obsidian eyes framed by blond hair and pointed ears. "Oh, Elton. It's good to see you again."

To my relief none of his clothes were frog-green. He had an equally beautiful woman on his arm, another elf. He tossed a coupon and a $20 bill onto the table and gave a small, unpleasant smile. "For Augusta. I believe I'm still a member."

"Hi, welcome. I'm afraid we don't take cash. It says here on the coupon..."

"How quaint," Augusta said. "Elton, you didn't tell me what a cute little place this is." She looked at me. "I love that dress. I thought it was so darling when it came out last year."

"It's my sister's," I said and could have kicked myself.

Harriet growled at their backs.

"Don't let them bug you," I said, hoping they wouldn't bug me, either.

But despite the unwelcome presence of Elton and Augusta, the conversation level in the room behind us was warm and friendly, lots of laughter and the sound of chinking glasses. I did a quick magic scan and couldn't detect anything unusual, other than a bit of magic showing-off by males trying to impress females—tricks with ice cubes and cutlery and so on. The evening was going well. More regulars arrived, and a few more who had been lured in by the advertisement.

As usual I heard Missy Bates before I saw her.

"...oh, I am so clumsy—Jane if you could just—Knightley you are so very—oh and look there's our Emma, how are—you see how my shawl caught on the purse and I—but of course Knightley—and then Frank..." A tightly knotted group approached, Missy and Jane, and to my surprise, Frank and Knightley.

"Twenty-buck special." Knightley offered his credit card. "Hi, Harriet. You're looking good."

Frank, engaged in disentangling Missy's shawl from the clasp of Jane's purse, looked up and gave me a smile that tingled all the way to the soles of my feet. "Emma," he purred.

"Hi, Frank." I dropped Knightley's credit card and

scrabbled beneath the table to retrieve it in an undignified way. Knightley was busy introducing Jane to Harriet; I didn't think he'd noticed.

"I thought I'd like to see you in action," Frank said. He offered his credit card. I waved it away.

"I'll be rather busy. I don't know if I'll have time to talk to you much."

"I'm sure it will be worth the wait," he said with a smoldering look that almost made me giggle.

"You shouldn't turn down business," Knightley addressed me for the first time.

"And how are you, George?" I responded. "I didn't know you were available."

He put his arms around Jane and Missy's shoulders. "I've come to keep these two lovely ladies company."

Missy squealed a little in excitement and the unfortunate shawl began a downward slide, as did her bra strap. Jane, elegant and beautiful in a plain black dress that made me feel overdressed in comparison, seemed indifferent.

"I think I'll go inside and make sure things are going okay," I said to Harriet and followed the group inside. I ran through my usual checklist—made sure waiters were distributing trays of canapés, that people had drinks and that no one stood terrified in a corner. Those, I dragged out from their isolation and made introductions. After all, they were there to meet new people, and I'd spent a long time memorizing details about my clients so I could introduce them and get them talking to each other. I left Elton and Augusta alone. I also left Jane and Missy alone—Missy was running off at the mouth as usual, and I figured that if Jane did want to be an observer only, then she was about as safe as she could be from unwelcome advances. Very few dared breach the Bates conversational defenses.

And, to my annoyance, I had Missy Bates on the books for at least three more months since she'd brought Jane in as a client. Not for the first time, I wondered why Isabella had tolerated Missy for so long. Generally, Isabella would have had a quiet lunch with a client like Missy and explained that it wasn't fair to keep taking her membership fee. Missy never had more than one date with a prospective mate—males ran from that continuous prattle—and it didn't seem fair to keep her hopes up. It wasn't fair to the agency, either, I reasoned, having someone as dowdy and vocal as Missy around. On the other hand, she seemed quite happy hanging out with Knightley and now with Jane.

I saw Harriet enter and sniff the air. I'm not sure how she could detect Bob Martin among the many scents at her disposal, but she did—I saw her start across the room.

I got there first. "Bob! Are you having fun? I'd love you to meet Celia." I led him to the naiad whose breasts had achieved their former centerfold glory.

He stared at her and spilled some beer.

"You're both new, so why don't you tell each other a bit about yourselves? Great!"

Harriet stopped in midstride and glared at me. At the same time, Augusta seemed to notice her for the first time, and said, quite loudly, "That one? Oh, my God, Elton. That funny little furry thing?"

They sniggered with each other, their heads bent together. I started toward Harriet but Knightley got there first. He took her hand and led her onto the open space near the speakers where a few couples were already dancing.

Knightley, dancing? He never used to dance. He was quite good at it, too, twirling Harriet around and then bending her into a sort of modified tango swoop that made her giggle.

The two of them made me feel like a chaperone at a high-school dance.

I needed a drink. I made my way to the bar, where Frank sat, and ordered a martini. Hoisting myself onto the barstool I slid off my shoes and wiggled my toes. All in all, I was quite pleased with the way the evening was going. People seemed to be enjoying themselves; a few couples I had introduced had retreated to corners for quiet conversation. Celia, the naiad, had abandoned Bob and was winding herself around someone who could only be a vamp on the dance floor. Bob had found some other werewolves to hang out with. I deserved a quick break, after which I planned to make a few more introductions.

Then it struck me that Frank hadn't said a word. I turned to him and saw he was staring at Missy and Jane.

He noticed me looking at him and smiled. "Sorry. I was miles away. Is her hair real, do you think?"

I looked at Jane's luxuriant dark waves of hair. "I guess so. I hadn't really thought about it."

My first reaction was to wonder if I'd overdone the protective spell I usually assumed for gatherings that would involve vamps and elves. Although the spell would wear off as the evening progressed, I really hadn't expected to find Frank so, well, dull tonight. His dangerous vampire charm had evaporated and he seemed to be finding the ice cubes in his glass more interesting than me. At any moment I expected him to go home, claiming his fangs ached.

I placed my empty glass on the bar, consulted my

folder, pushed my feet back into my shoes and, with Harriet's help, searched out the clients who'd requested one-on-one meetings. We settled them at tables in the courtyard, where there were fewer distractions and a more romantic atmosphere, and supplied them with scorecards. They had five minutes to impress each other.

I watched nervously. Some people could do this well; others went into babbling rants of the best and biggest spell they'd cast or a quick delivery of their resume, as though they were applying for a job. Their scorecards had suggested talking points, to which some clients stuck with dogged determination.

"I have a cat," a witch sitting at a table nearby blurted out to the vampire who sat opposite her. "Do you like cats?"

"I've never..." he replied. "I've heard their blood is... I mean..." They both glanced at their scorecards. "Do you attend sports events often?"

I restrained myself from slapping my forehead. I wasn't trying to listen in, but I did like to keep an eye on things. Celia had signed up for a membership, to my delight. I paired her first with a cute elf who proceeded to lecture her about his job writing government proposals, which she met with an equally tedious account of day-to-day life at the Federal Reserve. All going well, in fact.

My stopwatch beeped and I signaled my clients to move to different tables.

Harriet appeared with a plate of canapés that we shared, and I had another martini. As our clients met their last prospective partner, I could overhear Jane and Missy preparing to leave.

"I'm fine. We can walk."

"But your shoes—they're so cute but I—or a bus, it's

only a few—but then we'd have to—or maybe Knightley can give us a ride—although—"

"I expect he'll want to stay. It's still quite early."

"Oh! You mean—well, I have to get up early tomorrow but maybe—or do you think Emma may—"

"I don't think she drove. No, it's okay, really. We can
walk. When I've bought a car—"

"Oh, but parking is so—and the one-way streets are—
you know what Knightley said—it was when we—oh,
no, it was after that, I think, because I remember he offered to—I couldn't walk in those heels, Jane, but then
you're—"

At this point Knightley joined them and gallantly offered them a ride home. My stopwatch beeped again,
I collected my clients' scorecards and Missy, Jane and
Knightley moved into the courtyard. Missy started on a
long-winded discussion on how she and Jane really didn't
need a ride home.

Knightley insisted and Missy shut up for a few minutes. The three of them paused as Missy began to rum-
mage through her capacious tapestry purse.

Frank wandered out into the courtyard and came to
my side. He gave me a light kiss on the cheek. "Shall we
leave soon?"

Jane slipped in her high heels on the cobbles of the
courtyard and Knightley moved to her side, taking her
arm.

"Well," said Missy, "I wonder if—but that's what you
do—Emma, I do hope you will find Jane—she's shy but
some people think she's—she doesn't talk much, although
as I said to Knightley—you had to laugh, Emma, I—"

"Lovely to see you," I said firmly. "I might have someone for you to have lunch with soon. I'll call you. Thanks again for bringing Jane." My duty was done.

"Give me five minutes," I said to Frank.

Oh yes, my spell was definitely wearing off. I was aware of Frank's warmth and his hand briefly on my hip; the flash of fang in his smile. I touched base with Harriet, who was deep in conversation with a pack of werewolves, with Bob Martin gazing adoringly at her, and retrieved my purse and laptop from behind the bar. After I'd settled up with the restaurant, I did one last round of the room, promised to call people who had met someone they really liked but whose name they couldn't remember and finally escaped.

Frank stood in the courtyard, light from a lantern glinting off his hair and accentuating the handsome bones of his face. I stopped for just a moment to admire him. Oh, God, he was gorgeous. Tall and lean, elegant in a dark blue shirt and dark pants, with his suit jacket slung over one shoulder. I'd never gone much for men in suits before—possibly because I didn't know how good a man in a well-cut suit could look (besides, men in suits reminded me of Knightley when he wasn't in janitorial mode). He didn't wear a tie; his shirt was unbuttoned at the neck because vampires liked to show off their own throats. I'd never really seen the appeal before myself.

I was quite sure he knew I was looking at him: that stillness, the pose, was for my benefit. He turned a little so that the light caught his throat and smiled at me. Oh, yes, very definitely a vamp on the prowl.

"Are you hungry?" I asked.

He raised his eyebrows. If he'd been human, my question would have been the equivalent of asking him if he had an erection (and to be honest, I was quite interested in that, too).

"Uh, I mean, it's late for dinner, but if you like we could… I have some stuff at my apartment, or…" I was embarrassed now by my tactless question. "I've pigged out on canapés, so I'm okay." Real attractive, Emma.

He crossed the courtyard to my side in that unnerving flash of movement I could never get used to in vampires. "You're more than okay." He took my chin in his hand and turned my face to his. I fervently hoped that my canapé pigout had not included anything with garlic.

And then he kissed me to stop me from blurting out anything else that was stupid or not in the Big Book of Vampire Etiquette and the entire world shrank to that moment, the man whose mouth caressed mine, and his feel and taste. I was dazzled.

"I think," he murmured, "we should go to your apartment as soon as possible. And, yes, I'm quite hungry."

Oh, my God. He was everything my mother and sister had warned me against, the big, bad sexy vampire, and my protective spell had almost entirely faded away.

His arm around me, we went onto the street where he did the vampire-cab thing again.

We kissed all the way to my apartment and I noticed that Frank made no effort to hide his fangs from me—although how could he have done so when they grazed my lips and tongue. The cab driver flashed his own fangs at us when we arrived and growled something that made Frank laugh.

"What did he say?"

He grinned. "It doesn't translate very well, and it's rather crude. He was, er, congratulating me on my fangs and wishing me well for the night."

JANET MULLANY   359

"You're very sure of yourself, aren't you?" I fumbled for my keys, wishing I hadn't asked.

"I'm a vampire. I can't help my biological destiny."

"You mean I'm your biological destiny tonight?"

He grinned again, all charm and fangs. "Exactly. Don't look so annoyed."

I didn't stay annoyed for long, not when Frank kissed me in the elevator and we emerged, me dazzled and weak-kneed, on the fifth floor. My hands were shaking so much I could hardly unlock the apartment door. I led him into the large living-and-dining space and placed my laptop and purse on the table.

A chorus of whistles and hoots met us from the gargoyles.

Frank strode to the window. "Shut up! One more word from you lot and you're gravel!"

There were some awed whispers and then dead silence.

A little light from outside filtered into the room, and I'd left a lamp on in the bedroom. Frank tossed his jacket onto a chair and turned to me, eyes glittering in the dim light.

"You asked me before if I was hungry."

"Yes." I backed against the refrigerator door, the metal cool against my shoulders. I should really move away if I wanted to open it, but my brain didn't seem to be working very well. "Can I get you anything?"

He walked toward me with the cool, male strut of an aroused vamp. Oh, he was hungry, definitely hungry, fangs out, and hard when he pressed against me. "I think…I think tonight I'll have dessert first."

I shivered with fear and desire. "Frank, I'm not using any protection. My spell for the evening wore off."

He nibbled at my mouth, my neck, my ear. "Don't worry. You haven't dated a vampire before, have you?"

"Not really. No." There was no point in lying to him.

"Two things to remember, Emma. I won't make you do anything you don't want to, and I can guarantee you won't think about Knightley anymore."

"I don't think about Knightley!" I exclaimed with great indignation.

"You thought about him in the lobby."

"Well, yeah. I did, but… Here's a third thing to remember, Frank. You don't read my thoughts."

"Okay. Do you want to cast yourself some protection?" This was the most awkward question of a paranormal encounter, which made the condom thing ludicrously easy in comparison.

"No." I unbuttoned his shirt and touched his hot skin. He smelled delicious, of sweat and male and arousal. Now I wanted to bite him.

"Okay." His hands slid up my thighs, under my short polka-dot dress. "I've been wanting to do this all night. I watched the way your dress moved when you walked. I loved watching you cross your legs when you sat."

He hooked his thumbs into my panties.

"Condoms are in the bedroom," I gasped.

"We won't need them for a while."

He was right. I stopped thinking about anyone except Frank. And then I stopped thinking at all.

CHAPTER 4

"Emma?"

I opened my eyes. The darkness of night had given way to the slate gray of early morning. The sound of traffic outside had diminished and from the direction of the zoo, a gibbon gave a tentative early-morning whoop.

"I have to go." Frank sat on the edge of the bed, wearing his shirt and boxers. His hair was mussed and he looked sleepy and rumpled.

"Okay. I could make coffee," I said, hoping that he would make me coffee and bring it to me in bed and then I could get his clothes off.

"No, it's okay. You go back to sleep."

"What do you have to do at…" I squinted at my clock. "At four in the morning?"

"Racquetball at five, then get a couple of billable hours in before a breakfast meeting."

"I'd love to make you late, counselor."

He leaned over to kiss me in a friendly sort of way, not a fang in sight. "I'd love that, too, gorgeous, but I have to get going."

I watched him step into his pants and button his shirt,

and then pause in front of the mirror, although I wasn't quite sure what he could actually see there, to shove his hair into a semblance of tidiness. All very graceful and sexy, just a normal vampire morning after. He sat on the bed again to put his socks on, keeping out of my reach.

I would have loved to pull him back into bed with me, but I felt tired and sated and slightly sore—naturally a vamp would know some positions I'd only seen on the Internet, and some that I don't think anyone had seen anywhere. And I liked to look at him, this exotic male creature wandering around my bedroom.

"I'll text you." He bent to kiss me and nuzzled my neck. "God, you're so sexy."

I heard his footsteps across the parquet floor then muffled by the rug in the living room, followed by the sound of the door opening and closing.

Frank's most recent nuzzling at my neck seemed to have resulted in a sting rather like a minor burn. I touched it with my fingers.

Oh, holy shit. I leaped out of bed and ran into the bathroom. God, I looked a mess, mascara ringing my eyes and my hair on end, no wonder he couldn't wait to get out of the apartment. And there on my neck, were two little puncture wounds and a trail of dried blood. No bruise— a vamp who knew what he was doing wouldn't bruise you.

I couldn't believe it. Sometime during the night I'd let him bite me. He must have thought I was an absolute slut, and by vamp standards I was, letting him bite me on the second date. Oh, God. Would my name and number be written in vampiric runes on the walls of every legal office men's room in D.C.?

Worse yet, I couldn't remember him doing it, let alone

giving him permission. What was that he'd said? *I won't make you do anything you don't want to.*

So I could only conclude that I'd allowed, or, worse, asked him to bite me. And while Frank was busily fulfilling his biological destiny I had had unprotected (in the magical sense) sex. What else might I have done, or said, that I couldn't remember?

At least I didn't feel light-headed—he couldn't have taken very much blood. It was more of a token bite, a vamp marking his territory, a cute little drama starring Frank as a mutt and me as a fire hydrant.

What an idiot I was.

I returned to the bedroom, stripped off the sheets and hurled them into the laundry basket, trying to ignore the seductive wafts of male vampire and sex that rose from the linen.

Then I stepped into the shower, turned on the water as hot as I could stand and stayed there for a very long time. Never again, I swore. I would not let Frank Churchill's fangs, or any other part of his anatomy, near me. I would keep my clothes on and swaddle myself in enchantment when in his presence.

Pink, squeaky clean, wearing a fluffy blue bathrobe that dated from my undergraduate days and that only one man had ever seen, I wandered into the kitchen and made coffee. My cell phone, lying on the table, made the annoying buzzing sound that indicated I had a text message.

If it was from Frank, I decided, I'd delete it immediately. Fervently hoping that his opponent would crack his handsome skull during his racquetball game, I pressed the plunger of the coffee press down and splattered hot liquid down the front of my bathrobe and all over the kitchen counter.

R U OK?

It was my sister. I couldn't say I was relieved, because if she had picked up on my distress, I'd have to offer some sort of explanation. Or maybe there wasn't anything witchy in Isabella's message at all, only that she was concerned because I hadn't emailed or called in the last few days. I'd been too busy sending flirty little messages to Mr. Frank the Fang.

I mopped up the counter, poured myself a cup of coffee and decided to delay things by sending her an email. I then made the discovery that my laptop, half in and half out of its bag, was turned on, the lid cracked open. I was sure—fairly sure—that I'd put the bag down on the table when Frank and I entered the apartment. I knew my thoughts had been on something other than checking my email or playing computer games.

Maybe Frank had woken even earlier than I thought and checked his email, but he had a highly sophisticated cell that did everything except make toast. So why would he want to use my laptop? And not say anything about it?

I touched my fingertips to my violated neck. This wasn't good, any of it. And I wasn't going to email Isabella, because she'd immediately wonder what I was up to before six in the morning—she knew better than anyone how I could hardly bear to drag myself out of bed before it was fully daylight. No, I'd drink my coffee, do the laundry and go to the gym. I would not hang around the apartment becoming paranoid and imagining the worst. I'd made a mistake, that was all, and I hoped I'd learned something from it.

And, however much I might deny my stupidity, I'd

had a terrific time in bed with Frank (the bloodsucking creep). I almost regretted that I couldn't remember the biting.

"OOH, FLOWERS!" SAID HARRIET with her usual grasp of the obvious.

They were indeed obvious, a small forest of sunflowers, roses and hydrangeas, a few birds of paradise poking out of the top, and some orchids to round everything off. I hoped they weren't for me. The bouquet, which lost a few blooms squeezing through the office doorway, screamed *Put a ton of the fanciest flowers in the biggest vase you have to impress the little lady.*

Frank's pre-deflowering bouquet had been an understated cute masterpiece of Shasta daisies.

"Who are they from?" Harriet was almost jumping up and down with excitement.

"Frank," I muttered as I opened the card.

For my delicious sexy Emma.

I sent him an email: *Thanks for the flowers. Emma.*

A perky out-of-the-office reply bounced back to me. Frank, it appeared, was out of town until after the weekend, something he'd neglected to tell me this morning. A night of great sex did not compensate for being made to feel like a fool the next morning, something I'd learned ten years ago, or thought I had. A pen cracked in my fingers with a small flash of fire. I was reminded of Jane Fairfax's sparking ice cubes.

"I like your scarf," Harriet said. Obviously, she was dying to know if there were any telltale marks beneath.

I took cover behind the monstrous blooms that took up most of my desk. "Thanks. We have a lot of emails to answer from last night. Can you see if you can find a nerdy sort of male for Missy Bates? I more or less promised her a lunch date."

I made my obligatory gushing phone call to the restaurant to thank them for last night and see if anyone had left any personal items behind—cell phones, the occasional dental retainer or pair of eyeglasses, and once, according to my sister, a single shoe, as though Cinderella had attended.

"Thanks again, and we'll see you in two weeks," I finished, about to disconnect the call.

"Two weeks?"

"Is that a problem?"

I could hear the rustling sound of pages being turned. "I'm sorry, Miss Woodhouse. I have it here that your next event was canceled."

"Canceled? How about the next one?"

More rustling. "We don't have any more bookings for you until September."

"Oh, no." This must have been something Isabella forgot to tell me about. Maybe the restaurant had misunderstood, thinking that with Isabella abroad, the agency's bookings should be canceled. "Do you have any evenings this summer where we could have the party room and a few tables in the courtyard? Please?"

They looked, I begged, cajoled and threatened, but it was no use. Hartfield's bookings, if they had ever existed, had disappeared into thin air. I glared across the office at Harriet who was making soft amorous growling sounds on the phone, and finally plucked a flower from the bouquet and threw it at her to get her attention.

"What's up?" she said.

I explained the situation to her.

"Why would Isabella do that?"

"I don't know." Maybe it was why she'd called this morning. "We'd better get to work on finding another location. Can you call the *Washington Paranormal Paper* and the *Post* about our ads, please—keep the space but tell them we'll send new copy. And let me know if you think of somewhere suitable—you know the city better than me."

Two hours later my desk was giving off occasional sparks and a bird of paradise wasn't looking too good after spontaneous combustion followed by a dousing with cold coffee.

"Nothing," I said. "They're either too expensive or they just won't work. Any luck?"

"Well…there is one place."

"Great! Where?"

"The roof of your building. I know Knightley rents it out on weekends and it's really nice."

"Harriet, you're brilliant! Did you call him already?" She shook her head. "I think you'd better talk to him."

"Why? Okay, no big deal."

I left a message on his work phone, thinking feverishly. We could have an awning for shelter against the evening sun—the vamps would throw hissy fits if we didn't provide some shade. There was a clubhouse on the floor below we could use for the one-on-one, five-minute sessions, or if it rained, and we'd have the events catered, get some pretty flowers in containers for decorations—it would work brilliantly. Just so long as Knightley agreed, and if Thursday nights were available. Or at this point, any night. I scribbled figures on my notepad, figuring out the cost of more email blasts, bigger ads, more promotion.

Right on cue the agency's bookkeeper, Larry, called. "Hi, Emma. We have a few problems."

"Problems? What sort of problems?"

"I'm having trouble reconciling things. I'll email you the details. I'm fairly sure we can sort it out easily. Take a look and get back to me."

My heart sank. From only my few weeks at the agency I knew I was in for hours of cross-checking and poring over reports.

I took a break and tried calling Isabella, but got her voice mail. I assured her I was fine and so was the agency, and that we'd talk soon.

Finally, I retrieved a message from Knightley saying he'd drop by my apartment with contracts over the weekend and to call him back—our first piece of good news all day. I called back—straight onto his voice mail, of course—and told him I'd be home the next morning.

I asked Harriet what she was doing for dinner.

She smirked. "I have a date."

"Not that Bob Martin guy, I hope."

"Actually, yes. Is there a problem with that?" She bared her teeth.

"So long as he isn't a client. He seems really nice, but don't you think he's a bit—" short, shy, hairy "—I mean, I think you might get bored with him."

She shrugged. "Maybe. What are you doing?"

"Going out to dinner on my own." It was a split-second decision. I didn't want to talk with anyone—Harriet would have been okay because then we could have talked business and I wouldn't have had to put on a front of everything being great. I wanted some good food and wine and solitude.

"Not with Frank?"

"He's on a business trip."

She nodded. "How about Knightley, then?"

I made a face.

ISABELLA'S EMAIL THE NEXT morning made me whoop with glee and hit the print button.

Knightley knocked on the door at almost exactly the same time.

"Look!" I flung the door open and handed him the picture.

He frowned. "A snowstorm in a cone?"

"You have it the wrong way up. Look. It's a baby. Isabella's baby. I'm going to be an aunt!"

He gazed at the picture, now the right way up. "That's a...?"

"Yes. That blob is my niece or nephew. Isn't that great?"

"Oh, wow," he said, his voice soft. "A baby."

"You are such a girl," I said, elbowing him. His gray eyes were filled with tears.

He sniffed. "It's amazing. Do you think that's an arm or leg?"

"Possibly. I think it pretty much looks like a shrimp."

He laid a manila folder on the kitchen table. "Do you want to call her? I can always come back later."

The phone rang and I grabbed it, thinking it might be Isabella.

"Emma? Oh, Emma. You'll never—I can't believe—I said, 'Jane, there must be a mistake, you—' but the guy from the dealership—and we don't have a—you must come—" the sound became muffled.

I waved at Knightley who was edging toward the door. *Missy Bates,* I mouthed. I covered the phone. "I think

she's in some sort of trouble." I took my hand away.
"Missy. Missy? Are you there? I think you have the phone
upside down. Okay. What's wrong? Take a deep breath.
Start over."

She responded with another flood of words. Even for
her, this was incoherent.

Knightley took the phone from me. "Knightley here.
Calm down, Missy, tell me what's wrong."

He frowned as she shrieked and babbled. Eventually,
she had to pause for breath. I heard, quite clearly, "And
you're in Emma's apartment? Oh, that's—I've always
thought—but…" and she was off again.

"Okay," Knightley said. "We'll be over. Twenty minutes."

"What's going on?" I said. "Is she hurt? It's not one
of her cats, is it? Have they called 911?"

He shook his head. "No, it's not that sort of emergency.
No one's hurt. It's something to do with Jane. Come on,
I'll drive."

I stuffed the ultrasound picture into my jeans pocket
and we ran out to the elevator. Knightley's BMW was
parked a couple of blocks away.

"This is very impressive," I said, settling into the
leather seat. "No Doritos on the floor. No apple cores in
the ashtray. You've come up in the world, Knightley."

"Put on your seat belt." He eased the car out into the
Saturday-morning traffic.

If we hadn't been on our way to help a distressed
friend, with the additional worry of not knowing exactly
what her problem was, I would have enjoyed the ride. In
a year or so, when Isabella and Jim were back in town, we
could bicycle, towing a toddler in a brightly colored cart,
or take him or her to a café where we'd sit at an outside

table in the sunshine. They might even have a dog, like the couple running with a golden retriever loping along beside them. Later, my niece or nephew could be one of those kids in a car crammed with sports or music gear, on their way to soccer or orchestra. And me...Aunt Emma. I liked the sound of it.

But I wondered where I'd be then; would I still be in D.C.? Would I have found someone special and be contemplating a family of my own?

Knightley tapped his fingers on the steering wheel as he expertly steered the car west across town. We turned onto Wisconsin Avenue, sleazy and cheerful, tourists browsing sidewalk displays of watches and beads and designer knockoff purses, and then onto one of the picturesque cobbled side streets.

"I've always liked these old houses," he commented. "Not worth what you pay, though. I'd like something with a bigger yard."

I wondered if he, too, was daydreaming about a future family.

A few more turns and we were on the block where Missy lived. Knightley slowed as we both started to look for a parking space.

To my surprise Missy and Jane were outside on the brick sidewalk. For a moment I wondered if they'd locked themselves out. I could hear Missy talking and talking, and still hear her when Knightley squeezed his car into a tight parking space and we opened the doors. As we walked toward them, I could see that Missy was excited rather than agitated.

She ran to us, talking all the while "...such a surprise—I have no idea—but Jane, do come here and tell—I was

outside picking up the newspaper when—and this weekend she—"

"Someone gave me a car," Jane said.

She gestured at a bright, yellow, shiny VW Bug parked
outside their house.

"That's so cute!" I said. "Lucky you! Who's it from?"

"We don't know!" Missy cried. "Such a surprise—
they delivered it this morning and Jane and I were getting ready to—you know she's been looking at cars, and I
said—and the insurance is paid for a year—" She tugged
at my sleeve and whispered, "Emma, I think it's from her
ex-boyfriend—you know, the one who—but she's probably told you already, and my feeling is she—oh, look at
Knightley, he's so cute…."

I didn't often agree with Missy, but the sight of Knightley, sleeves rolled up and peering inside the hood at the
Bug's engine, in serious conversation with Jane, was
rather nice. His butt, a little too skinny when I knew
him, had improved immensely.

"Congratulations, Jane," Knightley said, rolling his
sleeves down and buttoning his cuffs. "Welcome to driving in D.C."

"Oh, you're so funny! You must have some iced tea—
coffee—no, stay to lunch. Jane, do we have some—or
maybe we should celebrate by—Emma, you must be—"

"We're fine, Missy," I said, knowing that once trapped
in her cat-filled house we would be there for hours.
"Knightley and I have something to do. I mean, I have
and so does he," I added, noticing her look of delighted
interest. "Congratulations, Jane. It's a lovely car."

"Thank you," she murmured. She stroked the car's
shiny surface and looked at Knightley with a shy smile.
"You didn't need to come over, but it was great to see

you. It's just that Missy was so excited and we wanted to share the news."

"No problem," Knightley said, grinning back like a fool. "We'll see you later." Out of earshot, he muttered, "That's absurd. She'll spend hours trying to find a parking spot near the house and the shocks won't last a month on those cobbles."

"It's a great car," I said.

"Maybe, but whoever gave it to her wasn't thinking straight." He clicked the remote to unlock the car doors. "Do you want to grab some lunch?"

"What?" I stared at him. "You're asking me to have lunch with you?"

"Whatever," he muttered and opened the car door for me.

"I mean, it's only ten-thirty."

He shrugged and pulled away from the curb with a screech of tires. "Take a look at that contract and give it back to me," was all he said on the ride home. "Call the office next week if you have any questions."

Back in the apartment I called Isabella and we squealed together on the phone, talking about her due date and if she'd be back in the States by then, and how soon she'd know whether it was a boy or a girl. I assured her that the business was going fine, just fine, and that yes, I'd met Frank, and he seemed like a really nice guy, Knightley was fine and the gargoyles were quiet.

I had to go through the same sort of subterfuge when Mom and Dad called a bit later that day. By then, I sat at the dining-room table scattered with reports and statements and saw that, indeed, in the last few weeks, something had gone very wrong with the business's finances. Money had disappeared, apparently into thin air. I'd have to tap into the savings, and lose considerable interest, to make the expenses for the rest of the month.

The worst thing was that I couldn't talk to anyone about it. Normally I took my problems to Isabella, but she was so happy now I couldn't tell her I'd possibly screwed up her business. I hadn't been in town long enough or had enough leisure time to make friends, real friends in whom I could confide. The only person I knew well here was Knightley and there was no way I would share this misery with him. He was far too fond of taking over. Just a few hours ago he'd taken the phone from me and calmed Missy down—something I might have been able to do without his interference, given time and patience. And someone like Missy, creating crises and fluttering around helplessly offering iced tea and adoring giggles, only made him worse.

Knightley hadn't really changed much in the past ten years. He was still the superior, arrogant privileged male, and, worse, he could still jerk my chain.

CHAPTER 5

"You look tired, Emma." Frank Churchill, his face full of concern, put his hand over mine as he slid into the leather booth opposite me. When he'd called and asked to meet, I'd suggested this bar on Capitol Hill where dark oak paneling, leather and the dark-suited clientele precluded any sort of romantic atmosphere.

I was protected by so much magic I could as well have been wearing armour. His touch had absolutely no effect on me; today, he looked like a fairly good-looking guy and that was all. I had only agreed to meet him because after my weekend with the books, followed by a meeting on Monday with my accountant and another this morning with the bank, I needed lunch and a break. I didn't want a big helping of vampire charm; I wanted a burger and fries.

"I am tired," I said after we'd ordered. "Things are pretty busy. How was your trip?"

"Oh, good, good." He nodded. His face was unreadable behind his wraparound mirror sunglasses. "That's actually why I wanted to meet."

The waitress placed our burgers on the table, mine

cooked medium-well and Frank's rare. I started in on the side of onion rings I'd ordered.

"There's something I have to say to you, Frank. I don't remember giving you permission to bite me, although I suppose I must have done, but I'm wondering what else I don't remember about that night. If there's anything else you think I should know, please tell me now."

He ran his finger around the neck of his beer bottle. Without any protection I think I might have swooned. As it was, I saw it only as a cheap vampire trick.

"I'm sorry. You were so sexy, Emma. You smelled so delicious. I asked when—when I thought you wouldn't say no to anything."

"I trust you're not implying it was my fault—that I was so sexy and delicious I made you do it? And you waited three nanoseconds before I had an orgasm to ask me? I was really upset when I found the bite marks."

"Give me a break, Emma."

"No, Frank. You give me a break. Give me some honesty here, or I'll order a stake, and it won't be one with fries."

"Christ," he said. "You're so hostile."

"Do you blame me?" I eyed the furniture in the bar, wondering if I'd worked out enough recently to rip off a chair leg and plunge it into Frank's immaculate shirt front. "So was there anything else unusual that you or I did that night? You didn't invite any of your buddies in, for instance, and put a spell on me so I'd blank that out, too?"

"Of course not! I can understand that you're mad," he said, and I wished I could believe what he was about to say. I didn't really think I'd been the victim of some vampire orgy, but I wondered what I might have said to

him. "You were gorgeous, we had a great time and I...
well, I am what I am, Emma. A shallow bite, a little blood,
is very erotic during sex for a vampire. I think you must
know that. I gave in to temptation, and I'm sorry. You're
pretty magicked up at the moment, aren't you?"

I nodded, my mouth full of burger.

He sighed. "I'm sorry I've lost your trust."

I waved the waitress over. "Can you bring us some
ketchup, please? No big deal, Frank, it's not as though
we have any sort of future together."

He dipped a fry into the bloody juice on his plate.
Eeew.

The waitress returned with the ketchup and Frank
looked appalled as I slopped a generous amount onto
my fries. "Remind you of anything?"

"Emma, what can I do to convince you that I am sorry
for upsetting you?"

I considered what he could do. I couldn't bitch at him
indefinitely; it seemed childish. He knew now I was mad
at him, and I hoped he had some idea why, and that he
wouldn't do the same thing to another nonvamp. I'd prefer to end our relationship, such as it was, on a friendly
note. "Are you going to eat that pickle?"

He smiled and turned his plate, pickle side toward me.
"Help yourself."

"But why did you want to see me, Frank?"

"Well..." he picked at the label on his beer bottle.
"When I went back to the L.A. office this weekend, they
offered me a partnership."

"Congratulations."

"Thanks. But the problem is..." another pause.

He leaned forward and gazed into my eyes. "You know
why this makes things complicated for me. I don't have

to explain it to you. You're so intuitive and smart and I'm sure you've already…well, I don't need to say any more."

In my opinion he'd have to say a lot more to explain whatever it was he was trying to say, but he nodded emphatically as though he'd given me a perfectly adequate explanation. Enjoying my sudden and unexpected reputation as a person of high intuition and intelligence, I could only murmur that of course I understood, before diving into my fries again.

We parted with a friendly kiss on the cheek—there was no dangerous vamp sizzle at all, to my relief—and I returned to the office to find Harriet in tears.

"Clients have been calling me up and complaining," she wailed.

"About what?"

"They said we sold their email addresses."

"What?" This was serious. We never, ever sold or traded an email address. "What sort of material have they been getting?"

She sniffed and showed me an email that had been forwarded to her.

Attention, Washington DC paranormal singles!
A new sophisticated urban solution for finding that special someone!
Save the date now for our debut event, Friday, June 17, 6:30 at the Vineyard Restaurant.
www.elfinlove.com.

"What lame copy," I commented. "And that's at our location—our old location. What's going on?"

Harriet clicked on the link to a site full of gorgeous

swirly patterns and tinkling music. "Oh," she sighed. Her eyelids fluttered and her head dropped forward.

I caught her before she fell out of her chair, and clicked her browser off.

Harriet blinked and shook her head. "Sorry, what did you just say?"

"Please don't visit that site again. It seems to have some sort of magic virus. Are you feeling okay?"

"I'm fine. I was having a great dream about me and Bob. We were dancing in a beautiful cave hung with satin and velvet drapes, and elves were giving us goblets of wine and delicious cakes."

"How clichéd," I commented. "You'd think elves could have come up with something different in the past thousand years or so. But that's not what worries me."

Harriet gasped. "Oh, no, Emma, do you think my computer is infected?"

I assured her it wasn't her fault, while hoping we wouldn't lose too much data. Once I'd started the enchantment virus application, I told Harriet to take the rest of the day off, since it would take several hours of computer time.

After she'd left I began to shake. What if we'd both looked at that site and I hadn't been protected? Would we be lost in some sort of romantic elven dream, sprawled helpless on the floor?

I was pretty sure Elton, with his IT background, had something to do with this nasty trick, but I'd already had one uncomfortable confrontation that day and didn't have the energy for more. By Friday, though, I'd be ready to get myself magicked up and attend the debut event of elfinlove.com, just to see what was really going on.

The enchantment virus application popped up its report

on the screen and I breathed a sigh of relief. Everything was intact. So something had gone right—actually two things had gone right this week: I'd messengered over the signed contract and a deposit to Knightley for the rooftop rental, and Harriet and I had worked our way down the list of extra services we needed for the location—catering, plants, awning, valet parking and so on.

On an impulse I picked up the phone and called Knightley.

"I didn't thank you for the roof rental."

"That's okay."

"No, really, it's going to be great. And you gave me a very reasonable rate."

"You'll have more overhead there. You won't save a whole lot. In fact, it may cost you more."

"Maybe." I examined the chipped polish on my toenails. Another thing to do. My legs were looking a bit prickly, too. And then something made me ask, "What are you doing on Friday evening?"

"This Friday? What do you have in mind?"

I told him about the spam, but glossed over the possible misuse of my client list, and that now Hartfield Dating Agency had competition.

I heard clicking sounds. "Yeah, I got it, too. It's in my spam folder. They probably hit every known paranormal single in town."

"Don't click through! You'll wake up in seven years and a day with your keyboard attached to your forehead and a fried hard drive."

He laughed. "I'm tougher than that. Sure, I'll go with you on Friday. Sounds like fun."

"A singles' bar full of elves? I don't think so. This is business, Knightley."

"Oh, yeah. Sorry, I forgot. I'll meet you in the bar."

I said goodbye to him and disconnected. A date with Knightley—what was I thinking? But it wasn't a date. It was business, as I'd told him. Harriet would probably have accompanied me, but she was out of her depth with elves—I'd learned that the hard way. I could have gone on my own, but I was finding out that although I might pride myself on my self-sufficiency, sometimes it was nice to have a friend.

Or, if not a friend, someone who knew me.

KNIGHTLEY, BEING A GENTLEMAN, had arrived at the bar early so I wouldn't have to wait alone at the mercy of prowling elves. Sure enough, a group of them were having an impassioned conversation about something highly technical—I know it involved Java, and I didn't think they meant coffee, but I couldn't understand much more than that. I could have walked in stark naked and they wouldn't have noticed.

I'd put quite a bit of thought into what I should wear. Not the short-skirted polka-dot dress that I'd worn (for the first part of the evening) when I'd taken Frank home. A suit looked too formal. Definitely not jeans or shorts. Remembering Jane Fairfax's elegance, I finally settled for a plain black linen dress, chunky bracelets that looked like ivory and small gold earrings.

Knightley sat at the bar, one ankle propped casually on his knee, reading the newspaper. A glass of beer stood at his elbow. Now and again an elf or vamp, usually a female, glanced at him, but he paid them no attention. He looked good in a pair of khakis, a blue-and-white striped shirt, his bare feet in loafers. I felt myself give a little sigh.

He looked up as I approached. "Why, Miss Moneypenny!"

"Very funny. Is that beer shaken or stirred?"

"What are you drinking, Woodhouse?" He pulled out a barstool for me with his foot.

I ordered a zinfandel.

"Did you see this in the paper?" He pointed to an article in the Metro section of the *Post*. "A lot of people fell asleep at their computers on Tuesday afternoon. Some odd phenomenon, apparently."

"The junk mail."

"Yeah. Not good. And now it looks like you have serious competition." He folded the newspaper and laid it on the bar. "Are you magicked up?"

"Yes."

"Shall we go in?" He stood and offered me his hand.

I hadn't touched his hand in that way for years. I'd forgotten how my hand, not particularly small or delicate, felt that way when his long fingers were wrapped around mine.

"I'll get this," I said as we approached the check-in table. "Business expense. Oh, hi, Augusta. Fancy seeing you here."

Augusta, wearing a tight strapless violet leather dress, sat at the check-in table. "Thirty dollars, please. Oh, Knightley," she cooed. "We don't have nearly enough males here. Don't you look good enough to eat!"

"And I don't?" I said. "Oh, hi, Elton. How are you?"

"What are you doing here?" Elton gripped my elbow and steered me to one side.

"Research," I said. Being manhandled by a beautiful, blond, pointy-eared thing with such gorgeous, fathomless dark eyes wasn't so bad, even if it did make me think in clichés.

Someone else grabbed me. "Go magic up some more," Knightley hissed in my ear. "You're not even in the door and you're falling apart."

"Oh, bite me," I muttered, and saw a male vamp look at me with interest. I shot into the bathroom and locked myself into a stall—I'd never been much good at administering self-enchantment in public.

When I emerged, to my surprise I saw Jane Fairfax applying lip gloss at the mirror.

Our reflected eyes met.

"Is Missy here?" In a way I hoped she was, because then she'd become Elton and Augusta's problem, not mine.

"No." She didn't sound very friendly.

The door opened and Augusta sashayed in. "Oh, there you are, Jane. Don't hide in here, honey. There are lots of lovely males out there." She admired her own size-two reflection, and whined for our benefit, "God, I look huge today."

Neither Jane nor I supplied the obligatory cries of how thin she looked, and, on the contrary, we were the fat ones.

"I wish I had your hair," she said to Jane.

"Your hair is great," Jane said dutifully.

I was tempted to tell Augusta that I wished I had large, pointy ears like hers.

"You haven't called the senator yet," Augusta said.

I busied myself with mascara to disguise the fact that I was blatantly eavesdropping.

"I'm not sure whether that's the sort of job I want. My background is—"

Augusta interrupted with an elvish tinkling laugh that set my teeth on edge. "Oh, honey, it's a fabulous opportunity. I've told him all about you and—"

"I'll think about it," Jane said.

"Let's have lunch soon. I'm really concerned that you haven't been making the right sort of contacts." This with a nasty look at me.

"Jane, come and say Hi to Knightley." I zipped up my makeup purse.

She gave me a cool glance. "Maybe later, Emma."

"Okay." Thinking the two of them probably deserved each other, I joined Knightley outside.

He handed me my glass. "Mostly elves and vamps. I don't know how many of your clients are here."

"I met Jane Fairfax in the bathroom. Augusta is trying to get her to take a job with some senator."

"You should make friends with her. She doesn't need to hang out with someone like Augusta."

"I don't think she likes me very much. I don't know that she likes anyone much."

"I guess you know Frank Churchill's leaving town," he said, a little too casually.

"Yes, he's going back to L.A."

"Are you okay with that?"

"I'm fine."

"Good. I always thought he had a thing for Jane."

"Jane?" I stared at him. "I don't think so. She doesn't even like vamps."

"Didn't you notice the way they looked at each other? She used to live in L.A., too."

"It's a big place." He was kidding. *Jane Fairfax?* "I thought you had the hots for Jane."

"She's nice enough," he said. "But a bit tight-lipped. I

took her out to dinner the other night and she didn't have much to say."

"That's normal if Missy was talking all the time."

"Missy wasn't there."

And then I got it. Knightley had had a *date* date with Jane and the realization made me feel odd, even though I'd joked about him being attracted to her. I remembered the way he'd smiled at her when we went to see the new car.

We entered the party room, which had an entirely different atmosphere from Hartfield's mixers. Magic was thick in the air, and waiters circulated with drinks that sparked and smoked. Vamps lurked with blatantly exposed fangs. Elves shimmered with danger and beauty, and as we entered, a couple of females approached Knightley, tossing back their manes of gorgeous blond hair.

I grinned. "Looks like you'll be busy. I'm going to take a look around."

He winked at me.

I made my way through the room and looked for current clients.

"Ah, a sweet little witch," a vampire crooned.

"She is bitten," another commented. "But not taken."

In other words, I was a slut who put out for vampires. My vamp clients would know, too, although I hoped they would never be so crass as to mention it to me.

"Come play with us." An elf stroked my arm.

"No, thanks. Hey, do elves like blonde jokes? I have a really funny one—" He snarled and turned away.

I placed my empty wineglass on a tray and looked around to see what Knightley was up to. He was at a table with a female elf draped all over him and a female vamp, fangs bared, on his other side. He had a big stupid grin on his face.

In front of him was a goblet of one of the sparkly blue drinks, half-full.

I hoped he knew what he was doing. I made my way through the room, noticing that most of the crowd were vamps and elves, with a few witches and wizards—not a werewolf or naiad or dryad in sight. In other words, Elton and Augusta were after an elite, powerfully magic clientele, and so far, none of my clients had bitten (so to speak).

That could change, however. I resolved to do more targeted promotion to vamps and elves.

Swatting away a few heavy-breathing vamps, I returned to Knightley's table. "Are you ready to leave?"

His eyes were heavy-lidded and sleepy. He blinked at me.

"Knightley!"

"Ignore her," cooed one of the vamps at the table—he'd accumulated another one during my trip across the room.

I resorted to a spell that had been common in our college days—a simple enchantment that made the recipient feel as if their head had been dunked in a bucket of ice water, recommended for friends falling asleep in class.

The effect was electrifying. Knightley shot to his feet, shaking his head. His chair tipped over behind him with a loud clatter, and the two vamps, hissing, jumped back.

The elf pouted and tossed her hair. "He was mine," she said, as though she was in first grade and I'd taken away her candy.

"Sorry. Come on, Knightley, let's go."

"Sure. See you later," he said to his companions. "Where did you get that spell from, Woodhouse?"

"From you. You taught me that one in college."

"Yeah, but…" he followed me outside, where the polluted night air of Washington smelled almost sweet after the heavy, magic-charged atmosphere we'd just left. He took a deep breath, as though clearing his head. "I was protected. You shouldn't have been able to break through that."

"Not protected enough. They were all over you like a cheap suit."

"Bull. I was having a good time. They were nice girls."

"*Nice girls?* Those vamps were about to have you as a late-night snack and the elf—God knows what she had in mind for you."

"Shall we get a cab?"

"Don't change the subject. No. I want to walk."

We walked together in silence for a while.

"The thing is, Woodhouse," he said as we turned onto Connecticut Avenue, "is that they were pretty potent—"

"Aha! You admit it!"

"Well, yeah. Okay. But I let them, to a certain extent. I was having fun."

"Yeah, I did notice that."

He ignored me. "And, as I said, I was magicked up."

"Sure."

"Sarcasm isn't attractive, Woodhouse. So you used a very primitive spell that broke through the magic of two vamps, one elf and my protection. I wouldn't have thought you had it in you."

"I don't. I'm not much of a field practitioner. Teaching the Theory and History of Magic 101 is about my level."

We walked up the steps to the building, and Knightley fumbled with his keys.

"You're saying it was a fluke?"

"I guess."

Knightley held the door open and we walked into the lobby.

"But maybe I shouldn't have done it," I said. "There's an equally good spell that makes the recipient think they're asleep and their hand is being dipped in water."

He grinned. "I remember that one."

We lingered, waiting for the elevator. "Come up to my place," he said. "It's early and I need a drink to wash away the taste of that blue elfin martini."

Why not? I was curious to see his apartment anyway.

I don't know what I expected, but it wasn't this. True, there was some sort of weight-lifting arrangement on view through an open door, but the living room was furnished with a blend of antiques and dark green leather. Oriental rugs lay on the wooden parquet floor, and paintings and prints hung on the walls. Not a flat-screen TV in sight, although I suspected it was kept in the huge antique armoire against one wall.

"This is really nice," I said, sinking into one of the leather couches.

Knightley handed me a glass of wine. "Is this okay?"

"Thanks. Great furniture," I said, wondering what we were going to talk about.

He sat beside me. "A lot of it's family stuff. My mother asks after you now and again. She always liked you. She said I shouldn't have let you get away."

"Your mother liked me?" I couldn't believe it. "Do you remember when we met your family for brunch? She spent half her time looking down her nose at me and the other half waiting for me to use the wrong fork."

"That's just her way." He shifted beside me. "Why did we break up, Emma? I never really understood it. I liked you. You liked me. And I thought, for a first time, we didn't do so badly."

"It wasn't my first time."

"Oh, yeah. The captain of your high-school debating team." He made a face.

"Chess team, actually. Wait, what are you saying, Knightley? I got your cherry?"

He rescued my wineglass as I whooped with laughter. "Well...yeah. It was my first time. I mean, going all the way. So why did you break up with me right after?"

"It wasn't the sex." I really shouldn't be sitting next to Knightley talking about sex, whatever his taste in interior design, or, more likely, his taste in interior designers combined with a huge budget. "That was perfectly fine, in my rather limited experience at the time."

"Thanks. I guess." Then he said, "I was actually rather relieved you broke up with me. You scared the hell out of me. You were so smart and self-sufficient and I felt inadequate."

I stared at him. "*You* felt inadequate? God, Knightley, if you knew how scared I was then of—of everything. I was terrified of everything, including you."

He gave a rueful grin. "It's a pity we didn't ever talk to each other properly."

I shook my head. "It wouldn't have worked. We would only have gotten ourselves more scared."

There was a pause while I tried not to look at him. I was finding Knightley, the grown-up version, that is, disturbingly attractive.

"I'm hungry," he said. "How about you? I'll get us something."

He went to the kitchen. In a very short time he returned with a plate of cheese and crackers and another plate of grapes and cherries. The wine bottle was tucked under one arm.

I stood to help him. Oh, God, I was standing perilously close to him, and our knees, mine bare and his khaki clad, brushed against each other.

I took the plates and placed them on the coffee table.

I sat, a little farther from him, and to my surprise, talked about that night.

"I knew it was magic. I knew that with your family you'd be able to do stuff like that at the drop of a hat. And it was great—the candles and the flowers all over the room—all those orchids and flowering vines and the music. I mean, no one has a room like that unless they're gay and majoring in botany with a minor in drama. It was gorgeous.

"And then I woke up in the morning and the illusion had faded. All I saw was a college kid's room, with your socks on the floor and your lacrosse gear on the wall and…"

"Wait. You're saying you wouldn't have broken up with me if I'd put my dirty socks in the hamper?"

"No, they were last night's socks. Mine were there, too."

"At least I took off my socks. You have to give me some points for finesse."

"You're so obsessed with your performance. Like I said, it was okay."

He grimaced.

I continued, "I thought, Why did he bespell the room

with all those candles and flowers to impress *me?* I was scared. I couldn't live up to those expectations. So I got up and left before you woke, and then broke up with you in the cafeteria."

He shook his head. "Oh, shit," he said. "And I thought you couldn't possibly want to have sex with me unless I put on some amazing magic show for you. I can't believe we were both so dumb."

He leaned forward and kissed me.

CHAPTER 6

"Sorry," we both said.

Then we kissed again, a sweet welcome-home kiss after ten years apart. He still tasted as good and he made that familiar, purring sound in his throat. But he kissed now with authority, cupping the back of my head in a wonderfully gentle and possessive way, the fingers of his other hand trailing on my knee.

"I really don't think this is a good idea," I said, breaking away from him.

"Absolutely." Knightley got very interested in the cheese and crackers and I watched his hands with some regret as they cut cheese into neat slices.

Sighing, I took a cherry and raised it to my lips.

He laid down the cheese knife and took my wineglass from my hand. "Allow me to assist you with that."

I nearly swallowed the cherry pit in my surprise as Knightley rolled me onto my back and kissed me for real, wet and hungry and urgent, our mouths open to each other, his hands at my breasts, mine clamping onto that butt I'd admired a few days ago.

He raised his head, the cherry pit clamped between his teeth.

"I was about to tie a knot in the stem with my tongue," I said.

"I'm sure you could. Shut up, Woodhouse." He got rid of the cherry pit and we kissed some more. He felt great, hard and muscular and insistent against me, one thigh between mine. I pulled his shirt from his pants and ran my hands over the smooth skin of his back.

His hands fumbled at the zipper the back of my neck. "Honey, you'll have to sit up if I..."

"You'll have to get off me...."

"No." He rolled me to my side, undid the zipper in one smooth motion and fumbled at my bra strap with the other.

"Front loader, Knightley."

"Nice." My dress at waist level, he viewed my black lace bra with approval before unfastening it. "Oh, very nice," he mumbled, my breasts in his hands.

"You have more hair on your chest." Having unbuttoned his shirt I shoved it off his shoulders.

"I'm older. More mature. Much better in the sack." He lifted my hips to get the dress, hopelessly wrinkled now, out of the way. "Pretty boring panties, Woodhouse. You weren't planning on getting lucky tonight."

It was the most erotic sight in the world, Knightley kneeling between my outspread thighs, his fingers hooked in my white cotton panties, and pulling them down, the leather of the couch smooth and supple against my skin. I worried for about a tenth of a second that I might be developing a leather fetish.

I changed my mind. The most erotic sight in the world was Knightley, with cherry smears around his mouth, bare-chested, unbuckling his belt, unzipping and freeing himself from his boxers.

"I've missed you so much," I gasped.

"Which bit of me?" And he was on me again, and this time there were no clothes in the way, but the slide of our skin together, a perfect match, and his mouth on my breasts. He dipped his fingers between my legs and I took his cock in my hand, silky smooth, familiar. Welcome home, Knightley. We kissed again, and it was clumsy and exciting, the first time all over again, but better.

"Wait a moment." He snapped his fingers and muttered a few words.

Something flew to the table, splashed into a wineglass and bounced into the brie.

"Show-off," I muttered as Knightley retrieved the condom. "You couldn't have just fetched it like a normal person?"

"What, and waste more time?" He ripped the foil open. And then he was inside me with one glorious smooth slide. "Oh, Emma. Oh, my God, you're so lovely." He stopped. "Is this okay?"

I hooked my legs around his. "More than okay. Can I go on top in a bit?"

"Sure. Anything you want. Use me. Plunder me."

I giggled. I'd never had sex like this with anyone, I'd never laughed while feeling that I could cry as easily, or lost track of time in the contemplation of a man's skin and hair and smell. Yet it wasn't perfect. We almost fell off the couch, scrambled around into other positions and knocked the plate of crackers onto the floor. He wanted to climax, I could tell from his breathing and the sweat that broke out on his chest and arms, but I wanted to savor each thrust, each long slide and retreat.

And then I felt the urgency, too, and pressed his fingers where we were joined and rode him to a fast, hard climax that made me yelp in pleasure and surprise and a little pain, too, as everything clenched and released and clenched again.

"God, Woodhouse," he said, and thrust into me, his eyes widening and then fluttering closed. "Oh, God, you'll kill me." And he went perfectly limp and laughed, just as he'd done ten years ago.

Only now he made love like a man, not like a boy.

After a while Knightley eased himself off me. Something warm and soft floated onto me, a throw of some sort, and I lay in a pleasant stupor, eyes closed, listening to the sounds of Knightley moving around, the toilet flushing, the click as he turned on a lamp.

He sat on the couch next to me, lifting my legs onto his lap. I opened my eyes. To my disappointment he'd put on his boxers again, but he looked good. Really good. Even better, he'd brought more condoms with him.

"That was nice," he said.

"It was."

He bent to pick spilled crackers from the floor. "So what happens now?"

"We do it again?"

"Great, but I thought we'd better have a talk about things in case I meet you in the cafeteria tomorrow and you've changed your mind."

"I doubt it. I don't find you nearly as threatening now." I rubbed my foot along his thigh.

"But I don't know if you're ready for a relationship with me," he said.

"You don't know if I'm ready?" This was an interesting reversal on the usual excuse. "What makes you think that? It wouldn't have anything to do with Jane, or Missy, or any of the other women you're dating?"

"I have been dating other women. I expect you've had relationships with other men, too. We're both adults. But I know I'm ready to commit myself to someone in a real relationship, when the right woman comes along. I'm just not sure whether it's the right time for you."

"Oh." I remembered how I dumped Knightley in the cafeteria, how his goofy grin had faded to a look of hurt and bewilderment. Now I knew how that felt. "And why don't you think it's the right time for me? What makes you think you know me better than I know myself?"

"Okay. Let me ask you— Are you ready for a relationship with me?"

I hesitated. "I don't know. It's not you, it's with anyone. But if it was with anyone, it would be you. Probably."

He gave a pained grin. "See? At least you're honest."

"Oh, shit, Knightley. I'm sorry." I knelt and put my arms around him. Here I was, hurting him again.

He hugged me back and wrapped the throw around me. "Besides, I think you might have to sort out your career priorities, too. You have a lot of untapped, undisciplined power you're not even aware of."

"I don't think so." I felt even more uncomfortable.

"Others agree. Isabella, for one. Missy."

Missy! What the hell did she know? She probably used magic to open the cat food if she lost the can opener.

"I really don't want to talk about it right now," I said.

"Okay. Come here," he said, and pulled me onto his lap. The throw slid to the floor.

We kissed, quite sweetly and gently, for a time.

"Maybe I should go," I said.

"You don't have to. I have more crackers."

"I really can't resist that, Knightley."

"About your magic powers… Do something for me. Make something move. Go on, show off some." He grinned at me.

"Sure." I stroked his thighs and licked his ear, letting my bare breasts press into his arm. "How about this?"

"Inside my shorts doesn't count." He pushed me away, giving me the chance to see that things were indeed on the move in his boxers. "Try across the room."

"Okay." I focused on a vase on top of the armoire and concentrated, letting the words of the spell form in my mind.

The vase wobbled, shifted.

We both ducked as it launched on an impromptu circuit of the room, scraped a couple of pictures off the wall and smashed into pieces on the parquet floor.

"Christ! I didn't say wreck the joint, Woodhouse. Moving it a couple of inches would have done quite well."

"Sorry. Was it very expensive? It was real ugly."

"Family heirloom. I never liked it much, either."

Waving away my offers to help clean up, he fetched a broom and dustpan and swept the floor. "If we have sex again, Woodhouse, should we wear hard hats?"

"Come here and find out." I grabbed him as he approached and yanked down the boxers.

He gave a happy groan as I took him in my mouth and stroked him with my tongue. I'd been too shy and inexperienced that first time—*ew, who'd want to do that?*— but now I knew what to do. I wanted to give him what I could, without reservation, without expectations.

He groaned some more and placed his hands on the back of my head, guiding me.

398 LITTLE TO HEX HER

"Get a condom," he said, his voice breathless. "I have a bed. It's bigger than the couch."

"There's plenty of room here once I'm on top of you." I let out a moan as I lowered myself onto him.

He moaned back.

We both laughed.

"That's so good." He nuzzled my ear, my neck, then stopped. He was absolutely still.

"What's wrong?" I said, although I knew. Those small purple marks on my neck had not faded.

"Did Churchill do that?" His voice was dull and angry at the same time.

"Yes."

"You *let* him?"

I wasn't about to admit that I'd been fooled, or, worse, that I probably would have let Frank do it anyway. "I don't think it's any of your business."

He pushed me off him. I wouldn't have thought a man wearing only a condom could look intimidating or superior, but Knightley managed to achieve both. "How could you have been so dumb? You're dealing with vamps on an everyday basis and they'll know. It explains why you had so many vamps checking you out tonight—"

"Nothing to do with my natural attraction, of course." I grabbed the throw and covered myself, feeling stupid and exposed and vulnerable.

"Realistically, no. You're pretty enough but you're nothing compared to most vamps, or even most elves."

"And naturally you'd know."

"And that's none of *your* business."

I grabbed my dress, dropped it over my head and zipped it up enough to stay on me. I found my bra and balled it up into my hand. My panties were somewhere on the floor, but I wasn't about to start crawling around to find them.

Knightley pulled on his boxers. "You need to set a spell—normal protection won't help. I'll email one to you."

"Thanks, but you really don't have to bother." I found my purse and shoes and headed for the door.

He got to the door first and opened it for me. "And there's another thing you're not being honest about, Emma. I had a chat with Harriet the other day and from what she told me, I think your business is in trouble. Stop flouncing around and ask for help, for God's sake. I can—"

"Things at Hartfield are fine, just fine. You know Harriet isn't the sharpest knife in the drawer—"

"Maybe not, but she has a great deal of smarts in her way. More than her employer, in my opinion."

"Thanks a lot, Knightley. Like you said, I don't need a relationship, particularly with you. Thanks for the drink."

I turned and ran, but the last thing I saw was Knightley standing in his doorway, looking like a *GQ* model in his boxers, but with a look of desolation on his face that shocked me. The last thing, that is, until my eyes blurred with tears, and I jammed my thumb against the elevator button, praying that he'd come after me and praying equally hard that the elevator would arrive first.

I heard his door close.

I cried in the elevator, and when I got to the apartment collapsed onto the kitchen floor and cried there.

Outside the gargoyles whispered and giggled.

I was too wrapped up in my own misery to tell them to shut up.

CHAPTER 7

"It's gorgeous, Emma. You're so clever."

As Harriet and I gazed at the rooftop, I allowed myself a brief pat on the back. She was right. It was gorgeous. "Give yourself some credit, too, Harriet. You put in a lot of legwork on this and it was your idea. And you found us another caterer when the first one backed out."

She grinned. "And that dryad asked for a second lunch date with Missy Bates."

I shuddered. "He must be insane. Maybe he photosynthesizes while she talks."

Harriet turned away and fussed unnecessarily with a lantern on the table. "You've seemed sort of...down this week. You've been going to the gym a lot."

"I'm fine." After I'd been to the gym and been hit on by five vampires, two of them female in the locker room, I'd cast the spell in Knightley's email. I'd thanked him and waited for a reply. Nothing. I hadn't seen him around the building and I didn't know whether I wanted to.

What I did know was that in some strange sort of way I missed him.

SO WE WERE ALL SET for our first mixer on the rooftop of Box Hill Apartments, made gorgeous with plants and candles, a cheerful awning and, I hoped, lots of attendees.

My walkie-talkie crackled. Ramon, an employee of Knightley's who was stationed in the lobby, informed me that five guests were coming up in the elevator. Harriet positioned herself at the table to sign them in, and I went over to the boom box and selected a CD. Vintage Sinatra, I decided, right in keeping with the retro decor of the building. I slipped the CD into the slot and hit Play.

Seconds later I winced as very loud, very explicit rap blared out.

Missy—naturally she would be one of the first to arrive—mouthed something at me.

I hit Eject and shrieked, "Sorry!"

The rap kept booming and grinding, obscenely detailing what the rapper wanted to do to his bitch as the CD slid out.

I checked the CD. Yes, it was Ol' Blue Eyes, or should have been. It was fine last time I listened to this particular CD, spooning in Cherry Garcia and undoing a trip to the gym.

"Oh, shut up!" I screeched and pulled the power cord out.

Mercifully, it stopped.

I gave the boom box a dirty look. I'd never heard of an enchanted boom box, and besides, it had worked perfectly well just yesterday.

No need for music at the moment. I called the caterers, who were using the kitchen attached to the club room on the floor below, and instructed them to bring trays of hors d'oeuvres in. Drinks were set out on a table. I mingled with the guests, flirting slightly with vamps and elves, and

LITTLE TO HEX HER

discussed bark viruses with Missy's dryad. His human form was a slightly scruffy-looking professor type, whose fingers had a twiglike appearance.

To my annoyance, Augusta and Elton arrived, each with an arm linked through Jane Fairfax's. She looked as beautiful and remote as ever. Missy rushed over to them and started gabbing on about Jane's new car. Augusta and Elton exchanged a smirk over Missy's bobbing head.

"Emma?"

I almost jumped out of my skin. "Frank! What are you doing here?"

"Maybe I couldn't keep away." He leaned in and kissed my cheek.

I stepped back. It was such a fake theatrical gesture and I wondered who he was trying to impress. "I thought you were on the West Coast."

"Not yet." He looked over at Jane and Missy, who'd moved over to the drinks table.

"So who do you think gave Jane the car?" I asked.

He shrugged. "I think she has a secret admirer."

"Is it you?"

He laughed. "I think it's Knightley."

"Excuse me, I think I'd better put some music on." I was suddenly so furious with him I wanted to scream.

I fumbled through my collection of CDs. Something upbeat and fun, that's what I wanted. Something brainless.

To my horror, as the CD began to play, I realized that instead of hearing rumors through the grapevine we were witnessing the fall of Valhalla, all brass and bombast.

"Oh, Wagner—such an unpleasant man—did you see the—"

"Sorry, Missy." I hit Eject, thumped the boom box on

the top and broke a nail, and finally ripped out the power cord. "There's something wrong with—"

"Emma, I hope you don't mind me saying—I have always—that is—"

"I'll catch you later, Missy," I said firmly. "There are some new people here and I must say hello to them."

At that moment there was a piercing shriek from a guest. I rushed over to the naiad who stood staring horrified at the plate in her hand. "It moved!" she said.

"What moved?" I asked.

She screamed again, nearly deafening me. "It's doing it again!"

And then I saw it. The miniature crab cake on her plate shivered, broke and released a black, glistening slug that oozed out onto the white porcelain.

I screamed, too, and looked around wildly for a waiter as she dropped the plate. "I'm so sorry. That's horrible. I can't apologize enough. I—" A waiter, alerted by the screams and crash of breaking china, came to our side. "Clean this up, please."

Harriet put her arm around the sobbing naiad, whose watery state was returning with the excess of emotion. I called the caterers on my walkie-talkie and asked them to come and clear away the food immediately. As I did so, other people gave expressions of disgust and put their plates down fast. Something rapid and furry darted out of the fruit centerpiece on the drinks table with a whisk of long, naked, pink tail.

"Was that a rat?" someone asked in disbelief—the exact words you want to hear at a party.

"At least the drinks are okay," someone else said, and at that very moment the glasses of white wine on the table started frothing and steaming. Boiling liquid spread onto the white tablecloth, turned a lurid green and then burned through to the wood.

There were more screams now and a surge of movement toward the elevators.

"I'm sorry," I shouted. "Let's please all try and keep calm."

I was feeling anything but calm.

Next to me, a slender young witch grabbed my arm and shrieked.

"What's wrong?" And then I saw the tips of her toes trail along the floor and lift, as she was raised into the air. Still clutching my arm, her entire body lifted and for a moment her terrified face was level with mine.

Someone else grabbed me from the other side and pulled me away, breaking her hold. She floated away like a screaming helium balloon.

"Others are going up, too," Frank Churchill said, still gripping my arm.

I muttered a simple falling spell with no result.

"Emma, I think—if I may—you should—"

"Missy, I'll talk to you in a moment." I tried to stop panicking. A good half-dozen of my guests were airborne, others hanging on to the parapet of the building for dear life. A potted hibiscus rose into the air to join the floating men and women. From below, gargoyles compared views up skirts.

"Emma—" Missy hoisted a bra strap into position, adjusted her eyeglasses and cleared her throat. "When we have little unpleasantnesses at work—I think you know what I—don't you think you should—or maybe Knightley can—"

"Missy, I'm busy dealing with a crisis here, if you haven't noticed. Will you please just butt out. This really isn't the time for one of your dumb conversations about nothing. Would you mind going home and talking to your cats."

She flushed a deep red. "Okay."

It was the shortest statement I'd ever heard from her. She turned on her heel, tossing her fringed shawl over her shoulder with what might have passed for defiance from anyone else. She paused by Jane, who was hanging on to the parapet like grim death, and said something briefly to her. They both glared at me, and then left, arm in arm.

Missy wasn't affected by the magic. Why not? But I didn't have time to think about that right now.

I tried another spell, this time casting a net that caught my unfortunate floating guests and returned them to the rooftop. It was by far the most complicated and exhausting spell I'd ever cast. Dizzy with effort, I turned and collided with a waiter who held a large tray of plates and food. We both landed sprawling in a mess of lettuce, slugs, broken china and taramasalta, and his tray floated serenely into the sky. Beside us a vampire thudded to earth and thrust his business card into my hand. I wasn't sure whether he was offering to sue or represent me.

"Sorry," I muttered. I took stock of my ruined party. Harriet, muttering werewolf curses, clutched the parapet with one hand.

"What a disaster!" Augusta, who looked as though she had stepped from the pages of *Vogue,* not a hint of squashed slug on her, and, thoroughly earthbound, laid a hand on Elton's sleeve. "Shall we go home, darling?"

Harriet and I helped the last of our guests into the safety of the elevator, apologizing as much as we could.

"I suppose you'll fire me now," Harriet sniffled. "I

hired the caterers. I did check out their references, Emma. I swear it."

"It wasn't your fault." I wiped a smear of slug from her face with a relatively clean corner of a tablecloth. I thought it more than likely we'd both be job hunting pretty soon. "Why don't you go home."

What a mess. The caterer was also in tears. "There's no way I could have cooked live slugs into crabcakes," she said. "All of our ingredients are organic. I can't explain the rats. They must live in the building. I can't afford a lawsuit, Ms. Woodhouse. I've worked so hard—"

"I'm sorry. I really am." Nobody was sorry for me, I reflected sourly. "I don't know what I'm going to do. I'll probably lose my business, too, after this."

"And—and some sleazy vamp gave me his card and said he'd represent me pro bono in exchange for a little nibble!"

I shook my head and left her to clean up.

I knew who was responsible for this and I was going to make him pay. I grabbed my cell phone and called the number of Knightley's apartment, and then his cell when all I got was his voice mail.

I ran down the one flight of stairs to Knightley's apartment and banged on the door. "Open up!"

After a while the door opened. Knightley stood there, barefoot, wearing a pair of baggy khaki shorts and a ripped old T-shirt, with a pair of rimless eyeglasses on his nose. Even as mad as I was, the thought, *Aw, he's so cute* flew through my mind and then flew straight out.

"You bastard!" I spat out. "You fucking Neanderthal overgrown frat boy! You've just ruined my business. You bastard!"

"Emma?" He took off the glasses and slipped them

into the pocket of his T-shirt. "Emma, what are you talking about?"

"You know what I'm talking about. You—"

"Come inside. You're bleeding."

I was what? I glanced down and saw a trickle of bright red blood pooling on the floor at my feet and then I felt the sting on my knee.

"Come on, Emma." He took my hand and made a face, probably because my hand was covered with black slime. "What the hell have you been doing?"

He drew me inside and pushed me onto the couch.

"I'll bleed on your leather," I said stupidly. My knee hurt now, and so did my palms and one elbow.

"Stay there."

He went away for a couple of minutes, returning with a washcloth and a first aid kit, and attended to my cut knee and grazed hands. "That might need stitches," he said, applying a bandage. "Now tell me what's going on."

"No, it's okay."

"No, it's not, Emma. You come in here making wild accusations, and I've had the window open. I could hear all sorts of weird stuff and the gargoyles were going wild. I'm going to have a heck of a time getting them back in line." He glared at me.

Well, he had patched me up after I'd screamed at him. I guess I owed him. I told him about the magic tricks someone had played on the food and drink, and the enchanted boom box. And the floating guests.

"Are they still up there?" He interrupted me.

"No, I got them down using a spell from Hairy Elizabeth of Thycklewaite."

"Harry who?"

"A fifteenth-century werewolf mystic who specialized in net-casting spells. I think I could have improved the landings, though I don't think anyone got more than a few bruises. I——"

"Shit." He crossed the room to his bookcase and pulled out a tattered encyclopedia of magic. The last time I'd noticed the venerable leather tome was as he fumbled with my bra strap in his dorm room and then it had a gigantic orchid growing from the cover.

"Hairy Elizabeth of Thycklewaite," he read. "Few modern practitioners risk attempting the elegant complexity of Elizabeth's spells. Greatly respected during the fifteenth century for her skill with herding, fishing and knitting spells, Elizabeth also ran a successful perfumery business much favored by the local nunnery.... Okay. So why did you think I was responsible?"

"Because..." I leaned my head back against the leather of his sofa. "Because it seemed like a frat-house prank."

"A frat house prank that could ruin your business. Isabella's business. Emma, do you honestly think I'd do something like that?"

"No," I whispered. I couldn't figure out whether he despised me or whether I'd hurt him again, but now I was ashamed of my accusation. "I'm sorry."

"There's other stuff going on, too, isn't there? You got all riled up when I asked about your finances the other day. I know it was intrusive of me, but my offer to help still stands."

So I told him about the mysterious disappearing money and the other problems we'd had—the cancellation of our usual venue, the computer virus, the possible theft of our email list.

He nodded. "Do you see how this all adds up? Are you thinking what I'm thinking?"

I nodded. Now it all made sense, and it wasn't good. "Yes. A curse."

"Who the hell would want to put a curse on Hartfield?"

"Well…" I told him everything else. "Harriet did turn Elton into a frog a few weeks ago."

"She did what? Harriet? Oh, come on. She's only a friendly little werewolf."

"I let her look at my spell book and she was almost at her time of the month, so she had great power. I believe she used the Frog Variant of Buckaroo Velmsley Witherington-Hughes of Texas because it did wear off after a while, although—"

"And then Elton brings gorgeous Augusta back into town to start his own agency. Did he hack into your email list, too?"

I muttered, "I don't think so. I think he got Frank Churchill to do it for him. I noticed someone had been at my computer when he…when he was in my apartment."

"Oh, Christ," Knightley said. "Change your password as soon as you can."

"Okay."

He sighed. "You don't even have a password, do you?"

"Well, I—"

He reached for his cell phone. "We'd better get hold of Missy right away."

"Missy?" I said stupidly.

"Yeah, Missy, the most powerful witch in D.C." He had her number on speed dial. "Why else do you think she's on retainer at the White House? Hey, Missy, it's Knightley."

The White House? Missy?

A shrill barrage of sound emerged from his cell phone. "Uh…what? Oh shit, I'm sorry. Look, Missy, I… No,

I don't.... Yeah, of course. I'm sorry.... I'm sure she...
I understand...."

Missy's rant continued, Knightley nodding and making placatory sounds.

He turned off his cell and gave me a long, steady look.
"You've screwed up badly, Emma. That was the dumbest
and most unkind thing you've done in all the time I've
known you. She was crying."

"Look, she may be the power behind the throne, but
she's an embarrassment and a liability to Hartfield. I don't
know why Isabella kept her on the books so long. She—"

"Quit blustering," Knightley said. "Admit you've
screwed up and go do something about it. And maybe
when you've learned to ask for help, you can get your
life, and your sister's business, back in order."

"Okay, okay. Thanks for the repair job."

"Emma." He sprang to his feet and blocked my way.
"Just like the last time, off in a huff."

"No, you were in a huff."

"Yeah, I was. I guess I am now. I have good reason to
be. But I wasn't the one who flounced off."

"It's your apartment. Obviously, you wouldn't be the
one leaving."

"You know what I mean."

"No, Knightley. I don't. I'm sorry I doubted you, I really am." One quick step and we'd be touching. "Have a
good evening." I leaned forward and kissed him on the
mouth before running for the safety of the elevator.

CHAPTER 8

THE NEXT MORNING I WAS OUTSIDE MISSY'S HOUSE, WITH an apology gift—a large box of chocolates and a pair of guest towels embroidered with cats. I knew she'd be home, but she wasn't answering the doorbell. I wasn't sure, but I thought a lace curtain moved.

I plucked my cell phone from my pocket and called her number.

No reply, but I wasn't surprised.

One of Missy's neighbors, fussing over a boxwood in a pot outside his front door, gave me a curious look. Great, pretty soon someone would call the cops.

I gave the front doorbell one more push and then something brushed up against my ankles, making a soft crooning sound. I glanced down and met the green-eyed stare of one of Missy's cats, a gigantic calico that liked to sit on your chest and breathe cat-food fumes into your face.

"Hildegard!" I said. "Who's a good kitty, then?"

I scooped her up into my arms and stepped back from the front door, just to make sure Missy could see. Her windows were open so I was fairly sure she could hear.

"Shall we visit Uncle Knightley? You're his very favorite kitty cat."

I took a step toward my bicycle, parked on the brick sidewalk. "You'll fit nicely into this carrier...."

The front door flew open, revealing a stone-faced Missy. "That's a dirty trick, using my cat to gain access to my house, Emma."

Hildegard gave a mew of pleasure and poured herself from my arms onto the sidewalk and disappeared inside the house, while I stood there dumbfounded at the emergence of a complete and unfriendly sentence.

"And it's Ermintrude, not Hildegard." Missy turned and walked away back into the house, leaving the door open.

I took this as an invitation to follow, wheeling my bike into the dim narrow hall. I followed the whine of an electric can opener to the kitchen, a modern addition at the back of the house, where Missy spooned cat food into three china bowls. She set the dishes on the floor and the cats swarmed toward them.

I set the gifts on the counter. "Missy, I've come to apologize. I was way out of line. I'm very sorry I hurt your feelings."

She nodded.

I floundered on, "And I need your help. Badly."

"I see." She walked away from me into a tiny secluded walled garden at the back of the house. A small cast-iron table and chairs stood on a flagstone patio, and herbs and roses tumbled from containers.

I followed.

"Your sister and I are great friends," she said.

My face heated. "Yes, I'm sorry."

"She'd be very—how is Isabella?"

"Very well. In fact—" I reached into my backpack

"—I thought you'd like to see this. I'm sorry it's a bit crumpled. I've been carrying it around."

Her face softened as she looked at the picture of the ultrasound. "Oh! How—and when is she due—I suppose she doesn't know yet if it's a boy or—we must have a drink—and something to eat—I have a—no, I think Jane and I ate the last—let me have a look, or—"

"Oh, please, I'd like to take you out to lunch."

"How sweet, but Gregory—you know, such a lovely— he is such a—quite surprising, his—the girth, you know is so very—coming to pick me up at one—so Knightley thinks you have a curse—his email—I try not to be prejudiced against elves, but invariably they cause—it really is too bad—"

"Knightley thinks you can help, and I'd be very grateful."

"Yes, of course—I'll get my—I know I put it—" Still talking, she went back into the kitchen and came back out with a cell phone and an appointment book.

She sat down at the table and gestured to me to sit. "Knightley? It's Missy and dear Emma is… That's what I thought…. Let me see." She flipped through her appointment book. "The sooner the better…. Tonight… And we need another… Oh—do you think…" She glanced at me. "If you're sure…. Yes, yes… Well, an academic background is very… But for this sort of… Of course I do trust your judgment…. If you really… Okay."

She laid the phone down on the table and gave me a long, speculative stare. "Most interesting—that is—certainly not my choice but dear Knightley—you are to be the third, Emma—if you agree, that is—"

"The third what?"

"The third witch of the three needed to break the

curse—but of course you know—that is, Knightley thinks it should—"

"Of course it should be me. It's my business—my sister's, I mean."

"That's not the—I don't know that—"

"You think I'm not good enough."

She nodded. "There are some dangers and—well, academic knowledge only provides—but Knightley thinks—he has some doubts, naturally…."

She thought I wasn't good enough. And Knightley hadn't even mentioned the possibility of me being the third of the trio of witches who would tackle a curse. The old, familiar resentment prickled and irritated. Once more he had made a high-handed decision without even telling me what he intended or consulting me. And then reason set in: he was right. I hated to admit it, but he was right, I hadn't asked for help when I needed to and I'd been stupid enough to think Missy a silly, long-winded twit.

Missy, a cat on her lap, was cooing over the guest towels. This, I reminded myself, was the most powerful witch in Washington, D.C. I'd had no idea.

"Moonrise, in the lobby of your apartment," Missy said, fingers buried in the cat's fur. I hoped she wasn't digging for fleas.

"Okay. And, uh, thanks."

"Variant seventy-three of Claudius the Unhealthy's Charm against Elfin Practices," Missy said.

"No!"

She raised an eyebrow making me want to squirm in embarrassment.

I said, "It's okay, but I think Variant seventy-five has the edge, and we should add in the postscript."

She nodded and I wondered if she'd been testing me,

particularly when she replied with complete coherency. "Absolutely correct. Now I remember that seventy-three has that unfortunate loophole regarding invisibility. Thank you for your timely reminder, Emma. Seventy-five, then. I'll brief Knightley."

AFTER SPENDING THE REST of the day in the necessary purification rituals, I waited in the lobby for Knightley and Missy that evening. My robe was bundled up under one arm—I didn't want to give the tenants any ideas. I'd already received a few curious glances after the catastrophe of the night before and my stomach rolled queasily at the thought of what might happen later.

The elevator door opened. Knightley, wearing shorts and a T-shirt, holding a rolled-up robe in one hand, stepped out.

"Woodhouse." He acknowledged my presence with a curt nod. He smelled faintly of mint and verbane and his hair was still damp. He sprang forward to open the outside door as Missy arrived.

This was a Missy new to me. She carried an aura of power that made my spine tingle. "Ready?" she asked.

We rode up to the rooftop in silence. Knightley produced a key to open the door, and as he inserted it, sprang back, swearing and shaking his hand. "Burned me," he explained.

Missy must have seen the look on my face. "Courage," she said, slipping her robe over her head. She took the key from Knightley and shook the loose sleeve over her hand to protect her skin.

The door flew open bringing a gust of wind and a swirl of dead petals and ash. Knightly and I, having donned our robes, followed Missy out onto the rooftop.

Yesterday it had been a scene of chaos and panic; tonight the air was thick with magic and menace. As we joined hands, a gust of foul-smelling wind blew in a dark cloud, blotting out the city lights and the stars. Elfin laughter rang out and thunder muttered and crackled.

As we chanted, the concrete surface of the rooftop changed, becoming soft and moist. Near us in the shadows something moaned and heaved. Knightley's hand gripped mine a little more tightly.

Missy and I exchanged glances. We couldn't interrupt the incantation, but we both knew something was getting at Knightley and gnawing at his defenses.

The wind rose to a howl and hail spattered and bounced around us. A bright crack of lightning was followed by a rolling burst of thunder.

Knightley fell to his knees. No, he wasn't falling, he was sinking—sinking into what had been solid cement a few minutes ago, as if he were in a quicksand. His hand loosened in mine.

"Knightley!" I screamed, hoping Missy's power was strong enough to do the work of three.

There was nothing else for it—I had to do what I'd only explained in classrooms, in front of yawning, sleepy undergraduates, as a very advanced technique that, should any of them care to pursue a higher degree in magic, might be within their grasp. I was pretty sure it wasn't within mine, but I had to try.

I left my body.

I hurtled up into the darkness, into the swirling clouds that stank of magic. Below me three figures stood, one glowing almost as bright as her head of vivid reddish hair—Emma Woodhouse. The second gave off a bright, steadfast light, and the other, Knightley, *oh, Knightley, please come back*—was half-transparent, battled by elfin malice. The two women chanted the spell.

From above, I concentrated on Knightley and spoke the words that would strengthen him, a spell of return and identity. A spark lighted on Emma's arm—my arm, the arm of the real Emma down below, and ran across our joined hands like flame running along paper.

Beautiful, vicious elfin faces appeared out of the darkness. *He doesn't love you, Emma…. He thinks you're second best…just like your family does…. Not as smart as Isabella, not as pretty… Why should he care about a girl who lets a vampire bite her…? Let it go, Emma, admit you failed….*

The spark of light that bound me to Knightley wavered and turned a pale, unhealthy blue. Knightley, who had gained a little more opacity, faded.

The elfin voices continued, whispering poison, sapping my resolve. *He's embarrassed he made love with you, Emma…. You were right, ten years ago…. You won't fit into his world…. He's wondering how to break it off with you now…. He feels sorry for you….*

I gathered my strength as the dark, evil-smelling cloud swirled around me, obscuring the figures below as they chanted the last lines of the postscript.

"You're wrong!" I shouted. "I take back what is mine, I declare your curse as worthless as your elfin mischief and fantasies, as puny and pathetic as my love for Knightley is strong. I love him even if he doesn't love me back. Now go!"

A bolt of silver blue lightning shot from the dark cloud, scorching my face and sizzling my hair, spinning me around in a vortex of pure energy and tumbling me head over heels down, back to earth, into the arms of a blessedly solid and real Knightley. The air was scented with the fresh, earthy smell of freshly fallen rain and the familiar city sounds, sirens and traffic, rose up from the streets.

"Shit, Woodhouse," he said, "what the heck did you do?"

"Very impressive," Missy said. "Most—well, I think that should—everything should be okay now—Isabella will be—Knightley, I think I should take a cab—no, no, I insist, there's no need for you to—or maybe Jane—but she has a date with—a cab will do quite—"

I was too tired to interrupt. There was something quite comforting in Missy's endless stream of chatter. I followed them to the elevator and pressed the button for my floor. "I'm really tired. I need to sleep. Missy, thank you so much. You, too, Knightley."

"Yes, but—" I couldn't tell what he was thinking or what he wanted to say. All I wanted to do was fall into bed and sleep and sleep. Something came back to me from my class notes, about how energy was depleted after performing a taxing spell, and there were various methods, herbal concoctions, for instance, that could help, and many witches developed their own recipe for such occasions....

"Emma!" Knightley had followed me into my apartment.

"Sorry, good night." I dropped my robe onto the floor, then my T-shirt. "Sorry, I'm taking my clothes off."

"Yeah, I— Emma, there's something I…"

"Go away." I fell into my bed.

Someone pulled the bedclothes over me, smoothing

my hair from my forehead—strange and scratchy, that lightning bolt had singed it. "Thanks," I managed. "Turn out the light."

OH, GOD. I REALLY HAD TAKEN my clothes off in front of Knightley last night, everything except for yesterday's polka-dot panties, which somehow didn't seem appropriate for the practice of complex magic. And now the phone was ringing and I was in dire need of a herbal concoction—a simple caffeine drink, coffee, lots of lovely hot coffee with huge amounts of cream—but I rolled over to get the phone anyway.

"Emma!" My sister's voice was high and strained.

"What's up?" I sat up. "You—you're okay? The baby?"

"Yes, yes, I'm fine." But her voice said otherwise. "Is Knightley there?"

"No, of course he isn't. Why would—" There was a sudden, thunderous knocking at the door of the apartment. "Hold on, Iz, someone's at the door."

"It's Knightley. Go answer it. Stay on the line."

"Is this some sort of variant of pickles and ice cream?"

"Shut up and do as I say."

I paid a quick visit to the bathroom and was greeted with the sight of charred hair and a red nose from last night, but I pulled on the embarrassing fluffy blue bathrobe and headed for the kitchen while Knightley—I supposed it was Knightley—continued to hammer on the door.

"Now what are you doing?" my sister said.

"Filling the kettle. I need coffee."

"Hurry up!"

I put the kettle on to boil and headed for the door.

Knightley stood there, unshaven and with dark circles under his eyes. "Has she told you?" he barked at me.

"Huh? You want some coffee?"

"Tell him I haven't told you," Isabella said.

I wrapped my head around that. "I'm to tell you that she hasn't told me whatever it is that's dragging me out of bed at…" I looked at the clock. "Oh. One-thirty in the afternoon. Here, talk to Isabella." I handed him the phone. "I have to grind beans."

The shriek of the coffee grinder filled the kitchen. I dumped the old grounds from the coffee press into the sink and rinsed it out. Knightley looked appalled at my unfastidious habits.

"Will you tell me what's up?"

"Isabella said I should be here when we told you," he said.

"Okay." I sat at the kitchen table, suddenly afraid. "Tell me what?"

The buzzer that indicated someone was calling me from the front door of the building went off, sounding horribly loud. It was a courier, demanding my signature on something. "I'll go," said Knightley, looking as though he'd rather be anywhere but in my kitchen, seeing my slatternly housekeeping and horrible blue robe.

"Okay," I said, in possession of the phone once more. "Will you stop messing around and just tell me, Iz?"

She made a strange bleating sound that included Knightley's name.

"Tell me, please."

"It's Frank," she said in a sudden burst.

"Look, I know he—" *He nearly ruined your business. So did I.*

"You don't understand."

"No, I won't until you tell me." I gazed at the kettle, willing it to boil.

"Frank and Jane Fairfax are engaged."

"What?"

"I'm so sorry." She was babbling now. "We had no idea—well, actually Knightley did and I think Missy might have had a suspicion. Missy called me about an hour ago and she was so very concerned about you because, well, I encouraged you to—"

"You didn't encourage me to do anything," I said. "You told me Jim's squash partner might call and it might be nice if he and I went out for a drink. Don't be dumb, Iz."

There was a strange gulping sound on the other end of the phone. For a moment I wondered if it was morning sickness before I remembered it was early evening in Brussels, and then, with a sudden, excited rush realized I had just accused my sister, the perfect, beautiful, clever Isabella, of being dumb (something I hadn't done since I was eleven).

"Okay," she said. "You mean—you mean it's okay with you?"

"I think he's a charming creep but okay as vampires go, and she's someone who can't ask for help." Just like me. "I think she could probably do better."

"Oh, thank God," she said tearfully. "I was afraid you'd be hurt. I mean, Frank is really cute, and…"

"I wouldn't throw him out of bed for eating crackers," I said with impeccable timing just as Knightley came back into the apartment.

She giggled. "I'm so relieved. We were all afraid you were involved with him."

"It explains why Jane was so cool toward me. Hey, Iz, will you send me your brownie recipe?"

"It's stapled inside my James Beard cookbook. I'm so glad you're okay. Give Knightley a hug from me. Jim and I have to go out and I'd better find something that fits. I'm eating like a pig and everything's too tight. I can't drink the beer here anymore but I'm still eating *frites* at every opportunity."

"She told you about Churchill?" Knightley asked when I got off the phone.

I poured boiling water into the coffee press. "Yeah. You are such a pair of drama queens."

"You mean—you mean you're okay about it?"

"Of course I'm okay about it. I wasn't in love with him or anything." I let him do unspeakable things to me up against my refrigerator and in my bed and enjoyed every moment, but I didn't think it tactful to say aloud to Knightley who was doing the possessive male glower, much to my delight.

"Ah." He nodded and looked considerably happier. "Good."

"So what was the courier delivery?" I hesitated, torn between grabbing the envelope from his hands and pushing down the handle of the coffee press.

"You're supposed to stir it after it's sat for three minutes," Knightley said, handing me an envelope.

"Too bad. Do you want a cup?"

He poured while I opened the envelope. Inside was a truly miraculous and groveling letter from the manager of the bank that held the agency's account, deeply regretting the unfortunate mistake that had been made, attributed vaguely to a computer error during a system update. The interest I had forfeited would be restored and our savings account given a higher interest rate backdated to the beginning of the year, and if there was anything else they could do, etc., etc.

"Good news?" Knightley asked.

"Oh, yes. Read this." I handed the letter to him.

He frowned as he read. "They're probably afraid you'll sue. Maybe you should."

"No way. I'd rather have an embarrassed bank that's desperate to keep on my good side. Besides, if I sued I'd have to hire a vamp."

"True." He became intensely interested in his coffee. "Emma, I have something to say."

"If it's about taking my clothes off last night, it's okay. Would you like an English muffin?"

"No, thanks. What I have to say, Emma, is..." he lowered his eyes and muttered, rather like Missy Bates in full spate, "I'm really sorry I underestimated you and I've been overbearing and you saved me last night and I wanted to thank you and—"

"Cool it, Knightley. Aren't you forgetting something?"

He looked panicked. "Uh. I... You're an amazing witch. You have extraordinary powers. Missy told me what you did last night. Even she's never dared try that. If you hadn't done it, I think I'd have...disappeared, or something."

"I had to do it, Knightley."

"Of course. To lift the curse." He nodded.

God, he was dense today. "There's another reason, too."

My English muffin popped out of the toaster.

"Oh, shit," he said. "I love you, Emma."

"I was wondering when you'd get around to saying it."

"Shut up. I love you. I've always loved you, even if you still have that ratty blue bathrobe—"

"I love this robe." I dropped a large dollop of jam onto my English muffin. "I've never worn it for anyone else."

"Anyone else would go screaming into the night. I'm man enough to take the fluffy blue robe, Emma. We've ten years of wasted time to make up for."

"I love you, too." I wished I hadn't chosen that moment to take a big bite of my English muffin. I swallowed, and said it again. "I love you, Knightley. I think you're right about my magic skills—I've never accepted that I do have talent in that area, so I'm going to ask Missy for some advice. And I really want to see Hartfield grow, and—"

"And?"

"I want you, too, if you've time for a very busy woman. And I'd appreciate it if you quit telling me what to do all the time."

"I'll try," he said. "I know I'm sometimes an arrogant, overbearing jerk. I want to look after you, Emma, but last night you looked after me, and it made me…"

"Humble?" I suggested.

"Happy. Horny. Hopeful." He took me in his arms, squishing the last of the English muffin between us. "Congratulations, Ms. Woodhouse. Hartfield Dating Agency has made another great match."

Outside, the gargoyles cheered.

* * * * *

REQUEST YOUR FREE BOOKS!

2 FREE NOVELS FROM THE PARANORMAL ROMANCE COLLECTION PLUS 2 FREE GIFTS!

YES! Please send me 2 FREE novels from the Paranormal Romance Collection and my 2 FREE gifts (gifts are worth about $10). After receiving them, if I don't wish to receive any more books, I can return the shipping statement marked "cancel." If I don't cancel, I will receive 4 brand-new novels every month and be billed just $21.42 in the U.S. or $23.46 in Canada. That's a saving of at least 21% off the cover price of all 4 books. It's quite a bargain! Shipping and handling is just 50¢ per book in the U.S. and 75¢ per book in Canada.* I understand that accepting the 2 free books and gifts places me under no obligation to buy anything. I can always return a shipment and cancel at any time. Even if I never buy another book, the two free books and gifts are mine to keep forever.

237/337 HDN FEL2

Name	(PLEASE PRINT)

Address	Apt. #

City	State/Prov.	Zip/Postal Code

Signature (if under 18, a parent or guardian must sign)

Mail to the **Reader Service:**
IN U.S.A.: P.O. Box 1867, Buffalo, NY 14240-1867
IN CANADA: P.O. Box 609, Fort Erie, Ontario L2A 5X3

Not valid for current subscribers to the Paranormal Romance Collection or Harlequin® Nocturne™ books.

Want to try two free books from another line?
Call 1-800-873-8635 or visit www.ReaderService.com.

* Terms and prices subject to change without notice. Prices do not include applicable taxes. Sales tax applicable in N.Y. Canadian residents will be charged applicable taxes. Offer not valid in Quebec. This offer is limited to one order per household. All orders subject to credit approval. Credit or debit balances in a customer's account(s) may be offset by any other outstanding balance owed by or to the customer. Please allow 4 to 6 weeks for delivery. Offer available while quantities last.

Your Privacy—The Reader Service is committed to protecting your privacy. Our Privacy Policy is available online at www.ReaderService.com or upon request from the Reader Service.

We make a portion of our mailing list available to reputable third parties that offer products we believe may interest you. If you prefer that we not exchange your name with third parties, or if you wish to clarify or modify your communication preferences, please visit us at www.ReaderService.com/consumerschoice or write to us at Reader Service Preference Service, P.O. Box 9062, Buffalo, NY 14269. Include your complete name and address.